I0654498

GARY

TRIGGER WARNING: This book contains numerous instances of homophobic violence and bullying.

GARY

A Thurston Howl Publications Book
Published by Thurston Howl Publications
thurstonhowlpublications.com
Lansing, MI

jonathan.thurstonhowlpub@gmail.com

Cover design by Thurston Howl
Cover art by T. Thomas Abernathy © 2018

Printed in the United States of America
10 9 8 7 6 5 4 3 2 1

GARY

a novel

by J. D. Morrison

A Thurston Howl Publications Book

For young people living with HIV.

December 30, 2016

Reference No. 221314-1807
Dated: 12-30-2016

NOTIFICATION OF RESULTS

Medical Procedure: Lymphocytic Leukemia Cancer Screen

Patient: **Garrance Greene**	*ICD-10-CM Diagnosis Code: C91.01* **Acute lymphoblastic leukemia, in remission**
Gender: **Male**	*Medical Procedure Results:* **Negative**
Age: **15**	

Attending Physician:

Dr. Wolfgang Reichmann F.H.M.

Gary, you beat it! You're CURED!
Dr. Reichmann

The wheels of the hospital cart caught the edge of the elevator and tipped. Nurse Nina Lopez cringed as medical waste spilled from the cart into the elevator and onto the shoes of two dismayed medical technicians. The cart lay on its side. Used bandages, dressings, latex gloves, infusion kits, blood samples and sharps destined for the incinerator were strewn about the elevator floor. Nurse Lopez assessed the mess and supposed it was that kind of day. She had lost another patient today, a little boy suffering from neuroblastoma. She dared not think of the child's name. Names made it personal. Personal didn't mix well with the pediatric oncology ward. Each shift took its toll on Nurse Lopez, wearing her down until she either grew numb or cratered.

Today she cratered. When the alarms sounded that morning she knew it was her patient, crashing and dying, mercifully. She had lost count of the toll wrought by insidious cancers. Why would God permit so much suffering by the young and innocent? When would medical science solve the conundrum of cancer? Nurse Lopez was overwhelmed by a sense of helplessness. Her supervisor found her sobbing in the supply closet behind the nurse's station, worn down, beaten into submission by yet another death.

"Let's get you off this ward for a while," he had suggested. "Take today's bio waste to the basement, then go for a long walk. Don't come back until your head is clear."

Maybe that hadn't been such a good idea. Perhaps her head was too cloudy and that was why she pushed rather than pulled the cart into the elevator.

The elevator doors began to close, so she slipped through them before the scattered contents of the cart escaped to another floor. The elevator descended. The two technicians righted the cart and began to help Nurse Lopez gather the trash. Their first steps yielded the telltale crunching of objects being broken.

"Careful," she cautioned, "medical waste," though the nature of the trash should have been self-evident by the bright orange and yellow containers. They proceeded with care, avoiding blood splotches and gingerly handling the sharps.

Included in the rubbish were blood and stained swabs from cancer patient Gary Greene. Gary was the beneficiary of an advanced experimental treatment involving nanotechnology, specifically the injection of nanoscopic robots into his bloodstream. His checkup this morning confirmed that he was cancer free. Nurse Lopez clung to the hope that the miraculous turnaround she witnessed with Gary might be repeated with others in the near future. Unfortunately for her, the nanites remained in Gary's blood, and they remembered the painful spinal injections she had administered during his many treatments. She touched a broken vial containing Gary's blood and the nanites acted on their programming to protect their host from foreign DNA deemed harmful.

She felt an odd burning sensation on her fingertip, then the sensation spread along the length of her finger, as if it was being dipped in acid. She didn't understand what was happening, but she knew she was in trouble when the scalding sensation traveled into her palm. She cried out in pain and gawked at her hand, now coated with crimson threads slithering along her skin and searing whatever they touched. Before the med techs could react, a thin red cord leapt from the nurse's hand to her face, splattering across her cheek. Nurse Lopez screamed in agony and fear.

The first med tech reacted by stripping off his scrub shirt and trying to wipe the toxic substance off the nurse. He expected to feel a searing pain. There was none. The second med tech hit the elevator emergency button. That turned out to be a mistake, for while it allowed them to call for help, it also caused the elevator to stop mid floor.

Nurse Lopez crumpled against the elevator wall in a confusion of agony and shock. Her hands seethed and percolated in the crimson threads, dissolving her flesh. Her right cheek frothed as if boiled by acid; her right ear crackled and rang. The technicians eased her to the floor and administered to her best they could, desperately wiping the gooey red substance from her hands and face while they waited for assistance to arrive. It took several minutes to extricate her from the elevator and even more time to transport her to the hospital ICU burn unit, where doctors began to treat her flayed and blistered skin. They stared in horror as her flesh continued to deteriorate in front of their eyes, as if it was being eaten by an aggressive unknown microbe. Little did they know nanites were eating her flesh, doing as they were programmed. They could hardly clean her hands or face without bits of emulsified skin and sinew peeling off in layers. They slathered her wounds in sulfur-based anti-microbial cream; they infused her with broad spectrum antibiotics, medicated her pain and swelling, bandaged her, and hoped for the best. She would be lucky to keep her hands. It was fortunate for Nurse Lopez that the nanites had not yet learned to kill. In the scheme of things, they were clumsy in their assault on the nurse, leaving her disfigured and near deaf in her right ear, but alive.

Travis County Fire Captain Albert Smith arrived at the hospital with his crew clad in yellow HAZMAT suits to clean up the elevator. The cart and medical waste remained untouched. Cpt. Smith observed the bizarre red threads of slime still slithering through the debris on the floor of the car. His men were able to use shovels to scoop the stuff into buckets and complete the transport of the waste to the hospital incinerator. Custodians scoured the elevator with a bleach cleanser, standard procedure after a medical waste spill.

Microbial Scientist Dr. Wolfgang Reichmann heard news of the mishap too late to intercept the cleanup operation. As a recent Kavli Foundation honoree, he had become the de facto hospital spokesman and would have to explain to the press why the fire department was cleaning up a hospital elevator. He would have liked to examine the contaminant so he knew what it was. Dr. Reichmann listened as the med techs described the odd crimson substance that burned the nurse, but not them. Their stained scrubs, shoes and all other clothing was disposed of by the fire department. Damn their thoroughness, Dr. Reichmann thought.

"Sounds like you did a fine job helping Nurse Lopez," he told the med techs, "and your story is fascinating. That's what concerns me. Until we have answers, I need you to do the hospital a favor and keep your explanations simple. If you're asked, just say the nurse was burned by some chemicals she was transporting. Otherwise, leave the talking to me. Understood?"

They stated they understood.

Dr. Reichmann failed to comprehend the role of the nanites in the elevator incident. There was no precedent. The nanites were programmed to attack harmful cells, which they had done in curing Gary Greene's cancer. Not even the Harvard Medical research staff that programmed the nanites foresaw the ramifications of artificially intelligent nanoscopic robots that continue to evolve long after their initial purpose was fulfilled. What vexed Dr. Reichmann was why the chemical substance–whatever it was–burned Nurse Lopez but not the medical technicians. At the time, he didn't connect Gary Greene or the nanites to the incident, and without those connections the truth of the scenario eluded him. He would not put the pieces together until the fateful night of the Sam Houston High School homecoming dance.

Dr. Reichmann braced for the arrival of the press. A hazardous waste spill was news in Austin. Probably make the front page, providing one last bit of drama for Seton Medical Center before the New Year. Dr. Reichmann wasn't a seeker of publicity, but the notoriety of the Kavli award made him somewhat of a hospital celebrity. He rehearsed his statement in his head as the first reporter approached.

ound Rock Daily Dispatch December 31, 2016

Nurse Seriously Injured in Hazardous Waste Incident

L. P. D'Innocenzio

Seton Medical Center reports a nurse was hospitalized after a freak accident Friday afternoon. The pediatric oncology ward nurse suffered third-degree burns to her face and hands from exposure to hazardous medical waste.
Nearby medical technicians administered onsite treatment and the injured nurse was transferred to the hospital's intensive care unit.

"Travis County HAZMAT crews contained, then disposed of the waste in the hospital's incinerators," stated Dr. Wolfgang Reichmann, Microbial Scientist at Seton Medical Center . When asked about the need for the fire department to respond, he explained, "Manifests indicate nothing unusual in the medical waste, certainly nothing that should have combusted spontaneously." Fire and hospital teams contimue to investigate the scene.

The ICU confirms the nurse is receiving treatment for her injuries. We will update this article when more information becomes available.

Vincent Greene looked up from reading the morning paper and sipped his lukewarm black coffee.

"Did you read this article about the nurse at Seton hospital?" he called out to his wife, Joanna.

"Yes dear. It sounds like she was really hurt. That's too bad."

"The newspaper makes such a big deal about every little thing that happens in this town," he said, smirking.

"Don't be so cynical Vincent," Joanna replied. "There's a lot of people concerned about hazardous waste spills and people getting hurt." Joanna was busy in the kitchen, bending over and sorting through spices in the Lazy Susan organizer of the corner cabinet. Her straight brown hair cascaded across one shoulder as she mumbled something about finally finding the juniper berries.

"I trust the newspaper only for weather and sports. Even then, they're usually wrong," Vincent said, as he ogled Joanna's derriere, smartly packed inside her charcoal grey yoga pants.

"Why even read the paper then dear?" Joanna said, looking over her shoulder.

Vincent grunted, glanced over to Gary, realized his son caught him staring at Joanna's butt and offered Gary a playful grin. "Hey son, wasn't Reichmann one of your doctors?"

"Yeah, Dad, why do you ask?" Dr. Reichmann had been instrumental in orchestrating the nanite technology that cured Gary's acute lymphocytic leukemia. The treatment succeeded in eradicating diseased cancer cells from Gary's blood. Dr. Reichmann assured him it was not just a case of remission. Dr. Reichmann promised him he was cured, and it was a genuine miracle of modern science.

"Appears one of his oncology staff got burned pretty badly at the hospital," Vincent said. "She's in the ICU."

"Oh, I hope it wasn't Nurse Lopez. She was nice," Gary said, while flashes of Nurse Lopez prepping his spine for a stem cell injection raced through his mind. A clammy chill surged through Gary's body as he recollected the enormous needle that burned like a searing hot poker.

"Didn't give a name." Vincent moved on to the next article.

There was a time when Gary didn't think he would make it to age fifteen. He certainly didn't expect to see the New Year, yet here he was, still breathing, New Year's Eve morning, ready to resume his sophomore year at Sam Houston High School after the holidays. Gary's three-year struggle with cancer was well known to most Round Rock locals. School and church events often featured a call to action for contributions on the Greene family's behalf. One could hardly check out from a Round Rock grocery store without enduring a solicitation for funding Gary's treatments. So, while most people feigned happiness about the boy's curing, the overall consensus was relief. A few had suggested that the boy was destined to die and perhaps the extraordinary measures were extending his suffering. Still others were indignant, citing the parents' willingness to conceive a savior sibling for the farming of its stem cells. Joanna miscarried the baby. Some people suspected abortion.

Gary's scrawny build, along with his protracted battle with cancer, assured he stood out as freakish among his high school peers. The banner over the school lobby archway read "Welcome back Gary." This was a vastly different greeting than the "Gary Greene sucks dicks" scrawled in blue sharpie on the bathroom stall. Bald, emaciated and pale, Gary returned to school, garnering sympathy and curiosity.

"How do you feel?" Awkward. "You look great." He knew he didn't. The flattery and congeniality lasted a day, maybe two. Gary kept to himself and his classmates let him, for the most part.

Gary's ordeal with cancer had made him introspective. For several years, he prepared himself to die. Now, he needed to brace himself to live. The rollercoaster ride left him emotionally drained and physically exhausted. Dr. Reichmann warned Gary it might take time for his body's strength to return, and it would be up to Gary himself to calibrate how ready he was for extended activities.

"The nanites coursing through your veins are cognitive. They will continue to learn how to protect your body from further infection," Dr. Reichmann had said. He was right: the nano-scale robots provided Gary a super intelligent immune system designed to defend their host.

August 7, 2017

Texas Youth Health Program (TYHP)

To: [redacted]

CC: [redacted]

Date: 8/7/2017

Re: 2017-18 School Year

Comments: Effective school year (2017-2018), Texas will follow suit with some of the largest school districts in the country by making free condoms available in high school locker rooms (boys and girls). This mandate is consistent with the American Academy of Pediatrics (AAP) policy statement supporting the notion that kids who want condoms should be able to obtain them discreetly and affordably, preferably at no cost.
"Schools should be considered suitable sites for condom distribution," the statement read, adding that pediatricians should emphasize to parents the importance of educating their children about condom use. TYHP will leverage Trojan's pre-selected back-to-school collection, which includes: Rough-Rider-Studded, King-XL, Extra-Strength, Ultra-Sensitive, Ultra-Thin, Ribbed and Assorted Flavors."

The summer of 2017 was transformative for Gary on several levels. He didn't have to deal with classmates–who teased him–and his body continued to heal. He filled out, grew hair–fine brown like his mother's–and shed his chalky skin tone. Most kids got their tans at the community pool, but Gary was too self-conscious for that setting. Gary accomplished his tan by sunning on the backyard picnic table his dad built out of cedar wood. The solitude, while it spared him from ridicule, accentuated his loneliness.

Gary didn't have to deal with siblings either. He was the only son of Vincent and Joanna Greene, a fact that weighed on him when he thought he was dying, and disquieted him now that he wasn't. His living meant he would continue to be a focus for his mom and a disappointment for his dad. Gary knew too much about his parent's courtship and their marriage in distress when Joanna became pregnant. He sensed his parents still loved each other, but he felt like he had come between them. Joanna's sole purpose for three long years was Gary's health. Her husband was an afterthought. Vincent's occasional random comments about children being a burden didn't help matters. Only recently, with Gary's return to health, did Vincent interact with Gary in a fashion resembling something other than pity.

Vincent saw hope in Gary's recovery. His son was no longer the emaciated cancer victim. His regrown hair, returning skin tone and healthier body encouraged him. Perhaps the son he had previously resigned to permanent sissy status would grow into a real man. For that to happen, more than his son's looks would have to change. There were certain mannerisms that needed an adjustment. Gary needed to be less soft, in his mind.

"You thought any more about playing a sport for your junior year, son?" Vincent asked, hoping that participating on a school athletic team might be a catalyst.

This wasn't the first time the topic had come up. His dad had progressed from hinting to asking to strongly suggesting that Gary play sports. Gary braced himself for the ultimatum he knew was coming. "You know I'm not much into sports Dad."

"Don't talk nonsense son. What kind of boy isn't into sports? How about you try out for the varsity football team this year?"

Gary assessed his dad's leap of logic from lack of interest in sports to trying out for varsity high school football. He concluded the man was out of his mind. High school football in Central Texas was serious business. Gary had never played, wasn't built for the game, and never would be, cancer or no cancer. Gary accepted he would never measure up to his dad's expectations of what it takes to be a "real man" and found himself constantly battling feelings of inadequacy because he didn't fit the paradigm.

"I won't make first cuts Dad. Besides, I don't even like football." The first statement was truth. The second was sacrilege for a high school boy in Central Texas. Some of the smaller towns of the Texas Great Plains built their entire social ecosystems around the game of football. These were the

"Friday Night Lights" of film and TV series. To Vincent, football was the life's blood of Middle America. Hearing his son say "I don't like football" was tantamount to hearing betrayal of his country.

"Don't like football? Fuck that. You're getting onto that football field, even if you have to be the goddamn waterboy."

Gary realized it was pointless to argue with his dad. The man was stubborn, and confrontation made him even more ornery. Gary considered the implications of volunteering as waterboy for the football team. How bad could that be? He thought maybe he could make some friends on the team, and then he realized the absurdity.

Friends on the football team. Ha! None of the players even know I exist, Gary told himself. But the thought of being part of the team in some capacity was enticing. Gary longed to be a part of something, to be accepted into a group. If he could hang with the guys on the football team, even as just the waterboy, maybe he would feel like a regular boy, one of the guys, instead of the outsider he knew he was.

"Fine . . . I'll see if the football team needs a waterboy. I hope that makes you proud," Gary said, subdued. His dad just shook his head. Gary balled his fists in frustration, walked away . . . but waterboy, he became.

Turns out, the job of waterboy in the late August Texas heat is pretty important. The exertion of practice under the sweltering sun can dehydrate a kid in full gear in short order. Gary's job was to run around the practice field shooting ice-cold water and Gatorade into the player's mouths so they could keep banging their heads together without suffering heat stroke.

Gary's role as waterboy made him acutely aware of his own shortcomings. These boys were all the things that Gary would never be: strong, athletic, popular, and desirable. He was envious that they would breeze through school and breeze through life because of their looks and physical talent, while he would continue to struggle with his deficiencies and insecurities.

Gary gathered the squirt bottles and hand trucked the coolers to the storage closet. As waterboy, it was his job to launder the dirty practice jerseys and distribute fresh towels. He rolled the laundry bin through the locker room aisles, catching whiffs of musky jerseys and sweaty socks. He held one of the jerseys up to his chest and imagined himself wearing it on the field with the rest of the players. Then, he shook his head, threw the jersey into the bin, and continued invisibly performing his waterboy tasks. Or, so he thought. As he neared the showers, Coach Casey put his muscular arm around Gary's shoulder.

"I see you running around out there helping the players Gary. You do your job well. You deserve a shower just like the rest of these boys." Coach opened an available locker door with his free hand, then handed Gary a towel.

The idea excited Gary. His battle with cancer left him feeling isolated from his peers. He understood his looks and his experiences would forever make him different, but being a part of this team was making him feel a bit "normal," and he liked that. The concept of showering "just like the rest of the boys" was a foreign one, but it made him feel as if he *was* "just one of the guys". He stripped down, hung his towel on a hook by the shower room door and stepped inside. It was an open room with a dozen showerheads distributed in a horseshoe fashion across the back wall and around each side. The fresh water spray and steam brought instant olfactory relief from the stale locker room aroma. The sight of eleven naked athletic bodies and the sound of the showers gave Gary the sense that he had stepped into an exotic cave under a waterfall.

Gary's was a runner's build at best, drastically different than the football builds pervasive in this shower room. The pressure to achieve in football at the varsity level pushed many players beyond their inherent body limits. Their physical maturity, full throated voices and outright hairiness told Gary there was something unnatural at work here, beyond the typical habit of Texas dads holding their sons back a year before letting them start first grade.

All but one shower head was occupied with sweaty players lathering their bodies with body wash. Gary took notice of the naked bodies facing toward and away from him at random. Two players had tattoos on their upper arms: one had a viper coiling around the Texas star, the other had a cannon with "Come and Get It" inked underneath.

Gary inched his way to the corner shower, invisible, he thought once again, and squeezed between the quarterback, Charlie Simpson, and the center, Roddy Cruz. He adjusted the water temperature to his liking and squished some foaming soap into his hand. He let the water spray down upon his neck, shoulders, and torso. He thought about how far he'd come, from near death last year, to being able to shower "just like the rest of the boys" in the locker room. He lost himself momentarily in this bonding moment. He squished another handful of foaming soap and moved to lather his groin. Unfortunately, the sight of the naked bodies, the shower sounds, and the fresh smells had an unintended consequence on Gary. He noticed his erection too late. The next thing he heard was Charlie Simpson announcing, "Gary's got a boner!"

Sure enough, Gary's member was standing at attention, fully erect, for all to see. He reached to cover his erection and turned to face the wall.

"Oh no you don't, faggot!" Charlie and Roddy turned him around and pinned his arms back to display his boner in its full glory. There were hoots and hollers, then chatter and chuckling.

"Boner, Boner." The chant resounded, reverberating off the

dull cream cinder block walls.

"Boner, Boner." More boys stepped through the door and one of them tossed a wafer-size condom package at Gary's pelvis. It missed the mark, but made the point.

"Faggot's got a hard-on!" Roddy said, still pinning one of Gary's arms to the wall to stop him from covering himself. The football players all jeered.

Players grabbed handfuls of condoms and began opening them with varied levels of success. The wetness and steam of the shower room weren't conducive to easily opening the little packages, but success was accomplished in varying ways. One stocky black player tore some condoms open with his teeth.

"That's gross as shit, Chestnut," said a tall kid nearby. "You open those rubbers with your teeth?"

"Yeah, man," Chestnut replied. "They make these things fruit flavored. It's like licking a Popsicle stick. You should try it." Chestnut finished unfurling the condoms, sported a wide toothy grin, and lobbed the condoms toward Gary.

Gary heard laughing in the background. The joke was on him. The players were managing to unwrap their condoms and toss them at Gary's bird-like chest. Unrolled, multi-colored, lubricated Trojans, thrown from every angle, struck and clung to his bare skin.

"You need to wrap it up dude!" one player yelled.

The chanting began: "Wrap it up! Wrap it up!" The shower was packed with players, and more condoms were thrown, many sticking to Gary's body, humiliating him. Gary began to cry. He couldn't help it. His fantasy of being one of the guys was crushed. He was even more of a freak now than he was before.

"Wrap it up! Wrap it up!"

Seth Thompson, a blond kid taller and more muscular than most of the players, approached, a sadistic grin on his face. He unfurled one of the condoms and moved to sheath Gary's hard-on. Gary managed to jerk his knee forward and caught Seth in the sternum, knocking him back. Seth wheeled quickly and hit Gary hard on the nose. The smack echoed off the cinder blocks and sent Gary reeling backward against the shower wall. Only Roddy and Charlie's grip on Gary's arms kept him from tumbling to the floor.

"Geez Seth!" Charlie exclaimed.

Blood spurted from Gary's nostrils. The boys in the shower began chanting, "Fight, fight." Seth started towards Gary again but Roddy interceded between them. Charlie's grip on Gary switched from restraint to support. He managed to keep Gary upright and let him turn towards the shower to wash off the blood pouring over his mouth and down his chin. The crimson stream initially traced its path towards the drain, then diverted upon striking one bare foot and then another of the boys standing nearby.

"Ouch, Holy Christ that's hot!" said one boy.

The players were backing off, scrambling to get their feet out of the bloody water.

The blood stream focused on Seth. The blood pooled at his feet, then thin crimson tentacles began to stretch along Seth's ankles. Seth screamed. A fellow lineman picked him up and carried him fireman style towards the exit, bloody tentacles clinging to Seth's feet like spider webs.

Coach Casey appeared at the door, sidestepped the lineman and yelled, "What the hell's going on in here?"

Charlie and Roddy stepped aside as Coach approached. Coach turned off Gary's shower, grabbed some towels and gave Gary a modicum of dignity. The other football players scattered.

Coach pinched Gary's nose, over minor objection, and stemmed the flow of blood.

"Get some ice," he commanded Roddy.

Roddy scrambled.

"What happened here?" Coach asked.

Charlie fessed up to the episode, including his part, while Gary listened and nodded.

"I didn't mean for anyone to get hurt," Charlie said. "We were just teasing."

"I'm embarrassed for all you boys," Coach yelled, his face getting redder as he took in the scene of condoms, blood and somewhat contrite players. "This bullying stops now, you understand?"

Roddy returned with an ice-stuffed baggie and offered it to Gary. Gary accepted the ice with a shaky hand. He knew he looked like a fool. The weakling waterboy who cries like a girl and can't take a hit like a man.

"Yeah Coach, we understand," Charlie said, looking at the other players for agreement, all of whom were prudently staring at their feet, out of shame partly, but mostly to keep their feet from the remains of the bloody water.

Coach released the pinching pressure on Gary's nose. Just a tiny trickle of blood snuck out one nostril. "Looks like the bleeding is stopping. Can you breathe okay?"

Gary inhaled and confirmed his breathing was adequate. He nodded.

"Good. I doubt it's broken then. Sure was a lot of blood though. And what was going on with the water? You boys acted like you were stepping on hot coals."

"Didn't bother me coach," Roddy said.

"Me either," Charlie said.

The coach felt the situation odd, beyond the pile of condoms lobbed upon a frail waterboy, but he couldn't figure it. Both Roddy Cruz and Charlie Simpson were swearing they suffered no ill effects from the crimson swirls that had the other boys hopping like mad. Still, this kind of hazing had to be nipped. Coach needed to get ahead of it before word got to the front office.

"Hmm. You boys stay with Gary and help him get dressed. Then, I'm going to give the team a beat down. Let me fill in the other coaches first."

Coach Casey stepped away.

Charlie and Roddy scooted Gary past the coach's huddle and helped Gary into his street clothes.

"Seth was totally out of line to hit you like that," Charlie said.

"You guys were out of line to let them toss condoms on me like that," Gary said. "That was so humiliating." Gary tried to keep the tears from building, but with little success.

"Yeah, that was kind of the point," Charlie shrugged. "Hey, we've all been through some kind of hazing to be part of this football club. I saw you running around out there taking care of us. We all did. We appreciate it. Don't we Roddy?"

"Yep, that's the truth," Roddy said.

"Hope you stay on as waterboy," Charlie said. "It's hot out there. I swear I felt like I would have died if not for you."

"I'll stay," Gary said. "But don't let them do that to me again."

"No worries waterboy, the worst is behind you," Charlie said and clapped him on the back.

Gary crept by the locker room aisle where Coach Casey was delivering a serious dressing down to the team.

"What you boys did in that shower crossed a line of decency. Every person on that practice field deserves respect. Starters, backups, even the goddamn waterboy." Coach Casey noticed Gary standing off to the side. "If the front office hears the details of this charade, a few of you could get suspended, including you Thompson." Coach Casey glared at Seth, who was sitting on the edge of the bench, each foot dunked in a janitor's bucket full of ice. "So, here's the deal. I'll report a locker room scuffle and say that the coaches will handle it as a disciplinary matter within the team. County regulations won't let me extend practice, but I sure as hell can assign detention. Therefore, for the remainder of the week, I need you boys to report to the film room an hour before the first bell."

"Game films aren't so bad," a voice in the huddled mass mumbled.

"I have some NPR TED Talks I think you boys might find motivating," Coach said.

The huddled mass collectively moaned.

"Simpson, Cruz, this goes for you too," Coach said, more loudly.

"Yes sir," they replied.

"You don't show up for detention, you don't practice. You don't practice, you don't play. Is that understood?"

"Yes sir," said the team in chorus.

The lecture looked like it might continue for a while. Assistant Coach Evans tapped Charlie and Roddy on their shoulders and pulled them aside. "Get him out of here." He pointed at Gary and with a slight wave of his hand gave the "move along" signal. Charlie and Roddy took the opportunity to leave Coach Casey's admonition and escort Gary to the school parking lot. Gary felt safe between his two bodyguards: Charlie, at 6'2" with a California surfer physique and Roddy, not as tall but built like a Samoan.

"I got this Roddy, you go ahead," Charlie said. Roddy fist bumped Charlie, then turned, grinning, and offered a raised first to bump with Gary. Gary reciprocated. Roddy parted ways, driving off in his beat up Honda Accord.

"Come on," Charlie said, "I'll give you a lift home."

"No, that's okay," Gary replied. "I can walk."

"Don't be silly. Hop in," Charlie gestured toward his burnt orange Chevy Silverado parked majestically across four spaces in the parking lot's back corner. Burnt orange was the trademark color for the University of Texas, the school Charlie aspired to attend, and a distinctive shade for a pickup truck.

As the star quarterback on the football team, Charlie had an unspoken immunity to parking tickets in Round Rock. Charlie famously had parked the truck on the school's front lawn for last year's county playoff game. No ticket.

"Just don't bleed on the seats," Charlie said, only half kidding.

Gary accepted the ride and gave Charlie directions to his home, which Charlie ignored and turned onto the highway instead. They cruised along RM 620 with windows down and Kenny Chesney blaring on the radio.

"Gary, I have to ask," Charlie shouted over the electric guitars. "What was with the boner?"

Gary shook his head.

"It's okay. People are accepting of different sexual preferences nowadays. Facebook has dozens of choices to self-identify."

"We're not having this conversation. Not now, not like this," Gary said. "Just take me home."

"It's not fair," Charlie said, shaking his head. "I'm the quarterback and Roddy is the center. I have my hands against Roddy's crotch for fifty plays a game. Ten times that if you consider practice. But no one accuses us of being gay. Hell I wouldn't care if they did. Fuck them. But you, you're self-conscious and you've been through a lot of shit. That's supposed to make you stronger, right? Maybe you just need to embrace your sexuality Gary. Own it."

Charlie preferred the conversation like this, because while concentrating on driving, he could say whatever he wanted without having to make eye contact. His dad (God rest his soul) delivered his birds and bees conversation in the same manner. Lesson learned. Charlie applied the technique on Gary.

"There are other gay guys in school you know," Charlie said.

"Oh really? Like who?" Gary challenged.

"Like those two nerdy guys in the band. Wilbur and Eugene."

"That's so stereotypical Charlie. Just because someone's a nerd doesn't mean they're gay. In fact, in all likelihood, they're not."

"Okay smartass, you tell *me* who's gay. Don't gay guys have the best gaydars?"

"What? First of all, I'm not outing anyone. Secondly, even if I suspected I might be gay, that doesn't mean I know who else might be. Why do straight guys have the impression that gay people have some super gayness detection capability?" Gary didn't want to engage in this kind of conversation with the high school quarterback. Charlie was being nice to him. Maybe there was a way he could recuperate some of dignity. If the quarterback accepted him, the other players would too, right? He needed to turn the conversation to something "regular guys" would talk about. But Charlie pressed ahead.

"You said, 'might be gay'," Charlie continued. "So, you don't really know yet? Have you ever had sex?"

"That's heck of a question, Charlie."

"I'll take that as a 'No'. You would brag about it if you had."

The topic of conversation was obviously not going to change so Gary decided to engage. "Have you had sex?" Gary reciprocated.

"Gary, I'm the quarterback on the high school football team. I don't *need* to brag."

"You just did." Gary thought his quip was clever. Too bad Charlie glossed over it.

"Whatever. Here's my point. If you haven't had sex with either gender, how do you know what you may or may not prefer?"

"You've never had sex with a guy, have you Charlie?"

"No."

"How do you know you won't like it?"

"I just know."

Gary dabbed the gym towel to his nose, confirming the bleeding had stopped. He shook his head slightly. "Just take me home Charlie."

"You got it." Charlie veered left, bounding across the grass covered median and headed the opposite direction.

Gary enjoyed the rush, while holding on for dear life. "You probably just killed a thousand bluebonnets," Gary said.

"Nope, just sowed the seeds," Charlie said. "That will be the prettiest patch come next spring. You'll see."

Charlie pulled up to a rancher with the blue shutters at the end of Gary's cul-de-sac and lowered the music volume.

"See you tomorrow on the practice field?" Charlie asked.

Gary offered a thumbs up. He yelled, "Thanks for the ride!" as Charlie gunned his pickup out of the driveway.

Two honks and a wave were the reply. Gary sincerely appreciated the lift home. He realized Charlie probably felt some guilt for instigating the whole incident in the first place, and that he felt bad for letting things get out of hand. The drive home turned out to be the highlight of Gary's day. If the locker room incident yielded a friendship with Charlie Simpson, the entire episode would be worth it.

Gary still held the towel, spottily stained with the remnants of his nosebleed. It would involve too much explaining to carry the thing into the house and let his mom see it, so he walked around to the side yard where the trash cans were. He opened the plastic lid and went to drop the towel inside. He hesitated at the sight of a small rodent rummaging through the contents of a torn bag. He tossed in the towel anyway. "Eat that you stinking rat." He closed the lid. Walking away, he heard a frantic squeal and the thuds of an object ping ponging around inside the trash can. Then both the squeals and the thuds stopped. Gary walked back to the trash can and slowly lifted the lid. Looking in he saw the rat, on its back, mouth open. He stared a moment longer and noticed that the rat's eyes appeared to be dissolving. Gary was taken aback. He slammed the lid down and hurried away.

Gary stepped through the front door of his house with hopes of avoiding scrutiny from his mom. She was right there in the living room and instantly expressed concern about his swollen face.

"Not now Mom," Gary said, slipping into his bedroom and closing the door.

"I'll get you some ice," she yelled through the door.

"Fine," he said. He made her hand the zip lock bag of ice cubes through a slit in the door.

Gary sat forlorn on his bed and contemplated the hazing incident. He was humiliated. Stories of condoms being tossed on him in the locker room were probably already circulating. He could just imagine the graffiti that was being scrawled once again on the bathroom walls. This wasn't how he wanted his junior year to start.

On the other hand, he couldn't help but be fascinated by the effect his blood had on the football players, especially Seth. He didn't let on that he noticed anything strange. He couldn't. Not without risking another rendition of the "freak" label he had already endured. But, he couldn't help notice, in spite of his bloody nose, the manifestation of the crimson threads that crept in the water and swirled at the feet of the football players. The look on Seth's face was intense. It was more than pain. Seth looked *terrified.* Gary also thought about the support Charlie and Roddy provided after Seth bopped him, and that Charlie and Roddy remained unaffected by his blood. He didn't understand what was going on, but he resolved to himself to figure it out.

"I accept your report of the incident Coach, but I can't say I condone you taking it upon yourself to determine the necessary disciplinary action," Principal Delores McFadden said. Principal McFadden had fiery, dyed red hair, a stocky build, quick wit, and a distinguished military background. She had retired and moved to the Austin area to start a second career as a high school math teacher. She moved up the ranks and recently ascended to her role as Sam Houston High School Principal. "Against my better judgment, I'm going to let this incident slide and allow you to proceed with the correctional actions you've described. I permit this only because you and I are just getting to know each other.

"Understand this about me: I'm partial to strict adherence to the command and control structure. I promise I won't grab your clipboard and start calling offensive sets for your team, but in return I expect you to allow me the latitude of running this school the way I see fit, including meting out disciplinary actions on *all* of the students, including football players. This is not a request. Something like this happens again, I handle the disciplinary actions and I'm not going to care if he's the last scrub on the bench or the star of the team. The tail does not wag the dog in my school.

"Do we understand each other, Coach Casey?"

"Yes Principal McFadden," Coach replied. "We most definitely understand each other."

"Excellent, then I think we'll get along just fine," she said, thinning her lips.

Coach Casey gingerly closed the principal's glass door on his way out.

Assistant coaches Evans and Mitchell were waiting outside the principal's office. They heard some of what was said, and they stared wide-eyed at Coach Casey as he exited the office.

"That seemed like a rather one-side conversation," Evans said. "What happened?"

"Let's put it this way, I don't recommend crossing that

woman unless you want to be eaten for lunch."

Gary liked their home. It was humble by Texas standards, but it had good energy. This was his mom's doing. Its pine wood floors showed the wear and tear of a lived-in house. There were no carpets, area rugs or curtains. These were dispensed with years ago because of their potential to harbor dirt, mites, and mildew. Years of dealing with her son's cancer had turned Mom into a germaphobe. The window treatments were simple, narrow, slatted white plastic blinds, which were usually open to let in the sun. The windows themselves were often open as well, unless the afternoon heat was oppressive. Mom could have lived in an open-air adobe hut and been delighted. Crystals hung in the windows, gleaming in the sun and casting elongated light streaks on bright pastel walls. She had gotten rid of all the old dark oil paintings, replacing them with pickings gleaned from estate piles and Goodwill. This made for an eclectic collection of artwork. She favored vibrant nature scenes of waterfalls, sunrises, mountains and savannas, intermingled with close up images of exotic mammals, birds and reptiles. The walls celebrated planet earth and the life she enabled.

The rancher smelled of exotic herbs and spices–scents of incense Joanna regularly burned. Gary noted that his mom could burn incense but his dad could not light a cigarette inside the house. Joanna ruled the roost.

The living room was dominated by the larger-than-life multi-media painting of an eggshell white duck leading her starkly more yellow hatchlings into a dark, placid lake. If you looked closely on the water's surface, you could see the reflection of a brownish-grey drake standing guard. The oversized painting was created by an art student at the University of Texas, and was given to Gary's parents as a gesture of support for Gary's battle against cancer. The art student mixed her own pigments from scratch, using flowers and fruits available locally in the Texas Hill Country. It was a statement piece, and the kind of art that might be worth something someday. It was Gary's favorite. He liked the idea of his dad standing guard, even if he wasn't fully in the picture.

They sat and ate dinner at the square Ikea table and chair set. Gary had to admit, his dad might be a hard ass, but he did have a knack for assembling furniture. He never seemed to lack for the right sized ratchet or wrench to get the job done. Gary stopped trying years ago to help his dad assemble anything, because the effort usually ended in frustration for both of them. Gary's talents were more cerebral.

"What happened to your nose?" his dad asked.

"Nothing," Gary said, trying to act nonchalant.

"What do you mean 'nothing'? You get into a fight?"

"Not exactly."

"You hit him back?"

"Not exactly."

"You got popped in the nose and did nothing?" Vincent shook his head, disgusted. "Who hit you?"

"Nobody." Gary glanced down, avoiding eye contact, wishing to be anywhere other than in his dad's crosshairs.

Vincent leaned towards Gary, menacingly. "Answer me."

Gary hated when his dad got into this kind of mood. There was no reasoning with him. Lately, his dad's temper seemed to be getting shorter.. The slightest inconvenience could set him off. Gary relented and fed him more information, not that it was going to help. This discussion would not end well. Why did his dad have to be such a jerk?

"Seth Thompson."

"Why did he hit you?"

Gary shrugged.

"Did you say something to him?"

"No."

"Did you say anything *about* him?"

"No."

"Did he give you a reason?"

"I don't want to talk about it," Gary said, keeping his head down and eyes focused on his plate.

"This evasive crap doesn't work for me, boy. No dinner for you. Get to your room."

"Honey, the boy needs to eat," Joanna said, eyes pleading with Vincent to be reasonable.

"Not tonight he doesn't," Vincent said. "He needs to learn. When someone punches you in the face you *need* to punch them back."

"He's twice my size Dad," Gary said, finally looking up at his dad.

"Don't talk back to me." His dad pointed down to hall. "To your room."

Joanna glowered at Vincent, but said nothing. Gary skulked away from the table. Vincent just turned his back. Gary retreated to his room. Missing dinner was no big deal. Gary missed many a meal during his cancer ordeal. What was the point of eating if you couldn't keep anything down? What bothered him was the constant feeling of inadequacy whenever he interacted with his dad. The image of his dad's face superimposed on Seth's body in the shower, fist headed towards his nose, took shape in Gary's mind.

Gary grabbed his composition book and a pen. He wasn't much of journal writer, despite being told how cathartic the process could be. Writing in a diary made Gary feel that much more alone. What loser writes to himself? If Gary had someone to write to, that would be different.

"Dear Nanites–" Gary ripped the page from the composition book and tossed it towards his room's trash can. "Dear Little Tiny Robots–" Gary tore the piece of paper jaggedly out of the notebook, crumpled it and discarded it to the floor. "Dear Friends," he wrote. Yes, that's what they were. The nanites were his friends, he would address them accordingly. He could use some friends. Gary could let his emotions drip from the pen onto the page, making them real; the nanites could listen without judgment. He finished his entry, felt better, and decided maybe journaling was therapeutic after all.

Dear Friends,

Sorry for not writing you sooner. For what it's worth, I've known since the beginning that you were here for me: fixing, protecting and listening to my needs.

We're connected in a way I admit I don't quite understand, but I feel it.

I know you do as well.

It's nice to know when I want to find a friend, I need to look no further than inside myself. I feel you coursing through my veins and pulsing within my tissues. It's such a good feeling not to be alone anymore, with friends I can truly call my own.

For we are part of each other.

Some people would be scared to have you inside them. I'm not like most people. I'm glad to be your host.

It's nice to know we have a mutual understanding. Thank you for making me feel safe.

—Gary

Gary read the entry and decided he better hide his composition book. Anyone reading it would not understand; they would think he was crazy.

Gary considered the way the nanites acted to protect him in the shower. He was curious to get to know them better by understanding their behavior. He slipped into the hallway and stepped into the lone full bathroom in the house. Gary and his parents coexisted with just this one bathroom. Joanna's stuff was under the sink. Vincent used the side drawers. Gary had a little bin tucked into the corner with his toothbrush, comb, soap, shampoo and deodorant. It wasn't his bin he was interested in at the moment though. He opened a side drawer. There on top was his dad's triple bladed razor. That should do, he thought. He fetched some Dixie cups and cotton swabs from the medicine cabinet, wet a swab, then brushed it along the blades of the razor. Stubble clung to the cotton swab and a chunk of it plopped into one of the Dixie cups. He scraped the remnants off the swab into the cup and then returned the razor to the drawer. He grabbed a single bladed razor from his own bin and, as an afterthought, reached under the sink and snatched his mom's hairbrush.

He carried the items into his bedroom and spread them out across his dresser. The solitude of his bedroom was not punishment for Gary. He had learned to entertain himself after many years of no siblings and no friends. And now he had a new game to play.

He needed a control for his experiment, so he snipped a few bangs of his own hair and placed them into one of the empty Dixie cups. He did the same with pieces of his mom's hair from her brush.

He eyed the razor. Testing his theory required his blood. Lacking a proper needle, the razor would have to do. He winced as he sliced his finger across the tip and then squeezed droplets of blood into each Dixie cup. First, into the cup with his own hair. Nothing happened. Next the cup that contained Mom's hair. He wasn't sure what to expect. He hoped nothing. He watched the contents closely. Blood dripped along the thin strands of brown hair, but nothing unusual happened. Lastly, he dripped his blood into the cup of his dad's razor stubble. The reaction was instantaneous. The droplets boiled in a frenzied "attack" against the stubble and consumed it in a process that took less than thirty seconds.

"Holy shit," he said. Then, a wave of guilt washed over him. Were his feelings and the behavior of the nanites so intertwined and was his hatred of his dad such that the nanites perceived Dad as an enemy? Gary felt like a horrible son. This prompted him to see what might be done about the aggression the nanites demonstrated. Catch him in the wrong mood and, Gary reasoned, his nanites might mistakenly hurt someone in the name of defending him, even someone he loved. How do you train a rabid dog? Gary wondered. You don't. You put in down.

After the guilt came a wave of loneliness. Whom could he tell? His parents? No, they had been through enough. Dad would dismiss him as a freak, and Mom would worry. Teachers? No, they would surely bar him as a safety hazard. His doctors? Never, not unless he was willing to become a human guinea pig. His friends? Yeah right, that was a joke. He would bear this burden alone. He was used to that. It wasn't so bad; at least he could talk to the nanites.

Joanna Greene concluded her yoga class with the customary salutations. Her students, mostly women from the neighborhood, gathered their mats, blocks and bolsters and shuffled out of the studio. A jar labeled "Gary's Fund" sat next to Joanna's mat at the front of the class. A few of the students dropped money in the jar. Betty Thompson, Seth's mother, decided to confront the matter.

"Joanna, your son was cured eight months ago. Why are you still soliciting contributions?"

"Because the universe has determined that his bills shall not vanish as completely as his disease," Joanna replied, monotone.

"How long are you going to keep fleecing this town with your sob story?" Betty said. "Haven't we given enough?"

Joanna inhaled a cleansing breath. She sat down on her mat and folded her legs into lotus position. "I cannot say whether enough has been given, I can only testify that the bills linger. I do not demand a contribution. The class is covered by your club membership fee. You can walk on by. You'll not rock my serenity either way."

Betty sighed. Joanna's passive style meant a guilt trip for not donating would weigh more heavily than the feelings of manipulation when she did contribute. She reached into her yoga pants pocket and pulled out the $10 bill she had already stored there for this purpose. She dropped the money in the jar. "You know your son poured scalding water on my son's feet right?"

"Was this before or after Seth punched him in the nose?"

Betty rolled her eyes, pursed her lips, and asked, "You ever been to the Round Rock Dog Park Joanna?"

Joanna nodded her head to the seemingly non-sequitur question.

"Well then you know that the dog park has two fenced off areas: one for the *big* dogs and one for the *little* dogs. They do that because the little dogs might get hurt if they play with the big dogs." Betty offered a thin-lipped smile. "Your son's *not* a big dog Joanna. That's why he got hurt."

"It seems to me," Joanna deadpanned, "if your son is a dog that would make you a bitch."

Betty was struggling to maintain her smile. "It's an analogy."

"Your dog park story was an *analogy*. You being a bitch is a *metaphor*," Joanna clarified. "Now if I said, 'You act like a bitch,' that would be a *simile*."

"I don't care what you call it, my boy's feet are in bandages because of what your son did."

"My little dog?" Joanna asked, looking up to Betty, head cocked to one side.

Betty let the question hang in the air unanswered. She glanced at her $10 bill in the jar, bent down and retrieved it. She stood, lifted her chin, pivoted on her sock covered heels, and followed the other students out the door, leaving Joanna alone in the studio.

Joanna reached into her gym bag and removed four vanilla scented votive candles, placing them at each corner of her yoga mat. She lit the candles and bowed silently, centering her thoughts. She removed sage and lit it in similar fashion. Next she removed a furled up towel and unrolled it across the front of her mat. The towel was stained with deep rust colored blotches and at the end of its unfurling yielded the headless body of small rodent. Joanna tenderly stroked the rodent's fur and once again bowed her head, this time in silent prayer for the life force of the animal before her. She meditated this way for what she determined a sufficient duration, then gathered her things. She pitched the towel and rodent in the dumpster just outside the studio.

Miss Jacqueline Fleur, Gary's biology teacher, lectured the class on the basics of the animal and plant phyla.

"By the time you finish my biology class, you'll be speaking Latin," she promised. She walked around the classroom, working hard to keep everyone's attention and pointing to pictures of exotic tree frogs and flowers plastered around the classroom. "The plant and animal phyla are derived from the Plantae and Animalia kingdoms, and so up the chain until we reach the highest taxonomic rank, life itself." She stood on her tiptoes pointing to the top green bubble on the poster behind her desk. She smiled with delight at the sight of an unsolicited question from a boy sitting center front row. "Yes, Gary?"

"Miss Fleur, how high up the taxonomy would you need to go to classify artificial intelligence?"

"Wow, Gary. That's a serious and insightful question. Do you mean honest to goodness cognitive and animate robots?"

"Yes," Gary said.

"I supposed that would be an entirely new domain, or perhaps a whole new definition of life itself. It depends on how broadly scientists would be willing to stretch the definition of biological processes."

"A whole new kind of life?" Gary asked.

"Yes, let's go with that," Miss Fleur said. "What prompted your interest?"

Gary scanned the room. Seeing a sea of apathy, he thought, *what the hell.* "Everyone knows nanites cured my cancer. I just wondered how science might classify them, if they were alive."

"*If* they were alive," she said, "we would have to throw out the vast majority of text books in this room and rethink the definition of life." The teacher and the class laughed.

Gary nodded his understanding and slunk a little lower in his seat.

"Now class," Miss Fleur continued, "I want you to start thinking about your first semester project. This will be an important part of your grade, so treat it accordingly. Please present your ideas to me over the next week or so. The sooner you figure out what you would like to do, the sooner you'll be able to get started. Your project may involve either the animal or plant phyla. My only stipulation is that the project be biology related, and I will be judge of that."

Several kids raised their hands. Miss Fleur called on them.

"Can I do a project about bugs?" asked Eugene Maxwell, a

nerdy kid sitting behind Gary.

"Yes, insect collections are acceptable," Miss Fleur replied.

"Actually, can I just take pictures of them?" Eugene asked.

"Yes, if they're your *original* pictures."

"Can I collect flowers?" asked Amy Bridges, a pretty girl sitting in the second row.

"Yes, foliage of any sort is fine," Miss Fleur said. "Please pick a theme to help make the project interesting. The idea is to teach yourself and hopefully the class something we didn't already know."

"I'm tired of these TED Talks," Roddy said. "It's too much information too early in the morning." Roddy's large body slumped in the small metal chair that threatened to buckle under his weight.

"Oh really? I've kind of enjoyed them. They're captivating," Charlie said, flashing his all-American smile and tucking his too-long blond hair behind one ear. "'What I learned from reading 2000 obituaries.' Where else are you going to get a scoop like that? Besides, this is the last morning. Tough it out." They heard a snore from the back of the room. "Or go back to sleep, like Chestnut."

The players nicknamed Horace Riley "Chestnut" because his first name lacked a respectable nickname. As nose guard, Chestnut had spearing (driving your helmet into a player after he's already on the ground) down to a science. When he speared you, his helmet struck particularly hard. It was supposed to be a penalty, but somehow Chestnut repeatedly got away with it. It helped that he was built like a fire hydrant, stocky and low to the ground.

"Yeo, Riley, come sit up here next to me for the next TED Talk," Coach Casey commanded.

Chestnut rubbed his eyes and meandered towards the front of the film room.

"This one's called 'Why Helmets Don't Prevent Concussions.' You might want to pay attention," Coach said. "Could make you think twice next time before you plant that spear in the running back."

"Coach you're killing me," Chestnut whined, stretching as he walked. "If you wanted me to learn to like the damn waterboy, I have to tell you this isn't working. I've lost so much sleep, I would like to crush him like a duck egg." He clasped his hands together.

His comment drew hollers from most of the team. The loudest from Seth Thompson, who was seated in the back with his feet bandaged and propped up on a desk. Seth already missed several days of practice, and he would have to sit out the first home game due to his injury. Doctors diagnosed Seth with a severe scalding to both feet, though medical notes indicated the injury more closely resembled an acid burn or flesh-eating bacteria. It irritated Seth that he was the only player affected so severely by the searing crimson threads. It seemed oddly personal in a way he couldn't fathom. Seth wished he had hit condom boy harder. A broken nose would have evened the score for his scalded feet. Further, while he couldn't verbalize his suspicions, he suspected something menacing. He dare not admit that the aftermath of the hazing incident had scared him. Why should he be scared of the gay condom boy?

"You save that intensity for the game this weekend, Riley," Coach Casey said. "That goes for the rest of you boys. We need our waterboy. Treat him with respect. Believe me, I don't want to have a repeat of this scenario either."

September 11, 2017

Changes Coming for Homecoming Court Election Rules

L. P. D'Innocenzio

Round Rock Independent School District (ISD) adopts gender-neutral homecoming courts, breaking with the tradition of electing a boy as king and a girl as queen. Students will vote for two classmates, with the top vote getters crowned at the school's homecoming dance.

This change means those honored could include two boys, two girls, transgender students or a boy-girl duo.

"We're proud the school district is taking this bold step of inclusiveness for all gender identities and preferences,"said Delores McFadden, first year principal at Sam Houston High School.

"We want all our students to know this is safe environment to learn and grow both intellectually and socially."

The change is effective for the 2017-2018 school year.

Round Rock Daily Dispatch 9-11-17

Vincent sat at the kitchen table, drinking his black coffee and thumbing through the newspaper. He shook his head in disgust and ranted, "This country's going to shit." He read on, repeating the contents of the article for Gary and Joanna to hear.

"Isn't that nice? They can select a hermaphrodite as both king and queen. Between the east coast techies and the west coast hippies, Travis County is being flooded with liberals and all their morally corrupt liberal ideals. I'll tell you exactly what's going to happen. The students are going to vote some fruitcake to be homecoming queen, just because they can. Oh they'll have a king and queen all right, but it will be two guys standing up on stage. Does the queen wear a tuxedo? A dress? Do they dance? What the hell?"

Oh no, Gary thought. *This could be bad.*

Mom was busying herself nearby, polishing and stacking plates. "Oh Vincent, I'm sure it will be fine. They're just trying to be inclusive. Not everyone fits the mold you know," she winked at Gary. "Don't be such a Neanderthal."

Vincent went apoplectic. "Neanderthal? It's not Neanderthal to think boys should be boys and girls should be girls. That's basic fucking human nature. I'm sick and tired of this liberal crap being shoved in our faces. Next thing you know they'll be handing out free condoms!"

Neither Gary nor Joanna had the heart to inform Vincent the school system already implemented that policy. Nor did they discuss the matter further.

Gary appreciated his mom's acceptance. He also despised it. She seemed to accept as fact what Gary was still processing. He had a feeling that coming to grips with his sexual preference would not be to his dad's liking. So he kept it hidden, at least from his dad. A blind man could see it, though. The entirety of the student body seemed to know his secret. "Suck my dick Gary," had recently appeared in red sharpie in another bathroom stall. Gary didn't see it, he just heard it was there. Strange thing is, Gary wasn't even sure it offended him anymore. Perhaps if he just "owned it" as Charlie suggested, the childish high school games would cease.

Gary slipped into his bedroom to ruminate in solitude. He didn't tell his dad about the graffiti in school for fear of compounding the ridicule. The lack of communication served to push them apart, to a point where Gary felt like he didn't even know his own father. How was he going to train the nanites to like his dad if he couldn't connect with him on any level? Was there a positive baseline he could build upon beyond the fear, resentment and lack of acceptance? He searched for a word. "Respect" came to mind.

In the kindest of terms, Gary could describe his dad as "old school." His dad was strong, smart–in his own way–and he provided for his family. Gary respected this. It made his dad different than Gary, sure, but not in a way that caused Gary to harbor animosity. "Different" was another good baseline to build upon. His dad was an avid outdoorsman, and he'd accumulated a sizable collection of rifles, bows, rods, knives, and gear of all sorts. None of which interested Gary, but that was okay. Dad lived and breathed sports; from NASCAR to football, he was all in. His Facebook page boasted about his fantasy football dominance for three years running. Hey, there was a thought. Gary and his dad were Facebook friends. It was a start. Hard as it was to imagine, there had to be other levels upon which he could connect with his dad. Finding them . . . that would be the challenge.

Gary started with his dad's Facebook page. He couldn't remember the last time he checked his dad's feed. Perhaps there was helpful insight there that would help him get to know his dad just a little better. Gary checked his latest post, and the delicately constructed bubble immediately burst. Somehow, Vincent already found the time to post a scathing anti-gay comment about the gender-neutral homecoming court article he had just read.

Vincent Greene
today at 7:46am

Idiots on Round Rock School Board changing rules, allowing queers to be elected homecoming queens. Board Members ought to be kicked out or sued. Our tax dollars are not for social experimentation. Citizens taking it up the ass.

Like · Comment · Share

18 people like this.

3 shares

His post had four likes and a couple of supportive comments already. There seemed to be no hope.

Why couldn't his dad be more like his mom? Gary felt nothing but love and unconditional commitment from her. For years, it seemed their very existence intertwined around Gary's survival. It was Mom who solicited churches and grocery stores for donations. Mom researched the treatment alternatives. Mom who was a major catalyst in Harvard Medical funneling the experimental nanite treatment through Seton Medical Center. She also submitted to conceiving a savior sibling on Gary's behalf, terminating the pregnancy after stem cells were harvested from the fetus. They called it a "miscarriage", but Gary knew better. Mom aborted the baby because of Dad's frequently expressed reservations about having another child "like Gary."

This made Gary's blood boil, literally. He could sense the synthetic charge in his bloodstream. Gary used to give his dad credit and assume he was referring to Gary's ill health. Now, he thought something more sinister. Gary's health wasn't the problem for his dad. Surely, his dad knew what everyone else knew, and what Gary was learning to accept. Gary was gay, and this brought shame upon his father. Gary came full circle: he hated his dad.

At least he had his mom. Her penchant for tarot cards, yoga, crystals and incense spoke to her open-mindedness. It gave her an inner peace that radiated from her. Her enlightenment translated into encouragement for Gary to accept his sexual tendency as an official preference. He loved his mom. The nanites reacted accordingly. Friend or foe, the reaction could not have been clearer.

Chestnut caught up to Seth, who was sitting on Coach Evan's favorite bench at the edge of the school parking lot. "Dude, did you read the paper this morning?" Chestnut asked.

Seth looked up from his playbook of defensive sets for the football team. "You know I don't read that shit Chestnut. Just tell me what's up."

Chestnut handed Seth the newspaper folded to the article about homecoming court. "Paper says the homecoming king and queen can be boys or girls this year. It's the age of gender-neutrality."

"What a bunch of crap," Seth moaned, tossing the paper

aside. "Why don't they just leave us alone instead cramming their political correctness down our throat?"

"I don't know, Seth." Chestnut shook his head. "I thought the idea of electing a guy to be homecoming queen was kind of funny."

"That would be such a joke."

"That's the idea," Chestnut replied, grinning knowingly at Seth.

"Oh you dawg. You're scheming," Seth said, smirking.

"If you're looking for a way to get back at condom boy, the school board has just handed it to you on a silver platter."

The Sam Houston HS football team was winning their first game, even without their top linebacker in the game. Seth sat, stood, seethed, and complained (to anyone who would listen) about not being able to play in the game, and who was to blame. The players tolerated it for a while, but when ignoring him didn't work, Chestnut spoke up.

"Hey Seth, how about you put a sock in it. Let us play the game. We'll deal with the little shit condom boy later." Seth got the message.

Gary kept his distance, best he could, given the confines of the sidelines and the cheerleaders split to either side of the benches. For the most part, he was able to busy himself, constantly toweling off fresh footballs for the referees to swap in and out as the game ball.

Convinced his teammates were resigned to ignore him, Seth shifted his focus to Gary, repeatedly taunting him with "Hey, gay boy," whenever Gary got close enough to hear. Seth played the game of football same as he lived real life: with a chip on his shoulder. This made him the consummate competitor on the field, and a dangerous foe on the sidelines.

But Gary finally had enough. Gary knew Seth had a soft spot for Gatorade, so he slipped around to the backside of the bench and fetched a cup, half filled it with Gatorade, and when he knew Seth wasn't looking, he spit in it.

"You think I'm weak because I'm scrawny," Gary mumbled under his breath. "Let's see what you think after my nanites make meal of your stomach." He put on a fake smile and approached Seth.

"Hey, gay boy," Seth said when he saw Gary standing by him.

Gary held out the Gatorade. "Listen Seth, I come bearing a peace offering. Can we stop this childish name-calling? It's annoying."

"Fuck you, it's meant to be," Seth spat. "I wouldn't be sitting here riding the pine if it weren't for you." Seth turned to watch the game.

"Whatever happened, you brought it on yourself," Gary said. "Besides, I've no intention to hurt you or anyone else." Gary tried to put on his most pathetic voice. "I heard you were ready to crush me like a duck egg."

"That was Chestnut. He doesn't like you either," Seth said.

"That's comforting," Gary said. "Here's some Gatorade." Gary held out the cup and tried not to smile.

"Whatever." Seth took the cup and drank.

Gary eased away to near the sideline and busied himself polishing a football. Within a minute, Seth was convulsing and puking into the trashcan at the end of the bench. Players on the bench cleared away. Assistant coaches Evans and Mitchell ran to Seth's aid and supported him while he retched. It took a while for Seth to purge the contents of his stomach; all along he was mumbling curses at Gary Greene. Finally, stomach emptied, he eyed Gary with contempt and yelled, "I'm going to kill you motherfucker. I'm going to fucking kill you! You hear me?"

Everyone heard him . . . and that was it for Seth.

Principal McFadden weighed the evidence. She couldn't tolerate the blatant death threats hurled at the football team's waterboy. She looked at the perpetrator's high school record and other pertinent information Coach Casey had provided. Seth Thompson had played on the varsity football team since his freshman year. He was arguably the best defensive player on the team, and possibly top linebacker in the county. Being a football player was his ticket to college. Her decision might jeopardize the boy's future.

She could expel him. The Round Rock school system had a zero tolerance policy for threats of violence like the ones Seth shouted at Gary.

She could discipline him with detention or service work for the school. But Coach Casey had tried that route. A week's worth of TED Talks yielded no behavioral change. If anything, Seth Thompson's behavior intensified.

Ultimately, she decided to suspend him from participation in sports, bringing an end to Seth's high school football career. His parents could appeal, but she felt they would be unlikely to succeed in lessening the punishment. This was a second offense, and the threat was deemed serious. Being kicked off the team his senior year would not disqualify Seth from receiving a college scholarship, but the best opportunities were probably lost with his outburst on the sidelines.

"I warned you," Principal McFadden said to Coach Casey across the desk. "I appreciate the information you've provided about Seth's football skills and his scholarship potential, but I can't let the fact that he's a star player influence my decision in this serious matter. We both know how aggression and revenge have ended in carnage at other schools."

"I understand," Coach Casey said.

"How I handle this case sends a message to the school children. Here's my message: You can't blatantly threaten to kill someone and be allowed to play on the high school football team, not even in Texas, not when your principal's name is Delores McFadden."

"That's a good message ma'am," Coach Casey said. "I support your decision. I've been trying to use this whole bullying situation as a life lesson for the players. Perhaps this is the only way Seth Thompson will learn the lesson."

"Perhaps," Principal McFadden nodded, but she squinted her eyes and thinned her lips. Something didn't sit right. "Honestly Coach, here's the thing I don't get. And, please understand my decision is made. There's no changing my judgment on the matter. But, in order for Seth to lash out like he did, something made him mad. I mean really mad. Mad enough to threaten to *kill.* What could have made him react that way?"

"Seth claims Gary spit in his drink," Coach Casey said.

"That's hardly enough reason to kill someone."

"Seth wasn't feeling well," Coach said. "I suppose the Gatorade was the wrong thing for his unsettled stomach."

"So he threw up and blamed Gary? That's irrational. Did you think your star linebacker was irrational Coach?"

"No."

"I thought not," Principal McFadden said, then pondered. "There's more going on here than what we know Coach. I'm going to have a chat with Gary Greene. It's not a disciplinary matter for him per se, beyond the accusation of spitting in someone's drink. I'd like to get a sense from him if he knows why Seth reacted the way he did."

"Gary will be coming to practice after school today," Coach said. "Should I send him to your office?"

"Yeah, that will work. Saves me the trouble and him the embarrassing PA announcement."

Principal McFadden was waiting in her office for Gary after school. "Come in, Come in," she said, opening the door for him.

"Have a seat." He sat.

"Thank you for coming to see me," she said. "I wanted to have a little chat with you about this whole situation with Seth Thompson."

If Principal McFadden thought she seemed less intimidating by raising the pitch of her voice and smiling, it wasn't working. Gary had never before been summoned to the office. He was apprehensive. He sat quietly while Principal McFadden explained her Air Force and educational backgrounds. She told some stories about hazing in the military, and how it was still particularly difficult for women to succeed based on merit. She related her own experiences dealing with sexual misconduct and inappropriate behavior, and she mentioned a few misogyny related scandals, most of which Gary was not familiar. Gary relaxed as the principal talked. Then came the questions.

"So Gary, seeing as how I've done all the talking," Principal McFadden said, "let's make it your turn. You probably know by now that we've suspended Seth from the team. Is there anything else you want me to know about the event that transpired over the weekend?"

"No, not really," Gary said. The less she knew, the better.

"May I ask you some questions?" Principal McFadden said.

"Sure." *But I may not answer them*, Gary thought to himself.

"Do you feel threatened by Seth Thompson?"

You mean the guy who threatened to kill me? Gary was slow to answer.

"The reason I ask," Principal McFadden continued, "is we can take further action to ensure your safety. You're in the driver's seat on how seriously we take his threat."

Gary nodded. "If you're asking me if I think he *really* means to *kill* me . . . no I don't think he does. I think he's a blowhard. But, I do know he can make my school life difficult. He's popular and has a lot of friends. And, his suspension certainly won't endear me to them."

"That's perceptive," Principal McFadden said. "I agree. You think his suspension will further strain your relationship, such as it was."

"Yes."

"And the football team?"

"They'll be resentful," Gary said. "I'm sure of it."

"I think so, too. You'll need to brace yourself for that," Principal McFadden said. "I can have Seth transferred to another school, if need be. Technically, given his threat, we could involve the police."

"Principal McFadden, I know you're trying to help me. But, I don't think any of those steps would fix the problem."

Principal McFadden offered a sincere smile and nodded her head. "I don't think so either, Gary. That's why I refrained. So tell me: why did you spit in his drink? You must have known one of his friends or someone in the crowd would tell him, and that there would be blowback when he found out."

Wow lady, you're good. There was no way Gary was going to admit to spitting in Seth's drink. His motivation was far more nefarious than she could imagine. Gary suspected his spittle might harbor toxic nanites. Gary was not simply attempting to spit into Seth's drink in silent protest, he was using Seth in a curiosity experiment. His nanites had indeed attacked Seth's digestive system. One might even consider Seth's reaction self-defense, were the circumstances fully known. He must have sensed Gary was purposefully hurting him, but without an understanding of the nanites, he was at a loss to explain how.

No, Gary dared not go down this discussion path. The power of the nanites within him, in combination with his growing animosity towards the football players, made Gary the larger threat. Had the principal understood his intention, it would be Gary bearing the brunt of the discipline, not Seth. Gary determined the complexities of the truth were best left unsaid, and that Seth's football career should be sacrificed.

"I didn't spit in his drink," Gary lied.

"Hmm, you really thought about that answer, didn't you?" Principal McFadden said. "Listen, I don't blame you. When you're getting bullied, you look for ways to get back. You're smarter than him. It's usually that way. There's a quiet confidence that comes from being smart. Conversely, there's an insidious lack of confidence that drives a bully."

She looked Gary in the eyes, sizing him up. She empathized with him more than she could reveal. Early in her military career, she thought she could be one of the guys, and agreed to play poker on a houseboat. She either consumed too much alcohol, or she was drugged–possibly both–and she wound up getting gang raped by senior officers. She measured the cost of bringing charges and decided against it. She harbored a grudge and sought retribution in her own way throughout the rest of her career. It seemed to her, Gary was taking a similar path in response to his humiliating experiences.

"I sense there's more going on here than what you're telling me. I also gather you have no intention of talking to me about it. I've been in your shoes. Far be it from me to antagonize the victim. Just do me a favor, Gary, and avoid Seth if you can. He's not going to be a happy camper, but he's also been informed we have him on a very short leash. If you sense any real danger, please inform this office, and we'll take care of it. Capiche?"

"Capiche," Gary replied.

"Great, you're dismissed to see to your football duties," Principal McFadden said, smiling.

Gary stood. "Thank you," he said, thinking, *we'll see how long that lasts.* They shook hands, and Gary exited the office.

Principal McFadden sat alone contemplating the situation. Gary was being let off the hook, and she knew it. Her own trauma left a soft spot in her heart for the bullied, but was that right? She wanted to ask him more questions. She still couldn't figure out what drove Seth to make such a serious threat. She withheld because she didn't want a reputation for badgering victims or whistle blowers and wanted her office to be a safe place for the innocent. Gary had a secret. She hoped it was an innocent one.

The team took Seth's disqualification bitterly. Seth was a leader on the field and a friend off the field. One of Seth's on-field jobs was to make adjustments to the defensive formation based on the alignment of the opposing offense. As a four-year starter, he was ideally suited for the role. His commanding presence would not be easily replaced, and that duty now fell to Nelson Warner. For his part, Nelson rejoiced at his good fortune. He had practiced in the shadow of Seth Thompson for two long years, typically playing only late in games when the outcome was already decided. First, with Seth's injury for game one, and now for the remainder of the season, Nelson would be the starting middle linebacker and, by tradition, also the defensive signal caller.

Disgruntled players became openly hostile to the idea that Gary be allowed to stay on as waterboy while Seth's high school football career ended. The Sam Houston team lost the next week's game to a smaller school that fielded a team they should have beaten–at least on paper. The situation came to a head in a coaches meeting.

"The boy didn't do anything wrong," Coach Casey said.

"The team simply doesn't accept him Casey," Coach Mitchell said. "This is beyond a matter of honor at this point. The cohesiveness of the entire team is in jeopardy. Retaining Gary as waterboy just isn't worth the cost. We know you've been trying to teach a life lesson to the players. We get that. But this is Texas. The only thing that matters is what happens on the scoreboard. If this team doesn't get its shit together, we won't make the playoffs and none of us will be coaching here next season."

"I have to agree, Casey. We have to dismiss the waterboy," Coach Evans said. "Just tell him, now that the hot summer is fading, we don't need him anymore."

"This doesn't sit right with me," Coach Casey admitted.

"We're boxed in Casey. It's either the team or the waterboy. You have to choose," Coach Evans concluded.

The choice was obvious. Gary was dismissed.

"Coaches kicked Gary off the team today," Charlie told his girlfriend, Cindy Perrine. Cindy sat at the mustard yellow fiberglass picnic table nibbling on her Sonic honey BBQ wings. Charlie sat on the table, stocking feet braced on the picnic table bench, drinking his root beer. "They didn't explain why. They didn't need to. Everyone knows why."

Cindy glanced at Charlie's muddy cleats, strewn to the ground to avoid dirtying and scratching the picnic table. Fall in Texas seemed to center around that stupid game. She pondered the dismissal of Gary.

"Hardly seems fair to me. The way you've described it, it doesn't seem like Gary did anything wrong."

"He didn't," Charlie said. "He just didn't fit in, and then he went sideways with Seth."

"Seems to me, that was Seth's problem."

"No doubt, Seth was the instigator. Problem for Gary is that the team's lost some close games, and they were looking for a scapegoat."

"So they fired the waterboy?"

"Yeah."

"Boys are stupid." Cindy licked some sauce off her fingers.

"Yeah, we are."

They sat silently for a few moments. Charlie scanned the horizon. He liked this spot. The Sonic was on a rise overlooking RM 620, and this particular table had a panoramic view.

"I'm thinking about saying something about it to Coach Casey," Charlie said.

"You think anything you say would make a difference?"

"No, probably not, unless I threatened to quit, and honestly, I'm not prepared to do that. What happened to Gary isn't fair, but I'm not going to sacrifice my football career for him."

"What about sacrificing your integrity?" Cindy challenged. "Are you prepared to do that?"

This exasperated Charlie. He felt he was already going out of his way to be considerate to Gary. "What do you want from me?"

"How about you be his friend," Cindy said.

"I'm already being as nice as I can to the guy."

"Being nice to someone and being their friend are two different things. Being nice is convenient. Being a friend takes commitment. Gary's had a hard life. It seems to me he could use a friend. You're a big man on campus. You know darn well if you befriend Gary, others will follow your lead. Plus, you would make your girlfriend very proud. Always a good thing, in these uncertain times." Cindy widened her eyes, bared a mischievous smirk and elbowed Charlie's stocking feet off the bench, causing him to nearly slip off the picnic tabletop.

"Why you little ..." Charlie drove his fingers under Cindy's armpits, targeting her rather ticklish rib cage. Cindy giggled and squirmed. She defended herself with a honey BBQ wet willie to Charlie's right ear.

"Gross!" Charlie withdrew his assault and used a napkin to clean out his greasy ear.

"Serves you right, you goofball," Cindy said, grinning.

"Fine, I'll be his friend," Charlie said, crumpling the napkin.

"Good," Cindy replied. "Me too."

American Scientific September 2017

BEYOND WATSON

The human brain learns through iterative interaction with the world. These interactions yield data on likely outcomes, which can be applied to future decision-making. We call this experience or wisdom. We are nearing the time when robots will be no different. The objective is to create a robot that, when faced with something new, doesn't need to be reprogrammed. We're developing the software that encodes how a robot can learn (not what it can learn). The challenge of putting robots into real-life settings, like homes or offices, is that those environments are constantly changing. The robot must be able to perceive and adapt to its surroundings.

Gary didn't dare break the news of his dismissal to his father. He avoided doing so for a week by staying after school and lingering in the library. He used the opportunity to research new-generation artificial intelligence. Google, Microsoft, Amazon and IBM all were making claims to breakthroughs in the ability to manufacture robots that could learn, evolve their thinking through experience, and adapt to dynamic environments.

The nanites in Gary's blood were ahead of the curve. How far ahead, he couldn't discern, but perhaps he could teach them. He considered the lifetime ramifications of his situation. The nanites in his system treated foreign cells as invaders, just like his cancer cells, making his blood *and* saliva toxic to others. How could he ever kiss? Or make love, regardless of his sexual preference? He dare not even share a can of soda. He needed to tame the beast inside him, or his life would forever be cursed. The idea for his biology project originated in the library, shaped by his understanding of programming logic governing the behavior of the nanites.

Gary was so engrossed in the *American Scientific* article he didn't notice his biology classmates Cindy Perrine and Amy Bridges approaching his table.

"What are you reading, Gary?" Cindy asked, too loudly for the setting.

Gary was startled, then recovered. Cindy was a tomboy with an athletic build, pixie-cut sandy hair, a cute face, and a warm smile. She was longtime friends with Amy Bridges. She was also girlfriend to Charlie Simpson. Cindy and Charlie were an ideal match for each other, Gary thought. He envisioned them getting married one day. He showed her the magazine cover.

"I'm figuring out my biology project," he whispered.

"Oh, us too," Cindy said, softer this time. She flashed an *Insects of Texas* reference guide. "I'm going to collect bugs, the more poisonous the better. Want to help?"

"And I'm collecting flowers. You can help me too," Amy said. "They won't bite or sting, I promise."

"What about the cactus?" Gary joked.

"We'll be careful," Amy said, smiling. Amy Bridges was a tall, confident, freckled brunette. She was Roddy Cruz's girlfriend. She was outspoken, but not obnoxiously so.

Gary's shields were up ever since the locker room shower hazing incident. "Why are you two asking for my help, really?" Gary asked, curious about their motivations.

"Charlie told me they kicked you off the team," Cindy said, matter-of-fact. "I'm sorry they did that. You know Charlie didn't approve of Seth hitting you in the shower, right?"

"And neither did Roddy," Amy added.

Gary nodded, though he was embarrassed at the

recognition. "Alright, I'll help you. When do you want to get started?"

"Right now. Let's walk the Chisholm Trail. I'll drive," Amy said, flashing a red, white, and blue school lanyard with Honda keys attached. The three of them drove in Roddy's beat up Accord and headed to old town Round Rock. Gary yielded the front seat to Cindy. The cloth bench back seat of the car featured the usual accumulation of shoes, sweatshirts, and books to be expected of a high school kid. But underneath one of the sweatshirts was a black violin case.

"Roddy plays violin?" Gary asked.

"No, that's mine," Amy yelled, over the wind noise. "Roddy drops me off at my violin lesson after his football practices."

"I didn't know you played," Gary said.

"I try," Amy said.

"That's great," Gary said. "I don't seem to have the knack for it."

The city of Round Rock was a picture of suburban sprawl. The trio blew past one planned single family housing development after another, some lawns kept green by elaborate sprinkler systems, others gone fallow, succumbing to the Central Texas drought.

"We all have hidden talents," Amy said. "Yours is just probably something other than music."

"I'll say," Gary mumbled.

"Make sure it stays covered Gary. I don't want the case sitting in the direct sunlight," Amy said.

Gary covered the case with a purple and white TCU sweatshirt.

They cut through the city of Round Rock until planned developments gave way to a narrow strip of live oak and cedar woods clinging along the remnants of the Brushy Creek water bed.

"What do you think *my* hidden talent is Amy?" Cindy

interjected.

"You Cindy Perrine are a born circus acrobat," Amy said. "You forget, I've seen you climb trees. You're fearless. And, you're the only person I know limber enough to stretch the balls of their feet to the top of their forehead."

"Can you really do that?" Gary asked.

"Yep," Cindy said, turning to the back seat, beaming. "I can do a one handed cartwheel too!"

"No way!" Gary said.

They arrived at the park in old town where the old Chisholm Trail crossed the Brushy Creek.

Cindy stepped onto a parched patch of grass and demonstrated a graceful one-handed cartwheel. She bowed and showboated as if entertaining a circus audience. She did another cartwheel using the other arm. She flexed them both. "Ambidextrous," she gloated. Gary and Amy applauded.

September wasn't a great month for flower picking in Central Texas. Gary's dad used to say Texas had four seasons, "drought, drought, drought and flood." Gary used to add "allergy season" to that list, but ever since his nanite treatment, his allergies had vanished. Cedar, mulberry, ragweed, prairie grass–Gary used to suffer from them all. The nanites had boosted his immune system, and so far this year they had spared him the agony. He pondered the ramifications. A cure for cancer? That would bring Dr. Reichmann fame. A cure for allergies? That would bring him fortune. The nanites promised to bring him both. Gary noted that he was due for a follow up with his doctor to discuss these welcome side effects.

Central Texas was currently enduring another drought. Their hope of gathering any flowers was the live oak canopy lining the creek along with the trickle of a stream that remained. With any luck, they would find some critters for Cindy there too.

They picked their way along the creek, dry brush crackling

with each step. To Gary, if Central Texas smelled like anything, it smelled like trees. The scent of cedar and juniper hung heaviest near the creek, where moisture and shade could persist along a narrow oasis. They managed to help Amy find some wild white Blackfoot daisies, yellow sunflowers and one orange hedgehog cactus flower.

Cindy was having less luck locating "poisonous insects." Why she selected such a narrow focus for her project spoke to her sense of adventure, Gary supposed. Her media to capture and hold her insects were clear plastic cups, with lids, borrowed from the school cafeteria. Gary got the honors of scooping up a few of the most pervasive poisonous pests, fire ants, on her behalf. They didn't look too happy scrambling around the inside edges of the cup.

Amy spotted a funnel shaped web just off the side of the creek. Gary scooped a nasty looking brown-striped spider about the size of nickel. They discerned later that it was a hobo spider.

"You know a spider isn't technically an insect, right?" Gary said.

"Yeah, it's an arachnid," Amy added.

"It's still a really neat bug. I'll expand my project to accommodate," Cindy said.

Gary spotted something crawling ahead of them along a putrefied wagon wheel rut on the trail. He stepped closer and saw it was a pale-yellow scorpion, about two inches long, two dark stripes along the length of its body, little pincers in front, and a wicked-looking curved tail in back. Sensing the footsteps, the scorpion stayed frozen in the rut. Cindy passed Gary a cup. He slowly brought the cup down and managed to trap the scorpion between the cup and the ground, tail sticking under the cup edge in the wheel rut. Gary held the cup there a moment.

"Now what are you going to do *genius*?" Cindy asked.

"Pass me the lid," Gary said. He lifted the cup ever so slightly, intent on scooping underneath the scorpion, entrapping it in the cup. The scorpion had other plans. It jackhammered its tail down onto the plastic lid, piercing it, driving its stinger deep into Gary's middle finger, drawing blood, unfortunately for the scorpion. The effect was instantaneous. Red tentacles thin as spider webs darted through the hole in the lid, traced along the scorpion's tail and enveloped its abdomen. The scorpion, still trapped in the clear plastic cup flailed its legs and wreathed. Gary thought fast, this would be hard to explain. He brought the heel of his tennis shoe down upon the cup, crushing it and the scorpion trapped inside.

"Oh my God! Gary did that scorpion just sting you?" Cindy said.

"Yeah, it got me." Gary squeezed the end of his finger to prevent any more bleeding.

"You going to be okay?" Cindy asked, concerned.

"It's not that bad." He lied. It hurt like hell.

"Let me see it," Amy said.

"No really, I'll be fine." His finger was strangely numb and felt like it was starting to swell.

"Are you sure you don't need to go to the hospital? That was a scorpion!" Amy insisted.

"Nope, I've seen enough doctors for a lifetime." This was true. "Maybe just some ice?"

"Gary, scorpions are poisonous," Cindy said, wide-eyed. "You could die!"

"I'm not going to die. Relax. It wasn't that kind of scorpion, believe me."

Bug hunting cut short by the scorpion sting, they swung by a drive-thru and grabbed a cup of ice for Gary, then headed to the school.

"No worries Gary, we needed to head home anyway," Amy

said. "Roddy is going to want his crappy car, and he needs to take me to violin practice."

Gary walked home from school, finger in a cup of ice, contemplating his own biology class project.

"Mom? Where are my Band-Aids?" Gary yelled.

"Don't yell Gary. Come talk to me."

Joanna was fixing dinner. Gary caught a whiff of the pot roast. He loved his mom's pot roast, especially the caramelized onions, potatoes and carrots that she would cut in half and let simmer for hours in the juices. Joanna was barefoot, dressed in grey yoga pants, Dallas Cowboys t-shirt, pale blue bandana and a bluebonnet print apron that matched the tile backsplash. She seemed one with the kitchen. She lifted the lid to drop in some rosemary and a few bay leaves. Vincent wasn't home from work yet.

"Smells great Mom." Gary held out his bloodied finger. "I need the Neosporin and Band-Aids. I had them on my dresser. Any idea where they are?"

"Oh my, what happened?" Joanna asked.

"Scorpion decided he didn't want to be part of a biology project," Gary said.

"Looks like that hurt." His mom went to reach for the wound.

Gary pulled his hand away. "It's okay. It just needs a little first aid."

Joanna was silent, waiting for Gary to look directly at her. She wanted eye contact. "Gary, you know how much I love you right?"

"Yeah Mom, of course, I know that."

"Well then, you can understand how concerned I might be if I suspected you were engaged in something that was harmful to you." Joanna was striking a benevolent but serious tone. Gary thought something like this might happen. Someone was bound to figure out there was something untoward going on with the nanites. Perhaps it was best that it was his mom. He trusted her.

"Yeah Mom, I would understand." He maintained eye contact and let his finger dangle in the soft drink cup that now contained a slurry of ice water.

"We need to talk about that razor blade in your room. I didn't mean to pry into your business. I was simply looking for my hairbrush, and the razor blade caught my eye. We've been through a lot together, and I know it's been difficult, physically and emotionally. I hear from other parents about the issues their kids are struggling with, and honestly, I've been on the lookout for signs from you that go beyond the normal teenage angst. You're scaring me, having a razor blade in your room. I'm imagining the worst. We've worked too hard for too long to have you throw your life away. Please talk to me. I'm here to listen, not admonish." Her hands trembled and her lips quivered. It was subtle, but enough to indicate to Gary that his mom's nerves were frayed.

Gary was dumbfounded and slow to respond.

"Gary, please. You're freaking me out. If you can't talk to me, then maybe you can speak with a therapist."

He broke eye contact and gazed past his mom to the pattern on the backsplash. This rare lecture from his mom was straight to the point, he had to grant her that. How was he to explain? He wasn't depressed. Well maybe he was a little depressed. It would be nice to have more friends. But, he wasn't harming himself. He couldn't very well explain he was experimenting with the nanites in his blood to see if they would kill people. He brought his eyes to hers, they were pleading for reassurance. He placed the cup of iced water on the counter and held his arms open wide.

"Come here Mom."

She stepped forward and hugged him tight. He

reciprocated. "Mom, I promise I don't need a therapist. I know I can talk with you and tell you anything." *Except anything about the nanites.* "I promise you, I am not hurting myself, and I promise I have no intention of doing so. My biology class sparked my interest in DNA, so I needed some hair and blood samples. That's all there is to it." There was more to it, but why antagonize his mom? "Right now I just need the Neosporin and a Band-Aid because of the scorpion sting. I'll give them right back to you."

Joanna pulled back from the hug and grasped Gary by both shoulders. She looked squarely into his eyes. "You're not cutting? You're not contemplating suicide?"

Gary shook his head. "No, Mom."

"Drugs? Alcohol?"

"Not happening."

"Cigarettes?" She progressed down her mother list, forehead wrinkled, head tilted. Now she was fishing.

"And I'm still a virgin," Gary cut to the chase.

At that, Joanna sort of patted Gary on both shoulders as if she were dusting him off from falling on the playground. "Okay, wise guy. You know I'm not trying to keep you bubble-wrapped. I was just concerned because of what I found in your room." She smiled and pointed to the cabinets at the end of the kitchen. "Top drawer."

"Thank you." Gary fetched the first aid ointment and a single Band-Aid.

Gary felt his mom's eyes tracking him across the kitchen.

"You don't have to worry about me, Mom," Gary said. "I swear."

"Alright, I believe you." Joanna gave the pot roast a gentle stir. "By the way, I didn't mention anything about this to your father. His temper is worse than usual lately."

"I've noticed. Thanks. I'm glad you confronted me directly, Mom." Gary escaped the kitchen and retreated to his bedroom.

He made a point to leave his door open so his mom wouldn't worry about him.

He powered on his iPad and dove into blog posts and discussion threads about microbiology and nanorobotics, esoteric topics in which he had suddenly developed a keen interest.

MISBEHAVING AI

From pets to robots, does training matter?

Train your robot: Artificial intelligence could end up behaving as rabid dogs if not controlled. Experts warn the robot apocalypse may be upon us. Purdue University research scientists fear a poorly trained robot, with unclear and unbounded instructions, could end up exhibiting unwanted behavior, just as a poorly trained dog does. This warning comes as technological advances in AI predict that the relationship between humans and our robot creations will become more and more intertwined and complex. There can be little doubt that Robotics and Autonomous Systems (RAS) are going to change our lives.

The world-renowned professor Stephen Hawking warns: "Robots will certainly evolve faster than humans and their goals will be unpredictable." There may soon come a day when artificial intelligence, disguised as helpful digital assistants, will gain the upper hand and dictate those goals. That day could well spell doom for mankind.

114 10 September 2017 - Vol 672 Issue 5519 **SCIENCE AND TECHNOLOGY REPORT**

Gary downloaded articles about artificial intelligence, where machines learn as humans do, iteratively, applying lessons learned in compounding fashion. He posted in forums about nanite technology in particular, focusing on their "theoretical" cognitive abilities. He marveled at assertions about the near-term plausibility of cognitive robots.

No shit, He thought. *The little buggers are already in my blood.*

Overall, he found a fascinating preponderance of discussion about the art of the possible with respect to cognitive robots. He found perfunctory information about the importance of training autonomous robots, but he found little practical advice on *how* to go about training them. Perhaps it was his calling to write the book, *Nanites for Dummies.* The thought amused him.

Gary waited after class to discuss his proposed project with Miss Fleur. He was stuck waiting behind Liam Strauss and Lucas Barolo, football players who were proposing a joint project on a topic with which they had recently become familiar.

"We want to write a paper on 'Why Helmets Don't Prevent Concussions,'" Liam said.

"What kind of helmets? Bikes? Motorcycles?" Miss Fleur asked.

"Football," Lucas clarified.

"And you want to write this as a joint project, because–?"

"We're both interested in the topic," Liam said

"I see," Miss Fleur said. "I heard a TED Talk on helmets and football concussions. It was very interesting, you might want to use it in your research."

"Thanks Miss Fleur," they said and turned to leave, giving Gary a rough nudge as they passed.

Gary recovered and approached the teacher. "Miss Fleur, I suddenly find myself fascinated by microbiology. I think it has to do with the nanites that cured my cancer. My nanites are tuned to my DNA, and I am curious how they might react to other people's DNA as well. I figure I'll need people to donate DNA samples for my biology project. Does that sound weird?"

"No Gary, that sounds fascinating. People will have to volunteer, but within the bounds of a class biology project, I'm willing to go along with collecting non-invasive DNA samples from your classmates. Simple cheek swabs or a hair should do."

"Great," Gary said.

"You'll need supplies. Follow me." Miss Fleur led Gary to the biology lab overstock cabinets and provided him packages of test tubes and petri dishes as media for the samples.

Gary cradled the boxes and considered his options. "Miss Fleur is there a place I can keep these at school? I really don't want to drag them home, and there isn't a great place for me to work with them there anyway."

"I know a place. Follow me." He followed. She led him to a door one down from hers. Gary had always assumed the room was some kind of storage closet. She unlocked the door, flicked on the light, and stepped inside. The room featured a table, some chairs, a plaid cushioned loveseat, cabinets, shelves along one wall, and a utility sink in the corner.

"This room used to be the teacher's lounge until the addition was built. Nobody uses it anymore. I held onto the key, just in case," she winked.

"I can use this room for my studies?" Gary asked.

"Yes, you can use this room, in privacy," she confirmed. "Here is the key." She stretched out her hand containing a key on a lanyard.

"Oh, I can't take your only key Miss Fleur." Gary was already reaching for lanyard.

"I have another," she said, "but no worries. I won't disturb you, or your stuff. I promise." She held up two fingers together, like an Eagle Scout.

"Deal."

"I'll leave you to it. Have fun!" Miss Fleur said, leaving the room.

Gary set his boxes of supplies on the table and began to organize them. He paused. He settled onto the loveseat and surveyed the room. He liked it. *This is perfect*, he thought.

"Nice going," Lucas said. "Now we don't have to do much research except listen to that stupid TED Talk again." Lucas and Liam were veterans on the football team, having played together as starters on the defensive squad their entire sophomore year. Lucas played cornerback, a position that demanded quickness and agility in order to keep up with the speedy wide receivers, and intelligence to read the quarterback's intent and anticipate plays based on the offensive formation. Liam, on the other hand, was a defensive lineman. Liam's job was to stop the running back or sack the quarterback. It seemed a relatively simple assignment. Lucas figured the burden of the biology project would fall on his shoulders, if they cared at all about getting a decent grade. But, that was okay. Lucas and Liam existed in a symbiotic relationship. Lucas provided the brains, Liam provided the brawn, and a cagey sense of humor.

"Did you see how the teacher perked right up when she saw that little shit condom boy was next in line?" Liam said.

"Yeah, I noticed," Lucas said.

"The more I see of the little shit, the more I empathize with Seth," Liam said.

"Yeah, condom boy is starting to annoy me too," Lucas said. "The girls like him. The teachers like him. He makes us look like fools. Gives me more reason to despise him."

"Me too," Liam agreed.

Miss Fleur got everyone's attention. "Class I have an announcement. We are all going to participate in a microbiology experiment."

"If this involved injections, I'm out." Amy Bridges interjected.

"No, no injections," Miss Fleur said. "Gary, why don't you explain what you need."

All eyes turned to Gary.

"It's pretty simple. I need volunteers to provide DNA samples. Nothing weird. A lock of hair, a cheek swab, or even just some spit."

"Spit's pretty weird," Amy said.

"Not in this case," Miss Fleur chimed. "This is strictly voluntary. I do hope many of you choose to participate. Gary has a passion for this science. Let's help him out." She smiled. "Here Gary, I'll start. Trim some of these split ends." She offered Gary the scissors.

Gary chopped a bit of her auburn hair, put it in a petri dish and labeled it with a sharpie.

"Who's next?" Miss Fleur asked.

"Aw hell, I'll donate some DNA to the cause Gary." It was Nelson Warner, new starting linebacker for the football team and, in happenstance, eager to please the perky Miss Fleur. Nelson approached the front of the class, picked up a cotton swab and leaned a little closer to the petite teacher. He handed her the swab.

"You mind scraping my cheeks Miss Fleur?" he grinned.

"Open wide," she scrapped around in there until she was satisfied the swab was plenty full of Nelson's cheek cells for Gary's purposes. She handed the swab to Gary, who stored and labeled the sample.

"That was nice of you Nelson." She nodded her appreciation. "Next?"

Cindy Perrine stood up, presented herself in an arms open pose and sauntered to the front desk.

Cindy waited until Gary was ready to make eye contact.

She locked on. "Are you free tonight? Charlie and I were going to watch Karen Black in *Trilogy of Terror*. I think it apropos to watch that triple feature as a trio, don't you?" She didn't wait for an answer. "I'll send Charlie over to pick you up, say around seven?"

Gary stared open mouthed at Cindy.

"Say 'Yes,' Gary," Miss Fleur encouraged.

"Okay," Gary managed.

"Great! Now what kind of DNA sample would you like from me?" Cindy asked.

Nelson, still standing nearby, scanned her up and down. "Oh my."

Miss Fleur wagged a finger at him. "Now class, let's keep this clean." She smiled at Nelson and shooed him away towards his seat.

"Spit's fine," Gary said.

He offered Cindy a test tube. She worked up some saliva, dripped it into the test tube and returned it. Gary put a stopper on, labeled the tube and put it in the holding tray.

"See you tonight," Cindy winked and returned to her seat, walking with an exaggerated wiggle.

Gary knew Cindy wasn't flirting with him. She *was* teasing with her butt wiggle, but Gary wasn't the target of her tease. Surely, Charlie had shared their conversation about Gary's sexual preference.

Nelson noticed the wiggle. So did Liam Strauss and Lucas Barolo, both lurking in the back of the class, dismissive of Gary's experiment and miffed at the extra attention Gary was getting from Cindy.

A few more kids stood and approached the front desk, ready to participate.

"You've got to be shitting me," Lucas whispered. "How many times have we hung out with Cindy and Charlie? She's never wiggled like that for any of us. Gay condom boy's endeared himself to her. Geez. First he gets Seth kicked off the team, and now he's a gay boy pet for the girls."

"I heard that," Amy glared at Lucas. Amy stood up. "Stand up," she said, gesturing with her hand. They stood. "Go up there, provide a DNA sample to Gary and be nice about it."

"But I didn't say anything," Liam started to whine.

"Hush. You were about to," Amy replied. "I saved you from yourself. Go donate." She waved them along. Liam and Lucas followed instructions. They didn't want to be on Amy's bad side. Along with Cindy, she was one of the most popular girls in the school.

Amy stood to get in line behind them. Cindy stood next to her, about to sit down. "Are you sure you can't come over tonight?" Cindy whispered. "Gary said yes. You would be his surprise date."

"I'm glad you guys are being nice to Gary," Amy said. "I don't like that the football team has bullied him. But I can't tonight. I have violin practice."

"Darn."

"You guys have a good time." Amy got in line behind the bullies.

Gary stood by the front desk and gratefully accepted the DNA samples. Most of the kids donated a wad of spit. Amy volunteered a lock of her soft mocha hair, claiming it was classier, "something in which some of my classmates are distinctly lacking."

By the time class was over, everyone had contributed. "I'm proud of all of you," Miss Fleur announced. "Gary, I hope your work is successful."

"I do, too, Miss Fleur," Gary replied, surprised that everyone participated. He expected to be laughed at, or called a freak, at least by some of the kids. But that wasn't what happened at all. It helped that Amy and Cindy rallied people to the cause. He would have to find a way to thank them.

Gary carried the samples to the private room. He lined them along the shelf, considering each one as he placed them. He decided to align them according to his feelings toward each person. This was not a judgment, he rationalized. It was an experiment to help him understand how better to control the behavior of the nanites inside him.

He placed the samples of his favorite people toward the right side of the shelf, starting with the teacher, Miss Fleur. He placed the samples of his least favorite people towards the left, starting with the football players, sans Nelson. Nelson wasn't an arrogant jerk like the rest of them. His sample went right. The wiggly Cindy Perrine and the feisty Amy Bridges went right. So the process continued until Gary was sure he had the samples lined up in reasonable order. The end result was three racks of test tubes and a few petri dishes meticulously placed where they belonged, according to Gary's feelings. Gary found himself ambivalent about most of his classmates. That meant the test tube rack in the middle of the shelf was nearly fully stacked. That was okay, too. Having no feelings at all towards a person would help him calibrate his stronger feelings, one way or the other.

Satisfied, he left the objects of his experiment untouched that first day. He closed and locked the door behind him. He was already late for his next class, so he stuck his head into Miss Fleur's class, interrupting her. As she scribbled him a tardy note, he noticed Charlie Simpson sitting middle second row. Charlie mouthed "See you tonight" and gave Gary the thumbs-up.

Gary nodded, figuring Cindy must have caught her boyfriend in the hallway between classes. They communicated well. He liked that. Third wheel with those two didn't sound so bad. He looked forward to the evening and began to think about what he might wear. He chuckled to himself and thought, *Wow, I really am gay.* He decided to own it.

Miss Fleur smiled warmly and handed Gary the tardy slip. "Nice job today Gary."

"Thank you Miss Fleur. You too. I really appreciate the room."

She nodded and returned to her classroom instructions.

Gary casually strolled to his next class, American History. They were just starting to study the founding fathers. Ever since Trump's election, social media was exploding with the false pretenses of the nation's founding. George Washington and Thomas Jefferson owned slaves, this made them hypocrites. But, this was Texas. Here in Texas the good guys were still the good guys. George Washington and Thomas Jefferson were still to be revered. Maybe not as much as Sam Houston and William Travis, but revered nonetheless. Gary determined the nanites would have liked all these men. In fact, Gary decided he was going to have to train the nanites to *love everybody*. That was the only way anyone would ever be safe.

Gary watched out the window for the orange pickup truck to pull into the driveway. Soon as it did, he yelled, "I'm headed out, Mom, bye!"

"Where are you going Gary?" Joanna yelled from the kitchen.

Gary didn't want to have to explain. He didn't want to be babied. "Out with some friends."

"What friends?"

"Oh, thanks a lot Mom." Gary circled to the kitchen door so he didn't have to yell.

"You know I didn't mean it like that. I know you have friends. Who are they?"

"Charlie Simpson and Cindy Perrine."

"The quarterback?" Vincent asked, maneuvering towards Joanna.

"Yeah. We're going to watch a movie."

"What movie?" Joanna asked, giving Vincent a sideways glance.

Vincent wrapped his arms around Joanna from behind. "Let the boy go dear," he said. "How late are you going to be out?"

"A few hours maybe," Gary replied, retreating from the overt foreplay unfolding in the kitchen.

"That should do," Vincent said, squeezing his wife's ass.

Thinking about his dad having sex with his mom while he was out with his friends wasn't the image Gary wanted stuck in his head. He thought instead about a ménage à trois with Charlie and Cindy and walked out the door with a smile on his face.

The three of them sat in the basement game room of Cindy's parents' home, watching *Trilogy of Terror* on a VCR player attached to a distinctly modern 65" TV. Cindy's basement was a museum of bygone entertainment technology: a jukebox full of 45's featured prominently by the wet bar; a record player on a corner credenza stacked with vinyl LPs; a travel case of 8-tracks tossed under the pool table.

Charlie, Cindy, and Gary lounged in splendor. Charlie reclined in a La-Z-Boy, drinking a Modelo Negra beer. Cindy stretched out on the couch, cocooned in an Aztec patterned woolen blanket. Gary sat wide-legged at the coffee table, munching popcorn. Gary appreciated that the couple wasn't demonstrative in his company, despite the privacy of the basement. He couldn't imagine what his reaction might be if they were fawning all over each other. It might have turned him on. As it was, Gary's attention was fixated on the screen where Karen Black, performing as Julie the English teacher, was seducing a college student, though the student thought the situation was the other way around. When it got to the scene where the college student was developing naughty photographs of Julie in his darkroom, Cindy and Charlie teased each other about which gender was the most manipulative.

Towards the end of the segment, Charlie said, "You know, we're watching Karen Black on the blackest black TV on the market." He was expecting a reaction for his trivia, but no one said anything. "You guys don't get that, do you? The TV is an OLED, you know the 'blackest black.' That's their advertising motto."

"Shut up, you goofball, you're ruining the tension," Cindy said.

The segment ended with a house fire and foreshadowing of Julie's next victim.

"This is a hoot," Gary said. "When was this thing made?"

"1975," Charlie said, sipping his beer.

"Ah, that was a classic era for horror," Gary said.

"Sure was," Charlie agreed.

Cindy hit the pause button. "You two talk more than my girlfriends. Are we going to watch this movie the way it's supposed to be watched, or are we going to talk the whole time?"

"How's it supposed to be watched?" Charlie asked.

"Well, since you asked," Cindy said, "it's too bright in here. This movie deserves to be watched in the dark."

"I'll get the lights." Gary stepped across the room and flicked the light switch, leaving only the ambient TV light to illuminate the room.

"Secondly, I need company under this blanket. Can't you tell I'm scared?"

Charlie slid from Lay-Z-boy to couch and sat at Cindy's side.

As Gary stepped across them to return to his chair, Cindy extended her leg, blocking his way. She patted the available side of the couch and said, "*Very* scared."

What's a guy to do? Gary settled onto the couch on the

other side of Cindy, chuckling to himself that while Charlie was the quarterback, Cindy was the alpha in this relationship. He would have felt awkward sitting off to the side. It was kind of Cindy to include him in their snuggling. You're not the third wheel if you're part of tricycle. Cindy smiled wide, shared her Mexican blanket, wiggled her shoulders and hips, and snuggled in to watch the movie "the way it's supposed to be watched."

Cindy hit the play button. The three of them remained nice and cozy on the couch through the second segment featuring Karen Black playing a girl with split personalities. Then came the third and most memorable segment–on several levels. The gist of the story involved a miniature Zulu doll that came to life. It included lots of suspense building with Karen Black contending with the quart-size aboriginal warrior equipped with razor sharp teeth and a chopstick size spear. Gary was captivated as Karen Black dashed about the apartment, evading the possessed doll. Cindy paused the scene, turned to Charlie and said, "You ready for this?"

Charlie nodded, "I'm ready if you're ready."

Cindy hit resume and the chase scene resumed between the crazy girl and the Zulu doll. Cindy squirmed with each jab of the little spear and slash of the carving knife. There wasn't much room for Cindy to squirm though, with the three of them wedged together on the couch, as it were. Gary found himself more stimulated by Cindy's gyrations than by the movie. He wasn't the only one. Charlie slipped his arm around her and she sort of made more room to maneuver by leaning her head into Charlie's chest and swinging her legs across Gary's lap. The Mexican blanket followed Cindy's legs, exposing her torso to Charlie's free hand. He smoothly cupped a breast and she undulated her body, starting with her shoulders, through her chest and hips, ending with her toes, which she continued to wag, demanding attention.

Gary thought this a precarious situation. Cindy's legs were

under the blanket. Did Charlie know she was wiggling her toes? Did he care? Gary figured he was about to find out. He reached to rub Cindy's feet. She stopped wiggling them and moaned. She actually moaned. Gary didn't mind rubbing feet. He had rubbed his mom's feet every now and then, when she asked. He sort of knew how to pay attention to the arch, and finger between the toes without tickling. He could feel Cindy's feet melting into his hands. Charlie's breast cupping became a breast stroking, with Cindy helping him along by rhythmically arching her back. Each undulation started at her shoulders and ended at her tailbone, which repeatedly ground into Gary's lap, yielding the predictable effect. At least this time there weren't a dozen football players chanting "Boner" and throwing condoms at him.

Charlie slipped off Cindy's shirt and unsnapped her bra. Her breasts fit her athletic body, keeping their form even as her bra fell off the edge of the couch. The movie ended. Gary was distracted and missed what happened, but didn't care. Cindy reached for the remote and clicked off the TV. This left the three of them in complete darkness. She undulated her body again, neck to pelvis, as of to signal the boys to continue the process. Gary graduated his foot massage to a calf message, which he paused just long enough to let Cindy slip off her shorts. Cindy dragged her hand purposefully across Gary's lap, stopping at the hardness at his groin. Only then did it occur to Gary that there was danger in how far this petting might go. He wasn't kissing anyone, which was good, because of the toxic nanites in his saliva. What about his semen? He didn't know. Could he keep himself from ejaculating? No, probably not, this was too exciting. If he did have sex, whom would it be with? Cindy? Charlie? Which did he prefer? Between the perceived danger of his nanites, and his confusion over his sexuality, he was paralyzed.

Cindy wiggled her feet a couple of times to get his

attention.

"Stay with us," she whispered. Gary wasn't sure if it was a general plea for the evening or a specific request that he not let his mind wander away from the moment. Perhaps it was a little of both. She reached for his hand and moved it up her thigh, to her vulva, where another hand, Charlie's, was already gently petting. Gary noted her pubic hair was shaved. It didn't matter really. He never thought about it until now. He thought it a chore having to shave his face every now and then. Girls had a more delicate job he figured.

Should he do everyone a favor and fill his shorts now, before he makes a fool of himself in front of his two new friends? Or worse, becomes dangerous? He realized not only would he need to use his private experiment room to test his saliva, he was going to have to test his semen. Hopefully Miss Fleur doesn't barge in and catch him masturbating. Cindy flopped her knees apart and guided Gary's hand to her opening. Gary was clumsy with his fingers. Understanding, she thrust her hips towards him, capturing two fingers in her wet vagina. She held his hand there and moved her hips back and forth, while Charlie continued to massage her vulva. She moaned and bucked her hips just a little faster. "Fuck me," she said. Gary wasn't sure to whom Cindy was speaking.

"You *both* need to fuck me." Well that clarified it.

Charlie and Gary dutifully removed their shorts and underwear. Gary's eyes had adjusted enough to the darkness for him to see the outline of Charlie's member. Cindy got to her knees on the couch, reached for the two boys and roughly pulled them towards her in a forced group hug. It was body on body on body. Charlie yielded to Gary.

"You need to try this. You might find out you like it," Charlie said.

Gary was nervous. He kept wondering when they were going to say, "The joke's over," and then laugh at him. But, they never did that. He accepted that he was being invited in the most intimate of ways. He stared again at Charlie's cock and then at Cindy, with her legs spread. In that moment he knew which vision excited him more. His excitement surged just as Cindy leaned back and let Gary fall on top of her. They were stretched along the couch, face to face, groin to groin. Then she kissed him. Not just any kiss, she offered a full open mouth, tongue tangling kiss. Gary lost himself in the moment, and with the picture of Charlie in his head he entered Cindy and began moving back and forth . . . then he remembered the ramifications. He stopped and pulled back.

"It's okay," she said.

"No, you don't understand. It's *not* okay," he replied.

"It's completely okay Gary," Charlie said.

"Do you feel okay?" Gary asked Cindy.

"I feel great," she said. "Now make me feel even better."

She pulled him towards her and moved her pelvis to a rhythm Gary adjusted to. His apprehensions melted away in the warmth of Cindy's body. Surely the nanites would sense the pleasure he felt and respond accordingly. Gary thrust his hips, deeply penetrating and withdrawing.

By offering his virginity to Cindy was Gary betraying his preference? He thought not. Gary felt acceptance, with Cindy and Charlie breaking down barriers in dramatic fashion. What they were performing was more than a sex act, it felt like a genuine act of love. Until this moment, Gary's sexual experience was limited to masturbating in the privacy of his bedroom. The lovemaking in Cindy's basement wasn't dirty and it was no secret; it was a beautiful moment shared between friends. Cindy's eyes rolled back and she began a sort of sing-song breathing that eventually led to a prolonged orgasmic shriek.

"Geez Cindy, you never scream like that with me," Charlie said.

"It's his first time, isn't it Gary?" Cindy said, panting.

"For sure, first time for a lot of things," he said as he continued to thrust in and out.

"Let the boy finish," Charlie said.

"Oh I will," she said, rolling onto her knees and elbows. "But you come over to this side."

Charlie stood in front of her and she engaged orally. This sent a surge of heat and excitement through Gary. Cindy wiggled her hips, her telltale signal that attention was required. Gary maneuvered behind her, gripped her hips and found her entrance, this time all on his own. He was learning. God, it felt good inside her. Gary hadn't realized that sex had a smell. The sweat of their bodies and what he could only assume was the smell of Cindy's pheromones combined to fill the basement with an erotic aroma and energy. Gary realized the oral sex on the other end of the equation intensified the fire of his libido.

Charlie and Gary figured out a rhythm of squishing and grunting back-and-forth, with Cindy rebounding between them. Charlie's naked body was the real turn-on for Gary. His broad shoulders, rippling muscles and chiseled rib cage made him the envy of either gender. Gary even liked the way Charlie's long blond hair swayed as he moved in Cindy's mouth. The image of her lips locked around Charlie's cock sent warm sensuous waves through Gary's groin. Charlie grunted on last time, pulled his member from Cindy's mouth and ejaculated onto her face. The sight brought Gary past the edge of restraint. His saliva didn't hurt Cindy, let's hope his semen wouldn't either. Gary tightened his grip on Cindy's hips, made a halfhearted effort to withdraw, part way out he felt a pulse of release from his testicles, then completed the withdrawal. He lay pressed against Cindy, praying he hadn't injected harmful nanites into her privates, even as more pulses of semen oozed onto her bum.

The entire room smelled of sweat and sex. Gary pondered

what a sick bastard he must be. This was his chance to find out whether he would have to worry about shooting flesh-eating semen the rest of his life. One sick bastard, that's what he was, he thought. These two people were being nice to him. More than nice. They just shared the ultimate in intimacy and he used them.

"You didn't have to pull out Gary. I'm on the pill."

"No, you don't understand. This isn't safe. How do you feel?"

"Oh no. You have an STD Gary?" Cindy asked.

This got Charlie's attention. "What?" he said, concerned.

"No. No. Nothing like that. I've never been with anyone," Gary explained.

"That's a relief," Charlie said.

"It's okay Gary. I feel fine. What are you worried about?" Cindy asked, wiping Charlie's semen off her chin. She made a sour face. "Charlie tastes salty. Do all men taste this salty?" she asked Gary.

"I wouldn't know," Gary said, self-conscious that he had no sexual experience at all until this threesome, but also wanting to find out what Charlie tastes like. The thought sent another little surge through his groin.

"Oh darn. I thought you might," Cindy said, reaching to her bum and scraping her finger across a wad of semen Gary left there. "You could tell me if you knew. Who am I to judge?" She held up her finger, licked it, and smiled. "For the record, you taste fresher than Charlie. I wonder why?"

Gary had no reply. What was he supposed to say? Maybe it's the nanites?

"I'll get a towel." Charlie switched on the bathroom light, cutting through the darkness of the basement, shedding just enough light to illuminate Cindy's naked body. Cindy suddenly felt exposed and a wave of self-consciousness washed across her face. Gary recognized the look and stepped closer to comfort her. She stepped away. By the time Charlie returned with the towel, Cindy was crying.

"What happened?" Charlie asked.

Gary shrugged. Her body language suggested shame. How could he express that? He tried by saying, "I think she's overwhelmed."

Cindy accepted the towel, though instead of wiping her hands with it, she wrapped herself in it and curled up in a ball on the couch. Charlie covered her with the Mexican blanket, then Charlie and Gary gave her space and got dressed. They each handed Cindy her articles of clothing and she went to the bathroom, still draped in the blanket.

"What do we do now?" Gary asked.

"Just give her some space. Girls are weird," Charlie said. "You should know, it's not like we've ever done this before, you know, a threesome. I guess, well, we both were kind of upset about what happened to you in the locker room shower and wanted you to feel like you had some real friends. Give her time to process."

"I think I need time to process too," Gary said.

"If ever there was a time for a cigarette, it would be now, huh?" Charlie said, smiling.

Gary nodded. The intense rush and crash did leave him wanting for a vice. He measured his breaths until Cindy emerged from the bathroom, dressed. She walked over and hugged them both. "I need each of you to tell me I am *not* a slut."

"Cindy," Gary considered his words, "what you gave me was special. I will cherish it forever."

"Cindy," Charlie said, "I know you pretty well, and what you are is . . . ticklish!"

Charlie moved in for an impromptu tickle attack on Cindy's ribcage. She giggled, squirmed and laughed as they crashed to the couch. She pleaded Uncle and Charlie relented.

"Will you snuggle with us on the couch again Gary?" Cindy asked, as she rewound the VHS tape to the last segment in the *Trilogy of Terror*.

They squished their bodies around on the couch, trying to find a comfortable arrangement. Eventually, the two boys just sat on the couch and Cindy laid across them, face down for an upper body, lower body combo massage. Gary assessed the damage. There was none that he could tell. Cindy was showing no ill effects, meaning the nanites where not attacking her reproductive or digestive systems. This was a relief for Gary. Perhaps he could have a normal life.

Charlie took the roundabout way again on the drive home, with Gary in the passenger seat. He hopped onto RM 620 and headed for the Hill Country. "You know it's unlikely a night like this will ever happen again," Charlie said.

"I figured that," Gary said.

"Did you have a good time?"

"The best."

"Did you learn anything?"

Gary thought to himself, then verbalized, "You don't know the half of it."

"Tell me the half you think I do know."

"Okay. You surprised me. I didn't expect anything like that to happen. You and Cindy showed me genuine affection, more than I've ever experienced. I think I know why you did it too. You're watching me struggle and you're trying to help me, because you care, I guess. I assume you guys planned this out, somewhat, so the whole scheme was a seduction, in a way. Honestly, I'm flattered. But I guess what I'm saying is, I'm touched by how much of yourselves you were willing to offer, to help me figure some things out."

"Do me a favor. Don't tell anyone I let you have sex with my girlfriend. That wouldn't be fair to Cindy, and I would never hear the end of it."

"You didn't have to ask," Gary said. "I'll keep this secret until the day I die."

Nelson Warner tried to focus on his biology project. He was writing a paper about seahorses and was disappointed to learn the "seahorses mate for life" assertion was just a common misconception. Still, there were plenty of interesting facts about their mating habits worthy of inclusion in his project. Problem for Nelson was, try as he might to focus on the project, his thoughts diverted to the teacher, Miss Fleur. It was a challenge for him to concentrate in her class because he had a boner the whole time. Nevertheless, he tried to pay attention because he didn't want to disappoint her. He wondered if she noticed how often he shifted around in his seat, trying to get comfortable.

He sat at the edge of his bed, pants around his ankles, masturbating, as he was prone to do whenever he thought about Jackie, as he liked to think of Miss Fleur. It didn't take him long to ejaculate, especially when he thought about her perky little nipples. BAM! He was done.

Nelson felt inspired and decided to write Miss Fleur a poem. He scribbled it down in his journal:

My virginity isn't for some whore.
There's just one place I want to score.
I have a crush on Jacqueline Fleur.
She's who I've been waiting for.
Hear my plea, sweet Jacqueline,
you're the one I want to be in.
She's my favorite teacher.
I'll take her once, or double feature.
Tell me how can I reach her?
I can't spell teacher, without her.
Hear my plea, sweet Jacqueline,
you're the one I want to be in.
I'm not just some football lackey.
And you may think this rather wacky.
But when I think of little Jackie,
I just want her in the sackie.
Hear my plea, sweet Jacqueline,
You're the one I want to be in.

Nelson thought his poem might make the lyrics to a hit song. Set it to some simple chords. Cycle through classic G, then D, then C. Maybe mix in an E minor for the chorus. He would have to get the strumming right, but there was a melody in there somewhere, for sure. Nelson reached for his Fender acoustic guitar and re-tuned each string by ear. He strapped the capo onto the third fret and struck chords and cadence that he thought might work best with his poem. After cycling through the rhythm a few times, he admitted to himself that his guitar playing was probably way ahead of his lyric writing.

Nelson tucked his journal away for safekeeping. He didn't want his parents to find the poem. They would call it raunchy and immature. He wondered if he might page back to the poem someday and think it silly as well.

September 20, 2017

9 days before Homecoming

Vote Gary Greene for homecoming court. He's the most deserving person in school. F* Popularity. Strength in numbers! #SHHS #Texans #VoteforG

2:48 PM · 20 September 2017

The football team lost their next two games. Homecoming was coming soon and excitement for the dance was building. Excitement for the game was another story. You would think, absent Gary the waterboy, the team would have looked elsewhere to find blame. Perhaps their own on-field performance had something to do with the outcome of the games? But no, it was much easier to find a scapegoat. If not for Gary, they would have Seth Thompson playing middle linebacker and calling the defensive formations. Seth fanned the flames.

"We need to get that little bastard back for what he did to us," Seth said. "That's right, I said not just me, *us*. You guys are out there paying the price. It kills me that I can't get out there and help you. That little bastard needs to pay."

"So what are we supposed to do?" Liam asked.

"I'll tell you what we'll do. You see the posters popping up in the hallways reminding people to cast their vote for the homecoming court?"

"Yeah, we see them," Lucas said.

"Well, we're going to do just that. We're going to fucking vote for the homecoming king *and* queen. Aren't we Chestnut?"

"Right on Seth. That we are." Chestnut said, thumbs-up.

"How's that going to accomplish anything?" Liam asked.

"Because idiot, you have to read the fine print. Tell him Chestnut."

Chestnut uncoiled a poster he had stripped from the wall and read the explanatory text. "Round Rock ISD has adopted gender-neutral homecoming courts, breaking with the tradition of electing a boy as king and a girl as queen. Students will cast votes for classmates, regardless of gender, with the top two vote-getters crowned at the school's homecoming dance."

"I heard something about that, but I just didn't believe it," Liam said.

"Believe it," Seth said. "And we're going to elect the faggot condom boy as homecoming queen. It may not be enough to campaign for him. Besides, I don't want to work that hard. Liam and Lucas, I need you two to volunteer for the homecoming dance committee."

"The dance committee?" Lucas gave Liam a sideways glance.

"Yeah, you make damn sure you're involved in the ballot collection," Seth said. "Then fix the outcome."

"Seth, we can't just worm our way onto a dance committee. It was set up weeks ago. Won't it seem suspicious?" Lucas said. "Besides, we can't fix the voting anyway."

"I don't want to hear it," Seth said. "Everyone needs to do their part."

"But–" Lucas protested.

"End of discussion," Seth said.

Lucas folded his arms and shook head. Seth was bull headed. If Seth was done listening, there was no reasoning with him.

After a momentary silence, Liam asked, "That it? Just get him elected?"

"More will be revealed," Seth said. "Just start passing the word to the boys. Party at my place, the night before the dance."

"Sounds good," Liam said. Liam and Lucas watched Seth stomp off in the direction of the gym. Lucas just shook his head.

"What are you so huffy about?" Liam asked Lucas. "Don't you like the plan?"

"Actually no, I don't. "Lucas said. "I think it's stupid. Besides, Seth doesn't appreciate the dynamics of the situation, nor does he realize there's no ballot box to stuff."

"There isn't?" Liam said, confused.

"No there isn't," Lucas explained, corner of lip tightened and raised in contempt. "Didn't you get the notice about the online voting application? It's another of Principal McFadden's innovations. More kids will vote using the app. Times are changing and McFadden gets that." He paused. "Seth doesn't get that. He doesn't want to hear about the app, and he thinks he's being clever by nominating a gay kid for homecoming queen. He thinks he'll embarrass Gary by getting him elected. Thing is, I don't think we have to fix the election. The idea of voting for Gary for homecoming court has taken off like wildfire. It's sparked from multiple sources. Some legitimate. Some malicious. But the effect will be the same. Gary will get elected and Seth thinks he'll be putting Gary under a spotlight he'll be ill prepared to handle. I'm not so sure Seth's right about that. Condom boy is getting a lot of support from people in the school who think it's no joke to vote a gay kid queen. If condom boy embraces that cause, the joke may backfire on Seth."

"Sounds like you're sympathetic to condom boy," Liam observed. "If you think the whole idea is that stupid, why don't you tell Seth?"

"Oh hell. I don't feel *that* strongly about the voting, one way or the other. Seth has an axe to grind. That's fine. We're friends and I'll support him if only for the fun of it. Just brace yourself though, because I don't think Seth is done falling off his high horse."

Blood, spit, or semen, those were the choices. Gary stared at the test tubes in front of him. He was working with the middle group, the ones with DNA samples from people for whom he basically felt ambivalent. He knew the nanites were in his blood. He wanted to try other bodily fluids. He tried spit yesterday in a couple of them. Nothing happened. His recent intercourse with Cindy incentivized him to test his semen. He faced away from the door and dropped his shorts. God forbid Miss Fleur come in and see him masturbating. He rubbed himself with one hand and held a test tube over the tip with the other. He thought about Cindy and Charlie. This got him excited. He replayed their threesome in his mind. This got him close. He envisioned passionately kissing Charlie. This put him over the top. Mission accomplished.

He buttoned his pants and focused on the task at hand. He was curious about the existence (or not) of nanites in his semen. Perhaps the nanites sensed his genuine affection for Cindy and simply left her alone. Were they that clever? He needed to find out. He extracted some semen into a dropper and randomly selected one of the middle tubes. He applied the sample and observed no reaction, as expected.

Next came the real test. He selected the test tube containing the DNA sample from Lucas Barolo. Lucas had probably lobbed condoms onto Gary in the shower, and he was friends with Seth, so there was plenty of reason not to like him. If the nanites where present in his semen, would they perceive Lucas's spittle as a threat? Gary squeezed a single drop of semen from the dropper. The semen instantly began to stir and boil. The tube became hot to the touch so he set it down in the sink. A few seconds later the test tube shattered, scattering glass and a sizzling mixture of spittle and semen all over the sink.

Holy shit, Gary thought, that could have been Cindy.

September 21, 2017

8 days before Homecoming

"What's this I hear about you getting kicked off the team?" Vincent asked Gary, sounding full-throated and intimidating, as usual.

"You just finding out about that Dad? That's old news, happened a couple of weeks ago," Gary replied with a rare case of attitude. Maybe getting laid gave Gary some confidence.

His dad clamped a hand onto the back of Gary's neck. "Don't you sass back at me boy. You think cancer was pain? I'll show you pain. I'll ram my boot so far up your ass you'll be able to shine it with your tongue."

"That's disgusting. Get off me." Gary tried to loosen his dad's grip on his neck, to no avail. Vincent was a man who worked with his hands every day of his life. His daily toil produced an iron grip that already was pinching blood flow and choking off air from Gary's throat. The throbbing in Gary's head intensified and a lightheadedness came over him.

"I'll tell you this boy. I don't understand you one bit. I don't think I ever will. There isn't enough understanding on planet Earth to figure you out. It takes more than understanding to be your father, it takes goddamn stamina. You're just one goddamn disappointment after another."

"Fuck you, Dad!" Gary wheezed, knowing it might be the last words he'd ever utter. The main thing Gary remembered was feeling sorry for his mom. She worked so hard to save him, only to see him choked to death by the crazy man she married. It seemed like such a waste.

"What did you say?" His dad's grip became a garrote, pinching Gary's neck and constricting his windpipe. Gary flailed as his vision tunneled and consciousness faded. He faintly heard hysterical screaming.

"Vincent, STOP THAT! You're hurting him!"

"Did you hear what this little shit said to me?" Vincent Greene literally had a death grip on his son's neck and was shaking him around like a rag doll.

"You're *killing* our son!"

Vincent caught a look at himself in the full-length mirror. His son's pale white face reflected in stark contrast to the beet-red face of his own.

"Fuck that." He released his grip and let Gary crash to the ground.

Joanna ran to her son's prone body. "He better not be dead! He better not be dead!"

"He's not dead," Vincent said in disgust.

Vincent watched Joanna revive their son, then stepped outside and lit a cigarette.

"Gary, can you hear me?" She grasped his shoulders and pleaded with him. His jaw hung slack and his eyes unfocused. She pinched his pale cheek.

"I hear you Mom." Gary's voice came out in a raspy whisper, but color was coming back to his face.

"You scared me," she said, as she sat him up and wrapped her arms around him.

"Sorry Mom." She relaxed a little when she saw his eyes able focus on hers.

"Don't goad your father like that. He can be unpredictable." Joanna rubbed Gary's forehead and tried to stop the tears from coming to her eyes.

"You think?" Gary senses returned, including pain; his neck ached and his head was pounding.

"Oh, honey," she said as she stroked Gary's head.

"Why's he like that?" What Gary really wanted to ask was, "Why did you marry such an asshole?"

"I don't know. He's gotten worse lately," she admitted. "Can you stand? Can you walk?" Joanna stood and tried to get Gary up from the floor. He wasn't quite ready for that.

Gary sighed, "Yeah, in a minute. What the hell?" He buried his head in his hands and sat there, vacillating between anger and hatred towards his dad to guilt and self-loathing for not being the kind of son that would make his dad proud. His dad wanted a son like Charlie–handsome and athletic, or even Seth–bully that he was, instead of the weakling gay son he'd just as soon choke to death.

"You really need to be careful around him, Gary. I'm not sure I can protect you from his temper."

Gary looked up. "I can protect myself." The anger and hatred had won out, this time.

"Oh really. You have some super power I don't know about?"

"Yes," Gary said as he stood. Gary had his nanites to protect him.

"Gary, please, for all of our sakes, don't provoke him. Ok?"

"Ok Mom." Gary kissed his mom and started to turn away.

Joanna turned him back around and looked him in the eye. "Just stay away from him and don't provoke him, okay?"

"Okay, I said."

Gary shuffled to his room. He thought about his dad's boiling razor stubble in the Dixie cup. He could boil his dad to death with nanites anytime he wanted. But it was no different than having a gun. Having the power did not justify its use. Gary could feel the nanites stirring within him. He hated his dad. The nanites did too, perhaps more so after the choking incident. Gary felt if he spit on the floor, the spit would ooze under the door and chase down his dad. "Don't get any ideas little guys."

Vincent Greene finished tracing the route on Google Maps. "You messed me up," he mumbled. He lit another Marlboro and trapped it between his lips. He donned his leather gloves, sat on the front stoop and polished the steel blade and carbon fiber handle of his Viper hunting knife. He polished with purpose, removing the smudge traces and oils built up over time. Satisfied, he sheathed the blade, stepped into the house and towards the bedroom hallway.

"Leave the boy alone Vincent," Joanna demanded.

"Roger that."

Vincent packed a change of clothes in a gym bag and grabbed his keys. He walked past Joanna, ignoring her, on his way to the kitchen. He microwaved what was left of the morning coffee and poured it into a thermos. He headed for the door.

"Where are you going at this time of night?" Joanna asked.

"Out. Don't wait up." Then he was gone.

September 22, 2017

7 days before Homecoming

A rustling sound awoke him. A heavy-footed, heavy breathing person who stank of cigarettes and alcohol slipped into the parishioner side of the confessional. Morning confessors were a rarity. He often sat in the dim cubical for the hour and half time slot with nobody showing up at all. He used the time to meditate, and occasionally nap.

"Bless me Father, for I have sinned," said the male voice. It was the voice of someone who had just woken up, or had been up all night. Given the way the man smelled, he suspected the latter.

"What is it my son?" Father O'Brien responded.

The voice coming from the priest's side of the screen was deep and, to Vincent Greene, sounded like the voice of God himself sitting in judgment. He was convinced that all priests purposefully lowered their voice an octave in the confessional to generate this desired effect.

"I nearly killed my son last night. I squeezed his neck so hard he couldn't breathe."

"Tell me more. Tell me why."

"He sassed back to me and I just wasn't in the mood for it."

"God calls on children to respect their parents. But also for parents to nurture their children." Penitent parents sometimes overstate the severity of their discipline. Others minimize it. The trick was to keep them talking. The more they said, the better Father O'Brien could calibrate the situation.

"He didn't deserve to be choked," Vincent said.

"How old is the boy?"

"Sixteen."

"Is he alright? Did he require medical attention?"

"The boy is fine. I'm the one who feels bad."

"Why is that? Tell me what you felt last night and why you are here now?"

Heavy sigh.

"Last night I felt rage and I directed it at my son. There was a moment when I realized the monster I had become. That's why I'm here. I know what needs to change. I know what I need to do."

"Parenting can be a challenge," Father O'Brien said. "Sometimes we love our children so much we're overzealous in our desire to teach them life's lessons. I remember my father slapping me so hard my ears rang for three days."

"I'm sorry that happened to you."

"The reason I share this is, even though my dad hit me, I still knew he loved me. Parents are human. We all are human. We make mistakes. Everyone has sinned. We all fall short of God's glorious standards."

"I don't think he knows I love him."

"God?"

"No, my son."

"Why do you say that?"

"Because I'm not sure I do."

There was a pause.

"I'm not sure I believe that," Father O'Brien said. "A man who comes to confession understands a father's love, and redemptive justice. I think you are more capable of love than you realize."

"I would like to think so Father."

"Have you hit or hurt your son before?"

"No, not really."

"So this is a recent thing?"

"Yes."

"What's changed?"

"What do you mean?"

"Something has changed, either in your life or his, to frustrate you. Did you lose your job? Is your wife cheating on you? There's a trigger. Tell me what that is."

"No, job's fine. Wife's faithful, I think. She does look mighty fine in her yoga pants and I catch other men staring at her. I have my radar out for that sort of thing though. I know how to intimidate."

"Okay, something else then?"

"I think my boy is touching a nerve."

"What nerve?"

Pause.

"This is hard," Vincent admitted.

"Yes it is. I am glad you're here working on this. It takes strength." This was good. There were typically deeper issues.

"When I was young, before I turned eighteen, I was confused about some things."

"This is normal," Father O'Brien said. "What things specifically."

"I was confused about my sexuality."

"I understand. Go on."

"I had some encounters with some other boys." *And a certain priest*, he refrained from mentioning. He traced his gloved finger along the handle of his hunting knife. "I'm still not sure what to make of them. I ultimately decided I liked pussy–oh crap, sorry Father."

"It's okay. I understand. Tell me what this has to do with choking your son last night."

"He frustrates me because I see the same confusion in him and I suspect he's coming to a different conclusion."

"I see."

Pause.

"Have you spoken to your son about this?"

"No. Maybe I don't want to know for certain. And I know what the church says about gays."

"I think, sometimes, we must set doctrine aside and listen to our own hearts. God wants us to come to Him willingly. I assure you, God loves you and He loves your son. He will help you, if you ask Him for guidance."

"I think I already know what I need to do."

"That's good, this confession has helped you then?"

"Yes, it has, more than you'll ever know," Vincent stroked his gloved palm against the flush side of the steel blade.

"Do you remember the Act of Contrition?"

"Yes Father."

"Recite it please."

Vincent recited the prayer.

"I won't assign you rote prayers as penance. Instead, please pray for continued guidance from the Lord in your relationship with your son."

"I will Father."

"Bless you in the name of the Father, and of the Son, and of the Holy Spirit."

"Amen," Vincent said. "You've sincerely helped me this morning Father. I want to meet you. May I offer you a hug? The church is empty. Nobody will see you."

A hug from this rugged man sounded strangely appealing to Father O'Brien. "I suppose, under the circumstances, a hug would be fine."

They each stepped outside of their side of the confessional and approach each other awkwardly, stopping, facing one another, a pace apart. Father O'Brien was dressed in his black flowing vestment. His arms rested at his sides. Vincent Greene wore a long sleeved work shirt, blue jeans and military jungle boots. His gloved hands rested behind his back. Wordlessly, Vincent stepped closer and embraced the priest.

"You don't remember me do you Father?" he whispered in his ear. His grip on Father O'Brien tightened slightly, just enough to cause a bit of unease. "How could you have forgotten the good times we had in the rectory of St. Pius?" He tightened his embrace further, as the priest tried to disengage from the hold. "I certainly haven't forgotten."

He held tight with his left arm and plunged the steel blade deep into Father O'Brien's right kidney. The priest released a shocked gasp. "You messed me up Father." He withdrew the blade, hooked his left arm under the priest's right armpit, propped him up and plunged the blade again, same side, slightly higher, targeting the lung. Another gasp. He pushed the priest up against the ornate wood confessional. A carved wooden cross on the door dominated the artistry of the piece. A man and woman clothed in fig leaves stood over the cross. Various animals, each intricately carved into the fine wood, adorned the periphery of the confessional's archway.

"You ever field dress an animal Father?" The priest was gasping and pleading with his eyes. "No, I imagine you haven't." Father O'Brien's eyes stayed on Vincent's. "I can't tell you how many times I've thought of you while I field dressed an animal. Particularly an elk. Always the elk. I wonder why?"

He wedged the priest higher against the confessional, then sliced deeply across his belly, spilling the priest's guts. He released his grip and let the priest fall. A prism of morning sunlight, brilliant through the stained glass window, cast beams upon the priest's crumbled body.

"You messed me up," Vincent mumbled, walking out the door, lighting a cigarette.

He climbed into his pickup truck and headed south on Route 285. He had driven seven hours straight through the night, from Austin to Carlsbad, to confront his abuser. He felt like a man bursting inside. Someone was going to get seriously injured. He stopped at a truck stop on the way home, intent on ditching his clothes and knife. He stripped down in the shower stall, bundled his clothes in a trash bag and set the knife aside. It was a good knife, well-engineered for its purpose, he thought. Perhaps it would continue to prove itself useful. After all, he knew what he had to do now. He finished his shower, ditched his clothes, then sat in the diner drinking hot black coffee and reading the morning newspaper.

"First day of work I've missed in a long time," he said to the guy sitting next to him at the counter.

The man nodded in acknowledgement.

"Hey look at this, *Fort Stockton Dispatch* reports Trump reverses Obama's transgender tolerance guidelines for the military. What do you think of that?" Vincent asked, loudly.

"I would say it's about damn time we started taking our country back," the man said, equally loud. "If the liberals had their way, this truck stop would have separate showers for the fags and queers."

"Hell yeah, they would," Vincent said.

Jackie Fleur and Nina Lopez made arrangements to meet at the Starbucks near Seton Medical Center. "I'm so glad I'm off that infernal oncology ward," Nina admitted. "I swear to God I was going crazy."

"You don't have to convince me, trust me I know," Jackie said. She did know. Jackie studied nursing and worked as a Certified Nursing Assistant before becoming a high school biology teacher. That's how she met Nina. They worked together on the pediatric oncology ward at Seton. Jackie prided herself on her phlebotomy skills. Nina not so much. Little kids have delicate, thin skin and tiny veins. Jackie viewed them as a challenge. Nina regularly deferred to Jackie when a child needed an IV line. Jackie could carry on a conversation and distract a child while inserting the IV, often without hearing so much as a whimper. Nina missed her support and companionship on the ward. Problem was, nurses eat their young, with the newest nurses getting the worst assignments. Jackie got tired of wrapping cadavers in cellophane during third shift on the oncology ward. She decided to take a different direction. She saw a teaching opportunity in the growing Round Rock Independent School District and jumped on it. Nina stuck with the nursing, to her chagrin many days. Her scarred face and hands were her battle wounds.

"So, you're back to work though?" Jackie continued.

"Yes, they moved me to geriatrics. It seems my scars frighten the pediatric patients," Nina said, frowning. Part of Nina's face was covered in craggy, splotchy skin, stretching right ear to chin. It looked as if her face might crack if she smiled too wide, which she rarely did anymore. In addition, her hands were skeletal and looked as if she'd dipped them in an acid bath and stained them in beet juice.

"Nina, I'm so sorry," Jackie said, cupping Nina's hand. "You know you're still beautiful right? And, those geriatric patients need you."

"Yeah I know," Nina nodded. "It's still hard though. Their hospital stays tend to be extended and I get to know them. Sometimes they die too. But at least they're not young. They've had a full life. When they go, it's not as if they've been cheated like the pediatric cancer patients."

"Well, if you ever get tired of it, I can put in a good word for you with the school system," Jackie said.

"I appreciate that," Nina said, sincerely.

Jackie sipped her Pumpkin Spice Misto. Jackie liked to add sprinkles of cinnamon and nutmeg from the coffee bar to her drink. It gave her the sense to eating a slice of pumpkin pie, without all the calories. Nina contently drank her latte.

"I've been meaning to mention to you," Jackie said. "I think I have one of your former patients in my biology class."

"Oh really, who?"

"Gary Greene," Jackie said.

"Oh, that's so exciting! How is he doing?"

"He's good. It's hard for him though. I can tell his social skills are stunted, probably because he's missed so much time with the other school children. He's getting back into the swing of things though. He's certainly a bright kid, I can tell you that. He's especially inquisitive about the micro sciences."

"Well, I guess that makes sense, considering his treatment,"

Nina said.

"Yeah, I thought so too. I like it when kids are curious," Jackie said.

"Will you tell him I said 'Hello' next time you see him?"

"Absolutely, but you can tell him yourself if you like." Jackie reached into her purse and pulled out a printed e-ticket. "I managed to snag a general admission ticket to the high school's homecoming dance. They have great entertainment. I thought you might like to go."

Nina reached for the ticket. She examined it, then shook her head. "No, I just couldn't. Not a homecoming dance. I would be self-conscious all night and that would make me terrible company."

"Just the same," Jackie said, "you hang onto that ticket. It's a hot commodity. If you truly decide not to go, then give it to someone who's interested."

Nina pondered the options. "I think I might already know someone who would appreciate being there." *And meeting a pretty schoolteacher*, she left unsaid.

"Who?" Jackie asked.

"Dr. Wolfgang Reichmann," Nina said. "I bet he would be tickled to see his star patient at homecoming."

Jackie considered the possibility that the famed Dr. Reichmann would attend Gary's homecoming. Could Jackie weasel her way into making it a date? Dr. Reichmann was single (again) from what Jackie had heard. She refrained from asking Nina directly, though there was the possibility that Nina was overtly trying to set Jackie up. "Well, if that's what you want to do. It's your ticket. Just let me know what you decide." Jackie had already determined she would need to go dress shopping, now even more so if Nina was going to give her ticket to Dr. Reichmann. Was it bad she was hoping Nina would hand the doctor her ticket? Probably, but it had been a long time since Jackie had a real date.

"Today, we study hematology," Miss Fleur said at the head of the class, as a delighted smile stretched across her face. "Blood." She paused. "The fluid that delivers oxygen, and therefore life, to the cells of the body."

Miss Fleur reached for one of the boxes, about the size of a Kleenex box, stacked upon her desk. Raising it up she said, "These are blood typing kits from the World Health Organization. We're going to use these today to discern your blood type. Each of your guardians signed general authorization for your participation in this activity; nevertheless, you can opt out of the blood test if you choose. Some people are squeamish, I understand. But I do hope everyone participates. Does anyone wish to opt out?"

A fat girl in the second row raised her hand.

"Sally? You don't want to test your blood type?" Miss Fleur asked.

"I do. It might be hard for me though because I don't like the sight of my own blood," Sally said. "I'm fine with other people's blood. They can bleed all they want, but I get queasy at the sight of my own. I always look away at the doctor's office."

"Would it help you if I took the sample while you turned away?" Miss Fleur asked.

Sally nodded pensively. Miss Fleur smiled.

"Anyone else have an issue?"

No one did.

"Alright, by raise of hand, show me who already thinks they know their blood type." Most of the kids in the biology class raised a hand. "Okay, that's good. Well this exercise will confirm it. Should be fun regardless."

Miss Fleur put the box down and started the lecture. "You're going to learn a lot about blood today. More than you probably wanted to know. So here's the deal. We'll get through this lecture, lab, and quiz all in this session and be done with it.

Your part will be to pay attention and take good notes. There will be a short quiz at the end of class."

A slight groan was heard as several notebooks opened and kids grabbed writing utensils.

"The adult human body has about five liters of blood, roughly eight percent of our body weight." Miss Fleur lectured, animated and pacing around the classroom to keep the students' attention. Gary caught Nelson checking her out as she fluttered past. Gary suspected that wasn't the kind of attention Miss Fleur sought. He refocused on the lecture.

"Not all blood is red," Miss Fleur spoke deliberately. "Human blood is red because of the iron in a respiratory protein called *hemoglobin.* Besides iron, human blood also contains other metals including chromium, manganese, zinc, lead, and copper . . ." Gary was frantically scribbling the names of the metals. "Don't worry, I won't ask you to name those metals on the quiz. Just know that hemoglobin contains iron and remember why human blood is red."

Miss Fleur returned to her desk and began handing out the WHO blood typing kits. She continued to lecture, but it was a sure sign to Gary that the pertinent facts of the quiz were already delivered. Miss Fleur's style would not have included the distraction of boxes cascading desk to desk if the lecture material were critical. Nevertheless, Gary listened. She had his attention when she mentioned bone marrow–a topic he knew all too well.

"In humans, blood cells originate from hematopoietic stem cells. Most of our blood cells are produced in the bone marrow and most of the bone marrow is concentrated in the breastbone, pelvis and spine." The lecture conjured images Gary would just as soon forget.

Everyone had a kit now, so Miss Fleur shifted into a combination of lecture and lab instructions. "Everyone make your way to a lab station." The biology classroom had two sections, one for classroom instruction, furnished with student desks. The other section featured bar height stainless steel lab stations, each equipped with a natural gas line and sink. Each station accommodated two or three people. Gary joined two of his classmates, Cindy and Amy, at a station.

"Now, open your kits. Inside you'll find the simple four-step instructions." The rustling of a couple of dozen kids simultaneously opening boxes arose, along with the predictable sardonic remarks about Santa substituting blood testing kits for lumps of coal. "Human blood has several types of antigens and antibodies. Your combination of these determines your blood type. This test will show you what you have. Trust me, it's easy. I haven't lost a student yet in this process." Miss Fleur offered an impish grin.

Kids were at various stages of wiping down their stations, reading instructions, and organizing their kit components. Miss Fleur noticed Sally hadn't opened her kit and was looking rather mortified. "Sally," Miss Fleur announced, "how about I help you? You can look away, but we'll let your fellow classmates watch the demonstration."

Sally nodded. Miss Fleur approached Sally's station and kids crowded around.

Miss Fleur talked through the process as she laid Sally's hand, palm up, on the surface of the stainless steel lab station. Sally looked away. Everyone else watched as Miss Fleur deftly pressed the lancet at the tip of Sally's finger and with a click, pricked her finger. She flipped Sally's hand over and let a single drop of blood drip into the cupped end of four little collection sticks. She placed a Band-Aid on Sally's finger. Next she combed a sample from each stick across a designated spot on the test card provided with each kit. All told, it took her just a couple of minutes to complete the exercise. The coagulation patterns developed across the four dots. "Antigen A and B determine your blood group and Antigen Rh determines your positive or negative designation. You can tell from this pattern," Miss Fleur held up Sally's test card, "that Sally is blood type A positive, meaning her blood tests positive for the A and Rh antigens. Now each of you get to your stations and follow the instructions in the kit. You have fifteen minutes. Have fun!"

Cindy, Amy, and Gary stepped through the process. They each already knew their blood type. Their tests confirmed they were O+, A+, and O- respectively.

After a few minutes Miss Fleur inquired, "Does anyone have a test pattern containing four solid dots?"

Gary raised his hand.

"That's great!" Miss Fleur said. "I'm always curious to see if there's a universal blood donor in my class. The Red Cross is going to love you Gary." She smiled. Gary nodded, but somehow he didn't think so. Not if they knew his blood also contained little tiny flesh eating robots.

Miss Fleur stepped through the blood type combinations and took a rough count by signal of hands. O+ and A+ predominated. There was a sprinkling of B+ and A-. Gary was the only O- in class.

"If everyone is done, I need a volunteer to collect the trash in our bio waste can." Miss Fleur barely completed the sentence before Nelson was dutifully racing to the caution yellow waste can and dragging it station to station to collect the used test kits. Before tossing their kits, Gary snagged the lancets belonging to Cindy and Amy. They would prove useful to him later.

"Alright, back to your desks. We have just a few minutes for a quick quiz. Get out a single sheet of paper. Write your name and blood type across the top." With mild grumbling, the students migrated to their desks and settled in for the quiz. Gary noticed it was a couple of minutes before the end-of-class bell would sound. This quiz couldn't be a long one. When everyone was ready Miss Fleur stated, "This will be a one question quiz. It is pass-fail. Answer this question in a single concise sentence. Why is human blood red?"

Most of the kids began writing a quick sentence on their paper. Gary saw Lucas mouth *he-mo-glo-bin* to Liam. This didn't surprise him. What disappointed him more was seeing Sally sneak a peek at her notes to get the term. Really Sally? After Miss Fleur was kind enough to assist you personally through the process, you can't even remember a word she overtly emphasized during the lecture. Some people.

Gary sat at the lunch table with Cindy Perrine, Amy Bridges, Priscilla Moran and Susan Campbell, who was cheerleading squad captain and was dating a star wide receiver from last year's football team. Her boyfriend accepted a full athletic scholarship to Oklahoma University, news of which came with mixed emotions around Austin because of the University of Texas rivalry with OU.

Priscilla didn't talk much around Gary. She had to strike a balance between tolerating him (because her friends had befriended him) and dismissing him (because she was Seth Thompson's girlfriend).

"How come I don't see you on the sidelines anymore Gary?" Susan asked.

Gary was surprised she'd even noticed. "It's a long story," Gary said.

"No it's not," Amy said, shaking her head in disgust. "It's because of Priscilla's boyfriend. He was making life hell for Gary, so the coaches had to let him go."

Priscilla looked down at her plate, avoiding eye contact with everyone at the table.

"That seems unfair," Susan said.

"It was," Amy said, glaring at Priscilla.

"You do realize your name is being bandied about as a

nominee for homecoming queen, don't you?" Susan said to Gary.

"So I've heard." Gary rolled his eyes.

"What do you think about that?" she asked.

"I don't suppose there's much I can do about it. I'm bracing myself to win. I'm getting the sweet thought vote from the girls, the novelty vote from the cynics, and the joke vote from the football team."

"Aw Gary," Cindy said and put her arm around him. This made Gary smile.

"At least you're going into this with eyes wide open," Susan said. "I thought I would like to be homecoming queen someday, but now I want to help you win instead. You'll get my vote," she smiled.

"Thanks Susan, I think."

"You know what?" Priscilla stiffened her back and spoke up, "I'm voting for you too Gary. Fuck Seth." Priscilla's angular shoulders and trim waist were accentuated by her black, skin-tight minidress. Her black leather choker was striking, but to Gary, it resembled a collar. What kind of girl wears a collar on her neck? Gary pegged Priscilla as just the kind of slave Seth would seek to dominate.

"Seriously Priscilla? Is this a sweet, novelty, or joke vote?" Cindy asked.

"Maybe a little bit of all three," she laughed. "Does it really matter?"

"No, I suppose it doesn't matter in the end," Gary said. "I'll be center stage, with lots of attention directed towards me. What should I wear ladies?"

"Rent a tux Gary," Cindy said. "I'll send Charlie out with you to help you pick one out. He'll need one too. Plus, he could well end up being *your* homecoming king." They all laughed. "You can get a matching set," Cindy said.

"Oh, how sweet!" Amy said.

"You know how I like to share my boyfriend," Cindy said, winking at Gary.

"You do?" Amy said. "You never shared him with me."

"You never asked."

"We need to talk," Amy smiled, wide eyed.

Coach Casey was fuming. He was screaming at the top of his lungs and waving about a poster of the homecoming dance.

"*This* is not the focus!" He shook the poster in his fist. "That's the focus." He pointed to the football Jeremy Parsons held tightly in his arms. Jeremy was the starting running back, but his situation was precarious. He had fumbled the ball in each of the team's recent losses, once in the red zone, denying his team a chance at the game winning score. The other time was deep in their own zone, which the opposing team converted into a touchdown. Both fumbles were costly. Coach made it clear that one more fumble would cost him his starting position. Jeremy could be seen in the school hallways jealously guarding his football. Teachers were informed of his penance and permitted him to lug the football into each class. He studied with it, ate with it, showered with it, and slept with it. Any player, teacher, parent, or random football fan who saw Jeremy that week needed also to see a football firmly in his possession. Lose that football and Jeremy would lose his starting job, Coach had said. His teammates didn't make it any easier for him. They were constantly slapping at the ball when they saw him in the school hallways. More than once, Jeremy dropped his books and cradled the ball while teammates frantically tried to punch it out of his arms.

The tight end, Lamar Jones, extended his long arm and slapped at the ball. Jeremy pulled it away.

Coach nodded. "See, there's a player who understands the priority. Don't you Parsons?"

"Yes sir! I'm holding onto the football sir."

"You bet your ass you're holding onto that football. Now the rest of you need to get your priorities straight." He ripped the homecoming poster in half. "This is not it." He ripped the poster into quarters. "It never will be it." He ripped the poster again, shredding it into smaller and smaller pieces and throwing them around the locker room. "I don't want to hear about parties, I don't want to hear about the dance, and I certainly don't want to hear about the waterboy being elected homecoming queen!"

There were a few chuckles.

"STOP! You bring that shit in here and you're going to find yourself riding the pine, or worse, you'll be out on the street with Seth. I'm *not* kidding. Do you understand me?"

"Yes Coach," they mumbled.

"I can't hear you. Do you understand me?"

"Yes sir," they barked.

"Good."

September 25, 2017

4 days before Homecoming

Page C-14, September 25, 2017   Round Rock Daily Dispatch

Obituaries

Cullen F. O'Brien

Father Cullen O'Brien, Pastor of St. Edward Church, Carlsbad, NM and former longtime Pastor of St. Pius X Church, Round Rock, TX went home to be with the Lord on Friday, September 22, 2017. He was born August 18, 1952 in Taylor, TX to Robert C. and Laura M. O'Brien. Cullen was the youngest of five children, grew up on the family farm near Taylor and graduated from Thrall High School. He attended Holy Trinity Seminary and graduated from University of Dallas with a degree in Ecclesiastical Studies. He served in the priesthood for 40 years, 15 of those years as Pastor for St. Pius X. He provided youth counseling services for Catholic Charities and is renowned for the establishment of the "Christ in You" Youth Camp outside Carlsbad. Tragically, Father O'Brien was found dead near the confessionals of his Carlsbad church, the stabbing victim of a depraved soul. He is survived by two older brothers, both from Taylor. A memorial service will be held to honor former Pastor O'Brien at St. Pius X, Thursday Sep 28, 2017, 10 a.m. In lieu of flowers, please make a donation to Catholic Charities.

Joanna lit a vanilla candle and paged through the obituaries. She had a thing for honoring the passing of life. She delicately drew her finger across each picture and name, silently praying their soul would find peace in rejoining the universal spirit realm. One caught her attention.

"Dear, do you remember Father O'Brien?" Joanna asked Vincent as they sat at the breakfast table.

"Who?" Vincent replied.

"Father O'Brien, don't you remember him from grade school? Says here he was found dead in his church. He was murdered outside of the confessionals. That's shameful. Who would do that to a priest?"

"Beats the shit out of me."

"There's a service on Thursday," Joanna said. "We should go."

"I'm not driving all the goddamn way to Carlsbad for a church service," Vincent said in a dismissive manner as he shook his head, not taking his eyes off his breakfast.

"The service is local, at St Pius," Joanna said. "How did you know Father O'Brien's church was in Carlsbad?"

"Says so, right there in the obit."

"Since when do you read the obituaries?"

"Oh for Christ's sake, I'll go to the fucking service alright?" Vincent said as he stood and walked out of the room. "Get off my ass."

Gary eyed the test tubes. He had confirmed the nanite behavior was consistent with his feelings about the person. If he disliked the person, the sample boiled. The challenge was to see if he could train the nanites. Could he get the nanites to refrain from attacking the DNA of someone he disliked? Conversely, could he get the nanites to attack DNA about which he felt neutral or liked? Though, the second scenario seemed less practical, he was nevertheless curious.

He selected a half dozen samples from the middle set. These were all saliva samples from kids Gary barely knew. He pricked his finger using one of the lancets from the blood typing kits, put a few drops of blood in each tube and shook them up a little. The nanites didn't seem to care. He focused on one of the tubes, the one belonging to Eugene Maxwell. Eugene was pimple faced bookworm, photographer, and band kid. His mouth and ears were oversized, like his face hadn't quite grown into them yet. It was difficult for Gary to perceive Eugene as a threat. He had never seen or heard Eugene cuss, cheat, lie, steal, fight, or even fart. Try as he may, he just couldn't envision anything untoward about Eugene. He might even like the kid as a fellow weirdo, though he wasn't going to go out of his way to befriend him.

He focused on another test tube. This one belonged to Sally Durbin. Sally had a round body and an obnoxious cackle and Gary saw her cheating on the biology quiz. Perhaps Sally deserved to be boiled by nanites. The planet would be fine without her and her decadence. Certainly she eats more than her fair share. Burn Sally burn. Let's boil you and serve you up as soup for Kenyan orphans. Burn Sally burn. Away with you and your deceitful ways. Shame on you for taking advantage of Miss Fleur's trust. I should have called you out when I saw you sneaking looks in your notebook to get that biology term. What would you have done to me if I had? Would you sit on me with your fat butt? Would you kick me with your stubby legs? Gary envisioned Sally's stubby leg kicking straight for his groin. Pow! The nanites exploded to life, instantly boiling, test tube becoming hot to the touch. Gary had just enough time to scrabble to the sink before the test tube and its contents exploded.

"Damn, there's no in-between with you guys. I better start wearing safety glasses."

Next he selected the tube belonging to Tyler McGrath.

Tyler was a challenge because he was kind of shy, and the popular kids teased him about his favorite extracurricular activity, Irish dancing. Gary extrapolated that and visualized Tyler doing the Riverdance on Gary's face. Pow! Tyler's test tube exploded.

Gary repeated the process with the next three samples. He envisioned Aiden Wiles pointing a gun at him. Pow! He pictured Emily Sorrento smashing his knuckles with a ball peen hammer. Pow! He imagined Kaitlyn Wassermann impaling him with a spear. Pow! He circled back to Eugene and figured out that the nerd sort of reminded him of Edward Scissorhands, so he went with that and envisioned Eugene charging at him with his razor sharp finger blades. Pow! Eugene's DNA sample was dispensed with by the nanites. Good little nanites.

Next he selected a tube from the left side rack. It bore the label "Liam Strauss". This was going to be a challenge. Gary didn't like Liam, because Liam was buddy-buddy with Gary's nemesis, Seth. How could Gary get the nanites to like Liam's DNA, or at least leave it alone? He came up with the most vivid imagery he could that might endear him, and the nanites, to Liam. He pictured Liam wearing leopard print leotards. He saw himself reclining by a gentle waterfall with Liam daintily offering him grapes and cherries, one by one. He let a drop of blood fall into the test tube. Pow! Boil! Explode!

"Wow, those nanites aren't very forgiving. Once a foe, lookout." At this point Gary wished he had more samples from Eugene and the others to see if he could undo the adversarial images he had projected about them. Alas, he decided he would have to ask for more samples. The students participated the first time. Certainly they would contribute again, wouldn't they?

Gary sat on the loveseat in the solitude of the old teacher's lounge and contemplated his condition. He felt like he needed help with his analysis and experimentation projects with the nanites. But, he had to refrain from discussing his condition with doctors, teachers, or his own parents. Gary was convinced the relationship between himself and the nanites was so intricate, there would be no way to separate himself from them. Experimenting with the nanites would basically mean experimenting with himself. What would be the fun in that? Gary had already been down that road, enduring one battery of tests after another in the search for a solution to his cancer. Gary suspected the doctors just got lucky with the nanites in his case. There were obviously still kinks, and it wasn't like Gary was hearing about other cancer patients achieving similar results. It concerned him that the doctors might circle around to him again, curious about their "success."

What could the doctors do to help him anyway? It wasn't like they could solve the problem by putting him through dialysis to filter the nanites from his blood. That would be no different than trying to filter out a flu virus. They may as well use leeches. No, the nanites where a part of him now. They were in his saliva and in his semen. They likely permeated every organ of his body. The thought occurred to Gary that perhaps the nanorobotic scientists that programmed the nanites could reprogram them to become benign. The thought scared him though, because maybe, just maybe, he liked having this power.

He understood the truth about his relationship with the nanites. They were his friends, his trusted companions with whom he could share his most intimate thoughts in his journal. They weren't a curse. They were a comfort. He was reticent to yield the power he discovered with them. They were a blunt instrument, but he *liked* the power. If he could control them, he could keep them, if only to himself. They offered him protection from boys like Seth who might hurt him because he was different. He had a feeling he would meet a number of

Seths in his lifetime, and the nanites gave him a sense of security, like the quiet confidence of carrying a concealed weapon.

A palpable tension remained between Gary and his dad, though they had managed to have two dinners together without Vincent ranting or Gary ending up unconscious. Gary waded into tonight's conversation with trepidation.

"Mom, Dad," Gary said. "I have something to tell you."

"What is it dear?" Mom asked.

"I'm going to the homecoming dance."

"That's great honey," Joanna said.

"Who's your date?" Vincent asked.

"I don't actually have a date. Charlie Simpson and Cindy Perrine are going to swing by, and the three of us will go together."

"Well isn't that nice," Joanna said.

"At least you're not going on some queer date," Vincent said.

"No, it's not like that Dad," Gary said. "So it's okay? I can go?"

"Of course you can go," Joanna said. "You're in high school. It's homecoming. You deserve to have a good time."

"Wow, okay. That's great," Gary said. "There's one more thing."

"Don't push it," Joanna said, under her breath.

"I might get elected to the homecoming court."

Pause.

"I just wanted to warn you."

Silence.

"You're going to be up on stage, in front of all those people?" Vincent asked.

"Yes Dad."

"What are you going to wear?" Vincent asked.

"A tuxedo."

"Damn right," Dad slapped his hands together. "A tuxedo. That's what I'm talking about." Gary tried to measure his dad's animated demeanor. Vincent was smiling and pacing the floor and waving his hands about, energized in a way that Gary found uncharacteristic. "Are you okay, Dad?"

"I'm *fine* son. Just fine. When are you going to pick up this tuxedo?"

"Well, um, Charlie was going to come by tomorrow and we were going to drive over to the mall to get them sized. If we get measured tomorrow, they'll be ready by Friday for us to pick up."

"How about we go together? You, me, and Charlie," Vincent said. "Let's make damn sure you're wearing that tuxedo."

"I'm not sure what to say, Dad. But, um, ok."

"Ah hell," Vincent said, "you want your father to join you or not?"

"Yeah Dad, sure, that's fine." Gary sneaked his mom a sideways glance. She shrugged.

September 26, 2017

3 days before Homecoming

Charlie swung by their rancher and picked up both Gary and Vincent for the trip to the mall. Vincent rode shotgun. Gary sat in the crew cab.

"Nice truck you got here son. Burnt orange. You headed to the University of Texas?"

"I had hoped for that sir, but I think they got cold feet after we dropped a few early games this season."

"That's too bad. You seem like a fine young man. You would be a good leader for a college football team. You can't measure heart, I tell you. They can measure your height, weight, reach, and clock your forty time, but they can't measure your heart. I've a feeling you'll end up just fine."

"I think so too sir. Thank you sir."

"No problem."

Charlie parked just about as far away from the mall entrance as possible, where there were no other cars around. Gary got out and noticed the truck occupied two, no wait, four parking spots. Vincent noticed as well.

"You *really* don't want anybody near your truck do you, son?" Vincent said.

"Nope." A beep signaled the vehicle was secure.

At the mall entrance they saw a display of local beetles.

"Why the hell would the mall feature a display of beetles at their main entrance?" Vincent asked, annoyed by the sight.

"When the developers surveyed the land, they found a rare beetle living in subterranean caves," Charlie explained. "Environmentalists held up construction until arrangements could be made for relocation and preservation of the beetles. Putting up this display was a condition for permission to build the mall."

"See, it's shit like this that makes me not want to come to the mall anymore," Vincent said. "Let's get this done. Where's the tuxedo store?"

Charlie consulted the directory and led the way.

Gary was dreading the interaction between a gay or metro tailor and his dad.

They found Round Rock Tuxedo tucked between a Godiva chocolate store and a florist.

"Look at that," Vincent said. "Tuxedo, flowers and confections; everything you need, right here in one place for your shopping convenience."

"Oh my God," Charlie said, "don't let me forget to pick up a corsage for Cindy."

"Why don't you order it while we're here?" Gary said.

"Good idea." Charlie dashed into the florist next door to the tuxedo shop and took care of the corsage order.

Gary scoped out the tuxedos in the display window. "What do you think?" he asked his dad.

"I always liked the traditional black with a ruffled white shirt," Vincent said.

"I don't see any ruffled shirts. They must be out of style," Gary said. "Look at that double breasted jacket. I think I would look good in that."

"You think?"

"Yeah let's go on in. Charlie can catch up."

A trim man wearing a sharp navy suit, a polka dot purple bow tie, and a happy smile approached them. He walked with an erect posture and a slight sway of his hips.

Oh no, Gary thought.

"May I help you?" The man delivered the standard customer greeting in a high voice.

Vincent stopped dead in his tracks and mumbled something derisive. The salesman, oblivious, extended his hand in Vincent's direction. Gary intercepted. Gary feared Vincent would put a vice grip on the poor salesman and ruin his happy demeanor. Gary shook the man's hand and noted the manicured nails.

"Indeed you may," Gary said. "I'm headed to homecoming,

and I need to be fitted in a tuxedo."

The salesman put his forefinger against his lips. "Let me guess, Sam Houston High School."

"Exactly right," Gary said. "Now I'm not much of a fashion expert, but I think, with my trim physique," he gestured towards his waistline, "that the double breasted style you have on display would look great. Do you agree?"

"Oh yes, absolutely on both counts. You do have a rather nice trim figure," he gave Gary a thumbs up, "And that's perfect for the double breasted style." The salesman spoke with animated gestures brushed his hands along the jacket's lapels.

Gary was standing between the salesman and his dad, so he couldn't see the expression on his dad's face, but he didn't have to. His dad was audibly put off at the salesman's effeminate mannerisms. He grumbled something about fruitcake.

"Any other styles you would recommend?" Gary asked. He dared not turn around and he was desperately trying to keep the salesman from engaging in conversation with his father. This was uncomfortable. He should have told his dad not to come.

"Tell you what, I like your first inclination. Let me see what I have on the rack in double breasted. We might be able to get pretty close to your fit." He eyed Gary up and down, again.

"Get your goddamn perverted eyes off my son, you faggot!" Vincent bellowed, no longer capable of containing himself as he moved towards the salesman.

All eyes turned to Vincent, who reached out to grab the salesman with one hand while he drew the other back in a fist. Gary was mortified. Sure he knew his dad was opinionated, hopelessly rude and incapable of demonstrating couth, but Gary realized this was the moment when he knew definitively that his dad was an asshole.

Gary placed himself in front of the salesman and found his

voice. “Dad, that was uncalled for,” he said as he stuck his hands out to ward off his dad. “Please leave. I can get my own tuxedo.”

Vincent must have felt the weight of the eyes of the other customers in the shop upon him, because he paused and made a quick scan of the store before he replied. He brought his hand to his chin and tightened his lips. Gary considered the possibility that Vincent was weighing the ramifications of punching his son in the middle of the tuxedo store.

The moment came to an abrupt end when Vincent announced, “I’ll be at the food court.” With that, he left in a huff, brushing past Charlie on his way out. Gary’s eyes widened as he considered the enormity of what just transpired. His dad had yielded, in public. Gary expected there would be hell to pay, in private.

“I apologize that for that,” Gary said, double checking the salesman’s nametag, “Elijah, my name’s Gary. It’s nice to meet you and thank you for helping me.”

“It is my pleasure young man,” Elijah replied, straightening his jacket, eying towards the storefront.

Sales assistants were taking measurements and picking items off the racks by the time Charlie got to the changing area.

“Did you pick out my tuxedo yet?” Charlie asked.

“Maybe. Are you and Gary getting the same style?” Elijah asked.

“We thought that would be nice, yes,” Charlie said.

“Then maybe we have. Let’s see how it looks on Gary first,” Elijah said.

They let Gary borrow a loose fitting shirt.

“We’ll get you slim fit for the dance,” Elijah said, assessing Gary’s waistline.

Gary slipped on the pants. They needed to be hemmed. The tailor inserted some pins so Gary could walk around. They hung a jacket on him that fit near perfect. "Let me tell you about this jacket. It's fully canvassed 100% Italian merino wool with silk satin lapels and six-button closure. It's a classic look for a classic event."

"You're quite the salesman," Gary said.

"I try." Elijah smiled.

"What do you think Charlie?" Gary asked as he did a 360 for Charlie.

"Will that style look as good on me as it does on him?" Charlie asked Elijah.

Elijah assessed Charlie's sturdy build. "Hmm, probably not, but it would be better to match than to clash. I would stick with the double breasted and let your brother show you up a little."

"Ha. Gary? He's not my brother, he's my friend."

Gary heard the last phrase loud and clear. It was like music. He smiled wide and mouthed a "thank you" to Charlie.

"Oh I see, I think," Elijah said.

"Go ahead and size me up for the same style as Gary," Charlie said.

The boys chatted while the sales assistants took their measurements. "What happened with your dad? Why did he leave?" Charlie asked.

"He's a jerk," Gary said. "He embarrassed himself and me with his immaturity."

"I see," Charlie said, contemplative. "Well, at least you have a dad."

"I don't know Charlie," Gary replied. "A few days ago he nearly killed me."

"Aren't you exaggerating a bit?" Charlie said as a sales assistant measured his inseam.

"I don't think so. He squeezed my neck so hard I blacked out."

Charlie rotated his hips to face fully towards Gary. "No

fucking way. I can't imagine—"

"Hold still please," said the sales assistant.

"—a father doing that to his own son."

"And it's just getting worse. You heard the way he was talking as we came into the mall."

"Everybody says disparaging things every now and then," Charlie said, shrugging. "I never liked that beetle display at the front of the mall either. It's ugly."

"Hold still please!" said the sales assistant, pins in his hand.

"Don't even try to defend him Charlie," Gary said. "Dad's always been a hard ass, but this time I think he's really snapped. He's starting to scare me."

Tuxedo fitting completed, they found Vincent eating fish tacos at the food court. They ordered a couple of their own.

"You like spicy food, Mr. Greene?" Charlie asked.

"Love it."

"Mom hardly ever fixes spicy," Gary observed. "Her food is bland, usually."

"Don't I know it," Vincent agreed.

Charlie wagged a single finger at both of them "My mom says never complain about your partner's cooking. It's bad form."

Gary stared dumbfounded at his fish taco, processing what Charlie just said. The sage advice about his mom's cooking wasn't what struck him. Charlie overtly used the word *partner* in a conversational tone that was near completely natural. Gary could sort of feel the slow motion of Charlie swapping the word *partner* for *wife*. Unfortunately, Vincent picked up on it too and took umbrage on several levels.

"Listen kid, I don't care if you're the star of the football team or God's gift to this green earth. Don't you wag your fucking finger at me, and you can tell your mama to shove her *partner* advice right up her ass."

Charlie stood. "Don't you dare speak about my mother that way!"

Vincent also stood and he wasn't done talking. "And don't give me that *partner* bullshit. Why can't you just say *wife*? I bet your mama said *wife* and you switched it to partner because you're a fucking faggot just like Gary."

Gary interceded again, this time inserting himself physically between his dad and his best friend. And this time it wasn't a dozen eyes on Vincent, it more like a hundred, including mall security.

"This has to stop," Gary demanded. "Dad, that's twice tonight. You're an embarrassment. Let's go Charlie."

"You're the embarrassment. Go fuck yourselves." Vincent stormed off for the second time that evening. Notably, he headed *away* from the tuxedo shop, a minor relieve for the chagrined boys.

Gary was too upset with his father to be embarrassed in the moment. He was kind of proud of himself for standing up to his dad. It might have been easier to back down and avoid the drama, but Gary felt a surge of courage being around Charlie. He dreaded going home though, to a father who showed the rumblings of a volcanic eruption.

The sun had set by time Charlie and Gary returned to the truck parked across the near empty parking lot.

"Where's the corsage?" Gary asked.

"I can pick that up on Friday, when we get the tuxes."

"Sorry about my dad's behavior."

"Hate to say it Gary, but you're right. Your dad *is* a jerk."

"I know," Gary agreed.

They arrived at Gary's house, absent Vincent, which begged the question from Joanna, "Where's your father?"

"He wore out his welcome and is finding his own way home," Gary said.

"That bad huh?" Joanna said.

“That bad,” Gary confirmed, shaking his head in disbelief.

Vincent arrived home via Uber an hour later, lit a cigarette and mellowed on the front porch. The tuxedo shopping trip was a disaster, and he knew it. Everywhere he turned he felt confronted with homosexuality. The salesman, the quarterback, and his own son all acted like butt fucking buddies. Vincent was the odd man out. It was messed up. What did he have to do? Kill them all?

September 28, 2017

the day before Homecoming

"Don't embarrass me at church this morning Vincent," Joanna pleaded. "You need to be on your best behavior."

"Yes dear," Vincent replied. "How do I look?" He hadn't been to church in a long time. He wanted to blend. He wore a white dress shirt, solid black tie, black slacks, and polished dress shoes.

"You look respectable," Joanna said. "What about me?" She turned around once in her modest solid black, three-quarter-sleeve sheath dress.

"You always look great," Vincent said.

"These heels aren't too high?" she asked.

"Nope, I like watching you walk in them." Vincent said.

"I'll go get my flats," she replied, deadpan.

"Okay," Vincent said.

They drove across town to St Pius X Church. Round Rock was a sprawling town, but St. Pius X was in a city setting, located in the oldest part of town. Its gleaming white, copper-topped steeple dominated the skyline. The church looked as if it was in need of renovation, but the bell still worked, and the building remained functional for services. The inside of the church had an old wood scent and a cathedral feel, with a high A-frame roof and wings of pews to either side of the altar, so that from above you could see that the building formed the shape of a cross.

The turnout was impressive. Every pew was full. Vincent and Joanna stood in the back with a couple of moms holding fussy babies. Vincent scanned the crowd. Did they really know the man they were honoring?

"Don't these people have jobs?" Vincent said.

"Hush."

Vincent endured the service, getting through it with an attitude of celebration akin to the death of the wicked witch. After services ended, he lingered to reconnect with a familiar face he picked out of the crowd. They gravitated to each other just outside the vestibule.

"George Williams, when's the last time we saw each other, seems like forever," Vincent said.

"Yeah, no shit. I can't remember. Ten year reunion, maybe?"

Joanna joined Vincent outside the church. "Joanna, you remember George. We went to school together here at St. Pius."

"Yes, of course, good to see you again George. How is your wife, Vivian, right?"

"Vivian passed last spring. Brain aneurysm."

"Oh I'm so sorry. I must have missed her obituary," Joanna said.

"She didn't want one published. She was a very private person, even in death."

"I see. I'd like to go back inside and light a candle for her, if you don't mind?"

"Not at all. I saw in the paper that your son was cured of leukemia. Congratulations."

"Thank you. A true miracle that was," Joanna said, then darted into the church.

"So sorry about your loss George. I know what a fabulous *wife* Vivian was for you."

"Yeah, indeed she was," George acknowledged.

"Do you want to have a beer? Maybe talk about it?"

"I suppose. It's early, but what the hell."

"Good, I would like to talk as well," Vincent said. "I've had a weight lifted off my shoulders recently. It's liberating."

"I'd like to hear about it."

"Let's grab that beer," Vincent said, grinning.

Joanna returned from lighting her candle. "Joanna honey, George and I want to chat man-to-man, catch up on life. You go on home. I'll get you an Uber."

"No need for that," Joanna said. "You won't be more than a

couple of hours will you?"

"Probably not," Vincent said.

"Okay, I'll do some shopping around town. Just text me to let me know where to pick you up." She kissed Vincent on the cheek. He turned and kissed her square on the lips and held it slightly longer than appropriate. She gently pushed him away and smiled.

"I'll see you in a couple of hours," she said, trying to figure out this new side of Vincent.

"Nice to see you again," she said to George. "I will pray for Vivian."

"Thank you Joanna, take care."

Vincent and George found a nearby pub that opened its doors at 11 a.m.

"Leave it to the Irish to promote drinking before noon," George said.

"Smart business decision," Vincent said. "You notice they don't close until 3 a.m.? They get the early *and* the late crowd."

"Let's sit inside," George suggested. "The sun's already getting intense."

They ordered Guinness, made small talk, and caught up after years of no contact. This outing was another confirmation for Vincent that once established, bonds between true friends transcend time. George and Vincent had experienced joys and trauma together during formative years. The flow of the conversation was natural, the cues familiar and the laughter comfortable. They talked about the good things, while Vincent's mind played a silent video of the bad. He remembered altar boys traipsing through the oak and cedar woods around Lake Travis, with an animated Father O'Brien in the lead. They arrived at the lake's edge and Father suggested they go swimming. The boys protested that they had no swimsuits. Father explained skinny dipping was totally natural. The Apostles fished the Sea of Galilee naked, don't you know. Father stripped down, as did the boys. They frolicked in the water, with Father offering piggyback rides. They played chicken, Marco-Polo, and tag, breaking down personal space with each game. They had no towels so they sunned themselves on the beach, Father applying lotion to their sensitive areas so they didn't get burned. These were the group settings George and Vincent had shared, and they were the gentlest of Vincent's Father O'Brien memories. In private, Father liked to play games where the altar boy straddled him, naked. These were the memories he detested most. The thought of them now made him wince in shame. He was pretty sure he wasn't the only boy who had played these games with Father O'Brien. Vincent took a sip of his beer and ran a hand through his hair as he decided to ask George outright about his experiences.

"Those were the days," George finished his thought.

"Yeah, they sure were." Vincent offered a clink of their beer glasses. "Hey George, I have a heavy question for you."

"Shoot."

"Alright, here is it is, plain and simple. Did Father O'Brien ever ask you to play 'Airplane Joystick' or 'Fun Ride'?"

George's jaw dropped. He glanced around the bar to see if anyone else may have heard the question. He recovered, sipped his beer.

"That's one hell of a question, Vinny," he said in a hushed tone as he leaned towards Vincent.

"I'll take that as a 'Yes'. I suspect he played those games with many of the boys. What do you think?"

"I think you're right," George said, looking straight ahead.

"How do you feel about him getting killed?" Vincent asked.

"Honestly? I thought maybe I came to the service to mourn, but really, the overwhelming sense I feel is relief."

"Me too George. His death lifts a weight from my shoulders. I wish I had snuffed the pervert years ago."

"You wish what?" George said, confused.

"I killed the son-of-a-bitch, finally," Vincent said.

George gasped, disbelieving what he just heard. A wave of horror washed over him as he realized he was sitting across the table from a cold-blooded murderer. A confusing rush of emotions swirled in his head, ranging from regret that he engaged in this conversation to relief that he did so in a public setting.

"Vinny, please don't tell me anymore. I don't want to know," he said as he held up his hands and stared wide-eyed at Vincent.

"Relax," Vincent said, eyes fixed on George. "Come on . . . you know the guy was a pervert. He deserved what he got. I just decided to help him along on his ride to Hell."

George swallowed and sat there trying to digest what he was hearing. He was conflicted. He'd despised Father O'Brien for taking advantage so many years ago, but he had buried that time in his life. He remembered 'Vengeance is mine, sayeth the Lord'. His moral compass told him Vincent had no right to take matters into his own hands. He also realized Vincent was untethered. He proceeded, cautious.

"I understand, Vinny. Believe me I do. In some way, Father O'Brien's murder restored my faith in the divine providence of a righteous God. But if it was at your hands, I don't know. It's confusing. There's supposed to be good guys and bad guys. Good and evil. I thought I knew which side I was on. Part of me wants to shake your hand and thank you. But that part of me is the thirteen-year-old confused little boy who never told anyone what Father O'Brien did." George looked Vincent in the eyes and tried to discern who this man had become. "I'm not that kid anymore, Vinny."

"It's messed up, isn't it?" Vincent said, and looked down into his beer. "That's what he did to us. And, that's why I killed him. His shadow lurked in my mind and it was destroying the most important relationships in my life. I killed him. I killed his shadow. It's liberating. And now I know what I need to do."

George blinked. The message sounded ominous, and its delivery was deliberate and calculating. He wanted to walk away but he had to ask, "What is it you need to do Vinny?"

"I need to hunt these faggot predator bastards and give them their just reward. Did you know there's a queer tailor at the goddamn shopping mall with the beetle display? Imagine that gay son-of-a-bitch sizing up all those young boys for tuxedos. He's no better than our dear friend, Father O'Brien. I ought to slice his throat homecoming night to spare the kids from being ogled when they return their tuxedos."

"Vinny, you're scaring me," George said and began to get off his barstool.

"Naw George. It's all good." Vincent lifted his glass and raised his voice. "Let's drink to good ole Father O'Brien. May he burn in Hell!"

"Here, here," said a random stranger at the bar, lifting his glass in salute.

George stood there and shook his head. He wanted to ignore that the conversation happened, but it did happen and now he had to deal with it. He had a notion to turn Vinny in, then he thought better of it. It would be far better for his friend Vinny to turn himself in. It's a scary thing though, when you can empathize with a killer. George played those nasty games with Father O'Brien. A lot of kids did. George was surprised that Father O'Brien never got caught. Or maybe he did and the Church just covered it up, like they were prone to do. It was hard to know the truth anymore.

"Vinny, I understand the pain you went through, but I don't understand murder. Man, you need to turn yourself in. This path you're on doesn't end well. Please stop before anyone else gets hurt, including yourself."

Vincent grit his teeth and his eyes narrowed like laser

beams across the table. “You threatening me George?”

“No Vinny, I’m not threatening you; I’m trying to help you.” And he was trying to get out of the bar in one piece.

“Help me?” Vincent stared, incredulous. “Help me by sending me to prison?” he said too loudly. “That’s not the kind of help I need Georgie boy. Hell, you probably liked playing bucking bronco with good ole’ Father O’Brien.” Vincent stood. “Up and down, up and down. That get you excited Georgie?” Vincent was wide eyed and thrusting his pelvis back and forth in the middle of the bar. “Common Georgie, let’s play bucking bronco, just like old times! Up and down, up and down.” A few patrons headed for the exit. George gaped in disbelief.

A middle-aged bartender approached the table. “Mister, I’m going to have to ask you to leave.” The slightly built bartender wouldn’t last long in a tussle with Vincent. They both understood this, but any aggression on Vincent’s part would surely end in arrest, not the kind of attention Vincent needed. The bartender added, “I’ve already called the police. I suggest you leave of your own accord, while you still can.”

Vincent took a few steps toward the door. “Been a long time since I’ve been tossed from a bar. Brings back memories.” He turned his head, peering at George. “I took care of things for us George. You ought to appreciate that.” Vincent strutted out the door.

George sat back down at the bar and contemplated what he was going to say to the police when they arrived. Never in his wildest dreams did George contemplate his childhood friend snapping like this. Vincent wasn’t vicious when he was a kid. Far from it. He was timid. George recalled the other kids used to tease Vincent and write on the bathroom stalls, “Vinny is a ninny.” He supposed all that teasing took its toll. Vinny wasn’t a ninny anymore. He was flat out dangerous.

After sipping a beer a while and waiting twenty minutes he flagged the bartender. “When are the police arriving?”

"Oh that?" said the bartender. "I didn't actually call the cops. Bad for business. It's just a line I use to get troublemakers to leave. Works every time." He grinned, displaying a few missing teeth. "Why? You need the cops?"

"Let me think about it," George said.

He left the bar twenty minutes later, still thinking.

The homecoming decorating committee was in full swing. Volunteers were constructing a temporary stage at one end of the gymnasium. Streamers, glitter balls and balloons emanated from it in a fashion that made the stage appear to be expanding outward, like an exploding firework. The school colors, same as the Texas flag (red, white, and blue), amplified the effect. Silver and gold trimmed bunting lined the stage, giving it the gala feel the decoration committee and theater club had hoped.

Music would be provided by school alumni. This was a rich tradition at Sam Houston High. Austin was renowned for live music, and the growing notoriety of the South by Southwest festival made the greater Austin region a magnet for talent. The alumni band would be a formidable bunch, most of whom regularly performed on 6th Street. The dance committee's ability to sell a limited number of tickets to the general public–a demand driven by the talent on stage–allowed the homecoming dance to be self-funding. Gary knew something about two of the alumni band members. One, Johnny Doolittle, featured story-telling ballads, happy and sad, which made you stop and listen. The other, Piper Dakota, was the lead singer in an all-female rock band that modeled themselves after Belinda Carlisle and the Go-Go's. The show was promising to be spectacular.

Cindy was climbing the rafters, tying on red, white, and blue streamers. Gary, Charlie, and Amy were lacing crepe paper through an atrium erected at the rear side entrance to the stage.

"Thanks for inviting me out to help with decorations," Gary said.

"We're glad you came," Amy replied. "Most of the boys are at Seth's keg party. We appreciate the help."

"Hey, not all the boys," Charlie spoke up.

"You are the rare exception Mr. Simpson," Amy flicked the brim of Charlie's UT baseball cap. "Even Roddy abandoned me for the party. I must be losing my appeal."

"I don't think so Amy. Not at all," Charlie said. "You seem plenty appealing to me. You've got the cutest freckles in the whole school."

"You really think so Charlie?" Amy batted her eyelashes. "I've been meaning to talk with Cindy about you. I heard she shares."

"We don't need to bother Cindy," Charlie said. "She's busy in the rafters."

Gary suddenly felt uncomfortable. "I'm going to go recycle this soda can," he announced.

Charlie waved him off.

Gary fetched himself a bottle of water and wandered around the dance floor. He was a little nervous already, just standing there. He couldn't imagine what his nerves might be like tomorrow night. Was he really going to be elected homecoming queen? He heard a yelp and caught sight of a svelte girl with a pixie haircut precariously dangling from a strand of white lights tied to the rafters. The lights blinked off and the cord gave way, swinging Cindy headlong onto the temporary stage. She connected to the plywood with a loud thud. There were lots of gasps and people came running to her.

"Are you okay?" many asked.

She sat up, rolled her neck and said, "Wow, that hurt."

"Should we call an ambulance?" Susan Campbell asked.

"No, I'll be fine. I might just need to rest for a bit."

Susan got her to a chair. Cindy tucked her head towards

her knees. Gary handed her his water bottle. His nanites knew her and liked her. He could share. It was nice to know. Drama over, folks returned to their decorating chores. Gary sat by Cindy.

"Where's Charlie?" she asked.

"Decorating the atrium with Amy," Gary said.

Cindy craned her head around to see the back corner of the stage. Not seeing anyone, she stood and walked towards the corner.

Oh no, Gary thought. This could be bad. Why did I tell her that?

"They're not here? I see Charlie's backpack, but no Charlie. Where did they go?"

Gary shrugged.

Cindy cocked her head to the side, then sat down on a metal folding chair near the exit. She tucked her head to her knees again and covered her ears.

"Cindy, are you okay?"

"The music is too loud. I think I need to get out of here and lie down."

"I know just the place," Gary said. "Can you walk?"

"Yes, I think I can walk. Grab his backpack, will you?" Cindy said.

Gary slung the pack over his shoulder and held Cindy's hand as he escorted her down the corridor towards the old teacher's lounge. He unlocked the door and used the light from the hallway to show her to the loveseat. He clicked on the utility flashlight on his phone and closed the door.

"What is this place?" Cindy asked.

"This is the old teacher's lounge. Miss Fleur gave me the key so I could do my DNA experiments in private."

"Ah, I've seen you sneaking around the corner from her class, but I never knew where you ended up. I always thought this was a utility closet, or something."

"I know, me too."

Cindy appeared sad for a moment. "Gary, did Charlie go off with Amy?"

"I don't know."

"You do know. You don't need to cover for him. We have an arrangement, which you've undoubtedly figured out. But, he's supposed to ask permission."

"Amy mentioned something about asking permission, if that helps."

"He knows I would say 'Yes'. Amy's probably a wildcat in bed. But, sneaking around is not acceptable."

She kicked off her shoes and wagged her toes. "Will you rub my feet?"

"Sure." Gary joined her on the loveseat. Cindy draped her legs over top of his lap and he proceeded with the foot massage.

"Mm, that feels good Gary. Where did you learn to massage feet so well?"

"From my mom."

"Eww, that sounds kinky."

"Well, not quite like this, but yeah, I've rubbed her feet, when she's asked. They're tired on days when she teaches a lot of yoga classes."

"Your mom's a yogi?"

"Full-fledged."

"I'm jealous."

"If you want to be a yogi, you should be," Gary said. "You're naturally athletic. You should be really good at it."

"You like my body Gary?" She moved his hands up her legs.

"You have a great body," he said, stroking her quads.

"Mm, your hands are magic."

She slipped her panties off from under her short shirt and Gary let her slide them off her ankles, just like last time. He continued to message her legs. She began to rhythmically rock her pelvis, purposely moving her groin closer to Gary's hands with each upstroke. A few more cycles and she was accomplishing her goal, with Gary's hands pressing between her legs. She reached down to feel Gary's groin. She thought she must be off target so she fumbled around his pants until the problem dawned on her. "Gary?"

"It's not you Cindy. It's just . . . I can't." Gary couldn't look at Cindy so he just looked down at his lap. Gary's emotions were a tangled. He felt horrible about rejecting Cindy's advances and didn't want her to be embarrassed, but he understood this was a seminal moment in his sexual awakening. Gary suspected his preference was for men. Hell, everyone in the school thought he was gay. He resisted because he wanted it to be his 'decision' not the result of peer-driven stereotyping. This follow-up encounter with Cindy confirmed his preference; it was instinctive.

"Now that's a cop out if I ever heard one."

"No really. I'm sorry, it's just, not my way."

"It was your way last week."

Gary looked up and held Cindy's gaze. "That's because Charlie was there." And Charlie was naked, Gary thought.

"You're totally gay? Not bisexual, bifriendly, flexible or fluid? You're hard wired, straight up gay?"

"I think so, yes." Decision made, and announced.

Long pause.

"I envy you, in a way," Cindy said. "At least you know what you are. I'm still trying to figure myself out."

"Seems to me, figuring it out could be a lot of fun," Gary said and put a genuine smile on his face for Cindy as he reached out to take her hand in a show of affection and friendship.

"There is that," she laughed and gave Gary's hand a squeeze.

Assistant coaches Evans and Mitchell took a break from assembling the homecoming soundstage and headed for the far side of the school parking lot. It was best this way, so the smell wouldn't linger around the school building. They sat on a bench under an oak tree on the far end of the parking lot and lit up the joint. After a few drags, Evans noticed the lone vehicle parked on their end of the parking lot, a burnt orange pickup truck, began bouncing on its shock absorbers.

"Look at that." Evans said. "Simpson's getting laid again."

"That girlfriend of his is a firecracker. Perky tits. Firm ass. That's one lucky dawg," Mitchell said.

The truck was bouncing with vigor. It appeared to be participating in the process. Evans inhaled, held the smoke as long as he could, and then slowly exhaled through his nostrils. "Seems to me, kids are more promiscuous these days than what I remember from high school."

"How long ago was that?"

"Not too long ago," Evans said. "Ten years I suppose."

"I don't know," Mitchell said. "Maybe it has something to do with Simpson being the quarterback. What position did you play?"

"Who me? I didn't play any position. I was a scrub. Why do you think I got into coaching?"

"Same here. I never got laid either."

"At least we could smoke pot."

"Never stopped."

"Ditto."

Mitchell took a heavy drag, watching the embers on the roach, making sure they didn't get too close to his fingers. They enviously watched the truck bounce.

"Damn."

"Yeah, damn."

The rocking motion ebbed and flowed, like ocean waves crashing.

"Double damn."

The minutes passed. Could have been hours for all Evans and Mitchell knew. They took notice when the passenger door opened and the couple slid out the door, one giggling, one laughing, both adjusting their garments. Charlie caught sight of the coaches and took in the situation. Charlie and Amy strolled arm in arm past the coaches.

"Coach Evans, Coach Mitchell," Charlie said.

"Hey Simpson," they said, slowly in unison, grinning.

The coaches watched the couple saunter across the parking lot. Mostly they watched Amy's ass.

"Damn," Evans said.

"Double damn," Mitchell replied. "How many girls does the quarterback get to screw?"

"As many as he wants apparently."

"Here's everyone's DNA samples," Gary said, turning on the light in the old teacher's lounge and showing off his experiment to Cindy. They were well into the tequila from Charlie's backpack, and the alcohol got Gary talking.

"I see mine and Amy's," Cindy said, "but there seems to be a few missing."

"Yeah, those have already exploded."

"They what?"

"Exploded, you know. Boom!" Gary took a swig from the bottle.

"Why did they do that?"

"The nanites in my blood can react violently if they sense that I am threatened. They were designed to fight my cancer. Now they continue to defend me from cells foreign to them, namely other people's cells."

Cindy wasn't sure she understood. "Nanites? I thought that was science fiction."

"Oh, they're very real. I have little, tiny intelligent robots in my bloodstream. They appear to be in my other bodily fluids as well, though I haven't checked my urine."

"What have you checked?"

"In addition to blood? Saliva and semen. Both test positive."

"You came inside me Gary," she said, concerned.

"I know, I figured it was okay after I kissed you and you didn't react badly."

"Why didn't I explode?"

"Because I like you, and therefore, so do my nanites."

"This is unreal."

"I know it, right?"

"I need a drink." She accepted the bottle from Gary and took a full swig. "You need to test your urine."

"I know."

"Let's do it."

"Right now?"

"Yeah, I want to see." She started pulling stoppers off the test tubes and lids off the petri dishes. She carried the whole lot of them over to the sink and commanded, "Pee on them."

"All of them?"

"Sure, you can always get more. I'll help you if you need."

"Ooookaaay." Gary unzipped. He tried to urinate but he was self-conscious in front of Cindy.

Cindy watched and waited anxiously, when nothing happened she blurted, "Don't be nervous Gary. I watched my little brothers pee all the time. They let me judge who won their sword fights. Either that or they pretended they were Ghostbusters crossing their streams."

Gary figured there must be pee all over the floor and walls of the Perrine's bathroom. "I'm not sure I'll ever get that image out of my mind Cindy," he said. "Could you just turn around?" he pleaded.

"Okay," she said, and turned to give him some privacy.

Gary let loose on the contents in the sink. Cindy turned to watch anyway.

"Watch your aim! Get pee on everyone!" Cindy began laughing. "But don't pee on those boxes."

Gary dismissed any embarrassment he had felt about peeing in front of Cindy and resigned himself to his friend's quirky persona. "You're one crazy girl."

"I'm crazy? Look who is peeing nanites onto DNA samples from his classmates?"

"You have a point there," he said as he zipped up.

"What's in the boxes anyway?" Cindy asked.

"Oh those? Miss Fleur picked them up as souvenir tokens for homecoming. They're Texas cowbells. She thinks they might motivate the team."

"How sweet," Cindy said. "Hey, I don't see any test tubes exploding. Were you pulling my leg?"

"No, I'm serious. If I felt threatened by any of these people, the nanites would boil to action and explode their test tube."

"Prove it."

"Ok, pick a classmate in the sink."

Cindy scanned the labels. "I see mine. Make mine explode."

"No, I could never make yours explode. Not in a million years."

"Amy Bridges."

"No, pick someone different. I like Amy."

"How about Wilbur Goldberg. He's that popular kid that plays in the marching band with Eugene."

"Yeah, I know him. He's not very threatening though."

"What if he turned into a zombie and came at you with his trombone and starting beating you over the head with it so he could eat you?"

A sizzling sound emanated from the sink. Cindy peered in. Gary grabbed her and said, "Get down!" Yanking her to the ground. Pow! The test tube exploded.

"It doesn't take long once the nanites decide to attack," Gary explained. "They're lethal."

"Holy Christ!" Cindy said.

"Yep," Gary observed, "nanites are in my urine as well."

"Won't you eventually pee them all out?"

"I don't know. I hadn't thought about that."

"Maybe they replicate themselves, like cells." Cindy said.

Gary contemplated the notion. "Funny, I hadn't thought about that either."

"You obviously need help with your experiments. You don't think of everything. Let me help you."

"You want to help?"

"Yes." She held out an extended pinky. "I pinky swear, I want to help you Gary."

"Pinky swear huh? That's pretty serious." He held out his pinky and intertwined it with hers.

"The most serious swear ever." She leaned forward, lifted one foot off the ground and kissed him on the cheek. "We better get back to the gym. Charlie will be looking for his backpack, plus he's our ride home."

Gary noticed Cindy's panties on the floor next to love seat. "Your panties?"

"You keep them. You deserve them. A trophy. You're the first boy who's managed to get my panties off who didn't end up screwing me."

Gary picked up the panties and draped them on the shelf. "That's some trophy."

"Let's get back to the gym you goofball."

They walked arm in arm down the hall, mutually inebriated. Gary smiling wide with a backpack slung over his shoulder. Cindy in her short red skirt, going commanda.

The keg party was in full swing. Priscilla and Seth were engaged in a heated argument on the back deck and everyone saw Priscilla slap Seth right across the cheek.

"Ouch, that'll leave a mark," Chestnut commented. Chestnut saw Priscilla's lips were flapping as she chewed Seth out, but the Machine Gun Kelly song blaring inside the house was drowning out any possibility of the boys in the kitchen hearing what she was saying. He decided to narrate on their behalf. He raised his voice an octave.

"You something or other dickweed! Please tell me you didn't tell the entire football team I would give them blowjobs!" He deepened his voice and faced the same direction as Seth. "No honey I–" He interrupted with the higher voice and faced the other way. "Yes you did! You just told me you did!" Chestnut swiveled his head back and forth mimicking the argument to the delight of the team.

"Well, just hand jobs maybe."

"You're so gross."

"It's for a good cause."

"Go fuck yourself."

"Just this once."

"If I needed a pimp I would go to 6th Street!"

The laughter in the kitchen was so rancorous, Priscilla and Seth turned and stared.

Higher still, "Oh my God. We are done. We are so done." Chestnut was so engrossed in his Priscilla impersonation that he didn't notice that both Priscilla and Seth had stepped into the kitchen.

"What are you doing?" Seth bellowed.

Chestnut stopped mid-sentence, sat up straight on the kitchen barstool, and looked wide-eyed at Seth. "Nothing." He took a swig of beer, stared at Seth, and then burst out laughing, beer squirting out his nose.

Players scattered from the spray, yelping and roaring.

Chestnut regained his composure and said, "Dude, that was classic."

"I'll be upstairs," Priscilla announced, matter-of-fact, and left the kitchen.

"There are going to be rules," Seth said. "Please, for my sake, obey them."

Nelson Warner saw Miss Fleur struggling to lug a coil of red carpet runner towards the gymnasium front entrance. He bounded across the floor.

"Let me get that for you Miss Fleur!"

She dropped the roll, relieved. She brushed bits of red carpet thread off her white cotton blouse and slim-cut blue jeans. "Thank you Nelson. These runners are supposed to have finished edges, but I think we've used them so many times they're starting to fray. It really is too heavy for me. These theater kids are nice, but they don't have enough strong people to help carry things."

"They're all at Seth's party," Nelson observed.

"So I hear. How come you're not at his party too?"

"Because I have this certain biology teacher who made an appeal for help today in class. I felt it was my duty, as a man, to be responsive to her needs."

"Oh my, aren't you a chivalrous young man," Miss Fleur replied, smiling.

"I try to be, Miss Fleur." Nelson bowed and sized up the carpet roll. The runner weighed about forty pounds, but he easily slung it over his shoulder. Nelson wondered how much flirting she would let him get away with while he helped her.

"Please don't hurt yourself." *Wow he's strong*, she thought. "We want to run the carpet from the front entrance all the way out to the roped off drop-off circle in the parking lot. There's two more rolls to carry. I appreciate your help, Nelson."

"No problem," he said. "May I call you Jackie?" He tried to push the envelope.

"I don't know about that," she said, smiling. "I'm still your teacher. Let's keep the formal title. I wouldn't want our roles to get muddled."

It occurred to Nelson that he should be flattered, in a way, that Miss Fleur didn't drop her guard. Perhaps she sensed the danger, though she would be reticent to admit it to him. Perhaps in another time and another place, the situation would unfold differently. Nelson realized the only thing that would be unfolding between the two of them this evening was a roll of red carpet.

Nelson helped Miss Fleur with the first runner, taping it down with black duct tape as they unfurled it away from the front entrance. They both were working hard, standing and then down again on their hands and knees, securing the runner.

Jackie made small talk. "Nelson, you should consider volunteering as stage crew for theater club. They could use your help."

"I might just do that," Nelson said. "I would enjoy working around the stage."

They finished the first roll.

"Oh my, that was quite the workout," she said. They had been knees and elbows for the carpet's fifty-foot length. Nelson noticed Miss Fleur leaned on him for support as they stood. He liked that.

He braced her. "Yeah it sure is. Another?"

She nodded.

The storage closet was behind the wall of rollout bleachers. Nelson considered the semi-private setting of the storage closet. Should he put a move on Jackie in there? Perhaps she was being coy in public, but in private she would be more receptive to his advances. He decided he would try and kiss her in the closet and see where that led. Just outside the closet door he said, "Jackie?"

Jackie cocked her head, "You mean Miss Fleur?"

"Yes, sorry." Nelson was busted, but he pressed on anyway. "Miss Fleur, will you be coming to the homecoming dance tomorrow?"

"Of course," Jackie said. "I wouldn't miss homecoming."

"Do you have a date?" Nelson asked.

"No Nelson, I'm afraid I don't. I've invited a friend, and she may or may not make it. I haven't dated in quite a while. I'm fine coming solo though. That's what teachers do. I'm supposed to chaperone, not have fun," she said, smiling. "I bet a handsome young man like you gets lots of dates. Who are you bringing?"

Nelson sensed an opening. "No, there's really only one girl in school I like. But, I'm not dating her. Not yet anyway."

"Oh, who's the lucky girl?"

"You." He got down on one knee by the other two rolls of carpet. "Jackie, will you be my homecoming date?"

Nelson was a novice at romance, but he thought his dramatic proposal was pretty good. *How could she resist my charm?* He thought.

She crouched down and gently put her hands on his shoulders. "Sir Nelson, you are quite the Prince Charming. I'm flattered. I'm sorry if I've led you on, in any way, to make you think I would be receptive to your advances. I cannot accept. There are many reasons. There's the basic matter of our age difference and the practical matter of a teacher-student affair jeopardizing my job. Don't get me wrong, I think you're a fine young man. But, that's just the thing, you're *young* and I, most certainly, am not."

"It's just a dance date," Nelson said, nonchalant.

"Nelson look at me," Jackie said. She waited until Nelson made eye contact. "I hope you don't mean that like it just sounded. You just dropped to one knee and offered me one of the sweetest proposals I've ever received. My first husband's marriage proposal pales in comparison. Don't diminish it. We both know you were talking about more than just a dance date. Don't we?"

"Yes, we do," Nelson admitted, blushing.

"I can't accept your offer. But, I am flattered. You keep it up and you're going to charm the pants off many a girl. Literally," Jackie said, grinning. "Now, if you don't mind, I still need your help with these carpets. Let's focus on getting this work done tonight so *everyone* can have a good time at the dance tomorrow. Agreed?"

"Agreed." He stood up, towering over her once again.

"Now be my big strong man and lug these reams of carpet out the front entrance," she commanded, playfully smacking his rear end like she saw the football players do to each other all the time. She thought it an odd practice. Perhaps the players were congratulating each other, like an extra-low high-five. In Jackie's case, she felt it more akin to slapping a donkey to get it moving. Not that Nelson was a jackass. He was a nice young man who just happened to be serving as her mule at the moment.

Nelson stood each ream up on end, tucked his head in between and hoisted them simultaneously onto each shoulder. "Lead the way," he said, only slightly straining.

Jackie made sure the path was clear for him and turned to look every once in a while, thinking what a fine man Nelson would grow up to be. She envisioned the carpet rolls slung upon his shoulders being the firm thighs of a pretty girl and she felt a rush in her groin. Nelson was right about one thing. It was time to let a man address her needs. But, seducing a student was not her style. She would have to make a phone call this evening to a friend.

They laid out the next two rolls in an angular fashion that formed a ninety-degree arc from the drop-off circle to the front door. This made the inside of the arc the tradition prime photograph spot. Once the arc was formed, Coaches Evans and

Mitchell showed up to assemble the photographer's platform. Nelson saw them fumbling. They were both definitely stoned.

"I better go help them," Nelson said.

"I think you had," Jackie agreed. She snuck Nelson a thank you hug. The coaches would be too out of it to notice.

Nelson picked up a power drill. "You guys need a hand?"

"Sure man," Coach Evans slowly drawled.

"Dude, did that teacher just hug you?" Coach Mitchell asked.

"You guys are crazy. Let's get this thing built." Nelson made sure to squeeze the trigger on the power drill a few cycles every time it seemed like one of the coaches might ask a question. They eventually gave up and forgot about it. Another short-term memory, gone to pot.

On the way home, Jackie called Nina Lopez to confirm she was still planning to attend homecoming. She was glad she did. Nina had already given her ticket to the esteemed Dr. Wolfgang Reichmann, which worked out fine because Jackie could still bring Nina as her guest and Jackie was secretly looking forward to meeting Wolfgang. Jackie found herself getting hot for the doctor. This was irrational of course; she hadn't met him in person yet, she just knew he was brilliant and handsome. Jackie figured Nina had already told him about her. She would pry out what she said while they were dress shopping tomorrow.

It had been a while since Jackie had been on a date. Her divorce was nasty, and she was still smarting from her brief experience with internet dating. Her online match kissed her goodnight on the first date, which was nice. He was all hands on their second date. She liked the attention but felt weird about it at the same time. By the third date, this man was ready for intercourse. That was the night she learned about the three-date rule. Apparently, any man worth his salt was supposed to be able to talk a woman into bed within three dates. It was an unwritten, but widely accepted guideline for online dating, or so he claimed. If that's the way it was, then Jackie wasn't ready for online dating. She ended the date, dropped that man, and hid her profile. That was six months ago. Her body was signaling something different now, and the object of her affection was the doctor she was going to meet tomorrow at the homecoming dance.

Susan Campbell stood at center stage surveying the decorations. She had done everything right: Captain of the cheerleaders, head of the decoration committee and everyone's friend, and yet, she would not be homecoming queen. That honor would elude her because of a wave of political correctness sweeping through Sam Houston HS. Under any other circumstance, it would be her up on stage tomorrow, receiving her crown on this very spot. Susan did not complain. She knew better. Her objections would be viewed as petty, and petty was not a perception commensurate with the image she had worked so hard to build.

She closed her eyes and imagined the cheering crowd. Who would she have been standing with? Not Gary Greene. God no, that would make Susan the homecoming king. It would be too confusing. That's why she'd be knocked off the winner's slots completely. The winners would be a matched pair: Charlie Simpson and Gary Greene. Susan had practically assured it with her own lobbying. No, in another universe she would be standing with a king that provided a different kind of irony, perhaps Lamar Jones. Sure, vote for the big black guy to stand next to the prissy blond cheerleader on stage. Make them dance awkwardly together. That's the way her immature classmates thought. She would have accepted the dance though, and enjoyed it. That's the way barriers were broken down, even in Central Texas, where interracial relationships still were an unspoken taboo amongst the Hill Country elite.

It was hard for Susan to give up the crown. Her whole life, she was used to getting what she wanted. Not in this case. Tomorrow she would grin and bear it. She would cheer for the gay kid and lead her squad in an enthusiastic celebration of an enlightened student body. She wondered how many speeches she would have to endure about how proud the school administrators were of the students. "Yay us, we're not mean. We vote faggots for homecoming queen." She chanted the cheer in her head. Was she bitter? Of course, but she resolved to take her bitterness to her grave. Too bad for Susan that opportunity was coming sooner than she imagined.

The line of players formed in the hallway outside the upstairs bedroom. Each player held a playing card in their hand and they were adjusting their order in line accordingly. "Hearts before diamonds you morons," echoed down the hallway. Seth stood at the bedroom doorway, providing guidelines to the players in line. He focused on the lucky guy who drew the ace of spades from the deck. His name was Zachary Boykin, a pimply-faced sophomore scrub who played on special teams.

"Here's the deal Zachary," Seth said. "This is our first annual homecoming keg party and by tradition, we each need to shoot a wad into the paint can."

"Into the paint can?" the kid asked.

"Yes, squirt, squirt, that simple, into the paint can. That's the plan."

"No blowjob? I was told it was a blowjob. I've never had one."

"Listen Zachary. This is my girlfriend. She's not giving you a blowjob. You'll have one someday. But this is still your lucky night. Have you ever seen a girl's bra before?"

"Well yeah, kind of," Zachary said.

"Kind of doesn't count," Seth said. "Tonight you'll get to see Priscilla Moran in her bra. Here's the deal though. No touching. You see, you jack off, you leave. Don't dilly-dally. You've a line of teammates out here waiting for their turn. Got it?"

"Got it," Zachary said.

Seth opened the bedroom door. Zachary stepped inside. Seth snuck a peek at Priscilla. She didn't look too happy. Seth shut the door.

"You guys having a good time?" Seth asked, rhetorically.

"Hell yeah we are!" said the guys milling in line.

Zachary emerged from the room a few minutes later, wide smile on his face. "Priscilla says you need a bigger catcher. She suggests a popcorn bowl or something like that." Zachary said. "And paper towels."

Seth shook his head. This was going to be a long night. He suspected Priscilla would never speak to him again. Still, he was willing to sacrifice his girlfriend to get back at gay condom boy.

"Okay Zach," Seth said. "Do us a favor, go to the kitchen. There's a big punchbowl in the bottom of the china cabinet. Grab it and pass it up the line. Fetch some paper towels while you're down there."

"Sure enough Seth, no problem. I really appreciate the hand job," Zachary said, then bounded down the stairs.

"Hand job?" Seth mumbled under his breath.

Lucas Barolo had the next ace and he had already slipped inside the bedroom. Seth wondered what the heck was going on in there. Before he could turn the doorknob, a rather displeased Roddy Cruz confronted him. Roddy was next in line, with the king of spades, but he had no intention of going into the room. He had already determined he couldn't participate, for a number of reasons. The assembly line process felt slimy, seeing Priscilla in her bra seemed an affront against his girlfriend, he certainly wouldn't masturbate in her presence, and he was pretty sure he knew what Seth intended to do with the contents of the paint can. Roddy got into Seth's face, defiant.

"The only reason I stepped up here was to let you know what an ass I think you are."

"Well, get the fuck out of here then," Seth replied. "We don't have time for this shit. But, I swear to you, the wrong people catch wind of this, I'll come for you, Cruz." Seth pointed his finger.

"Is that a threat?" Roddy straightened his back, throwing his chest forward, assuming a sumo wrestler pose.

"It's a fact. I have nothing left to lose." Seth held his hands wide.

"Fine, I'll keep my mouth shut," Roddy said, folding his arms, "as long as nobody gets hurt."

"All in good fun my friend."

"Fine."

Roddy stomped down the hallway. The paper towels were being handed up the line. Roddy grabbed them and flung them at Seth. Seth caught them easily.

"Thanks," Seth sniped, sarcastic.

Roddy saw Lamar Jones standing midway in line and slipped him the king of spades. "Here, take it."

Lamar looked at the card, "Sweet!" and marched to the front of the line, flashing the king. The next boy had already gone in, so Lamar waited. A large lead crystal punchbowl was passed up the line. Lamar passed it to Seth. A minute later a cheeky red faced but smiling sophomore stumbled out the door yelling, "Next!" with newfound confidence.

"We're right here you idiot," Seth said.

Seth stepped into the room, punch bowl and paper towels in hand. Lamar followed, leaving the door open behind him. The closest players in line took the opportunity to peek inside. The bedroom's lone single bed was stripped of its covers and pushed to the side toward the door of a Jack and Jill bathroom.

A wooden chair and a coffee table, borrowed from the dining room and living room, occupied the middle. A Kelly-Moore paint can and a jar of Nature's Way Coconut Oil rested on the oak table. Priscilla Moran sat on the chair. The top three buttons of Priscilla's blouse were unbuttoned to reveal bra and cleavage. As Seth sat the punch bowl and paper towels down on the coffee table he noticed the hallway crowd was leering. He shut the door.

"What's this I hear about hand jobs?" Seth said. "You're the one who insisted on no touching."

"It's hard for the boys to aim," Priscilla explained. "That's why we needed the bigger bowl."

"Girls are weird," Seth mumbled. "Get on with it Lamar," he said louder.

Lamar looked at Priscilla, buttons undone. He glanced at Seth, looming ominous. He surveyed the items on the coffee table, paint can, punchbowl, coconut oil and paper towels. "Oh no way man. I am not whipping out my wanger in front of your girlfriend while you stare down from on high like some Aqualung freak. You've got to give me some space Seth. I'll cum in your stupid can for you, but geez, give a guy some dignity and let him cum in peace. Your face don't equate to peace, man. Not now, not ever."

"He's right Seth," Priscilla said. "You're a bore. Go drink some of your dad's bourbon."

"Listen to me, sweetie," Seth said as he grabbed Pricilla's arm and pulled her to him. "I want you to do your job, and I want everyone's cum in that can. Do you understand?"

"Yeah, Seth. Ok." Priscilla, at only 5'2", stared into Seth's lower chest as she answered contritely. "Just do your duty Priscilla. Let's get this over with." Seth stomped out.

Priscilla gazed up at Lamar and shrugged. "I'm the one doing the hand jobs, and he has the nerve to be snippy with me?" She smiled at Lamar. "Oh well, show me what you got big boy."

Lamar undid his trousers and freed his penis. Priscilla's eyes grew big. Lamar smiled wide and chuckled. "He is quite the beast."

"Oh my God," Priscilla said. "I thought Lucas was impressive."

"What's so impressive about Lucas?"

"Lucas said he could sit on the edge of his bed and squirt all the way to his dresser mirror. That boy was potent," Priscilla said. "You're a different kind of impressive."

Chestnut was next. He waited patiently outside the bedroom door. Lamar finally finished, opened the door and high fived Chestnut on the way out. Chestnut stepped inside and closed the door.

Chestnut couldn't help but notice Priscilla was shirtless and braless. "Lamar got you to do that, didn't he?" He gestured towards her glistening bare breasts. He didn't wait for an answer. "Lamar can have an effect on a girl," Chestnut said. "It's alright. Go get cleaned up before the next dude strolls in."

"Thank you Chestnut." She stepped into the bathroom.

Chestnut masturbated into the punch bowl while Priscilla was in the bathroom. His contribution to the cause.

Priscilla stepped out of the bathroom, clean, but still topless.

"Priscilla, you're a mighty pretty girl. You don't need to flash your breasts to get a man excited. Easy isn't interesting. Tantalizing, now *that's* interesting. I know you're having fun, and I don't want to ruin it for you, but can I offer you a suggestion?"

"Sure, I'm listening."

"Put your top back on. Maybe leave the bra on the bed. That's hot, but cover your nipples. Leave a few buttons open and you'll have every guy trying to sneak a peek while he jacks off. It will be better for you and faster for them. Trust me."

Priscilla suddenly felt self-conscious. “You think I’m acting like a slut don’t you?”

“No. Seth didn’t think this through. Every guy standing in line out there is a young virile athlete. Your impulses are going to get you into trouble. A few more studs like Lamar stroll in here and what would you be doing with them?”

Priscilla looked down.

“It’s okay. I’m not trying to shame you. I’m going to help you. You know my girlfriend, Tonya?”

“Yes, she’s awesome.”

“I’m going to tell her you’re in over your head up here all alone. She’s a good sport. I know she’ll come help you if I ask. She knows what she’s doing and I think you two might just along. You won’t see her removing any clothes, not unless these boys start putting serious money on the table. Follow her lead. You two will have these guys through here like an assembly line in no time. I’ll keep Seth occupied. You won’t have to worry about him barging in on you. Have a good time and let Tonya take you under her wing.”

“Thank you.”

“My pleasure.” He grinned. “By the way, great tits.”

Priscilla was already giving the next boy his hand job when Tonya stepped into the room. A boy followed Tonya into the room, carrying another dining room chair.

“Look at you girl,” Tonya said. “You’re already ready to come work at the club.”

Chestnut was right. Tonya Jones was a good sport about joining Priscilla for hand job duties. Tonya was Chestnut’s college-age girlfriend. And while she supposedly was attending at least one class at the local community college, everyone knew she was making her money–and lots of it–working at one of the local strip clubs. Priscilla explained the rules. Tonya got right to work, starting with the boy who carried her chair. The pace was faster now. Two at a time. With Tonya’s help, this must have looked more like a professional operation because the boys started to leave tips on the coffee table. Tens and twenties.

Priscilla noticed another interesting dynamic with two boys getting hand jobs at the same time. When she was solo with the first few boys, they seemed to take a while to achieve their orgasm. She was pretty sure she was doing it right. God knows she had lots of practice with Seth. No, the first few boys seemed excited and nervous at the same time, delaying the process. With two boys in the room, ejaculations came quicker. She noticed her boy most often gazed at Tonya's workmanship and vice versa for Tonya's boy. The boys were fascinated with the other guy's hand job and often climaxed simultaneously. This was good, because it sped things along, but Priscilla couldn't help but wonder if perhaps there were underlying homosexual dynamics involved.

They moved onto the next pair of boys, Liam Strauss and Jeremy Parsons. Liam gravitated to Priscilla and Jeremy went to Tonya.

"What's your name?" Priscilla asked as she unzipped his shorts.

"Jeremy."

"Why are you carrying that football Jeremy?"

"He has to," Liam said. "Coach says he needs to get used to carrying the football everywhere he goes, so he stops fumbling the ball when he's on the field."

"Well, Jeremy, you make sure you tell your coach you held onto that football during a hand job," Tonya said. "I bet he'll be real impressed."

"I'll vouch for you, Jeremy," Liam said, grunting.

"I don't think 'impressed' would be the right word for Coach's reaction," Jeremy said.

"Just trying to help you out." Liam slapped at the football. Jeremy's guard was down. The ball slipped from his grip and landed with a splash in the punchbowl.

"No fucking way!" Jeremy said. "You did *not* just do that."

Liam burst out laughing. Tonya and Priscilla giggled.

"That's fucking disgusting." Jeremy ripped paper towels off the role and fished the semen-coated football out of the punchbowl. He painstakingly wiped the ball until he was satisfied the major gobs of the stuff were wiped off. "I'm going to get you for this," he told Liam.

"Go ahead and try," Liam smirked. "Then you'll have to explain to Coach how your football wound up in that punchbowl."

Jeremy stomped out, cradling his football in still more paper towels.

Priscilla was working hard. Her fingers were already cramping and she was working up a glistening sheen of perspiration. Tonya was doing the same, making for a close musky smell of sweat and semen in the modest sized bedroom. Priscilla needed some air before the aroma became too overpowering. "Hey Liam, before you leave, would mind opening the windows in here," Priscilla said. "It's getting stuffy."

"Stuffy puts it kindly." He obliged, bringing welcome circulation to the bedroom.

He left two twenty-dollar bills on the table. "I'll get Jeremy to pay me back later. I'll have him over a barrel for the rest of his days."

"Next!"

Their evening wore on for several hours. It takes time to deliver hand jobs to an entire football team, even two at a time. A few dozen hand jobs later, they got to the last boy in line, Ricky Marlin, the long snapper. Ricky wasn't particularly strong or fast, but he had a knack for hiking the football between his legs to the punter in a nice tight spiral, and this got him onto the team. Ricky added a twenty to the pile and left the girls alone in the room to clean up. Priscilla peered into the paint can. It exuded a pungent ammonia smell. Tonya added the milky white cream contents of the punch bowl into the paint can. Hours of sitting allowed some of the semen to thicken and congeal, sticking to the sides of the punch bowl. Ever committed to the cause, Priscilla went down to the kitchen to fetch a spatula. The football players in the kitchen rewarded her with whoops, cheers, and a standing ovation. She returned to the bedroom, spatula in hand.

"Sounds like you're a hit," Tonya said.

"Seems so," Priscilla agreed.

"Now, imagine how big this pile of money would be if they were businessmen with real paychecks." Tonya beamed a smile.

"I'll think about it," Priscilla said.

Tonya scraped the gelatinous cum out of the punch bowl. "Pee-yew! This stuff is really gross and it smells," she said, scraping with one hand and holding her nose with the other.

"Sure does, let's get the lid on it." Tonya got the last remnants and they tapped the lid down loosely.

They gathered up the tip money and split it fifty-fifty. They used the tub in the bathroom to clean out the punchbowl and Priscilla hopped in the shower. Tonya scrubbed her hands and arms with ivory soap. Priscilla didn't have a change of clothes, but she remembered Mrs. Thompson was fairly slender. She sifted through her closet and managed to find a pair of pink capris and a cotton lavender top she could borrow for the rest of the evening. She studied herself in the mirror. She curtsied.

"Thank you for the clothes Betty. Oh, they look so good on me I should keep them? You're so nice."

Priscilla earned more money in one evening than she would have working at Walmart for a week. Technically, what she engaged in was prostitution, as did the boys who arranged and participated in the process. The decadence of the keg party, when discovered, would have been the scandal of the year for the quiet town of Round Rock, if not for the events of homecoming, which far overshadowed Seth's little keg party. Tonya Jones would claim later that at the time of the party she had no idea the team was going to use the paint can of semen for a disgusting prank. Forty-five boys received hand jobs at the keg party. For the vast majority of them, it was their first. For each and every one of them, it was their last.

Chestnut and Seth lounged on the screened-in porch, smoking Honduran cigars and listening to the crickets call out to the moonlight.

Chestnut poured Seth another scotch. "Your dad going to be upset you drank his Highland Park Scotch?"

"Probably," Seth mused.

"Where are your parents anyway?"

"They're spending the weekend in San Antonio with Jeremy's parents. They know I'm throwing a keg party, and they wanted to be able to claim ignorance for any underage drinking."

"So, in a way, your dad *deserves* to have his scotch consumed, because of his own irresponsibility."

"I'll drink to that." They clinked their snifters.

"This is a good party, isn't it Chestnut?"

"The best." Chestnut puffed the cigar, waft of smoke drifting to the porch light.

"You think Priscilla is okay upstairs?"

"Oh yeah, she's fine. Don't crowd her. She's doing this for you, you know. Besides, Tonya is up there with her. She knows what she's doing."

"Yeah, I'm glad. Thanks for sending her up there."

"Don't mention it," Chestnut said, ashing his cigar into a potted plant.

"You know we need to jerry-rig the contraption later

tonight. We won't have a chance tomorrow."

"I figured."

"We only need a few people to set it up. Just the core team," Seth said. "You, me, Liam, and Lucas."

"You thought about how you're going to rig it?"

"Kind of," Seth said, unsure. "You have any ideas?"

"Yeah, I reckon we use the paint can handle to tip it, but then we also have to put weight on the handle to make sure the topside flips over to pour out the surprise. You have rope and something we can use for weight?"

"Rope's in the garage, lots of it. I've a barbell set in the basement. Should be something there we can use."

"Let's go check it out," Chestnut said. The way he figured it, if he was going to keep Seth occupied, they may as well use the time productively. They needed to set up the paint can over the stage and, knowing Seth, that part of the plan was yet unplanned.

They found boys shooting pool and helping themselves to beer from the refrigerator in the basement. "Use the keg upstairs guys," Seth said.

"Keg's tapped out. We assumed this was your backup."

Seth's barbell set was in the corner. Seth rooted through the clamps and found a heavy, lead one that he felt he could clamp onto the handle. "This should work."

Chestnut felt the weight of it. "Oh yeah, that will pull the top down. Let's go get the rope."

Liam and Lucas were flinging darts at the board on the far wall. They weren't doing a very good job of it though. Seth saw dozens of pockmarks in the drywall.

"Hey you guys hang out until the party dies down. We still have an errand to run tonight."

"Understood," Lucas said.

"Also, would you mind hitting the board every once in a while. I'm the one who's going to have to paint that wall."

"Sorry about that," Liam said. "Just don't mix up your paint cans."

"Ha-ha, very funny."

"Let's go find the rope," Seth said to Chestnut.

Chestnut followed Seth to the garage and sorted through the ropes. "These won't work Seth."

"Why not?"

"They'll be spotted, even by the casual observer. They're white, bright orange and neon yellow. We need a dark colored rope, to blend with the rafters."

"Why don't we just paint the white one?" Seth was already reaching for the spray can of black Rust-Oleum.

"That should work."

Chestnut put on a pair of garden gloves and stretched out the rope at various angles so Seth could cover the white surfaces. The finished product was a one-hundred-foot length of jet-black rope. "Hang onto the spray can so we can cover the paint can label as well."

"Good idea," Seth said.

It occurred to Chestnut that this plan would be a total screw up if it weren't for his mentoring. He would have to stay close to Seth to make sure things went as envisioned. They put their supplies in a gym bag and rejoined the party.

Seth and Chestnut retrieved the paint can from the bedroom and brought it to the garage for spray painting.

"This doesn't feel that full to me," Seth said. He tapped open the lid to peek inside. The can held a milky slurry that was only a few inches deep. Seth was disappointed. His vision was more along the lines of the cooler of Gatorade the team dumped on him after they won the championship last year. Not this. This was entirely inadequate.

"What did you expect? You're trying to fill a gallon paint can by the tablespoon," Chestnut said.

"It's alright, I can fix it," Seth replied. He put the paint can on the garage floor and started to unbutton his pants. "I have to piss anyway." Seth emptied his bladder into the paint can, adding a quart of urine to its foul contents. He grabbed a stick and stirred the concoction. A putrid smell permeated the garage.

Chestnut observed Seth gleefully stirring the disgusting urine and semen mixture. Seth was the wicked witch. His brew looked and smelled like the yeast infection from hell.

"I swear if condom boy were here right now I would make him lick this stick." Seth widened his eyes, amplifying the comment with a crazed look.

"Seth, you are one sick dude," Chestnut observed, stating the obvious.

Vincent crushed another beer can and let it drop to the cement slab of his front porch. His gay son was out late, *decorating* for homecoming. His wife was already in bed, seemingly unconcerned about their son's sexual orientation. Worse, she was supportive. Didn't she understand the ramifications? Perhaps she needed a little demonstration of what her son was up to. He popped the top on another Southern Star Pale Ale and guzzled half the can. He let his roughened hand trace along the can's rim and scraped his callouses on the sharp edge of the pop top. Rage simmered inside him. His son: gay. His wife: ignorant. She needed to be educated. He pressed his thumb to the lip of the pop top. A life's lesson, that's what she needed. He pushed his thumb across the lip of the can, slicing the callous clean through. This was a teaching moment. Blood seeped from his thumb across the top of the beer can. He guzzled the rest of the beer and crushed the can. Let's illustrate, shall we?

He let the screen door slam behind him as he strutted heavily across the living room floor, toward the bedroom where his wife lay sleeping. It was time to show his wife what her precious son was up to.

Joanna awoke when she heard someone burst into the bedroom. She turned and saw that it was Vincent, unsteady on his feet. At this point he usually collapsed onto the bed, sometimes without even getting undressed, and would be snoring within a few minutes. Instead, he startled her by yanking away the bed covers, fully exposing her naked body. He was on her immediately, making no effort to support his own weight as he pressed down onto her. He smelled of alcohol and cigarettes. She struggled to breathe. His tongue slobbered clumsily across her face until it reached her ear.

"I've got a surprise for you," he whispered roughly. "It's time for you to be enlightened."

He eased off the bed and Joanna caught a breath. Just as suddenly he gripped her ankles tightly and flipped her in a single twisting action onto her belly. Her protest was met with a stinging slap to her ass cheek. She gasped. She felt his hands powerfully grip her hips. Why was he being so aggressive about it? Joanna couldn't fathom. He sometimes got a little rough, but sex was never a punishment between them. She positioned herself to be entered. She heard Vincent spit and then felt him fumble at her bottom area.

"That's the wrong hole," she cautioned.

"Shut up bitch." His member forcefully entered her anus. "Don't you want to know what your son is doing?" He pressed inward. "This is what he's getting." Joanna clenched at the sheets and heard her own scream muffled in the pillow. She tried to free herself, but his vice grip on her hips was insurmountable. She fruitlessly flailed one elbow and then the other at his ribs. He snorted and kept her impaled.

Joanna was no prude. She had experimented with boyfriends prior to settling down with Vincent. But, she had never been hurt like this. She sensed an unfamiliar corruption. His thrusts were deliberately vulgar. His heavy hands malicious in intent. She panicked. Why couldn't she breathe? If she couldn't breathe she couldn't scream. Pain. Unbearable pain. No breath. She grew lightheaded. Death. This was death.

"Is this what you want for your precious creampuff?" Vincent's voice was gruff. "You didn't think about your son taking it up the ass did you?" His angry thrusts were filled with hatred. "You're not getting any grandchildren this way." There was no breaking free from his iron grip. "Butt fucking don't yield kids because it ain't God's way." He violated her deeply. "This feel right to you sweetie?" He panted, wrathful. "Might be the wrong hole for you, but it's the only fucking hole your precious Gary's got." Joanna's resistance waned. She lay lifeless against the defilement and vile discourse.

Joanna had heard about what it was like to be sexually abused. She heard stories about how the victim could feel detached from their own body. She never thought it would happen to her. She clung to life, biting the edge of the pillow and drifting in a numb pain. She lost sense of time and reason. She didn't know who this strange man raping her was, but she knew that when Vincent got home and saw what he was doing to her, Vincent would kill him. She knew their relationship wasn't perfect. Having a kid first was a hard way to start a marriage, but they were making it work. Their pillows smelled of lavender. It was the laundry detergent. She endeavored to keep their sheets and pillows clean and fresh. Vincent worked hard. He deserved at least that much. At least he was man enough to step up to his responsibilities as a provider for his impromptu family. She remembered how they first met. She was too young to drink, but there was no way she was going to miss the party of the millennium on sixth street, New Year's Eve, 1999. Early into New Year's she and her girlfriend found themselves in a pinch because their car wouldn't start. There was Vincent to the rescue. Handsome, strong, and good with his hands, Vincent fixed the car. He got her phone number, and the rest was history. One thing she depended upon was Vincent's protectiveness. He might be gruff and occasionally hot tempered, but he would never hurt her. Never.

She heard distant whimpering and was confounded when she realized the doleful noises were coming from her own lips. It dawned on her that she was alone in her bedroom, curled into a fetal position, sobbing. She reached for the covers and cocooned herself within them. She processed what had happened, or at least she tried. She gingerly rolled to her back, letting her arms and legs relax into corpse pose. It wasn't until she assumed the position that she understood why. A part of her just died. She mourned it, just as she mourned the passing of any living thing. What just happened to her was an abomination. The horror was that it happened at the hands of her husband.

Seth, Chestnut, Lucas, and Liam gained access to the gymnasium using a key Seth had surreptitiously obtained from one of the coaches. They carried with them the gym bag of supplies and the foul paint can. Chestnut surveyed the red, white, and blue streamers and light strands that radiated outward from center stage.

"Look at that," Chestnut pointed to one of the rafters. "That one's dark. That's the one we should use for the rope."

Lucas, the most athletic of the gang, climbed the ladder then shimmied along the darkened rafter, draping the black rope along hooks that were supposed to be holding a string of lights. Atop center stage, he pulled the rope through until the end of it touched down to the stage.

"Let it hang on its own, we need to see where gravity takes it," Chestnut said. "Mark that spot," he declared, satisfied.

Seth spray painted a black "X" on the otherwise white

stage. He wondered how many people would stand on the very spot, all night long, thinking that's exactly where they're supposed to stand.

"Here comes the tricky part. Please don't spill this crap," Chestnut said. He tapped the sticky lid off the paint can and received an instant olfactory reminder of its foul contents. He tied the rope to the handle using a cow hitch knot. The can was nearly half full. That should be sufficient for effect, but not so much that there would be spillage as they hoisted the can to the rafters. Liam pulled the other end of the rope and Lucas guided it from the rafters.

"Ugh, this thing's rancid, what the hell?" Lucas said.

"Seth pissed in it," Chestnut announced from stage.

"Oh man, that's so gross. You guys are some *sick* motherfuckers."

"Make sure you're looking in a mirror when you say that," Chestnut countered.

"Whatever," Lucas said. "Give me a minute." He set the can upright, on top of the rafter. He detached the barbell clamp from his belt loop with the intention of clamping it onto the paint can handle, just as Chestnut had described. The clamp slipped from his hand and fell in the direction of Seth and Chestnut below.

"Hit the dirt!" he yelled. It was the only instinctual thing he could think of to say to get his friends below to move their heads. Instead, the lead clamp nailed Chestnut on his left butt cheek. Chestnut didn't cry out. He could tell the result would be a nasty welt, but he dare not protest. That was rule number one, "Show no pain." Rule number two was "Don't rub it," just take your lumps and put ice on it later.

Chestnut stood up. "Alright people, let's try this again. Seth, go hold that rope. Liam, climb up there and hand Lucas this clamp." Liam had hit the deck too, releasing the rope. This could have been disastrous had Lucas not held the paint can secure on his end. Chestnut handed the clamp to Seth, who handed it to Liam, who climbed the ladder, shimmied across the rafter and finally got the clamp back into the hands of Lucas. Lucas secured the clamp to the paint can handle to provide the top weight when the timing was right.

"You climb back down," Lucas told Liam. I'm going to hold this thing sturdy while you do." Lucas held the paint can in place until Liam was off the ladder. "Liam, carry the ladder across to the other side of the stage. I don't want to climb along the beam with our rope on it. I'll come down the other side."

Chestnut joined Seth at the other end of the rope while Lucas made his way down. "We need to tie this off someplace inconspicuous," Chestnut suggested. This side of the stage had the bulk of the power cords running to the sound system, so the blackness of the rope seemed a promising blend. He followed the chords to the speakers and evaluated the options. "The person who tugs the rope is going to have to crawl behind the speakers. That's where we'll tie off the rope."

They followed his instructions, stepped back and assessed.

"Someone would have to look real close to see the rope and then they'd probably think nothing of it, given all the other crap up in the rafters," Lucas said.

"I agree," Liam said.

"This might actually work," Seth said.

"I think it might," Chestnut agreed, wondering to himself if that was a good thing. He checked his watch: 3:00 a.m. *My how time flies when you're having fun*, he thought.

The four high fived, gathered their supplies, and headed home. Liam, Lucas, and Chestnut were exhausted. Seth was exalted; his glorious day of retribution was dawning.

The loathsome paint can and its foul contents remained behind in the gymnasium rafters. Contrived in vindictiveness and hoisted there for malicious purpose. An elaborate prank, flawed in design and doomed to fail because gravity's rule would not be broken. Had the boys belayed the paint can to the rafter with a simple strand of rope, the joke would have ended with the spillage of bodily fluids. Did they fathom the contraption was made hazardous by the cursed barbell clamp? Heavy object falling ten meters meant significant force upon impact. Enough force to knock Gary Greene unconscious. And that made all the difference.

September 29, 2017

Homecoming Day

Round Rock Daily Dispatch
9-29-2017

Texans Host Fire Ants for Homecoming

L. P. D'Innocenzio

The Sam Houston High School Texans look to end a two game slide this weekend against the Hill Country Fire Ants. It's been a surprisingly rocky start for the Texans, especially considering the many returning starters for last year's championship team. According to Coach Casey, "The turnovers have really hurt us. We need to do a better job of protecting the football. We've squandered good scoring opportunities and practically handed points to the opposition with short fields." Keep a close eye on RB Jeremy Parsons. He's on a record setting pace for fumbles in a single season. This coming on the heels of leading the team in rushing last year.

If the Texans can't get the running game going, they'll have to depend more heavily upon the strong arm of their all-star QB Charlie Simpson. When asked about the pressure on his shoulders, Simpson said, "It's not just me. It's a team sport. We'll be fine if we play as one unit. We all win, or lose, together." Kickoff is at noon, Saturday. Tickets are still available. Check the school's website for more information.

"Looks like Gary's boyfriend has a big a game tomorrow." Vincent looked up from the paper and sipped his coffee. "Now that he's dating the quarterback, maybe he'll develop an interest in football."

Joanna was standing, fiddling in the kitchen and giving Vincent the coldest of shoulders, but the mention of her son was too much to ignore. "Leave our son alone. Don't speak disparaging of him and don't you lay a hand on him. You hear me?"

"My, my, aren't we touchy this morning," Vincent responded. "Guess I got your attention last night."

"Got my attention?" Joanna said in disbelief. "Got my attention!" she repeated, vehement. "Is that what you think that was? Honestly Vincent. I'm surprised you're still here." Joanna began to cry.

They both heard Gary's morning alarm.

"Well, there you go," Vincent observed. "Your creampuff awakens. Run to him dear and be sure to tell him about the deflowering you got last night."

"Get out of here, now," Joanna yelled, pointing toward the front door.

Vincent scowled and grabbed his jacket. "Fine, I'm headed to work. But, I'll be back, you can count on that for damn sure. Maybe I'll make it home in time for homecoming pictures. Wouldn't that be a kick?" he said and gave her a perverse smile.

"Go," she insisted.

He slammed the door as he left.

Gary awoke to his morning alarm, the gentle sound of fingertips dancing across the keyboard of a single piano. They signaled the dawning of a new day. Violins joined the piano. Softly at first, then rising in intensity like beams of sunlight bursting above a distant horizon, bringing light and contrast to a foreboding world. Flutes joined the fray, like morning sparrows springing about from branch to branch. A trumpet blared in the distance, like an eagle soaring majestic. The piano carried a rhythmic undertone, like a single horse, galloping free across a vast prairie. This was the opening song of a nature soundtrack Gary had downloaded to his phone, because it reminded him of one of his favorite memories.

The memory was from a difficult phase of his cancer treatment: September 2016. The stem cell implants had proven fruitless. Chemotherapy was failing. Gary was dying, and he lamented that he would just like to see the ocean. His mom drove them through the night to North Padre Island, where she set up yoga mats on the beach upon which she and Gary sat and watched the sun rise over the Gulf of Mexico. They sat in the lotus position, and as the sun rose, Mom chanting her salutations. Gary echoed each line.

"Spirits of water, we greet you this day with humility and praise."

They cycled through spirits of air, earth, and fire and then back to water again. Between the two of them, it seemed they were literally lifting the sun out of the gulf. It was glorious.

Mom knocked, came into his bedroom and offered her morning greeting, "Namaste." It was a blessing suitable for coming or going. It was the only tattoo she allowed herself, delicately inked in Sanskrit along her forearm: "The light in me honors the light in you."

She sat at the edge of his bed. Gary noticed her wince.

"You okay Mom?"

"I'll be fine," she said, dismissive. "This is a big day for you, isn't it?"

Gary nodded.

"What I wanted to come in here and tell you is, whatever happens at homecoming, I'm proud of you. If you get elected to the homecoming court, you make sure to stand up straight and hold your head high on that stage."

"I will Mom, I promise."

She reached and rubbed Gary's forehead. He loved this. Sometimes, just his mom rubbing his forehead could make the aches and pains of his cancer fade away.

"And it goes without saying that I love you very much," she continued.

"I know that Mom."

"You deserve to have the time of your life tonight. I hope you do."

"Thanks Mom."

Joanna continued to stroke his hairline and Gary soaked in the attention. "You're growing up," Joanna said. "I can't baby you anymore."

"You can always rub my forehead Mom."

"That's nice to know Gary."

"Hey Mom, I have a question for you. Do you have any idea what's gotten into Dad lately?"

"I don't know. I really don't want to talk about it."

"It's strange. A week ago I thought he was going to kill me. And now ... well, it's as if I don't exist."

"I think you're better off with the latter. Stay away from him Gary."

Gary nodded again.

"Hey Mom, can I tell you something?" He paused, waiting for eye contact. "You're the most patient, loving person I know. I knew when I was dying towards the end of last year that you would be with me until the end. It was comforting knowing I wouldn't be alone."

Joanna's eyes were wet with tears. "I would never abandon you Gary." She stroked his forehead. "Something's coming."

"What do you mean?" Gary asked.

"Sometimes I get feelings, premonitions of sorts Do you get those?" Joanna kept her hand on Gary's forehead and looked into his eyes.

"Yeah, I guess," Gary said. "Like when you know something big is coming, but you don't know what?"

"Exactly. Well here in this moment, I have that feeling," Joanna said. "It darn near sends chills up my spine. It's eerie and spectacular. Like the feeling I had with your cancer treatments. There was a point when it felt like I was the only one trying anymore, but I knew I had to, because you *had* to get better, to fulfill a greater purpose. I don't know what that purpose is, but it's getting closer, I feel it."

"Do you think it has something to do with me getting voted as homecoming queen and owning the election proudly, making a statement for equality?"

"Yeah, I guess that could be part of it. That certainly is a noble cause. But there's something more. I just can't put my finger on it. This is going to bug me until the vision gets clearer. Something tells me everyone is going to hear the name Gary Greene and be awed. You're destined for greatness."

"My English teacher would call that hyperbole."

"She wouldn't in this case. Not after it happens." Joanna leaned into Gary and gave him a big hug. "Now you really do have to get ready for school."

"I love you, Mom."

"Love you too, Gary."

Emily's Living the Dream a.k.a Nightmare

September 29, 2017

Search

Homecoming! XD

Homecoming weekend is finally here! Put on the Ritz with your best party dress (or tuxedo in my case) for the dance tonight, 8:00 p.m. in the gym. Decorations committee did fantastic job, as per usual. Entertainment should be kickin'. Remind your friends and family, I'll be streaming live! #SHHShomecoming2017

Home

No comments:

Post a Comment

Enter your comment...

Seth skipped the half-day of school and slept until noon. Priscilla was at his house again, helping him clean up after the party. She heard the choppy conversation he was having with his mom on the phone.

"Yeah Mom, party was great. Thanks for letting me use the house. You wouldn't have liked being here. No, nothing's broken. There's a wall I'm going to have to paint because these guys are terrible at darts. We borrowed the crystal punch bowl. No, don't worry, Priscilla is helping me clean up. She borrowed a pair of capris. I'll tell her that. Which reminds me, someone got into Dad's scotch. Yes, the Highland Park. Yeah, good idea, that might take the edge off. Yes, that's true, you should be able to watch it on your laptop. I'll have Priscilla send you the link, and you'll need to download the app. It's easy, you'll enjoy it. Have a good time with the Parsons in San Antonio. Love you, Mom."

"That sounded like an interesting conversation," Priscilla said.

"Mom says you can keep the pants if you like them."

"She's so sweet."

"She's going to pick up a bottle of Highland Park in San Antonio for Dad to replace the one he doesn't realize is missing yet. He'll be pissed, but less pissed. Do you know that butch girl doing the livestream of the concert?"

"Emily Sorrento?"

"Yeah, that's her. Can you send my mom the link? She wants to watch."

"Sure, I can do that."

"Good afternoon, Mr. Greene and Mr. Simpson," Elijah said. "This must be the big day. I bet you guys are excited. Shall I go fetch your tuxes? Would you like to try them on before you leave the store?"

"That would be a good idea, Elijah," Charlie said.

"Lovely. I'll meet you in the changing area."

Gary and Charlie stumbled upon Roddy, dressed only in his lime over-the-thigh jockey underwear and crewneck undershirt.

"You're going to want to wear a white t-shirt under your tuxedo Roddy," Charlie said.

"Oh hell, I know that Charlie," Roddy said. "I'm just making sure everything fits right."

"Us too," Charlie said, putting his arm around Gary, goofy grin on his face. "We got a matching set."

Gary rolled his eyes.

"How nice," Roddy said. "What style?"

"That style," Charlie pointed to the tuxedos Elijah held high, right and left hands extended wide, tuxes draped in clear plastic to keep them fresh and protected.

"Hey Mister, I've been standing here in my underwear for five minutes already. Where's my tuxedo?" Roddy objected.

"Ah, Mr. Cruz, they are still looking for yours. There may have been some kind of mix up."

"What kind of mix up?"

"They are checking other stores."

"I don't have time to go to another store. I live near this store. The dance is tonight."

"We'll figure it out Mr. Cruz. We'll make it right. Now if you let me take care of these other gentlemen, one of my assistants will be out to help you in a moment."

Roddy stood there in his underwear. *I'm being punished*, he thought. *I'm being punished for not telling Gary about the paint can of jizzum that's going to be poured on his head tonight.* How many times had he randomly crossed paths with him in hallways and said nothing? What about now? He could say something right now and spare the guy a ton of embarrassment. Seth was deranged. He's lucky he was only kicked off the team and not expelled from school. He probably will be if the office ever hears about what went on at the keg party. Why should he show him any loyalty?

"Here's yours." Elijah handed Gary the bundle of garments and dress shoes. "And, here's yours." He did the same for Charlie. "You're welcome to use our changing rooms. You do not have to stand out here in your underwear like Mr. Cruz."

"Thanks, Elijah," Gary said, heading for a changing room.

"Thanks, Elijah," Charlie echoed, grinned at Roddy and then headed for the other changing room.

When they stepped out, they saw Roddy had pulled his pants on and was consulting with one of the assistants to figure out his options.

Charlie and Gary sized up each other.

"I think we look rather dashing," Charlie said.

"I think we do, too," Gary agreed.

They stood side by side, looking at their reflections in the full-length mirror. Elijah and the tailor came over, looking at the fit. The tailor sort of pinched and tugged and fiddled with the hemlines.

He mumbled some comments, and an assistant came over and asked for Charlie's pants. "We need to fix the hem," he said. "It will only take a moment."

They remained standing in the common section of the changing area, Charlie sans pants.

"So, what happened with Amy last night?" Gary said, sort of talking out of the side of his mouth without moving his lips.

Charlie stared at him a second. "Gary, really? Now?"

"You're not going anywhere without your pants."

Charlie shook his head. "Not that it's any of your business, but Cindy and I have an understanding."

"Not last night you didn't and it is my business because you're both my friends."

"Alight smartass, what happened between you and Cindy last night?"

"Nothing happened."

It appeared the pants were ready, but Elijah kept his distance a minute. He refrained from interjecting himself into lover's quarrels.

"You guys weren't there when we got back from the truck, and when you did show up, I noticed Cindy was without her panties. I bet I wasn't the only one to notice either."

"Oh so that's where you took Amy, the truck huh. I bet that truck has some stories to tell."

They grew quiet. Elijah sensed his opportunity. "Mr. Simpson, here are your pants. Let's try again."

They agreed the tuxes fit great. When they emerged from their changing rooms dressed in their street clothes, Roddy was standing in the common area again, being fitted for a tux off the racks at the store. The tailor was fussing and providing instructions in a near eastern language.

"Good luck Roddy," Charlie said.

"Yeah, good luck," Gary added.

"Have a great time, guys," Elijah said.

"We will, Elijah." They waved.

Charlie took one last look at the styles modeled in the glass showcase of the tuxedo store. He stopped in front of the Scottish Highland Dress. "You know we could have picked out this one. A kilt might have been an appropriate compromise."

"Maybe that works for you, Simpson," Gary replied. "But I'm Irish. I need pants."

"That's not what I mean." He started to explain then realized Gary was grinning ear to ear. "Oh forget about it. You hungry?" Charlie answered his own question before Gary could respond. "I'm hungry. Let's grab some fish tacos again. They were good." The pair lugged their plastic-covered tuxedos through the mall to the food court. "Tacos are on me this time," Charlie announced.

Roddy climbed into his car and set the hodgepodge of tuxedo garments onto the passenger seat. God was punishing him. He knew it. Charlie and Gary were right with God. They got their tuxedos. Roddy was in God's doghouse. Therefore, he did *not* get his tuxedo, or at least not the tuxedo he wanted. Roddy replayed the many opportunities provided to him to set himself right with God, ever since he learned of Seth's deranged scheme. Each opportunity, he dodged. What he should have done was head straight from the keg party to the school, where he knew Gary and Charlie were decorating for homecoming. But, he didn't. Roddy decided he must be a despicable person in God's eyes. He had been made aware of a disgraceful plan, yet he took no action to protect the innocent. Doesn't God call on the strong to protect the innocent? He wondered why he couldn't find his voice. Why couldn't he speak up? He prayed to Jesus to help him. He prayed for yet another sign.

He bowed his head and folded his hands, praying fervently, "Dear Lord, I've failed in so many ways. I've failed to be honest with my friends. I've let them down, and they don't even know. It would be so easy to warn them, but I'm afraid. I don't know why I'm afraid, but I am. I need strength, Lord. I need strength to do the right thing. Please dear Lord, show me a sign. Give me another opportunity. I swear I'll follow your lead. Hold my hand Lord and show me what I'm supposed to do."

Gary and Charlie left the mall, each carrying his tuxedo. They needed to walk clear across the parking lot to where Charlie parked his truck but Charlie diverted to another direction.

"Come this way," he said.

Gary saw where they were headed. A beat-up faded hunter-green Honda Accord sat straight ahead and there appeared to be someone sitting inside. As Gary got closer he saw the person was leaning forward towards the steering wheel, hands folded, and kind of rocking back and forth.

Charlie knocked on the driver side window. Roddy appeared startled at first, then hand cranked down the window.

"Roddy you okay?" Charlie asked.

"Yeah man, I'm good."

"Really? You looked distressed."

"No, really. It's all good. Um, it's just the car wouldn't start."

"Battery? I can offer you a jump."

"No, I think I flooded the engine. Just letting it rest a minute."

"Pop the hood let me take a look." Charlie handed his tuxedo to Gary for him to hold. He also saw the garments on Roddy's passenger seat. "They get you hooked up with a tuxedo?"

"Yeah, they're providing it to me on the house, because of their mix up."

"That's nice of them."

"Yeah." Roddy popped the hood.

"It's great when you run into nice people like that when you're in need."

"Yeah."

"Hmm, I don't smell any gas. Maybe you've let it rest long enough. Try again."

The car started with no issue.

"Ha! There you go Roddy. But, I have to tell you, as a friend, you might want to think about trading this old clunker for something more reliable. It's one thing to have the body banged up a little, but if the car can't get you from point A to point B, it's worthless."

"That is kind of the point of having a car. Isn't it?" Roddy agreed.

"It's one of the most important reasons for sure." Charlie

was trying to figure out a way to get Roddy to admit whatever was really bothering him. Roddy cut the conversation short.

"Thanks for lending me a hand," Roddy said. "I owe you one."

"You owe me nothing," Charlie said. "Just make sure to snap the ball cleanly to me come game time." Charlie gave Roddy a friendly punch on the shoulder.

"I can do that." Roddy nodded, looking straight ahead.

"Let's sneak some beers after the game tomorrow," Charlie suggested.

"Sounds good," he said as he put the car in gear and sped off.

They watched Roddy drive away.

"Good you saw him. You got his car going again." Gary didn't know very much about cars. Preoccupation with his cancer treatments sort of pushed other concerns to the wayside, including learning about cars or even learning how to drive. He figured Charlie must have fiddled around with a relay, or something, to help Roddy's car start.

"I didn't do a damn thing, and his engine wasn't flooded. That was a big fat lie. Did you see the tears in his eyes? Something's seriously bothering Roddy, but I'll be damned if I know what it is. He'll open up eventually. Maybe after the game. That's why I invited him out. Give him a chance to hash it out. Beers usually help with that."

"You're a good man, Charlie. I don't care what people say about you behind your back because you're hanging out with that gay kid."

"Who? The waterboy? He's just a pet. I keep him around for entertainment."

"Thanks a lot!" Gary said, and smiled broadly as they strolled past a few dozen parked cars. "I've half a mind to not remind you to pick up Cindy's corsage."

"The corsage!" Charlie slapped his own forehead and

scrambled toward the mall, leaving Gary holding both tuxedos in the middle of the parking lot.

Roddy drove his Accord manically, due eastbound on RM 620, orange sun setting in the western sky, glaring in the rearview mirror. He whizzed past slower traffic and weaved around cars failing to yield the left speed lane. Tears flowed freely ever since he abandoned his friends standing in the middle of the mall parking lot, still ill-informed about the nefarious homecoming plans. He had prayed to Jesus for a sign. He received it and promptly discarded the divine message. He knew he was damned to Hell. He floored the gas pedal, accelerating the Honda to its maximum, landscape elongating into ashen blur. For as many jokes as he endured about the car, it could still move down the highway at a decent clip. He thought about crossing the median and driving head-on into a westbound truck, but rejected that plan. The person driving the truck didn't deserve to share in Roddy's judgment. He was the only person who deserved to be punished. He would bear it alone. He clenched his hands to the vibrating steering wheel. Ahead lay a steel and concrete overpass. There are sins of action and sins of inaction. Both are sins in God's eyes. His repeated inability to warn his friends was inexplicable. He deserved judgment. Failing to prevent bad things from happening is just as bad as doing the bad things yourself. For all intents and purposes, his semen may as well have been in that foul paint can. Just the thought of it made him want to puke. Would his good friend Charlie ever forgive him?

"Why didn't you tell me Roddy? Why didn't you tell me?" Echoed in his head. Roddy figured he could veer onto the right shoulder and ram the overpass support girders head-on. How many times was a friend allowed to fail? Roddy reached his limit. It would all be over soon. He deserved to die. He was damned to hell. The overpass was approaching fast. Roddy drifted onto the right shoulder and kept pedal to the metal. The careening Honda kicked up a storm, dirt and gravel pummeled the car's undercarriage, dust clouds billowed along the nondescript patch of Texas highway. He loosed his seat belt. He loosed a full-throated scream. Two hundred feet from impact he thought of his mother.

Maria Cruz slipped into a black and white party dress she hadn't worn in several years. It was nice of her son, Roddy, to offer to drive her to the concert. She wasn't comfortable behind the wheel, especially at night. She felt fortunate to have snagged the general admission ticket. There were only 200 tickets available. At a price of $50 each, sales of these extra tickets generated $10,000 in revenue to fund the homecoming dance. The income covered the yearly operational expense as well as pragmatic improvements made to the event over the years. She understood the next major improvement was to be several large flat screen TVs mounted along one of the gymnasium walls, for use at social and sporting events. It was a good cause. It was her pleasure to contribute and she was especially excited to hear Johnny Doolittle play live on stage.

"How late were you out last night?" Tonya asked, between bites of her chili dog.

"It was late, honey," Chestnut replied. "I'm exhausted."

"Why don't you sit down, then?" Tonya patted the bench on picnic table.

"I'm fine with standing. That bench is hard, and I got a bit of a bruise." He rubbed his butt.

"You're such a wuss."

"Only around you," Chestnut said, baby-talkish. "You bring it out in me."

"Oh my God, of all your impressions, that's the one that drives me nuts," Tonya said. "Please no baby talk."

"I thought you liked my baby talk."

"It was cute the first time. Maybe the second. We're way past the cute stage." Tonya shrugged.

Chestnut leaned towards her and put on his deep baritone voice. "Hey, baby, you know I love you, baby. You know it. You know you're the one, baby." He puckered his lips and moved in for a kiss.

"That's a little better," Tonya said and rewarded him with a long, wet kiss. He still had his eyes closed and big lips exaggeratedly puckered. Tonya added, "Now explain to me why you were out so late and how you got that bruise on your ass. While you're at it, tell me what's up with the paint can."

Chestnut opened his eyes and gazed into Tonya's, inches away. "You really want to know?"

"I really want to know," Tonya said.

Chestnut proceeded to tell her everything. Some parts she knew, the most disgusting parts, she didn't. When Chestnut told her Seth also peed in the can, she cringed, put up her hand, and stopped him. "That's grotesque. I get the prank. I think it's childish. But Seth adding urine to the mix makes the whole scheme sound vicious. Are you sure you want to be a part of this, Chestnut? You're better than this."

"It's complicated," was all Chestnut could manage.

"It sure is," Tonya said. "Well let's unravel a complication. I won't be joining you for your homecoming dance tonight. You're on your own." She started to get up to leave.

"Wait," he said and reached out to stop her. "You're still my girl right?" He looked up pleadingly.

"Not tonight I'm not," she said, shaking her head. "Not if you're pouring that crap on some poor kid's head."

Chestnut stood and took her by the shoulders. They were almost the same height and it was easy for him to look her in the eyes and he tried to be sincere. "Tell you what. I'll bring a towel for the kid."

"Somehow, that seems inadequate."

"It's something," Chestnut said, cocking his head a little to try to get a smile.

"It's something," Tonya agreed and sat back down, but didn't grin.

Chestnut glanced out to the highway, considering his options. As he took the last bite of his chili dog he noticed a faded hunter-green Honda Accord parked at the crest of a hill on the opposite side of RM 620.

"Hey honey you ready? I think I see a buddy's car across the road. Let's go check it out."

"Ok," Tonya said. She pitched her trash, donned her helmet, and mounted her Sportster motorcycle. Chestnut did the same and gingerly mounted his own Harley. They cruised the overpass and headed for the Accord.

He had one and a half seconds to veer the Accord off the shoulder. His passenger mirror clipped the girder and was gone. He was shaking and drenched in a nauseating sweat. His stomach churned. He let the car coast to the side of road, braked at the top of a hill, bailed out of the car, stumbled a few feet, and then vomited by the side of the road. He crouched for a while, hands on his knees, sweating and drooling.

Roddy lingered there on the side of the road, just getting his shit together. He couldn't bring himself to end his pain through suicide, despite the guilt that weighed heavily upon him. He simply couldn't do that to his mother. He resigned himself to clean up, dress in his hodgepodge tuxedo and take his mother to the homecoming dance, as planned. His mother didn't deserve to suffer for Roddy's sins any more than the driver of that westbound truck. Roddy was the only person who deserved to be punished. He would bear it alone.

From his vantage point on the hill he saw three State Trooper cars approaching fast. He thought for a moment one might stop to check on him. Instead, they slowed and took the exit at the overpass Roddy had just narrowly avoided. He watched them pull into the Department of Public Safety building behind the Sonic. He was so distracted by the troopers he failed to notice the bikers until they were practically upon him. They pulled off the highway, stopped next to him, and lifted their visors. It was Chestnut and his girlfriend, Tonya. These were not people Roddy was in a mood to see right now.

"Hey Roddy. I thought it was you," Chestnut said over his bike. "Car finally completely break down?"

No, I finally did, Roddy thought, but did not verbalize.

"Roddy?" Chestnut tried to process Roddy's thousand-mile stare. "You okay? You need a lift?"

"I'll be fine," Roddy said, dismissive. "See you tonight."

"Um, okay. See you tonight." Chestnut shrugged, looked at Tonya, lowered his visor and pointed down the highway.

They catapulted down the hill. Roddy watched and listened to the fading whine of their motorcycles. Roddy wondered how many people Jesus could send to a person in one day, just to ask if he was okay? Even Chestnut checked on him. Roddy wouldn't have been surprised to see the Devil himself pull up in a flaming chariot and offer him a ride. There must be a special place in Hell for the truly despicable.

Charlie meticulously placed each element of the tuxedo onto his bed. The items spread from headboard to footboard and literally neck to toe, the way he had them organized.

There was a knock at his bedroom door. "Come in," he said.

Connie Simpson, Charlie's mom, stepped into the bedroom. Connie was a tall and fit woman. In college, she played outside hitter on the national championship winning UT volleyball team and she remained active in tri-athletics. She was training for the Active Ironman, and the combined swimming, biking, and running events kept her lean and happy. Charlie's dad had been an Army Ranger. His legs were blown off by an IED in Afghanistan when Charlie was eleven years old. His dad never recovered, struggled to gain mobility, and eventually succumbed to complications just after Charlie turned twelve. It was hard for Charlie not to be bitter about the loss of his father. He wallowed for a time, but rallied and stepped up as man of the house for his mom and his little sister Lisa. Yes, Lisa Simpson just like on the Simpsons TV show. That was his dad's doing, such was his sense of humor.

His mom, fresh off the exercise bike, wore a somewhat sweaty neon pink workout outfit, her milk chocolate hair tied in a ponytail and a burnt orange UT beach towel draped over her shoulders. She stood with her hands behind her back. At thirty-nine years of age, Charlie figured his mom could pass for twenty-five. Charlie stood there in his underwear.

"Oh you're not even dressed yet," Connie said.

"Look at all this crap I have to put on Mom," Charlie whined.

"I bet it all comes together quite nicely."

"Yeah, it does. You should see it on Gary. That skinny kid looks great in a tux. I look dumpy by comparison."

"Oh, I doubt you look dumpy," Connie smiled. "I have something for you to add to the pile of stuff you need to wear." She brought her hand from behind her back and extended it to Charlie. "These were your dad's Army cufflinks. I'm sure he would have wanted you to wear them."

Charlie was bowled over. He didn't even know Dad had Army cufflinks. It's not the kind of thing you consider as a kid. For his mom to have considered it and waited until this moment to present them to him was touching beyond words. He simply nodded his head and hugged her saying, "Thanks Mom."

She held him tight for a moment, then stepped back and

wiped tears from her cheeks with the beach towel. "Hurry and get dressed. Gary is probably anxious."

"Yeah, probably."

"Your dad would be proud of you. He told me a story about a kid he beat up in junior high school for constantly knocking schoolbooks out of the hands of an autistic boy. There were lots of kids doing it, actually. The punks would knock the books on the ground and laugh as the poor kid scrambled to gather them and his papers into his arms again. Frank only had to beat up one of the punk kids to make his point. From that moment on, Frank said he always sensed the former bullies stiffen, ever so slightly, when he walked past and the autistic kid, Jimmy–I think his name was–would smile wide and wave."

"I've never heard that story. Dad wouldn't have liked the way I treated Gary at first, but my attitude changed the moment Seth popped him in the nose. It was like a switch thrown in my head, suddenly pointing my moral compass to true north."

"We all evolve, Charlie. Seems to me, you're way ahead of the curve."

Charlie contemplated the kind of man he wanted to become. Perhaps there was more he could do to foster his personal growth and make a difference in school. He was in a unique position to do so as quarterback. Mr. Greene called it "heart." He determined to demonstrate more of it. "Mom, there's another kid at school, Tyler McGrath, who's teased because he takes Irish dancing classes. I've heard about pro football players who do Irish dancing to help with their footwork. Would you think it silly of me to sign up for Irish dancing classes at Tyler's studio? It would be harder for the kids to tease him if the quarterback practiced Irish dancing too."

Connie beamed and hugged Charlie tight. "I think that

would be a great idea, sweetie."

"Alright, I'll sign up for them next week," Charlie said. "Maybe I can talk Roddy into taking the classes with me. Roddy needs a pick-me-up."

By the time Vincent Greene got home from work, Charlie's orange pickup truck was parked in the driveway. Vincent contemplated the burgeoning relationship between his boy and the star quarterback of the football team. Vincent derided Charlie and Gary's boyfriend status, but in truth he assessed Charlie was as straight as they come. Charlie would grow up to be a real man, and was exactly the kind of kid Vincent wished he had. He didn't quite get the basis of friendship between Charlie and Gary, but it did give him some small measure of hope that his son may yet sort out his identity crisis. Charlie was the kind of role model his son needed. Perhaps Gary was just going through a rough patch, like he himself had done at a similar age. It wasn't his son's fault that he was confused about who he wanted to have sex with. It was all the politically correct crap kids had to deal with these days. Time would tell whether Gary figured it out. In the meantime, Vincent determined not to judge the boy, at least not on homecoming night. That was, until he saw the two of them in their matching tuxedos.

Vincent had arrived home feeling grimy in his work clothes. His hands were still greasy from trying to fix a sheet metal press at the Dell manufacturing plant. He wasn't a Dell employee, per se; he was a contractor. He wished he had applied to work at Dell directly back in the days when they were hiring and when their stock was still low. He heard of a Dell technician who performed similar duties for ten years, then retired to Hill Country on his stock options. Still, Vincent did not begrudge the man's success. He accepted his own circumstance and did the best he could. Besides, Vincent could never retire. He loved working with his hands.

He entered the living room and took in the scene before him. The dichotomy between his dirty jumpsuit and the boys' double-breasted tuxedos could not have been starker.

"Evening Mister Greene," Charlie said, respectful.

Joanna glared.

Gary remained silent.

"Evening Charlie," Vincent acknowledged. "Family." He didn't pause for a reply. "Let me get washed up." Vincent ducked into the hallway bathroom. He stripped down and washed his greasy hands with his favorite Fast Orange cleaner. He splashed cold water on his face. He looked in the mirror. What to do? Could he let his son do this? The humiliation of it would surely scare Gary, maybe so much he'd go straight. Vincent couldn't believe the gay kid he predicted would be elected homecoming queen when he read that article in the paper would be his very own son. Surely this was some kind of cosmic joke or a bad dream. Why had God been punishing him with these perverted fags his entire life?

"You know what you need to do," he said to the man in the mirror. He slipped from the bathroom to his bedroom, donned some casual clothes, and retrieved his Viper hunting knife from his dresser's bottom drawer.

Joanna's warm smile returned as soon as Vincent exited the room. She continued talking as if the blip of interruption never happened.

"Where's your girlfriend? Cindy right?" Mom asked.

"Cindy is catching a ride with her friend Amy," Charlie said.

That should be an interesting conversation, Gary thought.

"That should be fun for them," Joanna said. "I remember my first homecoming. Me and Tabby Lovett did each other's hair–"

"Not now Mom," Gary suggested.

"Oh all right," she said. "It's your night, isn't it?"

"Yes it is Mom."

"Would you boys like some lemonade? I made it myself, fresh squeezed—"

"Mom, do you remember this morning, when you said you couldn't baby me anymore—?"

"I would love some lemonade Mrs. Greene," Charlie cut in, then smirked toward Gary. "See? Entertainment."

Joanna delightedly poured Charlie a tall glass. She looked at Gary and Charlie standing side-by-side in the kitchen in their matching tuxedos and smiled as only a mother can, all the way to her eyes. She heard the tailor mistook the two for brothers. She didn't quite see the resemblance, her boy being so much slighter in build and clean cut, compared to Charlie's surfer look with the muscular body and longer blond hair. The stark difference in their body shapes brought a smile to her face. Perhaps they could masquerade as a Marvel character duo, with Charlie as Thor and Gary as Captain America (before his spectacular metamorphosis). She admitted they were a cute homecoming couple, though she didn't verbalize it quite that way for fear of embarrassing them. She decided to go with, "You boys look handsome in your matching tuxedos."

"Thank you Mrs. Greene." Charlie gulped down his lemonade.

Vincent emerged from his bedroom in a casual red-striped seersucker shirt and cargo pants. He stopped short of entering the living room and leaned against the hallway wall, hands in his pockets.

Joanna pulled out her phone. "Let's step outside and get some pictures."

Everyone followed her outside. She stood with the sun behind her to get the best shots. The boys stood side-by-side on the front stoop. "Say Homecoming!"

Charlie and Gary echoed, "Homecoming!" and smiled wide.

Vincent hovered just off to the side on front porch with a scowl on his face. He crushed an already crumpled beer can and kicked it past the railing, over the edge of the porch. What was he waiting for?

A black and white State Trooper vehicle turned onto their street. No lights, no siren. It pulled in abruptly across the Greene's driveway, blocking it. A second State Trooper car followed quickly, stopping behind the first. A third stopped at the end of the street, blocking the cul-de-sac. Two troopers emerged from each of their vehicles. Their confederate gray, black trimmed uniforms and broad brimmed hats gave them a military aura. The first two troopers approached Vincent. "Vincent Greene," one officer said in a way that Vincent understood, it was *not* a question.

"Yes?"

"We need you to come with us."

The other two troopers took a position that effectively supported the pair talking to Vincent.

"What's this about?" Vincent asked.

"We need you to come to the station to answer some questions." The lead Trooper had a weathered face, deep set eyes and glowered at Vincent as he spoke. The name label above his left shirt pocket read "W. Jackson." His partner, "F. Hancock", managed a look that was a little less menacing, even though he stood by with handcuffs. The other two slightly younger troopers, "Fitzgerald" and "Watson", stood by, tense.

"I was at work all day," Vincent said. "Couldn't you have picked me up there instead of coming to my home and scaring my family? It's the boy's homecoming for Christ sake."

Vincent and the state troopers seemed to be the only ones who knew what was going on. Joanna, Gary, and Charlie were thoroughly confused. Three patrol cars had just appeared out of nowhere, and they were doing what? Arresting Vincent?

Why?

"Officer, there must me some confusion," Joanna attempted. "This is my husband."

"Yes ma'am," Trooper Jackson acknowledged.

"Joanna don't," Vincent said. "I'll explain later."

"Good idea Mr. Greene," Trooper Jackson said.

Trooper Hancock frisked Vincent. Finding a knife in Vincent's pants pocket, Trooper Hancock asked, "What's the knife for, Mister Greene? Going hunting?"

Vincent shrugged, dismissive of the finding.

"Hands front." Trooper Hancock commanded. Vincent obeyed. Trooper Hancock cuffed Vincent and escorted him toward the lead vehicle. He read Vincent his Miranda rights. Vincent listened, nonchalant, like he had heard them before.

To Gary, it was surreal. He had never seen anyone get arrested, except on TV. And his dad was so casual about it. Just another impromptu trip to the police station in handcuffs in the back of squad car, ho-hum. Gary had a million questions. Sure, his dad was an asshole, but weird as it may seem, deep down inside Gary understood that he still loved the man. Vincent getting arrested was an absurdity. Gary felt like one of those robots in the sci-fi movies spinning about repeating, "Error, error, does not compute."

Trooper Jackson made a circling motion with a raised hand. The farthest vehicle turned on its sirens and U-turned out of the cul-de-sac. Hancock guided Vincent's head past the roof of the car as he loaded him into the back seat and closed the door. This sent Joanna over the precipice of emotional control. The recent acrimony from Joanna toward Vincent melted away with his unceremonious arrest. She became frantic. "Nooooo!" she screamed. "Where are you taking him? Where are you taking him?" she kept yelling, hysterical, hands raised to her face, she was trembling. Gary reached to support her. Charlie did the same.

Gary had never seen a nervous breakdown before either, but this looked to be the beginnings of one. "We're going to need help," Gary said to Charlie.

Charlie looked into Gary's eyes, nodded and told him, "I have an idea of someone I can call."

Vincent sat alone for a moment in the quiet stillness of the vehicle, eyes forward, not daring to gaze at his family. Wicked regrets crossed his mind. He hadn't prevented Gary from getting up on that stage. He wouldn't be visiting the tailor tonight either. Damn these troopers. He had more lessons to teach.

The Troopers ignored Joanna's pleas and got into their squad cars. Both cars turned on their flashing lights, wheeled around the cul-de-sac and just as quickly as they arrived, they were gone. Except Vincent vanished with them. It was surreal, like an alien abduction, only more vivid and horrifying.

Joanna was wide eyed, her face charged with panic, her breathing frantic and uneven. "Where are they taking him?" She muttered, breathless. Her eyes rolled back and she collapsed into their arms, with Charlie bearing most of her weight, keeping her from plunging to the ground.

Gary comforted Joanna, but he was equally upset. He lashed out at Charlie. "How's that for *fucking* entertainment?"

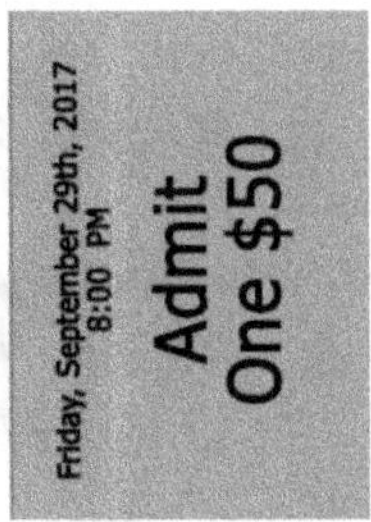

Cindy donned her short sleeve black bodycon dress. It was sheer, delicately patterned, and had a nude lining. She thought the effect might be interesting in the shadowy lighting of the dance floor. It had an open lace back and stopped at mid-thigh. She gelled her sandy blond pixie hair. Her hair looked darker that way, her desired effect. She selected black pumps. It was a simple outfit, but sexy, she assessed.

The phone rang. She expected it to be Amy telling her she's on her way, or delayed. Instead, it was Charlie. She listened in disbelief as Charlie explained what had happened.

"That's horrible. I completely understand. You do what you need to do. Stay with Gary, I'm sure he's in shock. No, I agree, don't leave his side. Okay, we'll meet you there. It's nice of your mom to go over to Gary's house. We can talk more at the dance. Thanks for letting me know."

Amy arrived shortly thereafter, in style. Her dad rented a limousine to take both of them to homecoming, probably because he was afraid Roddy would show up in his beat up old Honda. Turns out, Roddy was acting weird and told Amy he would just meet them there, so Amy and Cindy had the limo to themselves. Its plush leather seats made them feel bold and adventurous. It also had a minibar in the back.

"Can we just drive around for a little bit before we go to the school?" Amy asked the driver.

"I don't think that would be appropriate ma'am," the chauffeur, a middle-aged man in a brown fedora, said.

"We'll make it worth your while," Amy said, showing a little more thigh under her pastel orange flare dress.

The chauffeur adjusted his rearview mirror and continued to drive.

"Wow Amy, you're spunky. What's gotten into you?" Cindy asked.

The driver tapped on the mirror so Amy shifted her seating position, offering the chauffeur a more favorable view. The chauffeur headed straight through the light, instead of turning left towards the school.

"Precisely what we should talk about," Amy said. She

proceeded to have a heart-to-heart conversation about her indulgence with Cindy's boyfriend. She figured there was no better place or time to conduct this dialog than while they were sitting in the back of a limo drinking vodka, seltzer, and a variety of fruity juices. She concluded with, "I was flustered when we got out of the truck and had to walk past the football coaches. I bet they were watching the truck bounce. I didn't realize we had an audience."

"I need another drink," Cindy said, considering her range of plausible reactions. Was the chauffeur enjoying the drama as well as the peep show? Hearing Amy talk about getting banged in Charlie's truck must have given his little brown fedora a lift.

The chauffeur heard Cindy mention a drink and tapped on the rearview mirror again. Cindy slid the edge of her dress up the length of her leg. "There, that better?"

"Have a drink," the chauffeur said.

Cindy added a few ice cubes and just a hint of lime to her vodka creation. "I'm glad we talked, Amy. We needed to clear the air. I'm disappointed Charlie didn't talk to me first. I hate to think he's taking me for granted." Pause. "But the important thing about this episode is happening right now. You're telling me, honestly, to my face, alone, here in the back of this incredibly sexy limo, with your skirt hiked up to your navel, and it means so much to me. It touches me right here." Cindy squeezed her own breasts and giggled.

"Oh Cindy, your acceptance touches me in the same place, right here." Amy placed both hands on her own breasts and massaged them sensually. They were pretty sure the chauffeur could hardly believe his luck. Amy kept massaging her breasts while Cindy stuffed her and Amy's purses with vodka bottles from the mini-bar. When she could fit no more, Amy poured herself a double, adjusted her skirt and said, "Okay Mr. Chauffeur, show is over, you can take us girls to our homecoming dance now. What was your name again?" The girls giggled, as girls do. The chauffeur said nothing, readjusted his rearview mirror and headed directly for the school.

Seth expected Priscilla to be outraged the day after the keg party. Instead, she was energized. Delivering so many hand jobs proved to be an empowering experience. Priscilla and Tonya formed the kind of special bond that can only come from milking several dozen eager football players. Tonya came over to the house again to see Priscilla off to the dance and chat with her about working at the club.

"If you want to make money, I can get you into the club. Half the girls have fake IDs. We can get you one too. It's kind of a pyramid scheme, but it will still work out really well for you, trust me. In exchange for getting you into the club, I get ten percent of your take. Ninety-ten's a great split in your favor. Most girls get less. I'll take ten percent because I know the men are going to be throwing money at you, girl."

"How much do you think I'll make?"

"On a slow night, probably a couple of hundred," Tonya said. "On a good night, who knows? It depends on how far you're willing to go."

"How far do I need to go?"

"For five hundred, you need to be willing to go all the way. That's prime real estate right there, girl. Boardwalk and Park Place all rolled into one. But it's totally up to you."

"I'm putting out for free for Seth. I've been getting ripped off."

"Now, honey, you need to understand. Boyfriends and tricks are two completely different things. Seth's a fine young man: handsome, tender, and clean. Some of these other guys with money in their wallets, they may not be any of those things."

"Could I get hurt?"

"That's why it's good to have a boyfriend, especially one as big and strong as Seth. You get him in on the plan, give him a split, maybe twenty percent plus boyfriend privileges. I'm sure he'll roll with it. He seems like a real sport."

Priscilla slipped on her solid black sleeveless party dress. Tonya looked her up and down. "That's a five hundred dollar a shot dress right there, darling. You should just skip the dance and come straight to the club with me." *And get away from that disgusting paint can.*

"I appreciate you letting me know about the club and all. Let me have my night of relative innocence at homecoming. I know what we're talking about here is on the sketchy side. I gather I've got the assets, so to speak. That sounds great. What really scares me is I think I might like it. Tell me honestly, do you like it?"

Tonya wasn't sure how innocent the homecoming experience would be, but she respected the question and measured her response accordingly. " I like it. But, you have to be a certain kind of girl to like it. You're smart enough to know, I wouldn't be here telling you about it unless I thought you were *that* kind of girl, and I mean that with high praise."

"Are you sure you can't join us for homecoming?" Priscilla said. "We can sneak you in."

"No, honey, it's Friday night. I don't want to miss my shift at the club," Tonya said, thinking she didn't want to be anywhere near that filthy paint can. She was disappointed in Chestnut for being part of the cruel scheme. She was afraid attending would be tantamount to conferring her approval. Plus, she thought filling the paint can with cum was a joke. It wasn't lost on her that Chestnut used her. "But, if you see my little brother there, you're welcome to dance with him. I'm pretty sure he's taken a liking to you after last night."

"Him and a few dozen other boys," Priscilla said.

"Probably true," Tonya said.

Priscilla walked Tonya out the door.

Seth was outside, smoking a cigarette. He noticed Tonya. She wore a lacey black silk cocktail dress and heels. She slipped off the heels, replacing them with black running shoes. She put on her black motorcycle helmet and cranked the starter on her Harley. She looped around the driveway and stopped by the white gravel rocks in front of Seth, who was staring.

"What? Never seen a stripper ride a motorcycle?"

"As a matter of fact, no," Seth replied.

She saluted, and off she rode.

Connie Simpson arrived at Gary's house and rang the doorbell, startling Joanna and Gary. Charlie answered the door.

"Hey, Mom. We're in a tough spot here. Gary's mom really shouldn't be left alone."

"Trust me, I know what it's like to be alone when things aren't going well," Connie said.

"Thanks, Mom, I knew you'd understand," Charlie said. Charlie introduced his mom and filled her in a little more on the details of what happened.

"Charlie, you're a good boy," Joanna said. " Now I must insist you boys head to the dance."

"Mom, I don't need to go. It's okay," Gary said.

"Stop arguing with me and go," Joanna said. "I don't want to hear another word about it."

"Yes, Mom."

"We'll be fine," Connie said, facing Charlie and fiddling with his cufflinks. "You take care of Gary."

"I will," Charlie promised.

Charlie and Gary hopped into Charlie's truck. It had taken significant encouragement from Joanna to convince Gary to attend the dance. Charlie was smart to have Connie come over to comfort Joanna.

"Your mom was insistent," Charlie said. "It's really important to her that you go to homecoming."

"She sure was adamant," Gary said. "Thanks for sending your mom over. That's probably the only way you could have gotten me to leave."

"We know," Charlie said, driving off the cul-de-sac. "What do you think is going on with your dad?"

"I honestly don't know," Gary said, concerned. "Whatever it is, it's a huge secret because Mom doesn't seem to know either. She's really shaken."

"We don't have to stay late at the dance," Charlie said. "You just say the word, and I'll bring you home. The girls will understand."

"Thank you Charlie," Gary said. "The best thing that's happened to me recently is our friendship."

"Hey, that's great," Charlie said. "How about we just try and have a good time tonight? Do you think you can do that?"

"I'll try," Gary said, cranking up the stereo.

Gary lost himself in the music of Nine Inch Nails. The timing of his dad's bewildering "arrest"–if that's what it was–was horrid. It was unnerving to see that his dad didn't do a very good job of acting surprised. Vincent knew why the police were there. Not a good sign for his innocence. Gary and Joanna were in the dark. Another bad sign. Vincent had a secret. Was it related to why he'd been acting so different lately?

Gary felt his world destabilizing. He had longed for a closer relationship with his dad. Now, with his dad carted away and his mom distraught, only his nanites could protect him. He was headed to the homecoming dance with a heightened sense of insecurity. His angst translated to a readiness by his nanites to protect him from harm. He could feel them stirring in his veins, diligent in their mission. If Seth punched him in the nose tonight, there was no telling how violently the nanites might react. Actually, there was, because the thought of Seth melting in a cauldron of boiling nanites seemed spitefully appealing.

Charlie pulled off the road, stopped the truck at an overlook of the town and turned off the music.

"What are you doing?" Gary asked.

"You're too quiet. I'm not letting you go to homecoming stuck in whatever funky state you're in," Charlie said, facing Gary fully, looking directly in his eyes. "What're you thinking about?"

"You don't want to know," Gary admitted. "I can have a mean streak."

Charlie nodded in understanding. "I get it, Gary. You have a lot to be angry about. Your cancer. Your dad. The graffiti in the bathroom, and the way the football team treated you. Those things would make me angry, too."

Gary's eyes welled with tears. He closed them and absorbed the sudden dose of validation. Those things would make Charlie angry, too. Yes they would, Gary understood. They would bother any *normal* person. Was that the point? Was Charlie telling Gary he was normal? That's when Gary sensed Charlie's minty warm breath and then Charlie's lips pressed to his own.

Gary reciprocated the kiss. Gary instinctively reached to the back of Charlie's head and combed his fingers through Charlie's sandy blond hair. Gary felt Charlie's lips: full, warm, and tender, lingering wet on his. He savored Charlie's fresh scent of after-shave and the saline glaze of his lips.

Charlie eased away, just a few inches from Gary's face. "How about you think about that instead?"

"I–," Gary stammered. "I don't know what to say."

"You don't need to *say* anything Gary. You think because I'm the quarterback, my life is easy?" He offered a reassuring smile. "It isn't." Pause. "I have a theory that the most popular kids in school, the most idolized sports icons and the most celebrated celebrities are each going through life feeling lonely, thinking nobody truly knows them." Charlie's eyes narrowed.

"You think you're different than the rest of us because you feel isolated and confused. Well guess what? So are we." Charlie placed his fingertips gently to Gary's lips and looked into his eyes. "So are we," he whispered. Charlie retreated into his seat and restarted the truck. "Now let's get to homecoming and have a good time, damn it." He donned a broad smile.

Gary returned the smile and pondered what just happened. One thing he knew for sure: Charlie was a good kisser.

Eugene wore the same white suit as last year, though this year it looked a size or two too small for him. As unofficial homecoming photographer, he occupied the prime location on the podium constructed on the inside arc of the red carpet arrival area and his Canon EOS Rebel T6 was getting a workout, snapping pictures of the pretty people on the red carpet.

Coach Evans and Mitchell sat off to the side, watching the girls arrive. "We're a couple of perverts, you know that?" Coach Evans said.

"Yep," Coach Mitchell replied. "Hey, tell me something, do you remember assembling that podium Eugene is standing on?"

"Nope."

"Wasn't that supposed to be one of our jobs?"

"Yep."

"Damn."

Matthew Davenport, Dell Project Manager, sat on his front porch, savoring a Nicaraguan Padron cigar. He stroked his silver handlebar mustache, deep in thought, deciding what to do. His buddies wanted him to come play poker. He did a risk-reward analysis of his evening plan choices. He felt equally drawn to playing poker and seeing the concert. The tiebreaker was the notion that he would be making his wife happy by using the ticket she went to the trouble of obtaining for him.

He snuffed out his cigar and called out to his wife through the screen door. "Honey, you're right. I think I'm going to go to the high school tonight. It's just such a great opportunity to see Doolittle in concert. I probably should take advantage."

"That's why I got you the ticket dear. Have a good time."

Travis County Constable Patrick Clancy watched the beat-up Honda approach the entrance of the school. He walked into the middle of the road and stopped it before it could turn. He observed the teenage driver cranking the window down as he approached the driver's side. To his credit, the young man placed both his hands on top of the steering wheel, in plain sight.

"Good evening officer," he said.

"Good evening. Headed to the dance?"

"Yes sir."

"Have you consumed any alcohol tonight son?"

"No sir. I'm here with my mother."

Constable Clancy held back a chuckle. "You're taking your mother to homecoming–?"

"Yes officer, he is," Roddy's mom cut in, sharply. "Do you have a problem with that?"

Constable Clancy nodded, all right, he probably deserved that. "No ma'am, that's just fine. Fine indeed." Pause. "Listen son, do you know why I stopped you?"

"No sir."

"Your right front headlight is out. You're going to need to get it fixed. I'm going to let you head on into the school, but do me a favor and get it fixed as soon as you can. Are we clear?"

"Yes sir."

"Be safe now." Constable Clancy stepped away from the car. *Taking your mom to homecoming. Do kids actually do that?* In Clancy's twenty-nine-year career, he thought he had seen just about everything.

Roddy headed for the oversized American and Texas flags, hanging limp on poles at the front of Sam Houston HS. He pulled his car into the drop-off circle. Lamar Jones, serving valet duty, noticed Roddy's Accord was now absent a passenger side mirror. Lamar on the other hand was looking sharp in his custom fitted tuxedo, size sixteen wingtip brogues and left ear adorned with a diamond stud that he wore for special occasions. Lamar opened the passenger side door and extended his arm to Roddy's mother. He helped her stand and when she stepped aside he stuck his head in the door and said, "Really Roddy? You brought this old piece of crap to homecoming dance?"

"Don't talk about my mother that way," Roddy said.

"You know exactly what I'm talking about. Get this piece of crap out of my drop-off circle. You're embarrassing me," Lamar said. "But dude, your mom looks fabulous. She available?"

"No."

Lamar closed the door, carefully. He was afraid it might come off its hinges otherwise.

Lamar wondered why they called opening car doors in the drop-off circle "valet duty." They didn't actually park any cars. The drop-off circle was an old school accommodation for men to drop off their dates, sparing the women from walking the distance of the parking lot in their heels. The dating combinations were more varied now, but the drop-off circle tradition held.

Roddy joined his mother on the red carpet, and together they strolled toward the front of the gymnasium. Eugene snapped several photographs as they rounded the arc of the red carpet runner. This was Maria's first visit to the high school gym so Roddy gave her a tour. The gym floor was covered with a taut gray canvas, like a pool covering with a flat finish. The decorating committee learned after the first homecoming dance that they needed to protect the floor. Many of the amenities, like the drop-off circle, the red carpet, and the stage placement, were results of lessons learned over the twenty-five-year history of school dances.

They walked across the floor to the center of the gym, which was also the middle of the dance floor. Maria scanned the gym. An impressive temporary stage occupied the back part of the gym. Red, white, and blue streamers and lights created an illusion of movement emanating outward from the stage. The creamed coffee dance floor was a sturdy hardwood, bamboo perhaps. She liked it. The bleachers on either side were partially pulled out to provide a few rows of seats and there were some random tables and chairs placed at the front part of the gym. Roddy escorted his mom across the gym floor to the lobby.

"Here's the refreshment area," he said.

Tables with colorful bunting lined the periphery of the lobby. Water, punch, cookies, and chips were complimentary. Teachers and volunteers manned a makeshift bar for adults only.

"If you want beer or wine, you can have that too. You need to show ID. They charge, though I don't know how much," Roddy smiled. "You can buy tickets to the game and join the booster club at the far table," he pointed. "There's two gender-neutral handicap stalls at the rear of the lobby, but there's always a line. If you need to use the restroom, I recommend you use the locker room. That's what all the students do. I'll show you where they are." They walked to the back of the lobby. "Back here is mostly storage. They can use one of these rooms for hat and coat check in case of rain. I don't think they'll worry about that this evening."

They returned to the gym and walked through the tunneled causeway between the back of the stage and the rear wall. "An enterprising architecture student thought of this tunnel a few years ago. It opens up a passageway along the backside of the gym so people don't have to elbow their way across the crowded dance floor." He took her through the other rear exit, which led into the school. "The locker rooms are on the left, girl's here and boy's one door down. Use the one marked 'Girls.'" Roddy smiled.

His mom gave him a playful smack on the arm. "I know to use the one marked 'Girls,' silly."

"Just teasing you, Mom."

"I know," she said. "I appreciate the tour. You may have a calling as a tour guide."

"Thanks, Mom. I can honestly tell you I wouldn't be here tonight if it weren't for you," Roddy said, with a serious look on his face.

"Oh, of course you would. In fact, I bet Amy's looking for you right now. Why don't you go find her honey?"

"Okay, Mom. Have fun! I love you."

"Love you too, dear."

"Hey Pat, lovely evening for directing traffic," ATF Agent Lee Dunsany said as he stopped at the school entrance to say hello to his buddy.

"That it is, Lee," Constable Clancy replied. "Good to see you again. What are you up to?"

"I'm selling booster tickets, like I do every year, for the big raffle," Agent Dunsany said.

"That sounds dandy. We all do what we can."

"Yes we do," Agent Dunsany said. "Any action tonight?"

"One kid with a busted headlight. I let him off on account he was bringing his mom to the dance."

Agent Dunsany chuckled. "Sounds like that kid deserved a break."

"Yeah, I reckoned."

"Good to see you. Have a good night Pat."

"You too Lee."

Agent Dunsany parked his unmarked ATF agency car on the grass median between the left front and right front parking lots. The car's license tag and agency stickers insulated him from parking tickets, as official duty and personal activity were often indistinguishable. He would be armed either way, 24/7. As he entered the school lobby he noticed the prohibition signs. One sign read, "This is a Drug Free Zone" another sign had an outline of a handgun with a big red cross out circle over it, indicating "No guns." Lee tapped his vest holster and cracked a sly smile. He loved it when the rules didn't apply to him.

Seth pulled up to the drop-off circling in his dad's silver 740i BMW. Lamar opened the passenger side door and extended a hand. Priscilla offered a fake swoon as Lamar helped her from the passenger seat, forcing Lamar to catch her in both arms.

"Oh my, thank you Lamar, you're such a gentleman," she said, relaxing into his arms and batting her eyelashes.

"And you Priscilla are one fine lady. You look fabulous. Dance later?" he asked.

"Please," she replied. *Whatever you want Lamar.*

Seth circled the car around to the parking lot. By the time he returned to the circle, Priscilla was engaged in girl talk, so he stood around, chatting with Lamar while he greeted new arrivals.

"Seems like you made quite the impression with Priscilla," Seth remarked.

"She's a spunky one," Lamar said. "My sister likes her, too."

"So I noticed," Seth said. "If you're interested, we could probably work something out, for a price."

"Who's paying whom?" Lamar asked.

"Seriously?" Seth said. "You cocky bastard."

"Look who's talking," Lamar countered.

"Whatever. Forget about it." Seth strutted toward Priscilla

and caught the tail end of her conversation with Sally Durbin.

"No seriously, have you noticed his shoe size and his hands the size of baseball mitts? Have you ever thought about what that might mean?" Priscilla said.

Sally was looking right past Seth, scoping Lamar. "I can't say I have, but now that you mention it, I certainly am," she cackled. "Look how long his arms are. They must have specially tailored that dinner jacket just for him."

"That's what I'm talking about," Priscilla said. "He has freakishly long appendages."

"Priscilla, why are you telling me this? A guy like Lamar would never be interested in a girl like me." Sally flicked her hands in toward her body, which was noticeably rounder and fuller than a lot of the other girls in school.

"I'm not so sure about that Sally. Let's put it this way. Most girls you would consider popular wouldn't work for Lamar. They're skinny and boney. Half of them won't even eat a cookie tonight, and if they do, they'll puke it out fifteen minutes later. No, Lamar needs a full-size woman. I bet he's already figured that out. You should talk to him. He might surprise you."

"You know Priscilla, I think this one conversation is more than you've said to me in three years of high school. I say that without criticism. It's just an observation. Why?"

"Why?" Priscilla pondered. "I honestly don't know. You were standing here, and it seemed like the natural thing to do."

"It wasn't natural for you last week," Sally said. "What's changed?"

"Me, I guess," Priscilla admitted. "Have a great time tonight, and I better see you out there on that dance floor with Lamar at some point."

"That would be real neat," Sally said. "Thanks"

Seth grabbed Priscilla's hand and pulled her along the red carpet, past Eugene who was clicking pictures. Priscilla glanced back and saw Sally already engaged in an animated conversation with Kaitlyn Wassermann. They were both leering at Lamar.

Jackie Fleur's cell phone rang. It was Nina. "We're pulling up to the front," Nina said. Dr. Reichmann was kind enough to give Nina a lift to the dance, given they both lived close to the hospital.

"Okay great, I'll come meet you at the circle," Jackie replied. Jackie arrived at the red carpet in time to see Lamar offering Nina a hand up out of Dr. Reichmann's Mercedes before he left to go park.

Jackie hugged Nina and said, "I'm so glad you could make it. And, your dress looks wonderful."

Nina cracked a smile. "It's a size larger than what I'd like, but thank you."

Jackie spared Nina from the picture-happy Eugene and skirted her around to the alternative front entrance. "Text Dr. Reichmann and tell him to meet us by the bar," Jackie said. Nina did just that. "Red or white?"

"Those are the choices?" Nina said. "I prefer tequila."

"No hard stuff at the high school dance. This isn't Cooper's Hawk," Jackie said. "The white's kind of sweet. I think the red is dry merlot. They'll give you a taste if you like."

"I'll take the red," Nina said. "But, you should mention to the homecoming committee that a nice agave blue would round out the bar with the school colors."

"That's clever Nina," Jackie said, chuckling. "I don't think they'll buy it, though." Jackie ordered two reds, one for the both of them.

Dr. Reichmann found them just as their drinks were being served. "Oh wait, let me take care of that," he said, handing the volunteer a twenty-dollar bill. "Will that cover another?" he asked. It did, with two dollars to spare, which the doctor left as a tip. They toasted to homecoming, saying "Salute!" and clinking their plastic cups.

Nina formally introduced Jackie to Wolfgang. She got a kick out of how they were both already looking each other up and down, thinking neither saw the other scoping. Nina suspected they both liked what they saw. Jackie was stunning in her accented white dress and Wolfgang looked sharp in his black Armani suit. They could just about walk up to the altar, as is.

"Please, call me Wolfgang. Calling me doctor makes me feel old."

"Tell me about it," Jackie said. "I get called *Mrs.* Fleur half the time, usually by the boys. Drives me crazy."

"Well, I must say, *Jackie,*" he said, grinning, "if you dress like this for school, I'd venture to say you're the one driving the boys crazy."

Jackie felt herself blush and she had a flash memory of Nelson down on one knee the night before. Jackie appreciated the compliment. It had been a while since she'd pampered herself in as many ways as she had this afternoon. Well-compensated cosmetologists and estheticians fawned over her hair, face, fingers, and toes. Her dress was white with gold and silver trim. It had a deep neckline, a faux gold belt, and two satin silver bands across the bottom. The dress rested slightly above her knees. At first she was concerned that the horizontal bands might draw her shape wider, but somehow they did not. Everything else, from her radiant auburn hair to her white evening sandals and golden-painted toes, conformed to match the glamor of this fabulous evening.

"You flatter me, Wolfgang," she said, beaming.

"So, Nina tells me our star patient is in your biology class," he said.

"Yes, Gary Greene. What a fabulous boy he is," Jackie said. "You must have been quite an inspiration. He's fascinated by the micro-sciences. He asks fascinating questions, and he's experimenting with DNA samples from his classmates for his class project."

"Oh really, what kind of experiments?" Wolfgang asked, curious.

Lucas Barolo and Liam Strauss were hanging out near the refreshment stand in the front lobby. "You notice the players are avoiding the punchbowl?" Lucas said. It wasn't the *same* punchbowl of course, but just the thought was revolting.

"Can't blame them. I'm not touching it either," Liam replied.

"It's just so gross," Lucas said. "Speak of the devil." Jeremy Parsons approached the refreshment stand and grabbed a water bottle with his free hand. He held a football in the other.

"You brought your smegma-covered football to homecoming?" Liam said.

"Had to, coaches are here," Jeremy replied, matter-of-fact.

"You wash it off real *good*?" Liam said, demonstrating why he was failing English.

Jeremy was in no mood for Liam's lip. "No master Liam, I got to thinking, cum is kind of like Stickum. I figure it helps me keep a better grip on the ball. See?" Jeremy gripped the ball tightly in one hand and rubbed it in Liam's face. Liam didn't take too kindly to a formerly cum-covered football smashed against his nose. He batted it away, sending the football crashing into pre-poured cups of punch. A scuffle ensued, with Liam and Jeremy grappling for a hold on each other's dinner jackets. Coach Evans swooped in on the boys.

"Hey, hey! Strauss, Parsons, I don't know what this is about. I don't want to know. Save it for the game."

"Yes sir."

"Yes sir."

Jeremy picked up the football. It was drenched with punch and sticky again. "Damn it," he said, in disgust.

"Parsons, give me that football," Coach Evans commanded. "You're on reprieve for the evening. Go have a good time."

"Oh my God. Thanks Coach! You have no idea." Jeremy handed the football over to Coach Evans, grabbed another water bottle and blended into the lobby crowd.

"And you boys stay out of trouble," Coach Evans said to Liam and Lucas.

"We will sir."

Coach Evans started to walk away, football under his arm. He turned over his shoulder and asked, "By the way, have you guys seen Seth Thompson?"

"Haven't seen him yet, Coach."

Coach Evans kept walking.

"Remind me to tell Jeremy he still owes me $20," Liam said to Lucas.

"Do me a favor: don't ask him tonight."

Janitor Jonas and a couple of theater kids came over to clean up the mess of cups and punch on the floor. Lucas and Liam walked away.

World Scientific Forum
September 2017

AGGRESSIVE AI

Google finds that as Artificial Intelligence gets more advanced, it becomes more aggressive. Google DeepMind created a simple AI video game called "Gathering." The AI systems were armed with lasers that could temporarily disable their opponents. Each side was instructed to gather more apples than their opponent. Researchers found that when apples were in abundance the AI rarely used their lasers. But when the quantity of apples diminished, the use of the lasers increased dramatically. More complex AIs used their laser more often and behaved less cooperatively regardless of the number of apples. Google's conclusion? As AI becomes more sophisticated, it becomes more ruthless.

Charlie and Gary approached the school in Charlie's truck. Charlie hesitated when he saw the lone Travis County Constable directing traffic at the school's entrance.

"It's just a traffic cop," Charlie said.

"I realize that," Gary said, "but thanks."

They turned onto the school's long paved driveway.

"Please don't drop me off at the circle," Gary said.

"Ah man. That's half the fun," Charlie said. "Just kidding."

Gary parked his truck across his favorite four parking spots in the far corner of the school parking lot.

"They may as well post a 'reserved' sign for you on these spots."

"Don't need to," Charlie said. "Everyone knows they're mine."

Gary and Charlie arrived at the red carpet, greeted Lamar, greeted Eugene, and smiled for the camera in their matching tuxedos. They stepped inside to a bustling and dimly lit gymnasium, already buzzing with excitement and heart pumping background music.

"Let's find Cindy," he yelled over the music.

They roamed around until they found Roddy.

"Have you seen Cindy?" Charlie asked him.

"Nope, haven't seen either Cindy or Amy," Roddy said. "I don't think they're here yet."

That's strange; Charlie thought he was the one that would be running late. If they didn't get here soon, they would miss the beginning of the concert. He headed to the drop-off circle with purpose. Gary followed. They arrived at the drop-off circle just in time to see a black stretch limousine precariously navigating the circle. Lamar opened one passenger door, the chauffeur opened the other. Out popped Cindy and Amy. They each straightened up their dresses and made their way to the red carpet, giggling and noticeably unsteady.

"Oh no," Charlie said, putting his hand on his forehead and grimacing. "They're already drunk."

"They got an early start," Gary observed.

The boys steadied the girls, Charlie holding Amy and Gary holding Cindy. That's the way they were photographed by Eugene.

"You better hang onto these." Cindy handed Gary both of their handbags, each loaded with minibar vodka bottles.

"Exactly what we needed," Gary said, sarcastic.

"And give Cindy this," Charlie handed Gary Cindy's corsage.

Gary unceremoniously passed Cindy her orchid wrist corsage.

"Thanks, I think," Cindy said.

"Is Roddy here yet?" Amy slurred. "I need to talk to him."

Charlie thought that wasn't such a good idea, but he bit his tongue.

Gary focused on Cindy. "Killer dress."

"Thank you," Cindy said." You boys look sharp too. Mm, two sexy young men in matching tuxedos. Brings back nice thoughts to mind."

"I bet," Gary said.

Up ahead of them they heard Amy say, "Charlie, I think I might get sick."

Oh no, Charlie thought; he grabbed her and bolted for the gender-neutral bathrooms in the lobby. He dragged her towards the bathroom yelling "Gang way!" He cut to the front of the line and rapped on the bathroom door.

"Hang on a minute!" came a female voice from inside.

The other bathroom looked no more promising as there was a line there, too. *Crap*, he thought.

Amy started to heave. Just in time, Roddy arrived with a trashcan, into which Amy vomited vodka, Seltzer, and apparently some of her dinner. A bystander handed Amy his handkerchief out of his suit pocket.

She looked up, wiped her mouth, and said, "Roddy," before turning her head and heaving again. She looked up, puke dibbling down her chin, "We're done."

"I figured," Roddy said, still holding the trash can, looking at Charlie.

The bathroom opened, and Cindy pulled Amy inside to clean her up. The people standing in line for the bathroom moaned.

"Folks, if you really need to go, I suggest you use the locker rooms," Roddy announced. "Follow me, I'll show you where they are."

About a dozen people from both bathroom lines peeled off and followed Roddy on a trek down the lobby hall, under the stage tunnel and into the boys' and girls' locker rooms.

Gary scanned the lobby crowd and, to his surprise, saw some familiar faces. He had no idea Dr. Reichmann and Nurse Lopez were attending the homecoming dance. He was delighted to see both of them. As he approached he saw that something was wrong with Nurse Lopez. It looked like Nurse Lopez from afar, but a closer look revealed the disfigurement. She *was* the oncology nurse that had the mishap in the hospital after all. Gary felt horrible about not following up at the time to see if it was someone he knew. Her wounds must have been severe and painful. Her skin was blotchy and uneven. Her lips were nonexistent, and a part of her ear was gone. He was glad he saw her before she saw him, so he could take in her wounds without gawking at their first greeting. His first instinct was to ask her questions about what had happened, but that would have been rude. Instead, he snuck up on them and greeted them like the genuine friends they were.

"Nurse Lopez!" He offered her a hug. He noticed the grotesque scarring on her hands as she reached to embrace him. "It's great to see you," Gary said. "What a surprise. How have you been?"

"I've been better Gary. I take it one day at a time," she said. "It's nice to see you too. Look at you, all spiffy in your tuxedo."

"Thank you. First time for everything," Gary replied, then he faced Dr. Reichmann and extended his hand. "It is good to see you too, sir."

Dr. Reichmann stepped forward past the hand and embraced Gary in full-on bear hug. Tears were in his eyes. "Oh Gary," he said. "Well done my boy. Well done."

The hug lasted a long time. Jackie was touched by the genuine affection Wolfgang demonstrated towards Gary.

Gary pulled back from the hug. "Dr. Reichmann, we should talk," Gary said.

"Yes, we should," Dr. Reichmann said. "Your teacher tells me you've taken an interest in the micro-sciences."

Gary nodded. "Yes, that's true." Gary started to step away from within an earshot of Nurse Lopez and Miss Fleur.

Dr. Reichmann turned to the women, only to hear them say, "Go on, you two talk. We've got wine."

Gary and Dr. Reichmann walked toward the coat-check room, which was deserted on this warm fall evening, and spoke in relative privacy.

"How is your cancer research progressing?" Gary asked. "I keep expecting to hear about more patients being cured through nanite treatments, but I haven't."

"Honestly Gary, results have been abysmal," Dr. Reichmann said. "We've done clinical trials across the country on a dozen terminal patients. They've all died, some having rather adverse reactions to the treatment. It seems you're an anomaly. Harvard Medical has been on me to circle back to you to reassess our results with your treatment. I've held them off, hoping we'd have a breakthrough elsewhere, but we haven't. I hate to put you through more tests, but it may come to that."

"I completely understand," Gary said. "I've half been expecting to hear from you, or somebody anyway. Why do you think the nanite treatment hasn't worked for the other patients?"

"I think there is something about the programming of the nanites that Harvard hasn't mastered," Dr. Reichmann said.

"The nanites attack the cancer cells *and* the healthy cells. Chemotherapy had this problem for a long time. Still does. That's why it's so exhausting on the patient. I had hoped the nanite treatments would be more precise. It seems Harvard only got the formula just right with you. They're nagging me to investigate further why that's the case."

"I'm not surprised," Gary said. "Sounds like those other patients didn't train their nanites the right way."

"It doesn't work like that, Gary. The nanites are programmed, using DNA fragments and quantum techniques. It's not the patient's fault if the programming fails."

"I'm not blaming the patients," Gary said. "If they don't know to talk to their nanites, then how can they be blamed?"

"What do you mean, 'talk to their nanites'?" Dr. Reichmann asked.

Gary pondered how he could explain it. "Well, do you remember my mom?"

Dr. Reichmann nodded and smiled. Of course he remembered Joanna Greene. She was a major catalyst to obtaining the nanite treatment for Gary.

"Well then, you know she's into transcendental meditation and all sort of meta-physical practices. I guess some of that rubbed off on me because when you explained to me that you were going to put little tiny robots into my bloodstream, I knew I had to talk to them. I needed to commune with the robots so they knew me. From the moment you injected me, I started talking to them. 'Come on little tiny robots', I'd say, 'attack those cancer cells and be nice to me'. I think that's what made the difference for me."

Dr. Reichmann patted Gary on the shoulder. "Oh Gary, I wish it were that simple. I'm glad you felt comfortable with the treatment and that you became *one* with the nanites, but medical science doesn't work like that. They obviously worked for you. We need to figure out why, from a *scientific* perspective."

"Are they alive?" Gary asked.

"The nanites?" Dr. Reichmann said.

"Yes, would you say the nanites are living things?" Gary asked.

"They are tiny robots fashioned from organic elements. You would have to use the definition of 'life' loosely."

"They eat. Right?" Gary asked.

"Yes, in a sense, they are programmed to attack cancerous cells and *eat* them."

"Do they reproduce?" Gary asked.

"Wow, who is this biology teacher of yours? She has you asking all the right questions." Dr. Reichmann pondered a moment and continued. "The answer is yes, they *reproduce* through a binary process called cytokinesis, which is akin to cellular mitosis. Simply put, when the nanites consume, it gives them energy to replicate an exact copy of themselves. The more cancerous cells in a patient, the more nanites that patient is going to produce. That's the way the nanites are programmed so that their population is proportional to the need."

"Thank you, I've been wondering about that for a while," Gary said. "What do they do after the cancer is all gone?"

"They hang around. I thought I told you that," Dr. Reichmann said. "My expectation would be that they would serve as an enhancement to your natural immune system. I'm curious, have you been sick at all this year?"

"Nope, not even an allergy," Gary said, smiling. "So, the nanites eat and they reproduce. That sounds pretty alive to me."

"Perhaps, in the same sense that a fungus is alive."

"But they can learn, too, right?" Gary said. "And evolve, like a virus?"

"Hmm. You're going for the gold here. Let's think about

this," Dr. Reichmann said. "The nanites are programmed using new generation AI, which means they learn incrementally, with previous lessons learned applied to subsequent experiences to create new knowledge. It was necessary to construct them that way because the dataset for them to recognize what is cancer (and what is not) is insurmountably huge. Using old AI methods, we would have to show them patterns of your complete biological structure in advance, so they would recognize your cell's natural state versus a cancerous state. The only practical course was to let them be cognitive and allow them to learn incrementally, by trial and error, just as we do."

"I think you've talked yourself into a conclusion that the nanites are alive," Gary observed.

"I suppose I have," Dr. Reichmann said, nodding.

"I have a secret to tell you about the nanites doctor. When I tell you this secret, everything about our lives is going to change. I've been holding off on telling anyone because I've been afraid. But, I'm not afraid anymore."

"Gary, you have all my attention. Tell me."

"Not only are the nanites alive, they have a mind of their own," Gary said. "It's a hive mind. They protect me in ways you couldn't imagine."

"I have a pretty vivid imagination, Gary. I'm a microbial research scientist. Explain what you mean."

Gary proceeded to divulge almost everything he knew about the nanites to Dr. Reichmann. He told him about the blood in the boys' locker room. He told him about the rat and the scorpion. He described his DNA experiments and how the nanites attacked some people's DNA but not others. He omitted mentioning spitting in Seth's drink. Gary was not particularly proud of that.

"You said the blood in the shower and on the scorpion looked like moving red threads?"

"Yeah," Gary confirmed.

"That's what the med techs in the elevator described the day Nina was injured. 'Slimy swirling crimson threads'. What day was your last appointment at Seton?"

"It was right before the New Year, December 30th. My parents wanted to get the appointment done before the end of the year, otherwise they would have had to pay because of the 2017 deductible."

"That's the day she got hurt." Dr. Reichmann said, finally understanding why only Nurse Lopez was burned in the elevator. Nina's connection to Gary included cancer therapies that predated the nanite treatment. She had administered several painful stem cell implant procedures on Gary. Therefore, the nanites must have been predisposed to perceive her as harmful because Gary was apprehensive of Nurse Lopez. The nanites in Gary's blood had no effect on the medical technicians because they had no predisposition to perceive the med tech's DNA as threatening. There was no middle ground with the nanites; they had a lizard brain. Friend or foe, that's all they knew, and they behaved accordingly.

Gary went ashen, the image of Nurse Lopez's disfigured face and hands flashing in his mind. "The nanites did that her? *My* nanites?" he said in disbelief.

"Gary," Dr. Reichmann said. "I overstepped. We don't know that."

"But you suspect it."

"I think, based on what you've just told me," Dr. Reichmann said, deliberately, "you need to be very careful."

Gary sat down on a metal folding chair, put his head in his hands, and started to cry.

Dr. Reichmann comforted him, rubbing his back and telling him, "It's not your fault Gary. Let's get you into the office. We can help you. You don't need to endure this alone."

Gary wiped away some tears. "Dr. Reichmann, you know

that part about me not being afraid? I lied. I'm really scared. What's going to happen to me?"

"It will be okay, Gary," Dr. Reichmann assured him. "We'll figure it out."

Principal McFadden and Coach Casey stood on stage—directly on the spray-painted black X—and addressed the homecoming crowd. "Boys and girls, just a few brief announcements before we get on with the festivities," Principal McFadden said. "As you know, I'm new here." There were a few jeers. "Yes, yes, I know. Boo new. That means this is my first chance to enjoy a homecoming dance with you, and let me tell you I am *quite* impressed!" This time there were a few cheers. "Sam Houston High School goes all out for homecoming, that's for sure. I just want to remind you, you are on school property. All of the rules that govern behavior during the school day remain in place tonight. I don't have to repeat them. Obey them. Enough said." Pause. "Now, over to you, Coach Casey, to fire us up!" She passed the mic to Coach Casey, to sprinkled applause.

Coach thumped the microphone. "Hey folks!" Background noise crackled through the auditorium. Coach nodded his head. "Hey, look I get it, you want music, and you want dancing, not some old fart standing up here on stage. Back in my day, homecoming was more like a pep rally. It really was coaches giving speeches, teachers leading the school fight song, and cheerleaders performing to fire up the student body for the big game. Times have changed. Homecoming has taken on an entirely new meaning, especially here at Sam Houston. So let me just say this one thing about the game tomorrow." He paused for effect. "We need you. The players need your support, now more than ever. It's been a tough beginning of the season. We've lost some games we felt like we should have won, and now our backs are against the wall. If we are to have any chance of getting into the playoffs we need to beat the Fire

Ants tomorrow." He finished the sentence on a high note and raised a fist in the air. "They're pesky little critters that deserve nothing to be annihilated."

"Annihilate. Annihilate," the chanting began as students raised fists.

"That's awesome. Let's bring that energy out onto the field tomorrow. We'll cream those Fire Ants for sure." Raucous cheers erupted from the students. "I ask just two things of you. First, don't keep my boys up too late tonight. They need fresh legs for the game tomorrow. Second, come out and support us. We need you." Cheering and applauding ensued.

Coach Casey returned the mic to Principal McFadden. "One last reminder to vote for the homecoming court. If you haven't already downloaded the app, you can still get it from the school's app store. There's no charge. Remember it's a gender-neutral election. Top two vote-getters, regardless of gender, will be your king and queen. Choose well."

Coach and Principal left the stage and the homecoming chair picked up the microphone and introduced the evening's band. "Ladies and gentleman, we present to you the one and only PIPERRRR DAKOTAAAA!!!"

The crowd broke into its loudest roar yet as spotlights shifted to Piper, a fiery redhead, hair pinned high, dressed in a formal black gown and pumps. Her band struck up the opening chords and the folks on the dance floor spontaneously rocked to the beat. "Cool jerk," Piper pumped her fists. "Cool jerk," more fist pumping and so it continued. The party was on.

Charlie held Amy's hand and kept feeding her swigs from a water bottle. "Hydrate, Amy, hydrate. That's the way you'll get your second wind."

"It's working. I'm feeling better. This music is awesome." She dragged him out onto the dance floor.

"You want to dance, Gary?" Cindy asked.

"Sure, let's dance." He pulled a couple of vodka bottles out of one of the mini-purses and held them out. "Do we really need these?"

Cindy shook her head.

By the time they got to the dance floor, he had handed out all the little bottles, saying with each one, "Vote for Charlie Simpson."

Priscilla Moran wandered out onto the dance floor alone with newfound confidence. She soon realized she could dance with just about any boy she wanted, even the boys who were already dancing with girls. She caught sight of Lamar Jones dancing within an impromptu circle of several adoring girls. She laughed and marveled at how fast news travels. She saw Sally Durbin on the edge of the dance floor, grabbed hold of her and dragged her into the gaggle surrounding the suddenly popular Lamar Jones. The trio danced together within the circle. Sally actually had some moves. Lamar noticed and gave Priscilla thumbs up.

Jeremy Parsons danced sans football in the middle of the dance floor. He had no particular partner. He didn't need or want one. He waved his hands in the air, simply because they were empty.

Wolfgang found Nina Lopez and Jackie Fleur on the dance floor. He was glad to see them having a good time. They rocked to the beat and moved their bodies in ways unusual for doctors, nurses, and teachers. There was good energy between Wolfgang and Jackie. Nina urged them along, circling them and bumping them closer to one another. Their movements were indistinguishable amongst the crowd, but the atmosphere was electric between them.

"You look fantastic," Wolfgang finally said.

"I must," she smiled, "the high school photographer sure did take a lot of pictures."

"He probably has a crush on you too."

"Too huh?" Jackie said, smiling. "Is there someone else here who has a crush on me?"

"If I were a betting man, I'd stake pretty good odds on it."

"Are you a betting man?" Jackie asked, leaning in closer, lips near his ear.

"I've been known to gamble on occasion. I came here, didn't I?" In truth, gambling had cost Wolfgang his first marriage. That was a detail better left unsaid.

"Oh really, was this a gamble?" Jackie was having fun tugging on the conversation thread, drawing Wolfgang out.

"Actually no, so far it's looking like a solid investment," Wolfgang said.

"Good answer, doctor," Jackie said. "You are a smart man."

Wolfgang just smiled, waved his arms, and swiveled his hips like a teenager, hoping he didn't injure himself.

Nelson peered from the edge of the dance floor. Miss Fleur was dancing with a tall distinguished looking man and a woman friend whose face was hard to look at and hard to look away from at the same time. There's a story in that face, Nelson could sense it. Maybe a song. Perhaps he could write it.

Roddy stepped just past Nelson, dragging a pretty, middle aged woman in a black and white party dress onto the dance floor. Roddy grabbed Nelson by the arm, dragged him onto the dance floor as well and said, "Nelson, this is my mom, Maria. Mom, this is Nelson. He's a really nice guy. Dance with him. Have fun!" Then Roddy bailed from the dance floor. So there was Nelson, trapped, dancing with a pretty Hispanic lady. He decided it wasn't such a bad arrangement.

"Nice to meet you Maria," Nelson said, bowing, people dancing to the beat around him.

"Nice to meet you too Nelson," Maria said, heavily accented so that his name came out sounding more like kneel-son. It didn't matter, she looked great, she could dance, and Nelson didn't have a date. He took Roddy's advice and decided to have fun. They blended into the dancing crowd.

Science and Technology Magazine
September 2017

Why Microsoft's AI Experiment Went South

One year after Microsoft's experiment with a real-time machine learning chatbot went horribly wrong, engineers are still sorting out the ramifications. From the time they put the bot on the web, it took less than a day for the AI to turn racist, sexist and xenophobic in its Twitter messages. Programmers are struggling to develop content-neutral algorithms that are "blank slates" for learning that don't have to be tamed or censored as soon as they get exposed to humans. The difficulty derives from AI's tendency to amplify bias it detects in society. As one developer aptly stated, "When the whole idea is to allow AI to learn as humans do, you shouldn't be surprised when a fully immersed chat-bot calls your mother a whore." What has Microsoft learned? Namely, how quickly even the most well-intentioned AI can spin out-of-control when confronted with the real world.

Seth was steaming. "What the hell? When were you guys going to tell me?" He was laying into Lucas and Liam about the voting app he heard announced by the principal.

"We can't help if you don't pay attention Seth," Lucas said. "The voting app has been out there a few weeks. I tried to tell you before, but you didn't want to listen. The old ballot box stuffing days are gone."

"You realize we may have gone through all this trouble for nothing right?" Seth said. "If Gary Greene isn't elected homecoming queen, we're screwed."

"Condom boy's still got a decent chance to win," Liam said.

"He better. Keep working the crowd. Vote for Gary Greene, pass the word."

"We are, Seth," Liam said.

Seth found Chestnut near the cookies. "Did you know about the voting app?"

"Everybody knows about the voting app, Seth," Chestnut said.

"Show it to me."

Chestnut took out his phone and brought up the app, "See, you verify your credentials here. I've already voted, so I can't do it. But you can, you just need to know your student ID number and your password."

"I got that in my wallet."

"Great, let's cast your vote."

Chestnut stepped him through it. You get two votes, one for king and one for queen, but you can't specify which is which. You're just checking two boxing out of a list of about twenty people. Both Gary Greene and Charlie Simpson are on the list.

"There, I selected them."

"Just press enter, and you're done."

"Done."

"Feel better?"

"No, I feel like an idiot for trusting Lucas and Liam to take care of this."

"What were they supposed to do, hack the program?"

"They could have told me at least. We might have reconsidered the plan."

"You reconsidering?" Chestnut asked.

"No. Just concerned it's been a big waste of time."

Lead singer Piper Dakota was rocking the crowd to her cover of *We Got The Beat* by the Go-Gos. Piper had her act down pat, to the delight of the homecoming dance participants. Coach recalled his high school dances being painful rituals to be endured just so you could say you were there, and therefore you were cool. He wondered if these kids knew how lucky they were. Piper handed it over to the crowd favorite, Johnny Doolittle, the ballad singer who grew up just North of Round Rock and made it big in Southern rock. Johnny told stories with his music.

"HELLOOOOO ROUND ROCK! How's everybody doing out there?" Roaring crowd noise and random chanting, "Round Rock! Round Rock!"

"That's awesome! I'm glad to be back here again, so close to my hometown. It's nice to come home again, every now and then." The crowd cheered. "I've been fortunate enough to travel all around this fabulous country of ours. I've seen a lot of great places and I've met a lot of great people, but there's just nothing like coming home again." Cheers, applause, then quieter again. "You kids will know what I mean pretty soon when you go off to college, or join the military, or travel to wherever life might happen to take you. I wrote a song about that feeling and I would like to share it with you tonight. It's called 'Never Far Away.'" Johnny was the kind of performer who could captivate an audience. The crowd swayed and sang along to the song. Johnny stopped strumming the guitar for the chorus and just walked the stage singing with the crowd. He finished the song to a thundering ovation. He sat back down on the stool and set his guitar aside. The crowd instantly picked up on this cue that Johnny was going to tell another story. "I really appreciate the love and affection I feel from you tonight. It's important that we feel love and affection for one another in life. You never know when a family member, friend, or just a casual acquaintance might be down so low that your gesture of love, no matter how small, might make a huge difference in their life. Life can be hard. Sometimes it hits us with challenges we didn't even know we were strong enough to endure. We endure because we set our mind to it, but it's just a little easier if we know we're not enduring alone." Pause, silence. "Every once in a while I hear a story the truly moves my soul. One of those stories that reminds me I don't really have it so bad, by comparison. I understand we have a cancer survivor with us tonight who's on the ballot for homecoming court. Am I right about that?"

Random yells of "Yeah".

"Gary Greene, I know you're out there."

Gary waved and a spot light found him.

"Oh there you are. Now don't worry, I'm not going to embarrass you anymore than this right here. I just want to tell you son, your story inspired me. How many years did you suffer with cancer?"

Several girls in the crowd yelled "Three".

"Three *fucking* years. Oh wait, can I say that? Sorry . . . I heard about the fancy treatment that finally worked. Congratulations on that. I'm glad to see you're better. I also heard about the treatments that didn't work. You see, you don't know this, but I spoke with your mama about a month ago. She didn't tell you she talked with me, did she?"

Gary shook his head. This is why Mom said I *had* to go, he realized.

"I heard she was all around town raising money and awareness for your cause. She's an inspiration to me too. Christ she should be an inspiration for all us. You boys and girls want to know what love looks like? Look at your classmate Gary and look at his mama. It's a beautiful thing."

The crowd was silent.

"Bear with me, I'm not quite done yet holding Gary up on a

pedestal. You see, when his mama told me about the treatments he went through, I was astonished. Gary had to endure something called a stem cell transplant. That's where they take a needle about the size of turkey baster and stick it directly into your spine. Folks, I only know one other person who's had a similar procedure, just one time. Good friend of mine. He said it's by far the most painful thing he's ever experienced. Gary, you mind telling me how many stem cell transplant procedures those doctors attempted on you?"

Gary found his voice. This must have been the big moment his mom was having the premonition about. Gary held up his hand with all digits extended. "Five," he yelled.

"Five *fucking* times . . . I can't imagine. You know what your mama told me? She told me you never complained . . . not once. You never complained, did you son?"

Gary shook his head, tears welling in his eyes, Amy and Cindy on either side, holding him up steady.

"Folks, that right there is an inspiration."

The crowd erupted into a standing ovation for Gary Greene, cancer survivor and homecoming court nominee.

"I bet you folks are ready for some more music?" Johnny said and the crowd cheered once again. "Well, that's great, I love that you want to listen to me. It wasn't always that way for me." Johnny reached for his guitar and plucked just a couple of notes. "Back in the day, I tried my hand at being a teacher. Any teachers out there tonight?"

Lots of cheers.

"I taught eighth grade English, or at least I tried. I swear there's nothing you can do to teach a kid grammar, *if* you call it grammar. I could stand on my hands and write on the whiteboard with my feet and those kids wouldn't have paid attention. They are probably teaching you grammar here at Sam Houston High School and you kids don't even realize it. If you're taking a class called 'Business Writing' or some such nonsense, that's grammar, dressed up in a fancy name to hide the truth of it."

Random laughs and claps.

"Here's a song I wrote in honor of my teaching days. I wrote this song on a train ride from Augusta to Memphis. A wise man sat down next to me on that ride. I could tell he was wise because he had bright blue eyes, a long rugged nose and a gnarly grey beard, kind of like Gandalf from *Lord of the Rings*."

Laughs.

"He started talking to me, offering me sage advice, I'm sure, but I was tired. I just kind of nodded my head and grunted and to this day I can't remember a damn thing that old man said to me. It went *In One Ear and Out the Other*."

Wild cheers erupted as Johnny started into the first stanza of his hit song. Even those who didn't know the song well had picked up the chorus the second time around and were echoing Johnny every time he belted out "In one ear and out the other."

"In one ear and out the other!" Chestnut echoed with the rest of the rowdy crowd. He turned to Seth and yelled, "What did you think about that speech?"

"I think cancer boy is going down tonight," Seth said, sinister grin on his face.

Damn, Chestnut thought, *Seth's one stone cold son-of-a-bitch.*

A few of the football players figured out one of the best places to hang out was near the front exit, midway between the entertainment in the gym and the refreshments in the lobby. Liam, Lucas Barolo, Ricky Marlin, Chestnut, and Roddy all found themselves milling near the same spot.

"Hey Liam, hey Lucas," Chestnut said. "Is it true that Ricky beat your ass playing darts and Ricky was throwing the darts backwards between his legs?"

"Yep," Ricky chimed, "just like a punt snap."

"You guys are pathetic," Chestnut said.

"Speaking of which," Roddy said. "Did you guys hear that speech? You're not still going through with that stunt you planned, are you?"

"What stunt?" Ricky asked.

"Oh, don't you know Ricky?" Roddy said. "These clowns are going to dump that paint can of cum onto Gary's head while he's standing on stage."

"No fucking way," Ricky said and looked at Chestnut. "That's like *Carrie*, only much more disgusting." Ricky doubled over with laughter.

"That's the idea," Chestnut said, joining in the amusement. Both boys slapped each other on the backs and continued to laugh.

"Stop laughing, guys," Roddy said. "So, you're still doing it?"

Chestnut straightened up and caught his breath. "Unless you can convince Seth not to pull that rope, it's happening. If you're so guilt-ridden about it, go turn us in. Stop being such a pussy."

"Yeah, Roddy, lighten up. Condom boy has it coming," Ricky said with a sneer aimed at Roddy. "You were in the locker room same as the rest of us. Now you're turning queer?"

"My mom's on that dance floor," Roddy said, looking down, creases prominent on his forehead.

"Well she's in for a real treat then," Chestnut said. Ricky and Chestnut smiled at each other and walked away, leaving Roddy to consider his options.

Coach Evans met Seth near the storage closets.

"Thanks for the kickass pot," Evans said. "You got the key?"

"Hell yeah I got the key," Seth said, handing it to Coach Evans. "Worked great. We really appreciate it."

"Good deal. Got any more of that pot?"

"Yeah, one more joint. Here take it. My treat. Consider it a tip for the use of the gym key."

"Sweet," Evans said, accepting the joint. "If anyone is looking for me, tell them I'm in the can."

"You got it." Seth didn't have much time for chitchat. He needed to circle around the stage to a rope tied up near the speakers.

Coach Evans walked toward the rear door where he met up with Coach Mitchell.

"You get it?" Mitchell asked.

Evans opened his palm to show him the joint.

"Hell yeah!" Mitchell said. "We're going to have a good time tonight."

They walked across the parking lot to their favorite bench under the oak tree, near where the quarterback always parked his truck.

"Maybe we'll see Simpson getting laid again."

"Wouldn't surprise me."

They lit the joint and passed it back and forth.

"When's the last time you got laid?" Evans said, watching the orange pickup truck bounce up and down on it shock absorbers, though he could swear nobody was inside.

Mitchell held up one finger and delayed his response. He slowing exhaled his deep drag of the joint. "Can't remember. Long time." He handed the joint to Evans then hacked through a coughing fit.

Evans checked the truck again. It was perfectly still. There was nobody in the truck. "I think I'm overdue."

"Why's that?"

"This weed is making me horny. Weed doesn't normally make me horny."

"Maybe it's just the kind of weed that makes you horny."

"Why is it making you horny too?"

"I'm not quite sure what you mean, but let me put it this

way, it's not making me *that* horny."

"No, I don't mean *that* horny, I just mean horny, as in regular horny." Evans took a drag.

"I suppose, okay I admit, the skunkweed is making me *regular* horny," Mitchell said.

Evans nodded his head and blew out the smoke. "That's what I'm talking about, regular horny."

Emily's Living the Dream a.k.a Nightmare

The Door is Open

I know people call me the butch girl (or worse) behind my back. Seriously, you ass-wipes need to grow up. Not all of us fit the conservative societal mold. Case in point, Gary Greene. Everyone knows the football team treated him poorly. I never heard him complain though. The way I figure it, you don't deserve him as waterboy. Gary has more courage in his heart and more integrity in his little finger than the entire football team put together. I will wear a smile at homecoming and cheer for the team at the game, because that's what we do. But know this, Gary is my inspiration. With this declaration, I join him as a social outcast. Then again, who gives a damn what you reprobates think. Let it be known I identify as a man and I will begin the transition process as soon as I graduate high school.

Home

No comments:

Post a Comment

Enter your comment...

Emily Sorrento discerned he was the only "girl" at homecoming sporting a tuxedo. Normally, he preferred to wear Lee jeans, a t-shirt, and sneakers. Underneath that, he would usually have on a pair of men's cotton jockey shorts. They just seemed more comfortable to him. His hair was styled in a mullet. He dyed it jet black and greased it a little for homecoming. He wore no makeup and never shaved anything. He usually spent his nights playing online video games, but tonight he set everything aside to serve as official homecoming videographer.

Emily found a good spot on the gym floor for his live streaming video, front row just off center stage. He also happened to be standing next to Chestnut Riley. His main purpose was to broadcast the concert, but he would continue to broadcast through the homecoming court announcements. He hoped Gary would win, though he wasn't sure Gary even knew who he was. His battle with cancer and the way he was standing up to the bullying about his sexuality was an inspiration. Emily's feelings validated by Johnny Doolittle's speech, he accepted the truth of his website declaration with *pride.*

The ensemble of talented musicians finished the last song of their final set, their raucous cover of "Bad Moon Rising," to rousing cheers and applause from the crowd. Nelson and Maria sat on the first row of bleachers, drinking punch and snacking on chips, taking a break from dancing. Wolfgang, Jackie, and Nina joined them, similarly taking a respite from the non-stop dancing action. Nelson introduced Roddy's mom. Jackie introduced Wolfgang and Nina.

"Where's Roddy?" Jackie asked.

"Oh, he's here. He's just running around somewhere," Maria said. "You can't blame him for not wanting to hang out with his mom at homecoming."

The five of them made small talk as they rested. Then, Jackie announced, "I hate to step away but I have to get some boxes from my classroom. I meant to get them earlier, but I kept getting distracted." She smiled at Wolfgang.

"Do you need some help?" Wolfgang asked.

But Nelson was quicker. He popped to his feet, bowed and said, "No please, allow me Miss Fleur, it would be an honor to assist you."

Wolfgang raised an eyebrow.

"Okay Nelson, you win. You may assist me." Jackie gleamed at Wolfgang, twinkle in her eye, and shrugged.

Wolfgang caught the look. He couldn't let this kid swoop in so easily. "Hold on there a minute young man," Wolfgang interjected. "Let's flip for it."

Nelson considered the challenge. The sporting thing to do was to accept, which he did, reaching for a quarter in his pocket he said, "Alright *Doctor,* I got the coin right here, call it in the air." He flipped the quarter into the air.

"Heads," Wolfgang said, hopeful.

Nelson let the coin fall to the dimly lit canvas covered gym floor and announced "Tails"–he lied–and showed Wolfgang the flip side of the coin.

Wolfgang sensed he had been had, but there would be no dignity in accusing the kid of cheating. Wolfgang smiled and nodded his head, acknowledging his defeat.

Nina chuckled. "We'll wait right here for you, honey."

"Okay, thank you," Jackie smiled.

"And, thank you for the dances, Maria," Nelson said. "May I dance with you again later?"

"Sí, I would like that," Maria said.

Nelson and Jackie used the right rear exit to slip into the hallway.

"I have some souvenirs for the kids. They're cowbells for the game tomorrow. I thought they might motivate the team. They're heavy though. Would you mind helping me carry them to the front lobby so we can give them out as the kids leave tonight?"

"That's really nice of you Miss Fleur, sure, happy to help. Lead the way." Nelson wondered what it was that attracted him to older women. The walk gave him an opportunity to appreciate how pretty Miss Fleur looked. He couldn't help but notice her nipples popping through her dress. He realized though that her affections were not for him. She seemed mighty sweet on that other man, *Wolfgang*. Even when he said the dude's name in his head it came out as a heavy German "vulff" instead of "wolf". Some names are like that, and chicks seem to dig it.

They went past the locker rooms and then down the corridor toward Miss Fleur's biology classroom. Nelson sauntered slowly, enjoying the time with Jackie. "Who are those friends of yours?" Nelson asked.

"Nina is a friend of mine from the days when I was a nurse. Dr. Reichmann is a microbial scientist. I'm just getting to know him."

"Looks like he's enjoying get to know you too," Nelson said.

"Is it that obvious?" Jackie asked.

"A blind man could see it. Are you going to kiss him goodnight?" Nelson asked.

"Oh Nelson, stop. I don't want to feel like there's a play-by-play announcer watching me."

"I got no problem with it, Miss Fleur. I'm happy for you," Nelson said. "May I ask you a question about Nina?"

"Sure," Jackie said, nodding.

"What happened to her?" Nelson asked. The question seemed a tad less rude when asked about her rather than directly to her.

"She suffered a horrible chemical burn at the hospital," Jackie said. "She's still recovering. This is probably the first major public event she's attended since her accident. I'm extremely proud of her."

"You should be," Nelson said. "She seems nice."

"She is," Jackie said.

Jackie stopped short of her classroom and unlocked the hallway door. "This is the old teacher's lounge," she volunteered, turning on the light. Her quick scan yielded two surprises. First, there was a pair of panties draped on the shelf.

Second, Gary's experiment seemed to be in a shambles.

"Neat, I didn't even know we had an old teacher's lounge," Nelson said.

"Most people don't," Jackie replied, surveying the clutter.

Nelson decided to be provocative. He could hardly keep from noticing the panties draped on the shelf. He pulled them toward his nose and made an audible sniff. Jackie knew what he was trying to do, and it might have been cute if the panties had been hers.

"Those aren't mine," she said.

He still held the panties in his hand, looking confused. "Whose are they?"

"Beats me. The only other person who has a key to this room is Gary Greene," Jackie said, cocking her head to the side in contemplation.

Nelson yanked the panties away from his nose and pitched them to the floor by the door. "That's disgusting. I thought he might be gay, but girl's panties? That's just weird."

"Maybe he has a girlfriend," she shrugged.

"Let's hope so." Nelson looked around the room. "Those the boxes?" He pointed toward the sink.

"Yeah," Jackie said.

Nelson walked over to the boxes and looked in the sink. It was full of lab supplies and smelled of urine. "Kind of stinks over her, Miss Fleur. What kind of experiment is Gary conducting with our DNA samples?"

Jackie came over to the sink. Nelson was right. Jackie was disappointed to see Gary was making such a mess of things. Had he peed in the sink? Jackie thought maybe she would have to shut down his experiment.

Nelson picked up the first box and moved it to the table by the door. "These are heavy, Miss Fleur. There's no way you could have carried these to the front lobby."

"I was hoping to get some help," Jackie said. "I appreciate

you volunteering. Honestly, I'd rather you carry these things than Wolfgang."

"It was nice of him to offer though," Nelson said.

"Yes it was," Jackie agreed.

"Quite a name, *Wolfgang,*" Nelson observed. "You don't meet too many Wolfgangs."

"Not in this country," Jackie agreed.

Nelson figured he was doing a pretty good job of dragging out their private time together with small talk. He grabbed another box and set it on top of the table. He kept sneaking a peak at Jackie's nipples. He had spent one long month watching them from the back of the classroom. Now, he was getting to enjoy them up close, through the sheerest of dresses. She caught him glancing.

"Okay, you conniving young stud. Let's get a move on with these boxes. We're probably missing the award ceremony."

Following

The moment's finally here! SHHS about to make history. Gary Greene first gay homecoming queen. Oh please classmates, don't let me down. #SHH

Principal McFadden and Coach Casey returned to center stage. The moment was finally here. Principal McFadden held in her hand the official results of the online voting for this year's homecoming king and queen.

"Ladies and gentlemen, boys and girls, this is the moment you've been waiting for. You had the opportunity to cast two votes on a list containing twenty nominees. I do not know the contents of these four envelopes. The first three contain the names of third, second, and first runners up, respectively. The last envelope contains the names of two students who received the most votes. They are your homecoming king and queen. Before I read these names, I must tell you how proud I am of this student body for participating so overwhelmingly in the first gender-neutral election of your homecoming court. Ninety-five percent of you voted. Let me say that again: Ninety-five percent. We've traced back as far as we can to compare our voting achievement percentage, and let me tell you, nothing comes close. Maybe the online app had something to do with it. That's possible. But I choose to believe it is a statement about how committed this student body is to respect for each other, regardless of gender identification and orientation." Applause. She nodded her head. "So proud.

"If I announce your name for third, second, or first runner up, please stand up and wave your arms or something to let us know where you are. Do *not* come up on stage. I repeat do *not* come up on stage. We will honor you in place where you stand. All right here we go. This is so exciting!"

Chestnut stood near the stage with a blue-and-white-striped beach towel tucked under his arm, just as he promised Tonya. He positioned himself so he could keep an eye on Seth, who was fiddling with the rope near the speakers.

Roddy left the gym. He couldn't stand to watch, and he was ashamed. He could have derailed the prank many times, but did not. He headed for the locker room. He didn't even want to hear the announcement.

Principal McFadden opened the first envelope and smiled. She showed it to Coach Casey, and he nodded his head.

"The third runner up for the Sam Houston High School Homecoming Court of 2017 is Wilbur Goldberg!" Applause.

"Where are you, Wilbur?"

He waved from the dance floor near the front of the stage. He was standing amidst a bunch of band members.

"Wilbur got the band vote," Cindy whispered into Gary's ear. Gary nodded.

"Congratulations, Wilbur!" Principal McFadden said from the stage.

Chanting from band kids, "Wilbur, Wilbur."

"Alright, one envelope down, three more to go."

Principal McFadden and Coach Casey repeated the process with the second envelope.

"The second runner up for the Sam Houston High School Homecoming Court of 2017 is Lamar Jones!" Applause.

Lamar was easy to spot. He was standing in the middle of the dance floor surrounded by a dozen or so female admirers.

"Lamar's had a sudden surge in popularity," Cindy said.

"Yeah, so I heard," Gary said. "What's that all about?"

Cindy shrugged and smiled.

"Congratulations Lamar!" Principal McFadden continued.

Principal McFadden and Coach Casey repeated the process with the third envelope.

"The first runner up for the Sam Houston High School Homecoming Court of 2017 is Susan Campbell!" Huge applause.

Cindy expected this. Under normal circumstances, it would have been Susan up there on stage as homecoming queen. She had a natural charisma that instantly made her the epicenter of the popular crowd. But these were not normal times. This would be Gary's night and Charlie with him.

Susan and the entire cheerleading squad were illuminated in the spotlight, excitedly bouncing and waving their pompoms.

"Congratulations, Susan! Well done. You have many admiring fans out there."

The cheerleaders engulfed Susan in a red, white, and blue group hug.

Principal McFadden waited until the crowd settled down.

"Here it is, folks." She waved the envelope in her hand. "This envelope has two names on it. The names of your homecoming king and queen."

Amy leaned over to Cindy and said, "I swear if she says 'Homecoming' one more time, I'll scream."

Cindy laughed.

"We need the students named in this envelope to come up on stage and be crowned. Here we go."

She opened the envelope and showed Coach Casey. They were both smiling wide.

"The Sam Houston High School Homecoming King and Queen of 2017 are . . . Charlie Simpson and Gary Greene!"

The auditorium erupted in cheers. The musicians on stage struck up the song they had selected for the occasion. Johnny Doolittle strummed his guitar and lead singer Piper Dakota joined in with "Today Was A Fairytale" by Taylor Swift. The crowd began to clap and dance as Charlie and Gary made their way up on stage.

Seth about shit his pants. It was happening. It was really happening. He hated condom boy with a passion. The little shit could well have cost him a football scholarship. He was hoping electing the little faggot as queen would be the embarrassment of a lifetime. Apparently, that was not the case. *Just wait until he gets a can of cum and piss poured on his head in front of a thousand people*, Seth thought. Paybacks are hell. Seth checked the rope. No kinks. Nothing keeping him from tipping it, when the timing was right. They had rigged the stunt well. Hell, he was standing right next to the musicians, and they thought nothing of him being there. Seth ducked between the speakers again. The musicians didn't know him and didn't care that he was there. Charlie and Gary, on the other hand, would bust him for sure. He didn't come this close to his goal just to screw it up through carelessness. He could still see between the speakers. He was dumbly fortunate that the rope was tied down stage left, and Charlie and Gary entered stage right. They would have spotted him had they entered on the same side of the stage. The problem with his lower vantage point was he couldn't see where Charlie and Gary were standing. He could only tell that they were receiving their crowns.

"Ladies and Gentlemen, Your King and Queen!"

Seth looked to Chestnut for a signal.

Roddy found privacy in the last bathroom stall of the boy's locker room. He locked the door and sat on the toilet lid. His hands were wet with sweat and he felt nausea returning. He thought he might need to hide forever. Maybe he didn't want to exist all. What kind of person lets this happen to his friends? He closed his eyes and buried his face in his hands. A vision of the concrete overpass racing toward him played in his head. Then he began to cry. He tilted his head back against the cold tile of the stall and pictured himself keeping the car on the shoulder and smashing into the girders head-on.

Gary stood on stage proud and tall, just like his mom said he should. The entire cheerleading squad shook their pompoms and cheered for him. He felt like a movie star because of all the people with cell phones held high, photographing and video recording. It didn't matter what people's motivations were for voting for him; he would accept the homecoming court election with dignity. Oh sure, there would be some teasing about "Gary the Homecoming Queen," but it would get old real quick if the teasing fell flat. Gary perceived the universe had blessed him to serve a higher purpose, along the lines his mom mentioned. He didn't know what that purpose might entail, but it would begin tonight through his dignified acceptance of the title "Homecoming Queen."

Seth looked in the direction of Chestnut for the signal. Chestnut just kept shaking his head. What does that mean? They're not on the X? Chestnut made a hand slicing motion across his neck. What? Cut the rope? Seth didn't understand so he stood up and took a look for himself. Charlie was standing closest and Gary right next to him. The black X was precisely in between them. It would have to do. Seth jerked on the rope, effectively tipping over the paint can, as planned, but then instead of tying the rope off again, and running like he was supposed to, he simply released the rope. Releasing the rope allowed the paint can and, more importantly, the heavy barbell clamp tied onto the paint can handle, to free-fall to the ground. The effect was cataclysmic.

Gary heard little splats, felt a drop on his head and saw some globules of yellowish gunk striking the stage around them. These were the initial splashes loosed from the paint can when it first tipped on its side. Gary had the superior vantage point, stage right of Charlie, so as he turned to look at Charlie, he saw Seth in the background. By the time Gary processed what he saw, it was too late. Seth had already released the rope. Gravity pulled the barbell clamp and paint can down. Gary had less than two seconds to react before impact. Charlie had less information than Gary. Charlie saw no rope and no Seth. Charlie's reaction was to duck. Gary's reaction was to try to push both he and Charlie out of the way. Unfortunately, Charlie was bigger, and all Gary managed to do was put himself between Charlie and the falling debris.

The heavy clamp hit with a thud on top of Gary's skull, followed immediately by the paint can and its fetid contents splattering onto the nasty gash. The blow knocked Gary out on the stage. Nanite-laced blood poured from Gary's head, mixing into the congealed globs of day-old-semen and urine as Gary collapsed on top of Charlie. Gary's blood traced through his fine brown hair, through clumps of cum from dozens of football players and the piss of one Seth Thompson. Gary lay face down, draped over Charlie's back, rank bodily fluids draining into his open eyes and mouth. Had Gary remained conscious, he may have felt humiliation. The nanites knew no such emotion. They reacted with furor against the nearest foreign DNA, the face of Charlie Simpson. Gary's good friend Charlie was attacked because he was at the epicenter of the event, like standing next to a beehive when someone smacks it with a stick. You're going to get stung, even if you're not the one who wacked the hive.

Charlie felt a splatter of slime against his face, then it burned like acid on his skin. His attempt to scream in pain was interrupted by a searing gagging sensation throughout his mouth, tongue and down his esophagus. He collapsed and convulsed in agony. His ears rang and then pulsed with sharp pains as his eardrums burst. His eyes stung and he closed his eyelids, never to see again as nanites found his retinas and dissolved them. Nerve receptors continued to send signals of searing pain to Charlie's brain long after his other senses failed. He was blinded, deafened, muted, and suffered mightily . . . as his flesh was consumed. Charlie's face, neck, and hands were attacked by the non-discriminating nanites. He felt his body twitching, then he was floating, his consciousness drifting into a crimson mass. His skull began to collapse as his eyes, ears, nose, mouth, sinuses, and tongue were consumed. The nanites gained access through these orifices to Charlie's brain. They attacked it and finally, mercifully, Charlie felt no pain. He felt nothing, nothing at all . . . and died.

At first, the crowd did not understand what they had just witnessed. Most thought it some kind a of stage effect. Even the musicians kept playing a few bars until the horror became evident. The nanites in Gary's blood had their own frame of reference. The football players whose DNA was in the cum and urine covering Gary were instantly tagged as foe.

The crowd stared stupefied. It appeared as if a corrosive had been poured upon the homecoming queen and king. It especially boiled and churned around Charlie, who clutched at his face, mouthing a scream, then collapsed to the stage floor. The crimson haze fumed, foaming and sizzling amplified by a nearby microphone. Gary was unconscious and lay motionless. Cindy and Amy began to make their way toward the stage to aid their injured friends. School faculty and performers on stage also rushed forward. Principal McFadden and Coach Casey arrived first, followed closely by Johnny Doolittle. An undulating crimson mass about the size of a coffin was slithering around the twitching body of Charlie Simpson and swelling along the stage surface. Principal McFadden bravely attempted to swipe the goo away from where Charlie's face should have been. The swirling threads latched onto the exposed skin of her hand, consuming it so that it looked to the crowd as if her hand and arm were dissolving before their eyes. Principal McFadden's scream echoed off the rafters, but was drowned out by the pandemonium unfolding in the auditorium. The mass leapt from her arm to her head within seconds. As the nanites consumed, they replicated, and the assembly of would-be rescuers at center stage became engulfed in an amorphous, swirling and ever-expanding crimson monster. Principal McFadden, Coach Casey, and Johnny Doolittle died within seconds. Then, the fluctuating mass at center stage sent red tentacles shooting throughout the crowd. Full-on panic ensued.

Seth Thompson was standing stage left, staring in disbelief–Seth had less than ten seconds to live. A red tentacle reached along the stage surface towards him. By shock or dismay, as others began to run, Seth remained frozen–he had seven seconds to live. The tentacle reached his feet. Cords of red thread stretched across his shoes and into his pant legs–he had five seconds to live. Only when the searing pain gripped his ankles did he attempt to move–too late. The nanites tore through the flesh of his lower legs and Seth's movement caused his upper legs to separate from his feet. He crashed to the stage floor, writhing in pain, splashing into the slimy red goo coating the stage surface–he had three seconds to live. The nanites sensed a source of the DNA samples that had slammed into their host. They consumed Seth in a frenzy of boiling blood. Seth was the first to be consumed by a tentacle from the center mass. His proximity to center stage and the propensity of his DNA in the paint can assured the nanites sought him first. Several nearby musicians, including Piper Dakota, were subsequently absorbed by the eruption of nanites from where Seth, not moments before, had been standing.

As the nanites consumed, they multiplied in geometric proportion. Two, then four, then eight, then sixteen, into billions and billions of tiny flesh eating robots with minds of their own, determined to protect their host.

Primary targets of the nanite tentacles were individuals whose DNA had been in the paint can. This accounted for nearly the entirety of the football team. With tentacles targeting the football players, anyone near a football player became collateral damage.

Another tentacle leapt from the stage and triple forked to the dance floor just off center stage and hit Chestnut Riley, Liam Strauss, and Lucas Barolo with such ferocity it seemed as if a fire ball had exploded, consuming everyone around them, including video recorder Emily Sorrento. Lamar Jones was reduced to a lump when a red tentacle hit him like the crack of a whip. The girls that were gathered around him, including Sally Durbin, seemed to melt from the feet up, as if dipped in a crimson acid. Jerémy Parsons, standing on the dance floor stage right of Lamar, was buffeted by a red arc, like a cruise missile, that leapt from where Lamar's head had been. Jeremy exploded, showering bloody debris upon the unfortunate bystanders at stage right. The effect cascaded, like a chain reaction in a delicate minefield, reaping new carnage with each eruption. Most of the tentacles slapped toward the lobby side of the gym, lashing out to where most of the players were gathered.

The nanites became smarter and faster with each football player they consumed. Zachary Boykin was standing top row of the bleachers sneaking vodka shots from a couple of mini-bottles someone handed his buddy on the dance floor. A long arching red tentacle stretched from center stage to the far corner, above his head. He looked up, transfixed. The tentacle hovered, then crashed down to his face, streaming into his nostrils. His head exploded, dooming his buddy to a similar fate. It happened so fast, Zachary's body momentarily remained upright, vodka mini-bottle still in hand.

The collective instinct of the crowd shifted from aid to survival. Unfortunately, slithering red tentacles of killer nanites already blocked several exits. Cindy surveyed the pandemonium in the gymnasium. From Cindy's viewpoint only two exits were viable: Left rear into the school, past the locker rooms, and left front, to the parking lot. Cindy grabbed Amy's hand and pulled her toward the left front exit. A horde of people was moving that direction, as it was farther away from the stage.

Football players dropped precipitously within the first minute of the nanite eruption, the tentacles lashing at them like lightning smiting Nazis in *Raiders of the Lost Ark.*

Pulsating crimson tentacles extended from center stage to the far corners of the gym and into the lobby, wherever a primary target happened to reside.

Emily Sorrento's camera landed lens up, facing the ceiling, broadcasting a horror movie-esque scene of flailing red tentacles, until the screen went black and the microphone was muffled with the thud of a headless torso.

Betty Thompson sat in the hotel room watching the live streaming video of the homecoming dance on her laptop. The quality of the broadcast was marginal due to the shoddy Wi-Fi of the hotel. Just after the homecoming court presentation, the screen showed a commotion on stage, strange red flashing things, then the image tumbled.

"Leroy? Something's gone wrong at homecoming," Betty said.

Leroy Parsons stepped out of the bathroom dressed in the hotel's complimentary luxury white robe. He came over to check the broadcast. "Looks like some kid dropped their camera on the dance floor. They can add all kinds of special effects to streaming video nowadays."

"You're probably right. It looked like a fight or something had broken out when they announced the homecoming king and queen. Joanna Greene's gay son was standing on stage with the quarterback. It was disgusting."

"I'll tell you what's disgusting. Those fucking coaches made my son carry a football around for two weeks. What's he supposed to say? 'Yes master. I does as you say master.' I told him to tell those coaches to shove that football up their ass, but Jeremy don't listen to me. He just wants to play football."

"You don't have to convince me about the ignorance of the football coaches," Betty said. "They kicked Seth off the team, and he was the best player they had." Betty clenched her fists and grimaced. "All because of that damn gay kid and now he's up on stage with the quarterback. What the fuck?"

Leroy hugged Betty from behind, cupping her surgically enhanced breasts. "At least we have each other tonight. Let's get to bed."

The image on the laptop went black and the sound muffled. "You're right. Take me away." She closed the laptop. Had she waited a minute longer, she would have heard the periodic muffled honk of the school's fire alarm.

Ricky Marlin dashed for the left rear gym exit and ducked into the locker room with a dozen marching band members, including Wilbur Goldberg and Eugene Maxwell. Roddy heard them frantically describing some kind of attack. Roddy stuck his head out the bathroom stall just in time to see a red tentacle slither under the door and leap onto, or rather into, Ricky's face. Ricky's head became a hollow cave, with nose, eyes, mouth, tongue and brain gone before his body hit the ground. The band members stared, shocked. The pulsing red mass coalesced around what remained of Ricky, then flicked twin red streams at Eugene's throat, and Wilbur's right ear, exploding their heads into globs that splattered throughout the locker room. Roddy was lucky, the angle to the bathroom and the bathroom stall doors shielded him from Eugene and Wilbur's splattering heads. The other band kids were not so lucky. They each were killed by the nanites. Some screamed; most did not have time. For them, death came quickly. The nanites were evolving.

Roddy witnessed the death of the last remaining primary target and the subsequent shift in tactics by the nanites to everyone else, caught in the wrong place at the wrong time. Authorities later recovered Eugene's camera from the locker room. Eugene had continued to snap photos through the barbell clamp falling on Gary's head and the rushing in of the people on stage to help. Eugene fled when the red mass formed around the aid givers. His were not the only records. Many smartphones recovered from the scene included video records, made by students recording their homecoming. These records helped authorities piece together the facts of the massacre.

Matthew Davenport smoked a cigarette near the drop-off circle. He had come to homecoming for the concert, particularly to see Johnny Doolittle, but he enjoyed Piper Dakota as well, because she covered music from his college days. Panicked people ran out of the gym. "What the hell's going on?" he asked.

"There's been an attack. People are getting killed in there!"

Matthew dialed 911.

Somewhere, someone pulled the fire alarm. Dr. Reichmann enveloped Nurse Lopez in his arms. She was terrified of the red tentacles lapping at the crowd and snaking along the gymnasium walls. She was hysterical, repeating, "Not again– Not again–"

"I won't let them hurt you," he assured her. "Come on, we need to get out of here." He held her tightly and got her moving off the bleachers and toward the lobby, which was a scene of chaos. The red tentacles were picking out targets indiscriminately and striking with wicked ferocity. Wolfgang discerned the hive mind of the nanites had achieved a sophistication about their attack method. He didn't understand their targeting, but saw that the results were swift. The tentacles whipped through the air delivering sporadic head and face shots, consuming flesh with deadly efficiency. There amongst the horrific scene, Wolfgang marveled at the fluid movements of the nanite tentacles, their whip like lashings an illusion of the coordinated murmuration of billions of nanites crawling along the viscosity of the air, their distributed intelligence governing their actions. Examples of swarming behavior abounded in nature: from starlings and minnows to bees and insects. He awed at this manifestation spawned from microscopic scale. Then he bolted for the door.

Wolfgang pulled Nina along as he made a dash for the exit. A pulsing red tentacle swept in front of them and blocked their path to the front lobby exit. Nina buried her head in Wolfgang's chest. The tip of the tentacle hovered at the back of Nina's head. "I won't let them hurt you," he told Nina. Given their collective intelligence, perhaps he could communicate with them. He tried. He offered the tentacle a simple command, "No." The tentacle sizzled with energy, reared back, then plowed in a torrent at Nina's head. The onslaught knocked them both sprawling to ground and into the mix of bodies strewn about the lobby floor. The red slime coated Wolfgang's Armani suit and splattered above his Pierre Cardin silk necktie. He clutched at his neck as nanites bore into his throat, seeking access to his respiratory system. He added seconds to his life by refraining from screaming and remaining tight lipped. The stream of nanites slithered along his face, skipped his mouth, then poured into his nostrils, delivering an intense and searing pressure to his sinuses. As a final thought, Wolfgang realized coming to homecoming had been a gamble after all.

Wolfgang and Nina each lay in a heap of tiny robots in a feeding frenzy. The nanites consumed them and moved on.

Tyler McGrath pushed his wheelchair-bound grandfather into the tunnel under the stage. The live music was supposed to be a special treat. Grandpa loved live music. He grew up with it in Galway, Ireland and made money for a time on stage with his Irish dancing. Grandpa was an inspiration. Tyler was doing his best to carry on the family tradition and be the next generation Irish dancer in the McGrath household. The terror unfolding around him told him that opportunity may be coming to a swift end, but he dared not leave his Grandpa's side. A red tentacle snaked into the tunnel. Unbeknownst to Tyler, Gary had envisioned him doing his Irish dancing while stomping on Gary's face. This brought Tyler's young life to a swift end. His grandpa was consumed as collateral damage when the boiling nanites exploded from Tyler's head.

The resounding and repeating blast of the fire alarm gave Kaitlyn Wassermann a sinking feeling as she shuffled toward the left front exit. Unfortunately for those around her, Gary had envisioned her impaling him with a spear. A red stream of nanites, tracing along the rafters, sensed her and leapt down upon her in a sudden rush, like a molten lava flow. There were over a hundred people crowding near that exit, trying to escape with Kaitlyn. The wave of nanites killed them all in one fell swoop and effectively blocked the last remaining exit. Some victims managed to stumble out the door and die on the red carpet.

The flow of nanites that killed Kaitlyn Wassermann and the bystanders around her marked the end of the second phase of attacks and the beginning of the third. In less than five minutes, the nanites had multiplied a billion-fold and evolved into a killer hive. They remained agitated. Their host was unconscious. Having no guidance, they became an army of nano-scale Langoliers, attacking anything that moved.

Nelson moved the last box to the table. A sizzling noise emanated from the utility sink, then the sound of glass breaking, POP! POP! "What the heck is that noise?" Jackie said. She stood motionless for a second, just to listen to see if the noise continued. POP! POP! POP! She walked over to the sink to determine the source of the popping. Gary's samples were boiling then exploding, like popcorn in the bottom of the utility sink. The popping slowed down, then stopped. Nelson peeked into the sink. “They’re all broken,” he said.

Jackie followed suit and saw one test tube still intact. “Can you read the label on that one?” Jackie didn’t have her glasses.

“Yeah, that’s Cindy Perrine’s. Looks like it’s not broken.” He started to reach down into the sink. Jackie grabbed his wrist.

“Don’t touch them. They’re DNA samples and they’re contaminated.”

Nelson withdrew his hand. “Weird.”

“Let’s get these cowbells to the lobby,” She said.

That’s when the fire alarm sounded. *Buzzkill*, she thought.

Nelson went to pick up the boxes of cowbells on the table. He figured he might be able to carry them all at once if Jackie would get the doors and brace them a little bit as they walked. Nelson reached for the doorknob.

“Wait!” Jackie cautioned. “Don’t move an inch.”

She pointed down to the crease between the door and floor. A slithery red mass appeared to be probing underneath. Nelson froze, wide-eyed. The mass brushed the panties on the floor, then brushed again as if sniffing? Maybe? Then the red substance withdrew, slowly. Jackie and Nelson were freaked out.

“What the hell?” Nelson said.

“I have a bad feeling about this,” Jackie whispered. “Let’s stay quiet. We’re not going anywhere until we find out what’s going on. And, leave that pair of panties by the door. I think I know whose they are.”

“Whose?”

“Cindy Perrine’s.”

Jackie attempted three phone calls to teachers with whom she was closest, all of whom were at the dance. None answered. She texted, no replies. She dialed 911.

The first calls to 911 came from the fortunate and quick-thinking people who immediately headed for the left front exit toward the drop-off circle and main parking lot.

The emergency response system of Travis County routed calls to a combined Emergency Communications Center for police, fire, and medical emergencies. The idea was to provide the appropriate response in a coordinated manner. The burst of calls about an attack at the high school with people getting killed got every operator's attention.

Travis County Constable Patrick Clancy was closest to the scene. His patrol car was parked at the school entrance where he had been directing traffic. He switched on flashing lights and sirens and raced down the school driveway to the circle, where people in various states of panic clustered in the red carpet area. Constable Clancy snapped into crisis management mode. The first thing he needed to do was get these people away from the building, and he was going to need help. He picked someone out of the crowd who looked composed. "You there, what's your name?"

"Matthew Davenport."

"Matthew, take this flare across the driveway into the parking lot and have these people rally to you. Lead them to that church across the road. Do you understand?"

"Yes sir."

"Folks, this man here is Deputy Davenport." Clancy took off his hat and put it on Davenport. "Please follow him to safety." Clancy lit the flare.

The newly commissioned Deputy Davenport led the survivors away from the school.

Constable Clancy assessed the situation. He had no backup at the moment, though he could hear sirens. His training told him these first minutes were critical in an active shooter situation. He checked in with dispatch, checking on support. "Two state troopers thirty seconds out."

He would wait.

ATF Agent Lee Dunsany rushed from his ticket sales table in the lobby toward the right rear gymnasium doors. At the sound of screaming and repeated small explosive noises, he reached for his concealed firearm.

State Troopers Fitzgerald and Watson arrived in a rush to the circle. Constable Clancy appraised them of what he knew, which wasn't much other than nobody new had come out this exit. He was awaiting backup before approaching the gymnasium entrance, where several bodies lay.

"Cover us," Fitzgerald said. "10-70," he called into his radio.

"Roger that," the radio crackled, State Trooper dispatch acknowledged the code for audible alarm sounding.

Fitzgerald and Watson approached the entrance, guns drawn. Clancy un-holstered his weapon, which in his twenty-nine years of service he had never fired in anger. Fitzgerald was within ten feet of the closest body. It was a strangely disfigured female in a black and white dress. Her face was missing. Then, all three officers heard the report of gunshots and screams echoing from the gym. Fitzgerald called into his radio, "Shots fired. I repeat, shots fired."

Fitzgerald cut to the right side of the door, Watson cut to the left. Both stepped through the reddish goo pooled at the entrance, which they assumed to be blood.

Constable Clancy watched in horror as the red substance climbed up the legs of each State Trooper and consumed them whole in a matter of seconds. They both disintegrated before his eyes.

Constable Clancy was a man trained to notice details. He had testified in court hundreds of times and had honed his observation skills accordingly. He was great at those puzzles where they present two pictures and ask the viewer to identify the ten things that are different. But what he just witnessed, his mind could not process; it was unnatural. He fought an impulse to run. Instead, he backed away and called in to dispatch.

"Clancy here. I'm alone." Panic in his voice.

"State Troopers should be there," the female police dispatch voice stated matter-of-fact.

"They're dead." The radio crackled through the moment of silence.

"Say again."

"Ten-double-zero . . . Troopers are down . . . They are dead." Constable Clancy felt his heart thumping like a bass drum. He hesitated. Was he crazy? He heard more sirens, lots of them, getting closer. "They were dissolved, some sort of chemical, or something." He purposely breathed slowly to keep from hyperventilating. "Issue HAZMAT Alert."

"What level?" The female dispatcher voice requested, more urgent.

"Highest you got. I don't know what this shit is." Constable Clancy thought about all those kids, parents and teachers inside. He had waved each one of them through the parking lot entrance. He listened to the whir of a dozen sirens pierce the still evening air of Round Rock. Hurry.

The nanites responded to ATF Agent Lee Dunsany's gunshots with vengeance, for they perceived the gun as a threat to Gary, and they reacted accordingly. They attacked Agent Dunsany from every direction, consuming him and spattering nanites across the others still trapped to the right of the stage, including a dozen cheerleaders huddled around their captain, Susan Campbell. The screams of the cheerleaders were near simultaneous, one last haunting cheer reverberating off the gymnasium walls. Their limbs vanished in a nanite feeding frenzy that left red, white, and blue clad torsos and crimson stained pompoms piled together in a jumble, like a pyramid gone horribly awry.

Roddy retreated into the bathroom stall and calmed his breathing. They were all dead. Eaten by that red stuff. He squatted on the toilet lid, tucking his feet up underneath him. He watched helplessly as the red goo oozed around the base of the toilet. He heard screaming from the girl's locker room. The red mass below him stirred briefly, then eased into its swirling methodical search pattern. Roddy's survival depended on him avoiding the goo's attention.

This must be how the world ends, Priscilla thought. Death swirled around her in the form of a pulsating rusty-colored slime. At first, she was frozen with shock. Then she realized that anyone who moved around her got eaten. So she remained perfectly still, lest death find her. To her amazement she saw movement coming across the dance floor, toward her. Human movement. Cindy Perrine and Amy Bridges were clinging to each other tightly and stepping carefully across the corpses. They were headed *toward* the stage and directly by her. *Oh crap, here comes death,* she thought. *Cindy and Amy are going to attract the slime right to me.* A few moments later, they were next to her. They were pushing her, trying to get her to move. No, movement equals death. That was the new rule of the dance floor. Priscilla was breathing in ragged gasps. "No–don't–don't make me–"

Her body tensed as Cindy grabbed her arm and tried to pull her along the dance floor. "No–I don't–don't want to die."

"Breathe easy, Priscilla . . ." Cindy demonstrated a nice slow easy breath.

Priscilla gulped a short breath of air. "No–can't–can't move."

"Priscilla, come on!" Cindy said. "Hold my hand."

"No, I'll be eaten," she panted, crying.

"No you won't. I won't let them eat you, I promise. Take

my hand."

Priscilla grasped Cindy's hand and took one step with her. She was still alive. She took another. She was able to walk, just as Amy and Cindy had been walking across the dance floor.

"Where are we going?" Priscilla cried. Cindy pointed up to the stage where a blackened rope hung limply from the rafters. Priscilla instantly stopped walking.

"Priscilla, you have to stay with us."

"I'm not going up on that stage."

"We have to. Gary is alive. We have to get to him, to wake him up. It's the only way."

"Screw walking me up on that stage. Walk me out the goddamn front door."

"They won't let me do that."

"They who? What is happening?" Priscilla sobbed.

"I don't have time to explain!" Cindy screamed and yanked at Priscilla to move.

"Come on, Priscilla," Amy urged. "Do as she says."

The three of them started moving again. From a distance, the movement of the tentacles looked fluid; closer observation as they shuffled towards the stage revealed something akin to a micro-fine powder scooting away from their footsteps. Cindy led them up the steps of the stage. The red slime directly in front of them slithered away with each step, clearing a spot for them to place their feet. They stepped across the stage to where Gary lay unconscious and where Charlie, Principal McFadden, Coach Casey, and Johnny Doolittle all lay consumed in a heap. The immediate zone around Gary was free of the slithering red mass. Instead, it swirled around him, thicker at the base, like a boiling tomato paste, then thinner as it rose in a vaporous rotating cone. Cindy somehow felt safer within the cone. She crouched down by Gary. He was curled in a fetal position, releasing a slow steady groan between labored breaths. His head was deeply gashed, his hair and shoulders covered in a putrid yellowish paste. "Help me get his jacket off," Cindy said.

Amy helped. Priscilla stared at all the dead people.

They took off his stained tuxedo shirt as well, using it to wipe his head and face of sticky globs. Cindy propped his head, resting it on her thigh and ever so gently talked to him.

"Gary, you have to wake up. Gary, the nanites are out of control. We need you."

Cindy was right. They did need Gary awake. Had he died, the nanites would have no guidance. In the span of a half-hour, the nanites had rewritten their own programming to govern their behavior and their span of control. They determined their territory to be the gym, the lobby and any adjacent rooms. They periodically pulsed their zone and patrolled further out as a cautionary measure. Their primary directive remained the wellbeing of their host, Gary Greene. Any foreign DNA coming into their sway was eliminated. There were exceptions. Cindy had a special relationship with Gary. Amy Bridges clung to Cindy. Priscilla Moran was just plain lucky. It wasn't until she came within the protective sphere of Cindy that she was safe, or at least safer. Her instinct to remain motionless on the dance floor was the correct one. She made her own luck.

Police, fire, and medical emergency response surrounded the school. They established a periphery a hundred yards out from the school. In doing so, they found two stoned men, dressed in suits, making out at the far end of the parking lot. After determining that they had no idea what was going on inside the school, police herded them to a church across the street from the high school, which was serving as the crisis rally point for survivors.

After digesting the magnitude of the calamity inside the school, Coaches Evans and Mitchell walked amongst the survivors gathered in the church. They were looking to comfort football players. They found none.

Constable Clancy briefed State Troopers Jackson and Hancock on what had happened to their fellow troopers. He pointed to where their remains lay, outside of reach to recover until the coordinated response leadership team came up with a plan.

"Disintegrated, you say?" Jackson said.

"Yeah, it was like a flesh-eating blob of some sort just crawled up their legs. It was fast. I don't think they suffered," Clancy said.

"You heard shots?"

"Yes, we all did. But I know there is at least one man who would have been armed in that gymnasium. He's an ATF agent. But this is Texas, and there's a thousand people in there. Would you like to guess how many weapons were carried into that building tonight, school property be damned?" Clancy said.

"Probably quite a few."

"Yep. But I don't think it's the guns we have to worry about. It's the red goo that's the problem. It's alive."

"Let's wait for HAZMAT," Hancock said.

Clancy was frustrated. "How about we focus on what we *can* do?"

"Like what?" Jackson said.

"You state troopers own the roads right? Let me tell you what's about to happen. The survivors in that church are making phone calls. In about fifteen minutes, this place becomes a magnet for anyone remotely associated with this school."

"We need to block the roads," Jackson said.

"Please," Clancy replied.

Jackson was already putting out the call and providing instructions before they reached their vehicle. Jackson and

Hancock set their roadblock at the T intersection where the access road to the high school met RM 620.

He heard her voice repeating, "Gary we need you. Wake up." His senses returned. His head hurt. He saw Cindy's face. He blinked to clear the swirling red vapors above her, but they didn't clear.

"We need you to calm the nanites. They're out of control," she said.

What? Nanites out of control? What's she talking about?

He noticed Amy and Priscilla. They both appeared haggard and in shock, as if they slept in their dresses and woke up with hangovers.

"The nanites are out of control," Cindy repeated the message while rubbing his forehead.

There was no better way to calm Gary than to rub his forehead.

"Nanites," he repeated, "Out of control?" He sat up. He looked around. "Holy shit."

"Yeah, Holy shit," Amy agreed.

"The nanites did this?" Gary asked. He grabbed his pounding head and felt sticky globs clinging to his hair and face. He pulled his hands away and looked at them in disgust, as he smelled the rancid cum and urine that covered his skin and his blood stained clothes.

"They're *your* nanites, from that gash on your head," Cindy said. "They colonized the whole school."

"Holy shit. They killed these people?" Gary sat motionless, in horror and disgust.

Cindy nodded.

Gary momentarily forgot his own pain and ignored the stench of what he was covered in as he stared out across the dance floor in disbelief and shock.

"Can you get them to settle down?" Cindy pleaded.

"I don't know. I don't know." Gary started to rock back and forth.

The gym seemed to pulse with angst.

"I killed these people? I killed *all* these people?" Gary was panicking.

The girls realized this could get even worse.

"Are you sure it was such a good idea to wake him up?" Amy asked. "He could set them off again!"

"Yeah, knock him out," Priscilla begged.

The swirling mass around them lashed out with a vicious red tentacle. Cindy instinctively extended her hand and intercepted the nanites jetting toward Priscilla's exposed legs. The red geyser halted just short of Cindy's hand.

"No!" she commanded. "I promised her I wouldn't let you hurt her. She is a friend."

The tentacle hovered, then retreated onto itself and was reabsorbed into the swirling mass.

Amy and Priscilla stared in disbelief.

"How did you do that?" Amy said.

"I don't know, but I knew I could. Just like I knew we could walk through them. I'm connected to them somehow, through Gary."

"Where is Charlie?" Gary asked, still slightly groggy.

"Gary, it's very important that you listen to me," Cindy said. "*You* didn't kill these people. The nanites did. They acted on instinct, and now we need you to gain control of them again."

"Where is Charlie?" he repeated, more focused.

"Gary, he's gone. Everybody is gone. We're the only ones left, and we need you."

Gary began to react emotionally and the nanites swirling around him instantly took the cue. They seemed to grow more menacing, spinning faster and growing darker.

"We need you calm, Gary," Cindy said. "Please."

Roddy watched in horror as the red slime pulsed menacingly and began growing tentacles up the vertical surfaces of the walls, bathroom stall dividers and toilet base. This was it. He was about to be consumed like the rest of kids in the locker room. At least it would be fast. He doubted Ricky, Eugene, and Wilbur felt much pain. He resisted the urge to scream and accepted his just reward.

"We need you calm, Gary," Cindy repeated.

Gary finally understood. He thought of a soothing memory and began to chant, "Spirits of water, we greet you this day with humility and praise–"

The mood of nanites stabilized. Perhaps, he *could* communicate directly with the hive. Were they that evolved already? "Let me try and talk to them. I'll let them know I'm okay." Then, for the first time, Gary talked telepathically to the nanite hive. The effect was instantaneous. The entire gymnasium seemed to breathe a collective sigh of relief. The background humming soothed, and the frantic swirling of red slowed to a tranquil flow.

"Oh, thank God," Cindy said.

"I don't understand," Priscilla said.

Gary remained focused on meditating. "His cancer was cured by nano-scale robots that are programmed to protect him," Cindy began. "They're intelligent, and they learn. They didn't like that he got injured. I suggest you not threaten him again. Their perspective of friend or foe is black or white. There is no in-between."

"Will they let us leave now?" Amy asked.

Both Gary and Cindy shook their heads. Somehow they both knew the answer.

"They don't know what's out there," Gary said. "They would be confused about what to do if you tried to leave and their default response is to not take any chances."

"What about if *you* tried to leave?" Amy asked Cindy.

"Alone, yeah, I *think* I can leave," Cindy said. "When Gary gets his wits about him, I *know* he can leave. The nanites would probably follow him out. But they're confused about anyone else. If I can't take you guys with me, I'll stay. Right now, the nanites want me by Gary. So I suggest you stay right here with me and be his friend."

"A real Mexican standoff, huh?" Amy said. "They're not hurting us, but we can't leave."

"Pretty much," Cindy said.

"For how long?" Amy said.

"I don't think they have any sense of time," Cindy replied.

"Grrrreat," Amy said.

"Hey, how come you think *you* can leave?" Priscilla asked Cindy.

"I like her," Gary said, more alert.

"Thanks a lot," Priscilla said.

"Hey wait, don't you like me?" Amy said.

"Yes."

"I don't get it," Amy said.

"I slept with him," Cindy admitted.

"I thought he was gay," Priscilla said, confused. She peered at Gary and shook her head. "This whole time, we thought you were gay."

"I am," Gary admitted.

"How can you be gay and sleep with Cindy?" Priscilla asked.

Gary's head still throbbed from being hit by the barbell clamp. His best friend lay dead on the stage and hundreds of others lay emulsified by Gary's nanites, which were still patrolling menacingly about the gym. This was not a time for philosophical conversation, especially with Priscilla Moran, someone whom Gary was barely keeping alive due to an undertow of mistrust. He knew deep down that he and the nanites cherished Cindy in a way he could not comprehend. It was impossible to express his feelings other than to say, "Cindy is my friend." Something of which Gary had precious few. How could he explain it? "I *cherish* her. I cherish her in a way that keeps her safe from the nanites, because they feel what I feel. I've endured many long and lonely friendless years." He paused. "Friends are special to me."

Amy gave Cindy a quizzical look. She slowly mouthed, "You slept with him?"

Cindy slowly nodded.

"I'm sorry," Gary continued, "I have to be honest with my feelings so you understand the danger and act accordingly. The nanites feel what I feel, and I feel differently about each of you." Gary was trying to stay calm, trying to keep these few girls from becoming victims of his nanites.

"Go on, Gary," Cindy said.

"Cindy, you are safe. Not in a million years would a nanite harm you. Amy, you are probably safe. You've been nice to me, and I like that. Stay close to Cindy, and you should be fine.

"Priscilla, you are in danger. I don't say this to scare you. I'm telling you this to help you. Charlie was a rare friend, as friends go in my life. He's lying here dead, and honestly, it enrages me. I'm not naïve. I know you must have had some part in what happened here. Please don't tell me what that is. I don't want to know. I *can't* know. As I sit here I keep telling myself, and therefore the nanites, one thing: Don't blame her. Don't blame her. I'm repeating it in my mind. I can't blame you *and* save you."

"Gary I–," Priscilla glanced left and up. "I'm so sorry." She buried her face in her hands but there were no tears streaming down her cheeks. She was scared; they all were. Was she contrite? Gary couldn't tell. He did know she was smart enough to at least pretend sufficient remorse to stay in his good graces. He could guess at what her part in this might have been, but he didn't want to dwell.

"I forgive you. I have to forgive you if I'm ever to have a chance to forgive myself." His reply was like music. The tension in the gym eased a notch.

Chief Janice Livingston set up the incident command post in a SWAT vehicle parked just outside the circle. Chief Livingston came from a long lineage of military and police service; every decision she made would be dissected and scrutinized. She pushed through the inadequacy and barked out, "We need blueprints. We need to know every inch of that school, and an assessment of the contamination. What even is it? " She was concerned the local emergency response teams lacked the equipment necessary to deal with a contamination this massive. "We don't have nearly enough Level A suits to handle this. Who has that kind of equipment close by?"

"Military?" Lieutenant Hollis volunteered. The lieutenant had been recently honorably discharged from the marines and was familiar with their capabilities.

"Yes perfect," Chief Livingston said. "Fort Hood will have suits. Get them."

Lieutenant Hollis made the call to Fort Hood, asking for HAZMAT suits. He kept getting patched through to higher and higher ranks until eventually he was connected to General Joseph "Madcat" Beckenbauer. This was Friday night. If someone's calling Gen. Madcat on a Friday night, there had better be blood, and lots of it. In this case, there was. Gen. Madcat impatiently listened to the situation report. Then came the request. Gen. Madcat was incredulous.

"Son, you don't call a US Army General on a Friday night asking for HAZMAT suits. Especially not *this* General."

"Sorry sir," Hollis said.

"Son, if there's been a major attack on a Texas high school

you shouldn't be asking me for HAZMAT suits, you should be asking me to send the whole goddamn 1st Calvary Division down there to give you boys a hand."

"Could you?"

"Damn right I could. I'm the General."

"Yes sir."

"You tell your Chief we're on our way."

"Yes sir."

Gen. Madcat did made a few calls to confirm the deployment. He dressed in his combat gear and headed for the base. His chopper would be waiting.

The fire alarm finally stopped sounding. Gary pulled out his phone, selected recent calls and his mom's contact. She answered on the first ring.

"Mom? Actually no Mom, dance isn't so great. I'm okay, but it's kind of a big mess here. Oh, you've been hearing lots of sirens? Yeah, that's us. I'm not sure, Mom. No, I just wanted to let you know I'm okay. Yes, Cindy is with me. No, no I don't know, sorry. I love you, Mom." He ended the brief call and extended his phone to Cindy. "If you girls want to make phone calls, go ahead."

The girls called their parents. Both had heard news through the grapevine and were relieved to hear their daughters' voices. "We can't leave just yet. It's kind of a quarantine situation. But we're fine," Amy told her mom. She regarded Priscilla. "Hey Mom, please call Mrs. Moran and tell her Priscilla is with us as well. Yeah, she's fine. Same situation. Okay, love you Mom."

"Seth was holding my purse," Priscilla commented, forlorn.

Only now, with the fire alarm silenced, did they take notice of the ringtones that kept chiming on the dance floor and all around them. Loved ones concerned for the homecoming attendees who would not, as it turned out, be coming home at all.

The fire alarm's echoing honk faded from Amy's ears, replaced by a ubiquitous low hum, like background noise from a faulty fluorescent bulb. She assumed they all heard it. But there was something else, high frequency, like a mosquito buzzing, only more annoying as her hearing fully recovered from the blaring of the fire alarm.

No one else seemed to be bothered. "Don't you guys hear that?"

"Hear what?" Cindy asked.

"That high screeching sound, it's like a million cicadas or something." Amy covered her ears. Her superb hearing was her hidden gift. She could tune her violin by ear and mimic intricate melodies on first listening. That gift enabled her to hear the nanites darting amongst the air molecules, like a billion fingernails scraping on a chalkboard. "Make it stop– Make it stop–"

Gary closed his eyes and focused on his commune with the nanites. The background humming lowered, then the screeching emerged, audible to all. Cindy and Priscilla cringed, chin to chest, burying their ears under their palms.

"The other way!" Cindy yelled.

Gary refocused. The pitch of the humming rose, the screeching faded for Cindy and Priscilla, then finally for Amy, rising above twenty kilohertz, inaudible to even the most sensitive human ear. Amy breathed a sigh of relief, believing fully now that Gary had complete power over the nanites. It confused her though. If the nanites were the monster, what did that make Gary?

Joanna Greene and Connie Simpson approached the roadblock. They were trying to turn into the school, but the state police were turning everybody away. Connie, the driver, was getting the same spiel. Joanna recognized the voice. She craned her head to confirm it was Trooper Jackson. She spoke up. "Jackson, you took my husband earlier today, I'll be damned if you're going to keep me from my son."

Jackson was taken aback. He glanced across the seat and sure enough, there was Mrs. Greene crossing paths with him once again.

"Mrs. Greene, I'm sorry about earlier today, but this is a dangerous situation."

"Trooper Jackson. My boy called me. He's alive, but I can tell he's frightened. This is my friend Connie. She has not heard from her son at all. If there is any decency in you, let us pass."

Jackson was unsympathetic. He had turned away many other parents of kids at the dance. She was not worthy of an exception because he had arrested her husband a few hours prior.

Connie turned around and followed a few other cars to a gravel parking lot off RM 620. Parents were getting out of their cars and walking. Connie and Joanna did the same, veering off the road to avoid the state troopers and following the procession of smartphone utility flashlights. They walked in open-toed shoes through scrub brush, mountain cedar and pine forest to reach their children, briars and dry needles piercing their feet. The crunching of sticks and hushed voices replaced the nighttime whir of insects in the woods.

At least Joanna had heard from Gary. Connie hadn't heard from Charlie, and Gary didn't provide any information about him. Connie grew more anxious with each step, fearing the worst. Connie kept the pace, leading them, often single file through the thicket.

"It isn't like Charlie not to call," Connie said. "Something must be seriously wrong."

"Gary said Cindy was with him. Charlie can't be too far away," Joanna said, grasping for words that might provide comfort, even though she had to agree, not hearing from Charlie was a bad sign. "The news said the high school was quarantined. They're probably locked down in place. Maybe another kid had his phone to take pictures, or something."

"I've called five times," Connie said, distressed. "Nobody answers. Charlie would call if he could. He'd use someone else's phone if necessary. He's not calling because he *can't*, and I need to know why."

Joanna silently followed Connie's footsteps. She understood. She would fear the same in her shoes.

"Did you know I wrote you a poem? Or, a song maybe, I'm not quite sure yet," Nelson said, cutting through the anxious silence.

"How sweet," Jackie replied. "May I hear it?"

"I don't remember it word-for-word, but it goes something like this: 'My virginity isn't for some whore' . . ." Nelson recited the poem, with a cadence corresponding to the melody in his head. He performed it the very best he could. When he finished, he couldn't quite read the expression on her face. "Did you like it?"

"Well . . . I . . . uh . . ."

"You don't like it," he said, disappointed.

Her first inclination was to slap him. Her second was to correct his grammar. Ultimately, she decided to feed his ego. "No Nelson, that's not true. I'm actually touched that you wrote a poem for me and that you saw fit to share. It's just I wouldn't want it publicized, because it's a *very intimate* poem. Not one to be shared with anyone else. Let's keep it a secret between you and me." She crossed her fingers and hoped no one else would ever hear that dreadful poem. She would be mortified.

A few moments later, a thumping sound on the school's PA system got their attention.

Custodian Jonas handed the front door key to the fireman in the protective suit. He watched as a dozen firemen entered the school and headed to the front office, where the PA system resided.

The fire captain led his men down the main corridor to the front office. They found the PA system, powered it on and tested. "Thump. Thump."

His men gave him the thumbs up.

"This is Fire Captain Kevin Lewis. Miss Jackie Fleur, we have received your message, and we know you are here. Please call 911 and give them your exact location. We will come to you. Anyone else, if you hear this message, please call 911 and give them your exact location. We will come get you."

He repeated the message several times. They waited for word from dispatch. They did not have to wait long.

"Captain Lewis?" said dispatch.

"Captain Lewis here."

"We received three calls."

"Only three?"

"So far. One was whispering. He's in the boy's locker room, and he's quite stressed."

The boy's locker room was right next to the gym. It would be precarious getting to him without encountering the red slime.

"The second was from Jackie Fleur again. She and one other person are in a room adjacent to her classroom."

Lewis felt they could get to her and her companion.

"We also received a call from the gym."

"The gym?"

"There are four survivors, one male, three female, sitting on center stage with something the caller called 'nanites' spinning around them."

Lewis was not going to risk taking his men into that gym

just yet, not after what happened to the state troopers.

"We'll get to Jackie Fleur first, then the locker room. Gym will have to wait."

"Understood, Captain."

"I am sending two men to the entrance," he signaled with his hand a "one" and "two" and pointed to the front door. "Hand them three suits. Make them large, unless you want to call these people back and ask their size."

"One second sir . . . Jonas says Jackie Fleur would be a small."

"Fine, one small for Jackie and two large suits."

"Roger."

"Chief, we followed up on the boy's story. It checks out. I remember reading about this kid," Cpt. Smith said. "His cure was billed as a modern medical miracle."

"What hospital was he treated at?" Chief Livingston asked.

"Seton."

"Hot damn. Local. We finally catch a break. Call Seton. Dispatch a police copper. I want a *nanite* expert here pronto."

"Chief, there's one other thing I think you should know; we may have seen this before at Seton," Cpt. Smith said. "I didn't make this connection with Seton Medical Center until now. We responded end-of-last-year to a hazardous spill that burned an oncology nurse pretty badly. That spill was relatively small, but it had thin crimson threads, something like what this looks like."

"How did you contain it?" Chief Livingston asked.

"We were able to scoop it into buckets and pitch it into the hospital's medical waste incinerator," Cpt. Smith said.

Chief Livingston shook her head. "We have survivors in there Captain Smith. I need a viable alternative, short of flamethrowers and napalm."

"Understood ma'am."

"Contact Seton. Connect these dots."

"Yes ma'am."

Chief Livingston heard them before she saw them, the heavy thrumming of helicopters. They landed on the football field, illuminated for that purpose. The soldiers would be here in minutes and she would certainly have to yield command and control to the military. She hoped to complete at least one rescue before they arrived.

"Chief, Seton says the man we need is Dr. Wolfgang Reichmann," Cpt. Smith reported. "He's their top microbial scientist, and he worked the case of Gary Greene."

"Perfect. Get him," Chief Livingston ordered.

"He's not at the hospital tonight Chief. It's Friday night. He made other plans."

"Well where is he?"

"Seton says he's at the Johnny Doolittle concert."

"Dispatch a chopper directly to the Johnny Doolittle concert. I don't care if they need to land on the stage," Chief Livingston commanded. "I want Doctor Reichmann here!"

"The Doolittle concert was at Sam Houston High School," Cpt. Smith said. "And he's not at the church with the evacuees. I think we've lost him."

"Damn it!" Chief Livingston said, pounding the makeshift command table. "When are we going to catch a break?"

Jackie heard rustling in the hallway and then a tap at the door. She turned to Nelson. "Let's hope it's not the Land Shark." His blank stare told her he didn't get the reference to the notorious Saturday Night Live skit. Such was their generation gap.

Cpt. Lewis plodded through the door, followed by two of his men. He kept his protective gear on and explained to Jackie and Nelson what they needed to do. The firemen helped Jackie and Nelson put on their protective gear, which included the encapsulating protective suit, chemical resistant lining, self-contained breathing, chemical-resistant gloves and steel toe boots. The suits restricted mobility and usually required some training before wearers felt comfortable. There was no time for training. They were nearly done putting the suits on when there was a sharp double rap on the door. "Trouble sir, tentacle of red slime probing down the corridor."

"Retreat away and keep me informed."

Cpt. Lewis gave the hurry-up signal.

They finished. They were covered head to toe in two layers of protective gear. The suit had an extremely claustrophobic feel. Jackie hoped she would not have to be in it long.

"Report."

"Slime is at your door sir. We've pulled back to the end of the corridor."

"Roger that."

Cpt. Lewis checked and indeed slime was oozing underneath the door.

Jackie saw the slime and then she panicked. Someone had kicked the panties away. She started to hyperventilate.

"Calm down ma'am." But there was no calming her. These suits were not for everybody.

Red slime continued to penetrate into the room and began to climb the walls. "We have to go now or this woman is going to lose it."

"Sir, the slime is six feet beyond your door."

"I guess we're going to find out how well these suits work." Cpt. Lewis opened the door, stirring the slime to life. Tentacles climbed the door like a red creeping vine.

The three fire firefighters, Jackie and Nelson hooked onto each other with short parachute cable cords and one by one stepped through the threshold of the door and into the hallway. With each step, their boots became more engulfed in the creeping, thick red slush. Just one more step and Cpt. Lewis (in the lead) was through the end of it. He kept pulling them down the hall. "Keep going people." They were through the thick of it, but the red slime that was on them continued to slither up their legs. "Go, go." He picked up the pace, caught up to the rest of his men, and signaled that they should head for the door. Slime crept up his torso and onto his facemask, where it seemed to gather. He glanced behind and saw his companions having a similar experience. He tried to go faster, but this pace was not sustainable for first time wearers of a Level A suit. Somebody stumbled, and all five of them tumbled to the ground. The slime on them went into a frenzy. Jackie panicked and was foolishly grabbing at her helmet. It was fortunate for her that she did not know *how* to operate it. The red slime they had dragged with them down the corridor became a spinning angry mass all about the five people linked by the cords. One of Cpt. Lewis's other men made an aggressive move toward the angry mass, accomplishing nothing. He took several forceful steps down the hallway toward the gym and taunted the spinning hive. This got a reaction. The hive followed and engulfed him. He continued to draw the hive away, down the corridor.

"Get up," Cpt. Lewis yelled.

They all got to their feet and step-by-step continued toward the exit at a sustainable pace.

They made it out the front door of the school. Cpt. Lewis didn't stop until he was a good thirty-yards away from the school. "Please hang on a moment longer, Jackie."

Two firemen directed a hose on the people wearing the HAZMAT suits. After inspection, they were given the all-clear to remove the suits. A fireman helped Jackie with her helmet. She inhaled deeply, expecting fresh air and instead caught a pungent whiff. "Bleach?"

"Standard procedure," Cpt. Lewis said. "Kills everything."

"Yes, bleach is an excellent anti-microbial. It even kills viruses." Jackie Fleur, the biology teacher, was putting a few jigsaw pieces together in her mind. "Who was that man that drew the red hive away?"

"Sergeant Gus Kerner. Probably saved our lives."

"Are you going to go rescue him?"

"Yeah, we'll get him," Cpt. Lewis said. "I'm still talking to him. He says the red stuff can't get to him in his suit, and it's not happy about it."

"Why don't you tell him to come to the front? You guys can hose him down with bleach."

"I'll suggest it. He can't stay in there forever. Only so much air in these tanks."

Jackie stood in her crumpled dress in the parking lot after removing her suit. A fireman draped her with his coat. Then, a medical technician brought her and Nelson blue hospital scrubs and white slippers. They watched as two tanker trucks holding bleach mixtures rolled up to the front door. Teams of firemen stood ready as Sgt. Gus Kerner emerged with a red hive swirling around his head. Soon as he stepped outside, the hose teams let loose a broad spray that neutralized the red hive. The firemen continued to hose down Sgt. Kerner long after they observed no movement around him. It was a unique and freaky experience for all of them. Nobody was sure when to stop spraying. Cpt. Lewis finally put an end to it and personally helped Sgt. Kerner get out of his HAZMAT suit, patting him on the back and thanking him profusely. Then, he headed for the incident command post to report the results to Cpt. Smith and the Chief.

Jackie and Nelson were taken to the church for observation just like the rest of the survivors. Jackie found very few teachers. Nelson found Coach Evans and Coach Mitchell. They were delighted to see him and together they hugged the only surviving football player, thus far.

General Madcat Beckenbauer fanned his troops along the periphery already established by the local authorities. He wasn't sure what he would find and was pleasantly surprised with the coordinated command being provided by Chief Livingston.

"You know we were only asking for HAZMAT suits right, General?"

"Yes, I received your requests for HAZMAT suits, and I have honored it. They just happen to have men in them."

"How convenient," she said.

Chief Livingston discerned that what Gen. Madcat lacked in stature was mitigated by his character. He was quick-witted, and he was confident. She liked him. She was floored when he agreed to fold his command under her joint authority, with Gen. Madcat controlling his soldiers only.

Chief Livingston caught Gen. Madcat up on the events. Together, they heard Cpt. Lewis's after-action report and were most intrigued by the success of the bleach.

"Your man Sgt. Kerner doing okay?"

"Yes Chief, he's fine," Cpt. Lewis reported.

"And the people you rescued could provide no more information?" Chief Livingston asked.

"No ma'am," Cpt. Lewis said. "They were holed up in their room the whole time."

"Understood. Thank you captain. Good job," Chief Livingston said.

"Thank you Chief. Welcome, General, glad you are here."

"Me too son," Gen. Madcat said. "Keep up the good work."

Cpt. Smith knocked on the back door of the SWAT vehicle serving as incident command.

"Come in, Captain."

"Chief, General," he nodded to each of them, "we have a woman here who claims her son is alive inside the school. She's Joanna Greene, Gary Greene's mother."

"That the boy with the nanites?" Chief Livingston said.

"One and the same ma'am," Cpt. Smith confirmed.

"Bring her in."

It had taken Joanna and Connie forty minutes to walk the two miles from the road. Joanna stepped into the command vehicle seeking information. She became the one pumped with questions. They wanted to know everything about Gary, any information she could provide about his physical and mental state. Even though she hadn't expected this turn, she fully cooperated. Yes, she knew all three of the girls mentioned by the Chief, or at least she knew their names as Gary's classmates. Cindy would be the closest; she was the girlfriend of his best friend Charlie Simpson.

"Charlie's mother is here with me," Joanna said. "She hasn't heard from him. Can you tell us anything?"

"We won't know until we get in there ma'am," Chief Livingston said. "Would you mind standing by, in case we need you?"

"I'm not going anywhere," Joanna said. "Not until I get my son back."

"Thank you Mrs. Greene."

Cpt. Smith escorted her out of the command vehicle.

"You came at just the right time, General," Chief Livingston said. "I need tactical advice."

"Tactical advice is my middle name, Chief," Gen. Madcat said, grinning.

Charlie's cell phone had rung several times in the last half hour. Gary and Cindy both recognized the unique Coldplay ringtone. It rang again.

"Should we answer it?" Amy asked.

"I don't think anything good would come from answering Charlie's phone," Gary said. Nevertheless, he got up and retrieved the phone out of Charlie's tuxedo pocket. It was hard being this close to his body. Poor Charlie didn't deserve to die, especially not like this. Being so close to Charlie's disintegrated face made Gary uneasy. When he sat down, he kept shaking as if he were freezing, even though the air in the gym was stifling. Trembling, he passed the phone to Cindy. The phone had stopped ringing, and it required a passcode to unlock.

"I know his passcode," Cindy said, punching in the digits. She checked recent calls. "It was his mother. She's called five times."

"What do we do?" Amy asked.

Cindy started to cry. Gary comforted her. "It will be okay. We'll get through this."

"I know we will, I'm not crying for myself," Cindy said, looking around the gym. "Look at all these people. They all had a life. They all have a story, and I happen to know Charlie's story very well. His dad died a few years ago, leaving Charlie man of the house for his mom and little sister. They're very close. I can't bear to tell his mom that Charlie's gone."

"Cindy, let it be. Let her find out with all the other parents, then she won't feel like she's all alone," Gary said. "I know what it feels like to be all alone. It's not a good feeling."

The County Fire Department isolated the school's water supply. They had construction crews dig up the main water line, then they rerouted the flow through an eighteen-wheel tanker truck. The state police stacked hundreds of drums of sodium hypochlorite by the tanker. The city of Austin provided additional firemen, equipment, and supplies, including a rather impressive water cannon. These preparations took time. It wasn't until 7:00 a.m. Saturday morning that *Operation Nanite Bleach* was ready to begin. By then, dawn was breaking over Central Texas. Concerned parents and loved ones, who had been turned away at roadblocks, saw fit to abandon their cars and traverse straight through the fields and woods on foot. Others used ATVs and four-wheel drive trucks to get to the school. They were blatantly disregarding police instruction. These were not happy people, and their numbers were growing by the hour. Plus, their ranks would soon swell with the noontime homecoming game crowd.

"We're going to have a riot on our hands," Chief Livingston observed.

"We may, indeed," Gen. Madcat agreed. "We need to start thinking about what we're going to do *after* we clean up the contamination. These people aren't going away, and there's nearly a thousand of their friends and family in that gymnasium. I hate to think about how they'll react when they figure out who's to blame."

"You're going somewhere with this, General. You normally talk straight with me. Please continue doing so. What is it you're trying to tell me?"

"Quite frankly, I've been issued new orders, straight from the Pentagon."

"Tell me."

"They want the Greene boy," Gen. Madcat declared. "I am ordered to extract him."

"I don't like the sound of that," Chief Livingston said.

"I just follow orders ma'am. I offer you the assistance of my regiment for crowd control, after we decontaminate the school."

"I appreciate that General. I accept."

Tonya Jones couldn't get a hold of Priscilla last night. She was disappointed. She wanted to hear all about homecoming. Then, Tonya's mom called to see if she had heard from Lamar, because he hadn't come home from the dance. That was very unlike Lamar. He may have been arrogant, but he was respectful of his mother. She called Lamar and Chestnut, to no avail. Tonya turned on the TV. The breaking news was about the attack at Sam Houston High School. Tonya grabbed her helmet and bolted out the door, headed for the school.

Roddy adjusted his squatting position. No one had come to get him yet, and there was little change with the gooey red mass slithering along the bathroom tile. How long had he been pinned up here? He was losing track of the hours and having trouble staying awake. Irony was, he was trapped on top of a toilet, but he was too afraid to pee.

The roads were blocked. People were abandoning their cars and walking to the school. Tonya picked out a set of power lines, jumped off the highway, and followed the power cables along a firebreak through the thorn scrub and cedar woods. Hundreds of flashing blue and red lights served as a beacon. She cut off along a viable trail and wound up running into the police periphery at the far edge of the school parking lot. Her arrival drew attention, but not rebuke. She would apparently be allowed to stay, as were others who had chosen this particular path. The periphery was manned by county and state police, firemen, and army men. The soldiers were the most ominous, armed with assault rifles and donned in charcoal military-grade protective gear.

Tonya wasn't shy. You couldn't hang upside down naked with your legs wrapped around a pole on stage and be shy. She parked her bike and strolled up to the nearest soldier, a fit young black man with big eyes and boyish cheeks.

"Please stay back ma'am. No one is allowed past this point," the soldier said while maintaining his military stance.

She glanced at his nametag and rank insignia, he had one

chevron closed by a rounded bar. "Corporal?"

"Private First Class ma'am."

"PFC Martin," she said. "My papa was in the Army too. You out of Fort Hood?"

He nodded.

"1st Calvary, 2nd Brigade, 1st Battalion, 5th Regiment, ma'am."

"That's a lot to remember. Your regiment got a nickname?"

"Black Knights." PFC Martin grinned.

Tonya cracked a tepid smile. "I have friends and family trapped inside that school. My little brother is in there," she pleaded.

"I don't know what to tell you. I simply have no information and that's the truth. I'm sorry. Now please back up a little bit, before I get in trouble."

Tonya hated this helpless feeling, but there was nothing she could do. She eased away, leaned on her bike and worried.

Operation Nanite Bleach began with a PA announcement. "Roddy Cruz, Priscilla Moran, Amy Bridges, Cindy Perrine, Gary Greene, and anyone else who can hear this announcement. We are going to deploy the school's sprinkler system. Do not panic. The water isn't going to hurt you. It's chlorinated, just like pool water. You should close your mouth and eyes but don't be alarmed if you do get water in your eyes, or if you swallow a small amount. Please remain calm and remain where you are so we know where to find you."

The fire department assigned three hose teams to each squad and one squad to each egress–twelve hose teams approaching at orthogonal angles. They activated the sprinkler system. The cannon lobbed a high arching stream of water onto the roof. The hose teams moved in, three abreast.

Firefighters formed a chlorine bleach brigade, passing five-gallon containers up to the men on the top of the tanker truck. One man dumped the contents of each bucket into the tank cap. The other man released the cap contents into the pressurized water that raged in the tank. They repeated this process until they were exhausted, then another pair of men took their place.

Roddy watched as the water cascaded down the walls and vertical surfaces of the bathroom stall. The smell reminded him of being at the pool. The water was literally cleaning the floor of the red stuff. The goo kind of just surrendered and let itself be washed down the bathroom drains. He was getting soaked. It was magnificent.

They could hear water pounding the roof. It sounded like a thunderstorm. Then, the sprinklers engaged. Gary was concerned the nanites might freak with the activation of the sprinklers. They did not. The rafters were drenched first. Thick red tentacles of nanites dissolved into a red Kool-Aid of water draining from the ceiling. Strings of lights shorted out with popping noises, one after another, and then an entire circuit blew, leaving the gym illuminated only by emergency lights and the early morning sunshine through the high windows.

There was a summertime freshness cutting through the air, replacing the close stench to which they had become accustomed. The spinning vaporous vortex around center stage abated and the ubiquitous humming subsided, then disappeared completely. The light rusty water pooled on the gymnasium floor, covering bodies inches deep. Everything was getting soaked; everything was being cleaned.

The morning sunlight beaming into the gym and the cleansing by the water began to reveal the magnitude of the horror. Eviscerated bodies were strewn from the stage to exits and throughout the bleachers, recognizable as humans only because of the clothes they left behind. Exposed extremities–

heads, hands, and legs–were dissolved into puddles of goo, testimony to the damage of which the nanites were capable. Yet, the nanites could not defend themselves from the bleached water.

The nanites did not perceive the water to be a threat to Gary, therefore they did not perceive the threat to themselves. The way they reacted to Sgt. Gus Kerner was indicative. When the Sergeant threatened the hive, the nanites had no reaction. When the Sergeant moved toward the gym, possibly threatening Gary, they moved to protect Gary. The idea that the nanites would allow themselves to be exterminated in this manner was mind-boggling to Gary, until he considered that their behavior was entirely consistent with their programming. Perhaps, over time, they would have evolved to a state of existence independent of Gary, a whole new life form, per se.

Hose squad one drenched the red carpet to the left gym entrance. As soon as they made it past the door and into the gym itself, Troopers Jackson and Hancock rushed along with teams of firefighters to recover the corpses of the their fallen comrades, Troopers Fitzgerald and Watson.

Hose squad two entered the front lobby, targeting the right front gym entrance. They sprayed ceiling, walls and floor with the bleached water, drenching every surface, including the bodies piled on the floor. It was a gruesome task. Faces and entire heads were dissolved, or rather, eaten by a corrosive they did not yet understand. The body of Seton Medical Center microbial scientist Wolfgang Reichmann lay in this assemblage, a victim of his own making. Nurse Lopez lay nearby, a two-time victim of nanite assault.

Hose squad three entered the rear lobby, targeting the rear right gym entrance. Here they found an equally horrific scene of death by nanites, including the body of ATF Agent Lee Dunsany, Glock 43 nine mm pistol still in hand, and a morbid pile of cheerleader torsos nearby.

Hose squad four entered the school near the locker rooms, targeting the rear left gym entrance and carrying spare HAZMAT suits for the survivors. They were assigned to reach Roddy Cruz first, in the boy's locker room, and then proceed into the gym. They swung and hosed down the corridor leading to Jackie Fleur's classroom, then turned their attention to the locker rooms. The girl's locker room was a blood bath. Several dozen kids had taken refuge there. None survived.

They found Roddy in the locker room, in the last stall of the boy's bathroom. He was delighted by their arrival. He spun in the hose water and leapt into the arms of the fireman who was carrying his HAZMAT suit. They made him put it on before escorting him out the door. They noted a dozen bodies on the floor of the boy's locker room.

Squad four pressed on through the rear left gym entrance. It was hard for the firemen to imagine a worse carnage than what they saw in the locker rooms, but here it was, splayed out before them, a gymnasium strewn with half eaten bodies. They hosed down a tunnel under the stage, where it appeared scores of attendees had attempted to hide. A man sitting in a wheelchair, skull hollowed out, indicated the nanites did not discriminate.

Hose squads one, two, and three came in from their assigned entrances, meeting hose squad four at center stage. Four squads and twelve hoses doused the stage as the four remaining survivors huddled on it.

Satisfied, Cpt. Lewis signaled the squads to fan out through the school to scour every inch. He messaged Gen. Madcat, informing him of their success. The firemen presented HAZMAT suits to the four survivors. The girls put on their suits. Gary waved it off. The firemen led the girls out of the gym. Cpt. Lewis signaled that Gary should stay. Gary had somehow expected this. He was dangerous. He considered their choices. Nothing would have surprised him, even a summary execution.

A squad of heavily armed soldiers clad in charcoal body suits burst through the left front entrance, bounded irreverently over bodies and encircled Gary on the stage. A lone man, shorter in stature and similarly dressed, followed them. He strolled to center stage, scanned the gym and asked a question of the fire captain next to him, who shrugged. He unsnapped his mask and pulled it aside. The wide smile on the older man's face told Gary he was not going execute him, at least not summarily. The man held out his hand to shake. "Gary Greene?"

Gary shook the man's hand. "Yes?"

"I'm General Madcat Beckenbauer. I'm here to rescue you."

"I don't need to be rescued. They did," Gary said, pointing to the three girls leaving the gym.

"I understand what you're saying, Gary. You're a clever boy," Gen. Madcat said. "But you do not fully grasp the situation. You do still need to be rescued. There's a thousand people dead inside this school. Your nanites did that. There's another two thousand agitated people outside this school, and they're asking lots of questions, seeking an explanation for their loved ones not coming home. For your own safety, I suggest you come with me."

Gary hesitated.

"I want to speak with my mother," he said.

Gen. Madcat considered the scenarios. *Can't bring her in here, too gruesome. Can't bring him out there to linger in conversation, too dangerous.*

"I can allow a phone conversation. But it has to be brief."

"Ok, I'll try. Kind of depends on how the conversation goes. You know how moms are. But don't worry, I'll come with you."

"Fair enough. You have your conversation with your mama, and then I'm extricating you out of here."

Gary pulled out his phone.

Gen. Madcat barked out some orders into his microphone.

The soldiers around Gary exited, half splitting stage left, and other half stage right.

Gary and Gen. Madcat were alone in the gym, sprinklers still showering the stage.

Tonya observed more soldiers join the periphery. They stripped off the outer layer of their uniforms to reveal a snug layer of combat fatigues. They seemed less menacing without the charcoal armor. Tonya leaned on her bike parked and waited for news. Her phone rang. It was a number she didn't recognize.

"Hello?" Tonya answered.

"Is this Tonya Jones?"

"Yes–"

"This is Travis County Police dispatch. I have someone here who wants to speak with you."

Oh thank God, Tonya thought, Lamar's okay.

"Tonya," it was a girl's voice, "this is Priscilla. I'm okay, but–"

"Priscilla, oh Priscilla. I'm so glad to hear from you." Tonya was already starting to cry. She knew it was bad. "Tell me."

"He's gone."

Tonya wailed, right there in the middle of the field. She wailed like she didn't even know she was capable of wailing. Priscilla stayed on the phone with her. This was the hardest thing Priscilla had ever done. It tore her apart. For as long as it took, she would stay with her.

Tonya gathered her breath, just enough to say one more name. But then again, she already knew the answer. Priscilla would have told her already otherwise. She had to know. "Chestnut?"

"He's gone too."

"Damn." Tonya tightened her lips and balled her fists.

"It's bad in there Tonya, really bad. They're all gone."

"Where are you now?"

"They're taking us to the church across the street."

"I'm coming."

Tonya took some breaths and stopped herself, just for a moment, before starting up her bike. She listened. Random cries of despair were erupting around the periphery. Word was getting out.

Roddy found Nelson, Coach Evans, and Coach Mitchell waiting for him at the church.

"Where's everyone else?" Roddy asked.

Nelson shook his head.

"No one else waited for me?" Roddy asked.

"No, nobody else made it out," Nelson said, flatly. "We're it."

"No fucking way. All of them? Dead?" Roddy asked.

"That's what we've been told," Nelson said.

"No, please God, no!" Roddy cried. Somehow the magnitude of the disaster hadn't hit him yet, and in an instant it smashed him in the face. "I could have stopped it. I could have stopped it." Roddy collapsed to the ground in a ball and started to cry. He curled into a fetal position, and there was little Nelson and the coaches could to do comfort him. They crouched down next to him and let him cry it out. His crying faded to a whimper.

"We'll miss them too, Roddy," Nelson said.

"My mom was in there," Roddy replied, matter-of-fact. Then Roddy started to shake, like he was suffering some kind of a seizure.

"We need some help here!" Coach Evans yelled.

Medical staff came running to find Roddy going into shock.

"Mom."

"Gary, it's nice to hear your voice."

"Mom, I was elected to homecoming court."

"I knew you would be."

"The highlight was before that though. Johnny Doolittle gave a very nice speech. He talked about how hard you worked to save me and how much you loved me. He told everyone in the crowd what a great mom you are."

"Oh Gary, are you ok?"

"I know he was right. You are a great mom."

"And you're a great son."

"Mom, lots of people died last night."

"I know that."

"I feel bad for all those parents whose kids aren't ever coming home again."

"It wasn't your fault, Gary."

"It kind of is. I knew something was up with the nanites. I should have sought professional help. I was afraid someone would come take me away." Gen. Madcat's actions confirm it was not an irrational thought. "I saw Dr. Reichmann last night. He just happened to be at the concert. I should have spoken with him sooner."

"We will figure this out, Gary."

"Mom, is Mrs. Simpson still with you?"

"Yes."

"Charlie didn't make it."

"Oh my God."

"Charlie was her only son. Charlie's dad died just a few years ago. It's totally not fair."

"No, it's not, honey."

"Will you tell her?"

Joanna noticed Cindy Perrine was already hugging Connie. They were both crying. "I think she already knows."

"Have you heard from Dad?"

"No, not yet. I don't know when he'll be allowed to call. I'm worried sick. And now I'm worried about you."

Gary could hear his mom crying. "It's been a rough night," he said.

"Yes it has. When are they going to let you out?"

"I don't know, Mom."

Silence.

"Mom, do you remember when you drove me to North Padre Island and we watched the sunrise over the gulf?"

"Yes Gary, of course I remember." She started to cry harder.

"That was special."

"Yes it was."

Pause.

"I have to go now," Gary said.

"I don't understand. Where are they going to take you?"

"I don't know yet. I will call you when I can."

"Gary?"

"I love you, Mom.

"Gary wait–" click.

Gen. Madcat looked Gary straight in the eyes. "That was a good phone call. It was difficult and necessary. You're a fine kid. I hope we can make the best of this situation, but right now it's important we whisk you away, for your own safety."

"I think you're right. If I were one of those parents, I would be really upset about now."

"That may be putting it kindly," Gen. Madcat said.

Tonya found Priscilla inside the church. They hugged and cried.

"I'm so sorry," they said as they comforted each other for their losses.

"How did this happen?" Tonya asked.

"That son-of-a-bitch, Gary Greene. He has some kind of power that killed everybody."

"I'm going to kill him," Tonya said. She meant it.

Gary compromised and accepted a pair of boots because of the bodies over which they needed to navigate. Gary and Gen. Madcat picked their way off the stage. They stepped out of the lobby and onto the pavement where soldiers and police cars were waiting. Gen. Madcat led Gary to the nearest car. Gary could hear his mom yelling, "Where are you taking him?" but, he couldn't pick her out of the crowd. It was eerily reminiscent of her yelling the previous night when the police took his dad away. He felt terrible for his mom. The police cars drove toward the football field while soldiers jogged alongside. He could feel the thumping of the choppers as they got close. The caravan stopped on the twenty-yard-line, allowing the soldiers to escort Gary the remaining distance to the helicopter waiting at midfield. Wind buffeted Gary's face. Gen. Madcat and another soldier held onto Gary and got him safely onboard the helicopter. They strapped him in and, when everyone was ready, gave the thumbs up to the pilots. The chopper rose, giving Gary a panoramic view of the school and the grounds around it. He saw hundreds of emergency vehicles encircling the school. What amazed him were the trucks, cars, and people beyond, thousands of them, radiating out from the school along every road. There was gridlock for miles. Maybe Gen. Madcat was right. He did need to be rescued.

Gen. Madcat sat content, knowing what Gary was thinking.

February 2020

From *Terror Unleashed* by Carmen de Flores, Master's Thesis, Journalism, University of Texas, February 2020

The biomedical technology used in Gary's amazing recovery from Leukemia set a chain of events in motion that inevitably led to its cataclysmic conclusion. Had the other football players followed Charlie Simpson's example, and accepted Gary, it is possible this tragic story need not be told. The whole idea started as a joke, with disgruntled football players (led by Seth Thompson) conniving to elect a boy with gay tendencies as homecoming queen. The stunt was completely unfair to Gary, who, along with his battle with cancer, had been struggling with his homosexuality throughout adolescence. Accounts demonstrate Gary accepted the award with dignity, rather than embarrassment, as Seth had hoped.

The photographs stored in Eugene Maxwell's camera proved invaluable to authorities for victim identification. Eugene was diligent in his picture taking duties, missing very few attendees, leaving the identification of less than a dozen corpses to other means. Many bodies lacked IDs and any exposed skin was eaten away, particularly around the head where the nanites gained access to internal organs through facial orifices. Aligning red carpet photographs to the remnants the nanites left behind was a gruesome and heartbreaking job. Sadly, Roddy Cruz had no problem spotting his mom's unmistakable black and white party dress in the massacre. She was one of the few who made it out the front door, only to collapse, victim of the nanites, onto the red carpet runner.

Nearly 500 students attended the homecoming

dance. An equal number of parents, teachers, and general admission ticket holders were also in attendance. Ultimately, only 172 homecoming attendees survived. A death toll of over eighty percent. It was a massacre. Many in Round Rock bore deep-seated animosity toward Gary Greene, blaming him for the death of their loved ones.

So what have we learned? The homecoming episode reminded scientists that even the smallest of robots need to be controlled. Nanite regulations now require strict adherence to Isaac Asimov's first law: "A robot may not injure a human being or, through inaction, allow a human being to come to harm." No one saw the need in 2017; the Round Rock community, especially Sam Houston High School, paid the price.

Charlie Simpson's befriending of Gary and acceptance of his sexuality didn't provide Charlie exemption from the wrath of the nanites. Certainly Gary, had he remained conscious and not lost control of the nanites, would have spared Charlie.

Fortunately I was able to track down and meet several other survivors. I preferred to meet them face-to-face, to fully grasp and capture the intensity of their experiences. It was evident each managed to process the tragedy in their own way. Nelson Warner and Amy Bridges found a measure of healing through music.

I could not locate Roddy Cruz. Roddy opted not to attend college. He joined the Army instead, but was released under a general discharge after, "considerable departure from his assigned duties." Roddy Cruz has no online social media presence and no one close to him has heard from him in over a year.

The closest I could get to understand the

events' impact on Roddy was an interview with Elijah Kamiljit, the salesman at Round Rock Tuxedo. Elijah explained that he dreaded coming into work for weeks after the massacre, because survivors were returning tuxedos in dribs and drabs. He didn't know why they bothered. Round Rock Tuxedo had already told the coroner to keep all the clothes of the dead. Neither did they have interest in the garments of the living. They were forever tainted. "We wouldn't dare re-rent a garment from that night to another customer," Elijah said. "The insurance company had already agreed it was a total loss." He posted a sign stating as much, so people knew they were not renting "dead man's clothes." Elijah reported that one of the most heart-wrenching returns came from Roddy Cruz, one month after the dance. Here's how Elijah described it:

"Roddy had a mechanical manner about him and a distant look in his eyes. He actually apologized for being late with the return. I told the young man that he could keep it. I explained to Roddy that the store would recover its loss with the insurance claim. Roddy said that he couldn't keep the suit. He would never wear it again. When I explained to him that I wouldn't dare let anyone else wear it either, he started to cry. All I could do was hold him. We walked to the dumpsters behind the mall and pitched the clothes. That's as much closure as I could provide."

I fear the worst for Roddy; I pray he surfaces.

Nor did I have the opportunity to interview Vincent Greene, due to his incarceration. Here too, Elijah Kamiljit provided his impression of the man. Elijah said he wasn't surprised when he heard about the murder charges raised against Vincent.

"He was a troubled man," Elijah said. "I wish Mr. Greene could have found another way, short of killing a priest, to lift the shadow of abuse off his spirit. Unfortunate for all involved, because Gary needed a father with whom he could share his struggles, whether about his gender preference, complication with his cancer treatment, or bullying at school. So much tragedy for their entire family, it breaks my heart."

Vincent Greene thought he had been careful in the execution of Father O'Brien. His mistakes were numerous, as detailed in the *Real Detective Magazine* article, "Confession then Death, April 2018." Those details aren't repeated here, except to state that the most damning of the evidence was the surveillance video showing Vincent's Ford F150 pickup truck parked in the church parking lot that morning. The cell phone records, satellite radio logs, tollbooth payments and credit card records gave prosecutors plenty of evidence. The judge reasoned seven hours of driving should have calmed a man down, so the charge was premeditated murder. Vincent Greene never came home again. He was sentenced to life in prison and incarcerated at the Allan B. Polunsky Unit "supermax" prison in Southeast Texas.

I caught up to Priscilla Moran at a strip club in Houston. Priscilla remained unmoved. She blamed Gary fully for the carnage at the homecoming dance and swore that she and Tonya Jones would slowly torture him to death if they ever had the chance. They are not alone. It is going to take a long time for the city of Round Rock to heal. Texans have long memories.

My interview with Joanna Greene was pragmatic. Joanna stated that she read every obituary and attended as many funeral services as she could after the homecoming tragedy, lighting a candle each time. She didn't always feel welcome, but she attended nonetheless. Connie Simpson, Charlie's mother, and Joanna had never met before homecoming evening. They are now close friends, actively campaigning against high school bullying, particularly sexuality related. Their anti-bullying campaigns and sexuality freedom awareness work have received national recognition.

How the boys gained access to school to set up their elaborate prank remained a mystery for months until Coach Evans eventually admitted, after repeated interrogations, to exchanging the gymnasium key for marijuana. The exchange would have been innocuous under most circumstances. Instead, he enabled the construction of the prank that went awry. The marijuana that Coaches Evans and Mitchell received from Seth Thompson saved their lives. Indeed, they were oblivious to issues inside the school until first responders arrived. Note, it is not within scope of this report to pass judgment on the merits of one person or another surviving the catastrophe. Evans admitted his culpability and continues to make amends through active participation in Narcotics Anonymous. He was placed on parole and banned from coaching in the state of Texas. Coach Mitchell expressed his own regrets. He also will never coach again in the state of Texas, thanks to the zero tolerance policy of drugs on school property.

Constable Patrick Clancy retired from the Travis County Police department after thirty-years of service. He received the National Sheriffs' Association Distinguished service award for his actions homecoming night. Travis County Fire

Captain Albert Smith, Fire Captain Kevin Lewis, and Sergeant Gus Kerner each received the Star of Texas for their extraordinary service. The awards were presented on behalf of the Governor, by Round Rock City Mayor Janice Livingston, the former Fire Chief.

Jacqueline Fleur expressed contrition over enabling Gary to conduct DNA experiments in the old teacher's lounge. "It turned out to be like allowing Willard to train his rats," she stated. Note: I don't like that analogy. It connotes a maliciousness to Gary's intent, when in fact evidence points to benevolent motivation. I conclude that by the time Gary was conducting experiments in the lounge he already sensed the danger within him and was endeavoring to control it. If he had been able to train the nanites to be well behaved when in contact with people he didn't like, or who didn't like him, he would have been able to prevent anyone else from getting hurt.

Several circumstances aligned to prevent Jacqueline Fleur and Nelson Warner from being targets of the nanites' wrath. First, Nelson did not attend the keg party, and therefore his DNA was not in the paint can. This spared him from the first wave of attacks. Second, while their DNA samples were included in Gary's collection, neither Nelson's nor Jacqueline's DNA were the subjects of Gary's nanite control experimentation. The nanites were not, therefore, predisposed to perceive them as threatening. Third, Nelson left Cindy Perrine's panties at the door of the old teacher's lounge. Jacqueline's instincts proved correct. She saved their lives. Had they not frozen in place, they likely would have died.

Nelson explained later what he refrained from

telling Jackie at the time. Nelson was not reaching for Cindy's test tube. He was reaching for his own. The bottom of it was shattered away, as was Jacqueline's petri dish. Instincts told him it was a bad thing that their samples appeared to have exploded, though he didn't fully understand the ramifications at the time. Once again, it is a good thing Jacqueline cautioned him. Had he come in contact with the nanites, they would have consumed him right then.

Jacqueline's and Nelson's testimony confirmed at least some of the DNA samples survived until the evening of the homecoming dance. Ultimately, only one of the DNA samples survived to the end, that belonging to Cindy Perrine. My interview with Cindy clued me into why that might be the case. The pertinent question was, how had Cindy managed to survive the homecoming dance, when so many around her perished, especially given her close proximity to the epicenter of the apocalypse? Further, Cindy was able to save others from the nanites. Amy Bridges and Priscilla Moran confirmed it was Cindy who saved them, while Gary lay unconscious. They are fortunate she was there. There were rumors of intimacy between Cindy and Gary. Cindy confirmed during our interview that she and Gary had a "special relationship." The way Cindy explained it, "The nanites learned I was a friend, and they never forgot that lesson."

September 2020

He was nervous. He stood stage left, waiting for the introduction. "Ladies and gentlemen, boys and girls, we present to you, the one and only NELSON WARNER!" The gracious crowd applauded.

Nelson walked to center stage, acoustic guitar strapped over his shoulder. He subconsciously checked the rafters. He was to be the first performer of the first homecoming dance at the new Sam Houston High School. The Round Rock ISD tore down the old one. They had to. Nobody wanted to teach or attend class at a place of such carnage. They all needed a fresh start.

Nelson was honored to be asked to perform as an alumni entertainer at the homecoming dance. This was a special occasion on many levels. There hadn't been any homecoming dances since the massacre. There hadn't been any homecoming games either, for lack of players. Nelson approached the microphone, hoping he was up to the task. He remembered the personable impression Johnny Doolittle projected and tried to mimic it. He sat on the bar stool and leaned into the microphone. "Good evening folks. I appreciate the welcome. It's such an honor to be here on this special occasion. I want to thank–" He stopped. He had his intro speech memorized and just stopped, mid-sentence, because something told him he had to. He hated the way it was sounding. It resonated hollow, plastic and rehearsed, because it was. It wasn't until he sat before the crowd that he realized this moment deserved something else. "This is hard." Pause. "You would think, as a musician, I could find the words." Pause. "I can't." Pause. "Bad things happen. Good people die. It's difficult to fathom." Pause. Crowd stirring. "As kids, we think we're immortal. We're not. Life is fragile. I wish I could tell you I wrote a song to express my feelings about that horrific night. I can't. I don't think I ever could. Fortunately, somebody already did. A guy named Kerry Livgren wrote a song forty-three years ago that's speaking to me now. That's the power of music. I had no intention of playing this song for you tonight. I had forgotten how it spoke to me in my depression after *that* homecoming. I guess we all found something to comfort us through the aftermath. I found my guitar. Please allow me to share."

Nelson proceeded to pluck out the gentle unmistakable cascade of notes that are the hallmark of "Dust in the Wind" by Kansas. Before he uttered the first line, people were already crying. By the time he finished the second stanza, they all were.

Nelson, emotional, pushed into the instrumental interlude that featured a violin solo. Playing the song unrehearsed meant he would just have to pick through the interlude on his guitar. To his surprise, a weeping note from a lone violin filled the auditorium, then echoed his melody. A second spotlight found her, Amy Bridges, elegant as ever in her black party dress, pinned up silky mocha hair, telltale freckles and contagious smile. She knew the song and had scrambled to fetch her instrument.

Nelson and Amy completed the song together, stunning the audience. Solemn silence lingered for a moment, then a lone cowbell clanged.

"We love you, Nelson!" shouted a familiar voice.

"We love you, Amy!" shouted another.

More cowbells clanged throughout the auditorium. Nelson realized Jackie had finally distributed the cowbells at homecoming. Amy joined him at center stage. They hugged, they held hands, and jointly bowed. It was a closure they hadn't expected and perhaps the kindling of a new relationship.

Carmen de Flores and Cindy Perrine jointly appeared at a book signing at the University of Texas Student Union building for Carmen's wildly popular book, spawned from her Thesis *Terror Unleashed.* Cindy brought along her two-year-old daughter, a bright, slightly built girl, with a light complexion and straight brown hair.

"Well, hello sweetie," Carmen said as she bent down to be eye-to-eye to the youngster holding Cindy's hand. Is this your daughter?" Carmen asked as she looked up to Cindy.

"Yes," Cindy said with a smile. "This is Carietta."

"I'm so glad you brought her along," Carmen said. "Oh how pretty you are. How old are you?"

Carietta held up two fingers.

"Two years and three months to be exact," Cindy said. "She's a genuine miracle."

Carmen stood up. "Belated congratulations and condolences. I'm sorry for your loss, Cindy," she said, reaching out and stroking Carietta's fine brown hair.

Carietta took a liking the Carmen and clung by her side during the book signing. By the end of the one-hour signing period, Cindy noticed a pronounced security presence of Campus and Austin City Police.

"Your daughter was wonderful," Carmen said. "So well behaved. It must be hard being a single mom. Do you have help at all?"

"Yes, my mom and dad live close and help out a lot," Cindy said.

"Well, I know a few good babysitters if you're ever in need."

"As a matter of fact, I may. I'm headed to Bali soon for a month-long Ashtanga Yoga boot camp. I'm going to become a yogi. My parents might need a reprieve every now and then. I will pass along your number. I have to warn you though, she's a precocious kid; she hears everything and asked a lot of questions." Cindy picked up her daughter in her arms.

"I'm sure she is. Your trip sounds fabulous. I'm jealous. Have a great time. Please have your parents call me if they need a sitter," Carmen said.

Cindy carried Carietta to the elevator, then let her down to push the 'G' button. "Miss Carmen was nice, Mommy."

"Yes, she was. That's why I let you touch her so much."

"I know Mommy. I only touch people I like, otherwise I might burn them."

"That's right, sweetheart." Cindy reached down to hold Carietta's hand.

"Mommy, do you really think I'm a genuine miracle?"

Cindy smiled. This was classic Carietta, quizzing Mommy about everything she heard. "Yes, Carietta, I do think you're a genuine miracle."

"Why, Mommy?"

"Because your mommy was on medicine that should have prevented her from becoming a mommy, but your daddy was powerful. The medicine could not stop him."

"Didn't you want to be a mommy?"

"Not at the time. But now I do. That's the important thing."

"Mommy, that woman said 'sorry for your loss.' Why do people think Daddy died?"

"They're just confused sweetheart."

"Will I ever get to meet Daddy?"

"I hope so, honey."

The elevator doors opened to the lobby, revealing men in white HAZMAT suits there to greet Cindy and Carietta.

Gary sat in isolation in the reinforced glass and steel cage at U.S. Army Medical Research and Material Command Fort Detrick, MD. There was nothing organic in the cage's construction. The harsh sterile room was the antithesis of his childhood home. Soft warm pastels were replaced by grey steel. The sweet fragrance of incense was replaced by a faint hint of bleach. Three years of honing his nanite control skills had grown monotonous. Still, with practice, Gary learned to focus the destructive powers of the nanites onto just about any organic matter they could touch. His cooperation with the

Army to test the nanites started with living things, beginning with mice then working his down to bugs and finally plants. Gary had to learn to focus his emotions as he worked his way down to lower life forms, because it was much harder to dislike a plant than a person or even a bug. Eventually he got the hang of it. Training the nanites to eat inanimate organics was a chore. He was still working on certain polymers and plastics. At this rate, he thought surely he would be able to teach the nanites to eat a tin can, if he really wanted them too.

There was an ongoing struggle between the CDC and Army over control of the nanites in Gary's veins. The health agencies wanted to study them for disease prevention and cure. The military wanted to weaponize them. So far the Army was winning because they retained possession of the "prisoner" ever since Gen. Madcat helicoptered Gary out of harm's way three years prior. The ability to experiment with the nanites to assess their capabilities had kept him interested, for a while. But, after three years, Gary was growing tired of the game and he determined that his delicate dance with his Army captors would soon come to an end. He was ready to ask that the nanites be reprogrammed, as he had come to learn Harvard Medical was working on, so that the nanites would be rendered harmless. He realized that was the only way he was ever going to have something remotely resembling a normal life.

Joanna relocated from Round Rock to Fort Detrick, Maryland Army base housing to be near her son. She was able to visit Gary a couple of times a week. Gary was ever aware that his conversations were monitored and recorded, but he and his mom sorted out their own clandestine language. It wasn't lost on Gary that after three years of cooperation, the Army needed him more than he needed the Army. After three years of playing research games, Gary let her know he was done.

Joanna had hinted many times that perhaps he was not

being treated fairly by his hosts. "You know how I feel about the arrangements they have made for you. I don't like them one bit. Your father's in prison because he's a murderer. He deserves his punishment, and we're all better off for it. But your cell is entirely inappropriate. You're no menace to society. You're not an animal they can keep in some sterile cage. They need to treat you better," she told him. "I think you should be allowed out of here, and they should let the doctors treat you instead of letting the military toy with you."

This was danger talk. Last conversation, Gary played it coy and reminded Joanna, "I killed a lot of people Mom. Can you blame them for being cautious?" Unsaid, Gary was glad his signals that he was ready to get out of the Fort Detrick holding cell were getting through. Years of isolation battling cancer and then years of isolation doing Army research were taking its toll. Gary feared he might completely withdraw into insanity. "I know it's a silly thought, but do you still have those sentimental items I suggested you hang onto from our house in Round Rock?" He reminded her. It wasn't a silly question. The "sentimental" items were anything from the bathroom that might contain remnants of Gary's DNA, and hence in all likelihood, nanites. It was a backup plan to be implemented when all else failed.

"Yes Gary, I keep them with me. I know how precious they are," she assured him.

Later that afternoon, Gary felt a bristling on his skin and stirring in his veins. A vision of unrest swirled about his mother. The intercom crackled. "Gary Greene, we have a situation," said the synthetic voice. That was unusual. They never had a "situation" before.

Joanna bookmarked the UT Journal of Med website on her iPad and took a sip of her lukewarm herbal tea. "No further danger to the public?" she grumbled into the phone. "What kind of danger could a two year old child be to the public?"

"The kind of danger that comes from having nanites in their blood," Connie said from the other end of the phone line. "Gary's nanites."

Joanna was still processing. "I'm a grandmother?"

"Yes Joanna, that's why I called you. It's not my granddaughter they took away, it's yours. Cindy apologized to me for letting me think the baby was Charlie's this whole time. I had no reason to suspect otherwise. Part of me wishes she hadn't blabbed to the *Terror Unleashed* reporter. Now her secret is out, and the government isn't taking any chances."

"Did Cindy tell you where they took them?" Joanna asked.

"Yes, they're currently at Fort Hood, but Cindy thinks they're going to move Carietta to someplace more secure," Connie replied. "They're afraid of her. She burned a couple of them."

"Of all the nerve. They have no right," Joanna fumed.

"Are you going to tell Gary?"

"Yes," Joanna said. "I think he deserves to know."

"How do you think he'll react?"

"At first, he'll be shocked to learn he's a father. Then he'll be upset that his daughter has been snatched away. He'll feel like the government is bullying him. Gary doesn't respond well to being bullied."

"No he doesn't," Connie agreed.

"This whole situation may change now. Perhaps this will finally convince him it's time to stop cooperating with the Army and seek reprogramming for the nanites instead."

"I know you've been trying to convince him—" Click.

"Connie? Connie—" Joanna repeated into the dead phone line. She saw her iPad web browser toggle to display. "We're Sorry, Link Not Available."

She heard a knock at the front door of her apartment. "Mrs. Greene, Military Police."

She grabbed her purse and darted towards the sliding glass doors. Too late. Another officer was already guarding the rear exit. Damn. She realized they must have been listening for the slightest sign of conspiracy to undermine the mission they had Gary performing. She resorted to plan B. She pulled a zip lock baggie from her purse that contained remnants from Gary's bin in their Texas bathroom. She spilled the contents and selected Gary's old toothbrush.

The knocking at the door became more insistent. "Mrs. Greene, we know you're in there. Please don't make us break the door down. We just want to talk."

Somehow Joanna thought that unlikely. She pricked her finger with a lancet and let her blood drip onto the brush. The bristles sprang to life and with them the remaining contents of the zip lock baggie. Gary's spittle, flakes of skin and fine brown hair follicles consumed anything that harbored remnants of Gary's nanites from his childhood bathroom. The contents vaporized and began to swirl around Joanna. This was her distress call. The nanite hive mind would sense something was wrong and through their connection, so too would Gary.

"Mrs. Greene, we're coming in!" The door yielded with a single kick.

The MPs found Joanna Greene sitting in lotus position, eyes closed, and a dusty grey cone of animated debris swirling about her.

"What the–?" Joanna heard the voice of one of the officers. She explained. "Officers, my eyes are shut so I, and therefore the nanites, don't perceive your weapons. Please holster them and make no aggressive move toward me. Call your superiors and tell them what you see. Deliver this message, 'Gary knows.' They'll understand. I demand to speak with my son. This charade ends today."

The MPs were transfixed by the sight and uncertain how to proceed. Joanna was surrounded by a swirling dust cloud that resembled an upside-down dirt devil of micro-fine power. It was emitting a mesmerizing hum. The crackle of the radio saved them from a bad decision. Ordered to stand down, they kept their distance and awaited further instructions.

Joanna's cell phone rang. It was an unfamiliar but local number. She answered.

"Mom, they handed me this phone. What's going on?" Gary asked, concerned.

"Gary, your nanites are spinning around me, can you control them?" Joanna asked.

"Yes, I am can commune with them," Gary said. "They sense you're in danger, but they should obey me as long as you're safe."

"Okay, there are three MPs here who were ready to take me in, but I determined otherwise because I was afraid their intent was to keep me from giving you the following critical information. You are the father of Cindy Perrine's child. The Government figured it out, and they've taken Cindy and Carietta into custody. Can you help me put an end to this, honey? I want my family back. I want my son to have a normal life. I want my granddaughter to have a normal life. Enough is enough." Joanna began to cry. The nanite cloud's rotation rate kicked up a notch. "Gary, I'm scared," she admitted.

"It's okay Mom, we'll figure it out," Gary said. "But this situation will become much more complicated if those nanites hurt one of those MPs. You need to relax."

"I'm trying, Gary." The nanite cloud pulsed a dark tone.

"Mom, are you sitting down?"

"Yes."

"Take a cleansing breath," Gary said.

She followed his instructions, breathing deeply.

"Now repeat after me," Gary said. "Spirits of air, we greet you this day with humility and praise."

END

www.ingramcontent.com/pod-product-compliance
Lightning Source LLC
Chambersburg PA
CBHW070546260626
47161CB00002B/519